THE LONE WOLF

Some innocent people were going to be badly hurt. But he had to remember that there was no innocence in this trade, that anyone and everything touched by junk became irretrievably rotten and then had to pay the price. If he began to think of checks and balances, levels of thought, then he was beginning only to think like a cop or a bureaucrat again. That was why the enforcers were only another component of the disease; because they refused to accept responsibility and follow it through.

To fight vermin you had to be one.

Burt Wulff is beyond forgiveness, beyond vengeance. He is the Lone Wolf.

"Far far ahead of his time in both subject matter and style… Fans of Richard Stark, Andrew Vachss or Donald Goines should dive in without hesitation."
—Robert C. Giordano

D0988919

THE LONE WOLF #3:
BOSTON AVENGER

THE LONE WOLF #4:
DESERT STALKER

by Barry N. Malzberg

STARK
HOUSE

Stark House Press • Eureka California

BOSTON AVENGER / DESERT STALKER

Published by Stark House Press
1315 H Street
Eureka, CA 95501, USA
griffinskye3@sbcglobal.net
www.starkhousepress.com

ISBN-13: 978-1-951473-92-1

Book design by Mark Shepard, shepgraphics.com
Cover design by Jeff Vorzimmer, ¡caliente!design, Austin, Texas

First Stark House Press Edition: May 2022

Some Notes on the Lone Wolf

By Barry N. Malzberg

Don Pendleton's Executioner series started as a one-shot idea at Pinnacle Books in 1969. By 1972 George Ernsberger, my editor at Berkley, called it "the phenomenon of the age." Eventually Pendleton wrote 70 of the books himself and the series continues today ghosted by other writers. Mack Bolan's continuing *War Against the Mafia* (the working title of that first book) had sold wildly from the outset and less than three years later, when Pendleton and Scott Meredith had threatened to take the series from a grim and obdurate Pinnacle, New American Library had offered $250,000 for the next four books in the series. Pendleton stayed at Pinnacle—the publisher faced a lawsuit for misappropriated royalties and essentially had to match the NAL offer to hold on—but the level established by the properties could not fail to have inflamed every mass market paperback publisher in New York.

A few imitative series had been launched by Pinnacle itself—most notably The Butcher whose premise and protagonist were a close if even more sadomasochistic version of Pendleton's Mack Bolan. It was Bolan who had gone out alone to avenge his family incinerated in a Mafia war while Bolan was fighting Commies in Southeast Asia. Dell Books launched The Inquisitor, a series of books on the redemptive odyssey of Simon Quinn (by a then-unknown William Martin Smith, who under a somewhat different name was to become famous in the next decade), Pocket Books and Avon began series the provenance of which is at the moment unrecollected and Ernsberger at Berkley, under some pressure from his publisher, Stephen Conlan, was ready to start his own series.

What he needed in January 1973 was someone who could produce 10 books within less than a year and although my credentials as a Pendleton-imitator were certainly questionable (they were in fact nonexistent), there was no question but that Ernsberger had found one of the few writers close at hand who clearly could produce at that frenetic level. In 1972 I had written nine novels, in 1971 a dozen, in 1970 fourteen; ten books that quickly were not an overwhelming assignment. What he wanted was a series about a law enforcement guy, say maybe an ex-New York City cop, thrown off the force for one or another perceived disgrace, who would declare war upon the drug trade. The cop could be a military veteran with (like Bolan) a good command of ordnance; it wouldn't hurt if he had a black sidekick either still on or just off the force so that they could get some *Defiant Ones* byplay going in those pre-Eddie Murphy days, and the violence was to be hyped up to Executioner level as the protagonist, after an initial festive in New York, took his mission throughout the States and maybe overseas. Ten novels, $27,500 total advance with (it is this which caught my total attention) 25% of it payable upon signature of the contract. Only a brief outline would be necessary and the tenth book was due to be delivered on or before 10/1/73.

I had never read a Pendleton novel in my life.

Hey, no problem; $6750 for a five-page outline at a time when I perceived my nascent career to be in a recession-induced collapse cleaved away scruple and, for that matter, terror. I read Executioner #7, which struck me as pretty bad, mechanical, and lifeless (like most debased category fiction it depended upon the automatic responses upon the reader, did not create characters and an ambiance of its own), wrote the usual promise-them-a-partridge-in-a-pear-tree outline, signed the contracts and began the series on 1/16/73. The third of the novels was delivered on 2/14/73.

Incontestably I could have delivered the entire series by May (the early plan was for Berkley to bring out the first three novels at once, then publish one a month thereafter) but George Ernsberger asked me to stop after *Boston Avenger* and wait for further word. There was a problem, it seemed. In the first place, I had given my protagonist, Wulff Conlan, a name uncomfortably close to that of the publisher whose name at the time I had not even known, and in the second place Conlan's victims, unlike Mack Bolan's, were real people with real viewpoints who seemed to undergo real pain when they were killed which was quite frequently. Would this kind of stuff—real pain as opposed to cartoon death that is to say—go in the mass market? Berkley dithered about this while I sulked, wrote a novelization (never published) of Lindsay Anderson's *O Lucky Man!* for Warner Books, and waited around to accept an award for a science fiction novel, which award caused me much difficulty, you bet, in the years to come. (See the letter column of the 2/74 *Analog* for any further information you want on this.)

Eventually, Ernsberger called—during dinnertime, in fact, on 3/16/73—to say that I could go ahead with the series and would I please change the name of the protagonist? Grumbling, fearing that I might never get back to the center of those novels, I started again and in fact did deliver the tenth book on 10/1/73 after all. (The first three were published in that month.) As is so often the case with imitative series, sales steadily declined from volume #1 which did get close to 70,000) but held above unprofitability through all of those ten, and I was allowed two sequels in 1974 and then two more in conclusion (at a cut advance). I insisted upon killing off Wulff in #14 against the argument of Ernsberger's assistant, Dale Copps, who reminded me of Professor Moriarty.

I signed off on #14: *Philadelphia Blowup* in 1/75. That means that I am now at a greater distance from these novels than many readers of this anthology are from their birthdates ... and for that reason my opinion of the series is not necessarily any more valid than would be the opinion of Erika Cornell on her essays in ballet class in the mid-seventies.

The purpose and development of these novels would, in any case, be clear to anyone, even the author. It is evident to me now as it was then that Mack Bolan was insane and Pendleton's novels were a rationalization of vigilantism; it was my intent, then, to show what the real (as opposed to the mass market) enactment of madness and vigilantism might be if death were perceived as something beyond catharsis or an escape route for the bad guys. As the series went on and on and as I became more secure with the voicing and with my apparent ability to circumvent surface and not get fired, Wulff became crazier and crazier. By #13 he was driving crosscountry and killing anyone on suspicion of drug dealing; by #14: *Philadelphia Blowup*, he was staggering from bar to bar in the City of Brotherly Love and killing everyone because they obviously had to be drug dealers. Finally gunned down for the public safety by his one-time black sidekick, Wulff died far less bloodily than many of his victims while managing a bequest of about $50,000 to his overweight creator. The novels sold overseas intermittently—Denmark stayed around through all 14; the other Scandinavian countries bailed out earlier; the gentle Germans found it all too bloody and sadistic and after editing down the first 10 novels quit on an open-ended contract, paid off and shut it down. I haven't seen anything financially from these since 1979 but entries in various mystery reference sources and the invitation to discuss the series in this anthology suggest that it might have found a particle of an audience. (My real pride in this series, beyond its ambition and sheer, perverse looniness is that I was able to run it through the entirety of its original contract and manage four sequels as well; no Executioner imitator other than those published by Pinnacle went past four or five volumes.) The vicious Rockefeller drug laws ("drug dealers get life imprisonment") were being debated and eventually rammed through the New York State legislature at the time I was writing through the midpoint of the series. It was a propinquity of event which led to some of the more profoundly angry passages in these novels and imputed a certain timelessness as well. (The laws were horseshit and we are still living with their existence and terrible consequence.) Calling a crazy a crazy, no matter how anguished may have been the aspect of the series which was the most admired but for me the work lives in the pure rage of some of the epigraphic statements, notably Kenyatta's. Writing these brought me close to some apprehension of how Malcolm, how H. Rap Brown, how the Soledad Brothers might have felt and how right they were: The Lone Wolf was my own raised fist to a purity and a past already obliterated as they were written, rolled over by the tanks and battery of Bolan's ordnance. (Operating under Bolan's pseudonym: "U.S. Government.") Bolan killed to kill: I think Wulff killed to be free. It all works out the same, of course.

THE LONE WOLF #3: BOSTON AVENGER

by Barry N. Malzberg

Writing as Mike Barry

Boston: fair Boston
Home of the bean and the cod,

Where the Lowells talk but to the Cabots
And the Cabots talk only to God.
                    —*Old Proverb*

It's been the Lowells and the Cabots too long and now
the old order is changing. The scum think they're safe
here in old New England but I'll bring them a friend of
mine who I talk to quite a bit. His name is Mr. Death.
                    —Burt Wulff

For HWW: may he never have to read this!

PROLOGUE

TO: Chief
FROM: Information Division
RE: Burt Wulff
Our records indicate that the above-named resigned from the Department on 7/26/73 (Badge #1937567, Patrolman) for unstated reasons. Forms M31B and H261 were not filed. The subject did not await formal resignation-retirement procedures but quit by phone call to superior, Lieutenant Gage. He left last known address without forwarding information. Check in settlement was returned *unknown* and after efforts to locate the subject proved fruitless, was returned to the Finance Division.

Subject is 32 years old. Full physical description and medical history accompanies this report. He served in Department from 7/5/73 until resignation date with absence of two years (2/66–1/68) spent in active duty with USA, most of it in Vietnam. Although police personnel are specifically exempted from draft calls, subject volunteered for duty, stating, according to Request for Leave of Absence form filed 1-14-66, "I want to see what's going on there." Subject received an Honorable Discharge and obtained the rank of Staff Sergeant (E-6). It is indicated that he served in combat.

TO: Top Echelons Only
FROM: C
RE: Burt Wulff
Subject is thirty-two years old, former (ten years) police officer NYPD. Served on narcotics detail last five years until two (2) days before his resignation at which time he was transferred to patrol car. Subject is a combat (Vietnam) veteran with a highly sophisticated knowledge of weaponry. *He is extremely dangerous. A photograph accompanies this memorandum and the subject, upon identification, should be killed on sight, regardless of apparent risk.*

This man says that he is commencing a "war against the international drug trade." He has already killed at least six people, two of whom, identities not revealed in this memo, can be considered to have been at high organizational echelons. One of them was killed in a massive fire and explosion which demolished his townhouse on Manhattan's exclusive East Side. How Wulff was able to penetrate security is not yet known. *Extreme caution must be used in approaching the subject.*

Circumstances creating Wulff's decision to commence his "war against the international drug trade" (phraseology his) apparently trace to personal motives. Subject was engaged to a girl, name Marie Calvante, who was discovered to have died of heroin overdose on 8/12/73 in a furnished room on the West Side of Manhattan. Apparently the girl had died elsewhere and had been brought to this room by party or parties unknown where she was discovered by Wulff himself. *Wulff was in the radio car which took the call.*

It is not known and will probably never be known whether Marie Calvante's death was murder or whether, in experimentation with hard drugs, she misjudged and killed herself. Subject Wulff is convinced, however, that the girl *was* murdered in retaliation for certain prosecutions he had initiated as a member of the narcotics squad, and for his refusal to settle with various parties who wished to pay him well to have those prosecutions uninitiated. This is the apparent source of his goal to destroy the drug trade. Little else can be deduced.

It is obvious that Wulff is insane in this quest but he is *very dangerous.* Certain activities of his in New York have shifted the line of succession and created problems out of all relation to the subject's apparent powers to do so. It must be strongly emphasized that no known elements were connected in any way with the death of Marie Calvante, and the subject has thus from the beginning worked from a misapprehension. This however does not seem to be a matter which can be discussed with Wulff. He is, as stated, *extremely dangerous and cannot be approached.*

Based upon certain information in a stolen attaché case of one of our principals (whom Wulff murdered at close range before escaping with the case), the subject to the best of our knowledge has emplaned for San Francisco to continue his "war."

Reasons for subject's sudden, unexplained resignation from PD have been inferred from several sources. It is indicated that subject, who had been transferred to Narcotics Squad at his request, became involved in difficulties with superior officers there and was involuntarily relieved of duties and, pending further disposition, was returned to radio car. On the first and only night of said assignment, Wulff's car was sent because of an anonymous tip to a rooming house on West 93rd Street where one Marie Calvante was found by Wulff dead of heroin overdose.

It has been found through informal channels that Wulff and Marie Calvante were affianced. Whether Miss Calvante's death was murder by party or parties unknown or a genuine OD has never been established. It is known that immediately subsequent to this, Wulff threw away his badge and resigned peremptorily from the PD.

We can infer that subject is extremely embittered. Embitterment alone, however, would hardly account for his subsequent actions.

It is emphasized at this point in the report that everything which follows has been obtained through unofficial channels subject to your request to obtain as much straightforward information about Wulff as possible. The information comes from police informers and other sources similarly disreputable. Its credibility is, therefore, to be questioned although the sources utilized are considered to be reliable.

Wulff, as a result of his experiences, declared a "war on the international drug trade" and let it be known that his aim was to singlehandedly trace and smash the supply and distribution of drugs in the United States and territories. In New York City, within a period of several days, he was able to kill at least ten individuals, three of whom have been subsequently identified as being involved at the higher levels of East Coast distribution. In order to kill one of them, Peter Vincent, the subject bombed Vincent's three-story townhouse on the East Side of Manhattan.

Subject apparently then came into information advising of a large expected shipment in San Francisco. From this point, reports are hearsay, although there is considerable newspaper evidence as to some of his acts in San Francisco. In a major dock fire a freighter registered to the Government of Argentina was destroyed and fifty to sixty people were killed, including several law-enforcement personnel who arrived at the scene on a tip just as the ship exploded. (It is indicated strongly, however, that Wulff's "war" is upon illicit traffickers and distributors and he considers himself to be *aiding* authorities.) This freighter contained approximately one quarter of a million dollars raw price of uncut heroin. The ship sank and the heroin was not recovered. *It is possible that this quantity is in Wulff's possession.*

This man is extremely dangerous. He is obsessed by a sense of mission, his intellectual facilities remain completely unimpaired, and he appears to have easy access to heavy weapons and the knowledge of their use (probably acquired from his military experience). There is no question, however, but that in the few months since he left the PD subject has made a small but appreciable dent upon traffic in the areas which he has attacked.

It is agreed however that law enforcement personnel are not to assist him in any way and that he is to be placed under surveillance and apprehended as soon thereafter as arrangements have been made to protect the arresting personnel. Since the subject, however, is considered to be an enormous threat to traffickers it is quite likely that private assassination units will dispose of him before he can be apprehended.

According to unreliable sources who cannot be identified, subject was able to save the shipment of heroin from the fire and is now heading with it toward Boston, using it as "bait" to move to ever-higher levels of responsibility for the traffic. END OF REPORT.

PS: (*Handwritten*) This is the best I could dig up on such short notice; hope you'll find it useful. It probably is only FYI though. Nothing to put in effect.

I don't give this guy four days, now.

I

Wulff was numb after thirty-six hours non-stop in a 1965 Lincoln Continental, two thousand miles with only gas stops after a one-night stopover in Wyoming. He drove up to the toll booth on the Massachusetts Turnpike at three in the morning and fumbled on the seat beside him for the ticket which he remembered having tossed there two hundred miles back. On the back seat behind him the valise containing a quarter of a million dollars in uncut heroin joggled and then, on the sharp deceleration, slammed into the front, jarring him. "Fuck it," Wulff said absently and shook his head, trying to clear it. The damned valise belonged in the trunk, of course. But having gone through so much to get it, gone through so much to bring it here, he was damned if he was going to let it out of his sight. No. No way. He was going to take this mother with him all the way through Boston and convert it, before he was done, into a parlay of death.

The man in the toll booth looked sleepy. Little business at this hour; Wulff had probably awakened him. Scratching his head, he reached for the ticket which Wulff passed across to him. A short fellow, mid-thirties, thinning blond hair. Another civil service hack working down shift. Wulff logged the face and put it away where it would keep. An old police habit; you never knew when you might need a face.

"Three fifty," the attendant said.

Wulff went into his wallet lying on the seat beside him and got a five. There was only about three hundred of the New York stake left now. San Francisco had yielded heroin but Boston was going to have to give him money.

"Five," the attendant said. "That means fifty back."

"No it doesn't. It means one fifty."

"That's right," the attendant said. "Tired. Not thinking too well." He retreated into the booth, began to fumble at a cash drawer. Had anyone ever tried to knock over a toll booth? Wulff thought idly. Probably not; that kind of energy went straight to banks.

"Here," the attendant said, turning from the booth. "Here it is." His face broke into a peculiar smile.

He showed Wulff a gun held in his right hand. "Here's your change," he said.

Wulff, reacting if not thinking, dove, flattened himself on the seat. Someone yanked open the passenger door and hit him in the neck. He rolled to the floor of the car and found himself looking at another gun, this one held by a stocky, middle-aged man.

"Don't move," the man said. "Just tell me where it is."

Wulff held himself in place there. His own gun was where it should be, in his right coat pocket. He had no more chance of getting at it then he did of getting to the machine gun and full clip in the back.

They had him. He had rolled into it but good. Three thousand and eighty miles to dump into something like this. That took foresight. It really did.

The stocky man cocked the gun. Wulff felt it prod his forehead. "No bullshit," the man said, "where's the stuff?"

Wulff did not move, said nothing. The attendant was in the car now, leaning over the wheel, putting his gun into Wulff's stomach. His eyes were cold and furious.

"Let's not shoot the son of a bitch and then search the car," he said. "He's got it on him, we know that."

"Yeah," said the stocky man, "I suppose so—" and then his eyes fell on the valise in the back. He reached over, seized the handle and dragged it toward him. "I think we got it," he said.

"Open it you bastard," the blond attendant said. He seemed very nervous. "Don't tell me what you think you got, just get to it."

The stocky man fumbled with the clips, the pistol in his hand wavering. Wulff calculated a move but discarded it. He lay there, pinched up on the door. He could get to the stocky man the attendant would kill him.

The stocky man beamed as he saw what was in the valise. "We got it," he said.

"Close it and get it the fuck out."

"All right," the man said. He seemed hurt. Clumsily, quickly, he closed up the valise and maneuvered it out of the Continental, put it beside his feet outside the car.

"Come on," the blond man said, "shoot him."

"Me?" the stocky man said, "why me? You were supposed to shoot him. I was just standing guard."

"You stupid prick," the attendant said and raised his gun. Wulff compressed and closed his eyes. There was nothing else to do.

Behind the Continental there was a screech of brakes, the sound of a horn. "What is this?" someone was shouting, "what's going on here?"

"Son of a bitch," the blond said again, "they were supposed to block it two miles up. What's going on here?"

"Kill him," the stocky man said. His eyes were quite bright and he looked at Wulff intensely.

"I'm not going to kill him in front of witnesses," the blond said. He moved away, the gun going last, took his head out of the car. "That wasn't in the contract," he said.

The honking was more intense. Behind that Wulff could hear the sound of accumulating traffic.

The stocky man backed out, waved his gun, seized the valise. "Next time, sucker," he said to Wulff. He slammed the door viciously.

Wulff wrenched himself from the compartment, vaulted to the driver's seat and pulled the door closed. The toll booth was empty. In the dim light there, rising to his knees, he could just see the outlines of a form that might have been a man trussed.

Wonderful. That was just wonderful. Traffic was backed up now ten cars deep to the one entryway with a green light. Turnpikes were really amazing. Even at three in the morning, there were a lot of people moving into Boston.

Down the line people were starting to come out of their cars, some waving their fists and cursing. Wulff peered into the darkness beyond but he could see no indication of the two men or the valise. And he did not think that he was in any condition, on foot or by car, to pursue them at this time.

The motor was still running. Swearing, he took the car out of Park, in which the blond had thoughtfully put it, floored the accelerator and drove out of there. Stupid. He had been stupid. Three thousand miles and only for this.

And a quarter million dollars' worth of junk now back in the hands of the enemy.

"I'll make them pay for this," Wulff said quietly, coming to an intersection, turning right, ramming the gas to the floor as he drove at ninety through the back roads of Newton, Massachusetts. It might not have been in the contract but they had made an awful mistake not killing him.

The pain, the rage, his own sense of idiocy for being so exposed beat within him strongly. But, he thought wryly, there was one thing it could be said he had gotten away with anyway.

A quarter of a million dollars of death off into the night. But at least he had saved the toll.

II

Tucci got a call but refused to take it. No phones. Taps were everywhere, the sons of bitches were closing in. Reform district attorney, press calling for mandatory life, the usual hardline shit. It would blow away and the survivors would get fat but the heat had been on for months now and still no sign of easing. He had lived through these before, though. No calls. Everything face to face, in a public area.

He was at a luncheonette near Scully Square at midnight. A small man found him in the back drinking a cup of coffee and said, "we got it."

"That's good."

"No," the messenger said, "it isn't so good. They didn't kill the guy and they seem to have taken off with the valise."

Tucci's face suffused. "Son of a bitch," he said, "I don't believe you."

The small man was one of the few within Tucci's orbit in Boston who did not have to take crap from this bastard. "You better believe me," he said. "They missed the block and traffic got right through. Started backing up and they weren't going to do it in front of twenty witnesses."

"And they got the valise?"

"Put it this way," the messenger said, "it wasn't delivered. They're out there with it somewhere."

"Maybe Wulff got away with it," Tucci said almost hopefully.

"You kidding? No fucking chance. They spotted his car driving away with him in it but by then it was too late to do anything. Besides, what to do? They got the valise."

Tucci felt the anger assaulting him first as spots of dampness in the groin and underarms. He could feel the frustration, the rage. Everything he had done had been right. He had played by the book, controlled situations, worked his way along carefully until, he thought, he had placed himself in a situation where everything worked as it should. Now this son of a bitch across from him was telling Tucci that he had been wrong, the situation was uncontrollable after all. Furthermore, men he had trusted had turned out to be untrustworthy. That said a good deal about Tucci's judgment. It also meant that the entire organization was shaky. Hand-picked traitors.

"I want to hit that son of a bitch," he said. "I want him out of here within a day."

"What about the valise?"

"We'll deal with that later. We'll get working on that too. But it all starts with that bastard Wulff. If he hadn't headed this way it would never have happened."

The messenger shrugged, sipped his coffee, finished it. "That's all right with me," he said. "All of that stuff's out of my hands. I just wanted to bring you up to date."

"Nothing's out of your hands."

"Yes it is," the man said. He stood, looked down at the table. "I'm going to get out of here," he said.

"No you're not. I'm not finished with you."

"I'm afraid you are," the messenger said, looking at him. There was a glint of amusement in the man's face. Did he see weakness? Was that it, Tucci's failure had made him weak in the man's eyes? "You are definitely finished," the messenger said. "There is nothing more that I can do for you."

Tucci stood furiously, faced the man. His hand was already fumbling for the pistol in his pocket. He could feel the beat of rage within him; it would be insanity to gun down this man in a public place but Tucci had a violent temper. "Stay here," he said.

"Not really," the man said. He backed away three paces, looking to his left. Tucci followed the man's gaze, realized suddenly that the place was empty. The waitress and counterman were out of sight; the two customers that he had seen walled over in a corner booth when he came in had got out.

"Tucci," the messenger said, "Tucci, you're a stupid son of a bitch."

Tucci went for the gun, wheeling. The man threw himself to the floor. Two men came out of the kitchen holding guns. Before Tucci could reach his own pistol, one of the men fired, hitting him in the shoulder. Tucci, turned around completely by the pain, dropped his gun and stumbled into a wall. The place rattled.

"No," he said. It sounded like a protest but was a sound of futility. *Stupid.* He had thought himself insulated and all the time they were merely waiting. Tucci had not faced death since the old wars of twenty years ago. But it came back to him, this taste of death, like an old lover. He should have known. He always should have known.

The messenger stood, holding Tucci's gun. It must have slid directly into his grasp. He waved at the two men by the door of the kitchen. "Let me," he said, "this one is for me."

"No," Tucci said again. He was made rigid by the pain in his shoulder. It spun through him on little tendrils and he felt himself becoming dizzy and nauseated. "Please—"

"You're stupid," the messenger said. "You lost us the junk and you lost us Wulff. You can't cut it. You can't cut it anymore, Tucci. Right of succession."

He lifted the gun and shot Tucci in the eye. Tucci fell gasping across the table. The messenger hit him in the back of the neck. Already dead, the corpse contracted like a frog's leg and then rolled onto the floor.

"All right," the messenger said, throwing the gun on the body and motioning to the men by the kitchen. He gave the corpse a kick. "Let's get out of here."

The three of them massed near the door, walked out in file, quickly. After a time the waitress and the counterman came from the back and looked at the fallen Tucci wordlessly. "I suppose we should call the police," the counterman said finally.

The waitress shrugged. "You do it," she said. She stood there for a while and looked at the dead man, fascinated. She was only nineteen years old and had never seen a corpse before. She had always hoped she would see a dead man and now she had. What they said was right. It was as interesting as the movies.

Her breath began to move in her throat unevenly.

III

Wulff ditched the Continental finally on Beacon Street. It had been a pretty good car, much better than he had had any right to expect, but sentiment played no part in his new life; it was time to get rid of it. Everyone in town would be looking for it now. First there had been the matter of getting the machine gun and clips and the remaining grenades into his room at the cheap hotel, but the clerk downstairs had chosen that time to pass out completely, lolling stuporously behind the counter, a half-consumed bottle of gin beside his head, so no sweat on that. Boston, fair Boston. One thing Wulff was learning fast: the dirty sections of every city looked the same. Boston might have a reputation different from New York or San Francisco but when you were in the guts of the city, looking for a place to sleep or a connection, all of the territory was familiar. He felt right at home already.

He had pulled the plates off the Continental, raised the trunk and hood, left the keys in it. With luck it would look exactly like an old abandoned car and the scavengers would get into it before the police or the hoods did. Now he sat on the fourth floor of a Boston hotel, the machine gun held absently across his lap, the room secured by a chain bolt. For the first time in several days, Wulff allowed himself to think. The drive cross-country hadn't counted. He had been bombed-out, exhausted and the effort of pushing the old car all the way, half-expecting some Dodge Challenger to pull up from behind, outrun him and gun him down had kept all real thought from his mind.

But now, oddly, he was not exhausted. Fatigue and dread had been chasing one another in his skull so long that they had burned one another out, at least temporarily. He felt himself raised to that peculiar, burning sense of alertness he had felt now and then in the department when running down a call on an unknown assailant. And he had felt that way in Vietnam all the time; to be poised on the edge of dissolution was in a way a happy feeling because you knew that you could go no further, that you were, at least, existing at the limit of your possibilities and there were very few people who could say that. Stupid. He had been stupid.

He had been incredibly stupid to think that he would be able to get a quarter million dollars' worth of junk into this city or into any other major distribution point. Communications in the drug trade must have been at least as effective now as they were between nations and the word had been flashed by the survivors at San Francisco clear across the country: *get Wulff*. They must have figured that he was going into Boston because, as the dying mobster, Anthony, had told him on the burning freighter, Boston was the next point of distribution for the junk once delivery had been taken. It would probably have been flown there in bulk to be cut up and put into the pipeline there.

They already knew plenty about the Wolfs *modus operandi*. How could he have possibly thought that these men operated in a vacuum, that they did not know what was going on? He was going up against the shrewdest, most cunningly effective network in the history of cities; they had in only a decade managed to change and poison the nation: did Wulff really think that he would be able to slip by them undetected, undetectable? He had cut a swath of flame in New York, he had gone to San Francisco and killed fifty of them there, hitting the whole western axis in the solar plexus—but as far as the enemy was concerned, it only meant that they had not taken him sufficiently seriously. They had not put the proper troops into the fray.

Now, here in Boston, they would meet him in combat gear. Here in Boston, he would clash with the enemy for the first time in their full realization of the menace he represented.

Wulff, running his hands over his face, trying to restore some circulation to the spaces behind his burning eyes, decided that he was extremely lucky to be alive. It was only luck that the toll booth job had been assigned to men who would not murder in front of witnesses and that somewhere beyond that toll booth the men who should have blocked off traffic were incompetents. Failing either one of these two factors he would be dead now and his brief war over. A few quick flurries, a couple of minor campaigns won, to be a corpse on the outskirts of Boston....

Wulff shuddered. Dying was not so bad. He had been killed the day he saw a girl named Marie Calvante lying dead of a heroin overdose in a rotten furnished room on upper Broadway. Since then the life functions had worked, but inside, in all the places where a man lived, except for a few brief moments with a girl in San Francisco, he had been a corpse. All right. He had told the enemy that they could not kill him twice; he had not been lying about that.

But failure. That was something else. To be ambushed, to have the goods and his plan taken from him, to see everything that he had hoped to do collapse because of his own stupidity—that Wulff could not bear.

They should have killed him, he decided. The hit men should have gambled on the witnesses and shot him. The gang behind them should have closed off the damned road or come down the pike themselves to have shot him.

Because he was mad now. He was very mad. He could feel the anger pulsating within him and it seemed to stitch him together with a further intensity of purpose. They thought he had been serious in San Francisco or New York? They thought that he had been playing for keeps in those two cities?

Well that was nothing. That was absolutely nothing to what he was going to do now.

He was going to burn them out of Boston for this.

Wulff went to the valise. He still had the stockbroker's notebook, taken off the corpse in Manhattan. The notebook with names, addresses, points of location which the police in any city would have given up their pension plans to see, if only because they could sell it back to the racketeers for enough to set fifty men up for life.

He leafed through the notebook which had been arranged by the precise stockbroker by geographical area and then by city and found under Boston a name and address of a man who appeared to be important.

All right. All right, he would start there.

Henry Tucci, here come the Wolf.

IV

At about the same time or perhaps a little earlier, the bell rang at the home of a man named Phillip Sands who was an associate professor of linguistics at Harvard. When he went to the door, two men with grim faces were standing there, holding guns.

"Don't panic," one of them said, "this is no stickup, nothing like that at all. We just want to come in and have a conversation."

Sands held his ground and said, "My wife is in the living room. I don't think she'd appreciate the guns."

"That's all right," the man said, "you just go back there then and get her *out* of the living room and then we'll come in and talk. Meanwhile you can let us stand here in the hall. My friend and I aren't here for any trouble at all, and you'd make a big mistake if you started some on your own."

For a man holding a gun, this one had a surprisingly light voice, almost a lilt to it. The other one, a shorter item, stood behind the speaker in the hall, holding his gun firmly and pointing it at Sands with an almost demented expression. Sands decided that the speaker was not used to guns particularly but on the other hand this one was and would have to be carefully watched.

Not that he was in a position to do anything much besides watching. He shrugged and walked quickly back to the living room where his wife was sitting watching television and knitting. For a girl of twenty-two, a coed he had married in passion only a year before, she had certainly moved past the revolutionary stage quickly, Sands thought. What she was almost consciously trying to do, of course, was to disassociate herself from him—but there was no time to think about that now. A crisis was coming but it was months off, with these two guests in the hall it might be never. "Karen, there are some people here to see me," he said, "you'll have to shut that off and go upstairs."

She looked up, gave him a bright look of resentment. "I'm not good enough to listen to your discussions?" she said. "This happens all the time, Phil."

"We can't discuss it now."

"We're going to have to discuss it," she said, but she stood. "We can't go on this way. We have nothing to say to each other when we're alone and you're always dismissing me when people come around. We can't go on this way."

"We'll talk about it later."

"Don't think I don't know what's going on," she said. "I know what you're doing." She went to the foot of the stairs, balanced herself there, quite a pretty girl really, although Sands thought wryly enough, he had overrated her sexuality by more than a little, and what he had thought to be malleable raw material that he could mold to his needs had turned out to be a stubborn, fearful, resentful little girl. No time to think of that now.

"I'll be up as soon as I can, Karen," he said.

"Maybe you will," she said, "but don't expect that you'll find me up there just waiting. I can't go on this way, Phil, I really can't."

"All right," he said, "you can't go on this way." *Phil* she had always insisted upon calling him. No one else called him Phil: he was Phillip or Dr. Sands. He realized, almost absently, that she was right, things could not go on this way much longer; not if everything she did irritated him so.

The hell with it. He went back to the hall where the men with guns were waiting very patiently and motioned them inside. They followed him, guns dangling, seeming to be ill at ease in the relatively well-furnished apartment of an associate professor. That gave him a leg up, Sands thought, he was in his element, they out of theirs. On the other hand, this fancy speculation would get him precisely nowhere if one of them chose to pull a trigger. Guns had been created for people like this; they were the ones who needed equalizers. Sands felt an unpleasant tingle moving through the back of his neck and wrists, suddenly felt lightheaded and collapsed onto the couch behind him. The gunmen, seemingly less ill at ease simply by seeing this, took up positions against the wall, the one with the lilting voice even leaning against some bookshelves. "Let's get right to the point," he said.

"That suits me."

"We know who you are and what you can do for us. Now we've got ourselves a load of uncut heroin which may be one of the biggest hauls in history. Don't know and we're not going to run it through any chemists just yet. We need someone reliable to dispose of it."

Sands felt his knees shaking but he kept himself tightly in control. Control was the key to his life, he reminded himself of this. "I don't think I know what you're talking about," he said trying to keep his voice steady.

"Come off that shit, professor," the shorter one said. His face had become clotted with rage; his eyes were blinking rapidly. "We didn't come here to play cat and mouse or to go through any of this shit. Now you're one of the biggest pushers in the East, or at least the biggest one we can hang into on short notice. We've got some very hot, important stuff and we need it unloaded."

"My friend is a little abrupt," the other man said in that curious voice. *East European,* Sands found himself thinking with academic detachment, *probably came here at a very early age and doesn't even speak a second language, but can't lose the accent anyway.* "We wish we had the time to play it your way, professor, to drink some tea and get at the point longhand, but we're a little pressed for time so we'll have to take a rain check on that. We know your record and what you're doing; you can take my word for that. And we need some help."

Sands looked up at the serene, floating lights of his living room, looked up at the carpeted staircase which his wife had ascended, looked briefly out the window, but his gaze came back, as he knew it would have to, to this man. His hands clenched against one another involuntarily. "I don't know who you are or what you're after," he said, "but I won't touch a deal like this."

"We're not cops," the short man said, "if you're thinking that, professor."

"In fact," said the other, "we happen to be very much on your side of this, professor. We're allies, not enemies. We need you very badly and I'm afraid that there's no time to negotiate."

"Those guns are making me very nervous," Sands said, holding his palms to knees to lessen if not conceal the trembling. "Whatever you are or think you have in mind, it's impossible for me to discuss anything while I'm looking down the barrel of a gun."

The man seemed to shrug, looked at the other. "Don't do it," the other said with disgust but made no gesture to stop the speaker from opening the chambers of the pistol to show Sands that it was empty.

"Both are," the man said. "We're not the type of people who pull loaded guns on complete strangers, which so far unfortunately you are. We like to feel that there's some kind of a relationship before we start shooting people."

The stocky man said, "You're a great help, you really are," but put his gun away inside his jacket and, moving from the wall, went over to the doorway leading to the kitchen and then turned to look at Sands in an almost pleading way. "Please," he said, "don't play games. There's too much at stake for all of us here and we just don't have the time. We've got a quarter of a million worth of goods but unless we put it into channels it's worthless to us and it's just going to get a lot of people killed. We know that you can help us if you want to, it's your specialty."

Sands said, "Assuming that I could help you—and I still deny that because I am an associate professor at a major university and know nothing of drug distribution—but assuming for the sake of this discussion that I could help you, why the hell would I? You say that a lot of people may get killed because of what you've got. That means that you not only have what you have illegally and all of us could go to prison for life for possession or distribution, it means that there are other people who think that *they* should have it and they're looking for you. And, inevitably, they'll look for me. Do you think that I'd really put myself into a situation like that?"

Sands stood abruptly and walked past the short man at the door into the kitchen, feeling the fear ebbing all the time. These were not men who knew power; they had come into it by accident but they had no follow through. "I'm going to make myself a drink," he said. "If you want to give me your orders you can have one too. We'll all have a drink together to show that there are no hard feelings and then you'll go and I'll go upstairs and forget that any of this ever happened. You're obviously beyond your depth here and I don't blame you for anything."

"Listen," the East European said, with a note of frustration, bringing Sands around and yanking him into position, "I understand what you're saying. Of course I do. We've all got to protect ourselves and nobody's asking you to come out and admit anything until you have evidence of our own good faith." He turned to the other man. "Go to the car and get the valise," he said.

"I think that's a very bad idea. I think—"

"Shut up and get the fucking valise," the man said. "I'm handling this, so you just take fucking orders and keep your thoughts to yourself."

The stocky man seemed to dwindle. His body sagged, his eyes became dull. "All right," he said. He crossed quickly in front of Sands, went into the hallway and out the door into the night, not closing it. The East European took out his gun giving Sands a thrill of terror before he saw that it was a nervous habit and the man was simply using it to still his hands.

He looked up at Sands with a curiously open expression and said, "We're trusting you, you see. We're not coming in here with guns to threaten you or pistol-whip or hurt your family. You're in the driver's seat, we're the ones asking for a break here."

"A quarter of a million dollars?" Sands asked cautiously. "Of what?"

"Heroin, uncut. You know that."

"How do you know it's a quarter of a million dollars?"

"We don't," the man said. "That's what we've heard, that's what it's supposed to be. It sure as hell *looks* like a quarter of a million dollars. It might be twice as much as that, though. We just couldn't tell until we start to run it through channels and we can't run it through channels in our position."

"You stole it?" Sands said quietly.

"Not exactly."

"Not exactly?"

"We didn't exactly deliver it," the man said. "That's neither here nor there. I'm being honest with you and trying to come on straight now, but there are certain things we can't tell and that are none of your business. The thing to do is to get that fucking thing into channels and that's where you come in."

"That's where I don't come in," Sands said. "It's illegal merchandise that's been stolen. That makes it double murder and you must think that I'm a fool. I'm going to have a straight scotch, no ice, no water. What do you drink?"

"Just wait," the East European said. "You wait for the drinks, there's time for that later." He looked toward the hallway; there was the click of a door closing and then the stocky man came back grunting, carrying a valise. He put it on the floor, upended, then placed it on a side and looked at the East European questioningly.

"I still don't think—"

"Shut up and open the goddamned thing," the man said.

The stocky man fumbled with the clips and swung the top open. And Sands, taking three involuntary steps forward, found himself staring, almost with reverence, at more junk than he had ever seen in his life.

Raw, uncut heroin, it lay there arranged in neat little packets, glinting at the light. Sands took one more step, then another, and knelt by the suitcase. Almost unconsciously he extended a delicate forefinger, worked it within a bag just to the touching point and then withdrew it. He sniffed carefully, professionally, while the two men watched.

"I guess it's genuine," he said.

"Of course it's genuine, goddammit."

"There's no way to be sure unless you ran tests on it though," Sands said carefully, modulating his voice, keeping all excitement out of it.

"You don't have to run tests."

"Oh yes you would," Sands said quietly. "When you're dealing with something in this quantity of this alleged purity, tests would be absolutely necessary. There's too much involved." He paused. "Of course I wouldn't know anything about that," he said.

"Look," the stocky man said, apparently at the end of his patience, "let me slug the guy. Just once; let me hit the son of a bitch and then we'll get somewhere."

The East European made a quick, placative gesture, then turned to Sands. Sands, very carefully had taken a pack of cigarettes out and lit one cautiously, waving the match in a small circle, keeping the gesture as unobtrusive as possible. "My friend is over-anxious," the East

European said. "We've gone to a great deal of trouble to get this here and taken a hell of a lot of risk and he feels that we just don't have the time to circle around on this anymore."

"So get it out of here," Sands said, putting the cigarette to his mouth and inhaling delicately. No one could see the shake of his hands, he was sure of that. "I didn't ask you to come here."

"We may have to do that," the man said, "but you still haven't answered our question."

"What question?"

"Will you help us put this into the pipeline?"

"You want me to fence for you," Sands said. "That's what it comes down to."

"Something like that. Maybe. I don't know if we'd want to put that word on that."

"You know," Sands said, keeping his motions slow and quiet, sitting on the couch and leaning over to tap the cigarette into an ashtray, "even assuming that I could help you people, which I don't admit for a second, why should I? What would I get out of it tantamount to the risks?"

The stocky man said, "This is ridiculous. We're not getting anywhere with this clown and I think—"

"Give me a second," the East European said. His eyes were wide now and extremely alert. He kneeled easily, extended an arm, brought himself to eye-level with Sands. "Of course there are risks," he said. "With something of this proportion there would have to be risks. But think of the returns."

"What returns? There are people who would kill to get that stuff back apparently."

"Fifty percent," the East European said flatly. "Fifty percent and we'll take your accounting. Or you can give us fifty thousand dollars cash right now and we're out of it. That's all we want, fifty thousand dollars in bills and you can take it anywhere you want."

"That's crazy. I'm a professor, not even a professor, an associate. Where would I get that kind of money?"

"We're heard around that you have a pretty profitable sideline. That you might have that kind of money."

"Well I don't," Sands said. "I have about four thousand dollars in savings and a couple of thousand in stock warrants that I can't even *sell* and maybe a couple of thousand worth of furnishings. You're looking at most of what I've got."

"Are we really?" the man said quietly.

"I don't think we can do business," said Sands. He put out the cigarette with contrived casualness and stood, rearing far above the kneeling man. "There's nothing to discuss. Even assuming that I was everything you seem to think I am, I don't have any interest in buying this stuff and I don't think I want to take the risks. This is no straight deal; you've misappropriated that shipment."

"All right," the East European said. He stood, turned to the stocky man. "We tried. Let's go."

The stocky man came over, kicked the valise closed, snapped the clips. "I told you this was a waste of time," he said. "This is all bullshit."

"That may be."

"I have one suggestion," Sands said quietly as the shorter man hoisted the valise. The sight of it going away from him was suddenly intolerable but he held himself in check. Discipline. Everything was discipline. "If you want a suggestion that is. You're ready to rush right out of here now."

"Don't give me that shit," the man holding the valise said, "you're the one who—"

The East European made that placative gesture again, somewhat more abruptly. He seemed to be increasingly impatient. "Let the man talk," he said, "and just shut the fuck up now, I mean it."

"You can leave it here," Sands said, "leave it here and I'll see what I can do with it. Check back in twenty-four hours. I'm not saying for an instant that I *can* do anything but you could do that."

"You're crazy," the stocky man said, "you're out of your fucking mind. We're supposed to just *leave* that thing with you. Just walk out and leave it? Why, you're—"

"What choice do you have?" Sands said with sudden harshness. "Come on, tell me. You're the ones who have a problem here, not me and don't you forget it."

He clenched his fist, feeling a dim sensation of power rising within him. These men had the guns, they had walked into his home, they had begun by threatening *him* but Sands knew, looking at them as clearly as he had ever known anything in his life that he was in command. They were at his mercy. The guns had merely been masks for their condition because the fact was that they were beggars. "You give me twenty-four hours with that valise and I'll see what I can do," he said coldly. "I'm making no promises and making no commitments but at least I might be able to use certain contacts to get an evaluation. And not conceding for an instant, *for one second*, that I'm into the kind of things you think I'm into, I might be able to scout around and find someone who is and who could make arrangements." He stood, walked briskly toward the hallway, opened the door and motioned. "It's your decision," he said. "I don't want you in my house anymore. You can take the valise and get out or you can leave it here and trust me. Make up your minds now."

The stocky man, his face discolored, breathing heavily said, "It's a lousy deal, Paul. I don't like any part of it. Let's get the stuff and go."

"*Who told you to use my name?*" the East European said, "you stupid son of a bitch, keep my name out of it." He closed the distance between them in three strides and hit the stocky man full in the face, open-handed.

For an instant, Sands thought that the stocky man was going to pull his gun and that there was going to be, right in his living room, a small massacre. The man jumped, reached inside of his pocket cursed violently. "*Don't do it,*" the one named Paul said. His gun suddenly was in his hand. "Don't even think of it."

The stocky man subsided. He seemed to shrink. He shook his head, backed away from Paul, his hands flailing. "All right," he said, "all right, I think you're crazy, but not here. Not here."

Paul turned to Sands and said, "I don't like this. I don't like any part of it."

"I don't see why you should."

"But you're not giving us any choice here really, are you?"

"The choice is yours," Sands said. He edged all triumph out of his voice although the temptation was to giggle in a way that he had not for twenty years. If he did so, however, he knew that he would lose the control that he had so delicately asserted. "I mean that."

"The whole deal stinks," Paul said. "On the other hand we're supposed to trust you, to put this stuff into your hands—"

"Just for twenty-four hours."

"For twenty-four hours, for twenty-four minutes, what's the difference? We're supposed to walk out the door here, put the stuff in your hands and trust you. On the other hand, we're supposed to walk out with it."

"If I were in your position," Sands said, "if I were in your position, I think I'd rather leave it with me. Wouldn't you? Because if you walk out with it you're going back where you came from."

"We've got to go back where we came from anyway," the stock man said, and then subsided as Paul looked at him. "All right," he said, moving toward the door to join Sands, but in no aggressive way—it was apparent now that all he wanted to do was to get out—"all right, I don't care anymore."

"You can check back with me tomorrow night," Sands said with enormous calm. He knew now that control had passed entirely to his hands and his only emotion, strangely, was depression because he had a good idea of what he was taking on and it probably meant no more good for him than it did to this pair. "I'll be here. I'm not going anywhere."

Paul looked at him in an almost pleading manner. The man who had, with superb control, wedged his way into the household and shaken Sands so much was gone, he had been replaced by a cautious, tentative, almost desperate low-grade punk who now seemed to be trying to hold on to some piece of the situation. "We'll trust you," he said, "we've got no choice."

"That's good."

"But if you cross us up, you'll pay for it Sands. Remember, we know exactly who you are, where you live, everything about you. We know stuff about you you don't know yourself."

"All right," Sands said. "Whatever you say." Again, he had to resist a patronizing giggle. Fools: all of them were fools. If this was any true representation of the element which was responsible for procurement, Sands thought, he should have gotten into his own supply years ago. Well, no time to think about that now. "I'll be here," he said. "Believe me, I'm not going anywhere at all."

"You better go somewhere."

"I'll make a few phone calls," Sands said obligingly. He walked with determination through the hallway, yanked open the outer door. Night spilled into the hallway. He stood into one side of the hallway, feeling an umbrella stand press against his knees, and motioned for the two of them to leave. They did so, Paul first, leaving without a word, then the stocky man with a sidewise scuttle, looking up at Sands with the bright, uneven, demented stare of a sideshow freak being examined.

"Don't fuck around with us," this one said. "I don't work for him. I don't work for anyone. You fuck around with this stuff, I'll tear your balls off."

"All right," Sands said again. A small illumination of pain drifted from his groin upward but he was not going to grip himself instinctively or otherwise. Don't let them know that they have reached you and, in effect, they haven't reached you at all. All that they understand, he told himself, is the visible. No taste for abstractions. The stocky man went out into the night and Sands closed the door on them, locked it, put up the chain and then the police lock which he had had installed as a precaution three years ago but which he had never used until this moment.

He walked back into the living room slowly. The valise, closed down like a sleeping face, confronted him. He wanted to rip it open, tear at the clips and, lifting the lid, confront the treasure within, but he did not. Control: everything had to do with control. He merely stood there, confronting the valise and blanking his mind at the conscious level, while deep within the instincts and subliminal apperceptions ground away, telling him without inquiry what his next move must be.

Karen crept down the stairs and leaned over the banister. She had put on a pink nightgown and looked young and vulnerable, the fabric twisted around her, the shell of her body hinting at a softness he had never known before. "Phil," she said, "Phil, what was all that about?" He did not answer her. He knelt over the valise instead, looking at it. Inside the music beat at him. In the far background this woman was talking, she was talking away but it meant nothing. It was happening at a level from which he had long since ascended.

If she did not shut up soon he would throw her out, forcibly if possible. But just for the moment he blocked out everything, hearing the music rush at him, looking at the valise which when opened would confirm nothing more or less than the simple truth: the biggest, the most meaningful score of his life.

Fallen right into his fucking hands. He didn't even have to work for it.

"Come on," he said to the woman who might have been his wife, "get the fuck out of here."

He sounded, he realized, like the stocky man.

Junk could do that, even to him.

V

Wulff slept three hours, because it was either that or go under altogether, got up at three a.m., his anger congealed into a desperate fury. He lay awake in the darkness contemplating whether he should wait until dawn for his strike at Tucci, and then abruptly decided against it. He would go now. He would move in now. Better to move against these people at night, because he could catch them at the low ebb of their purposes. Even the vermin had to sleep; he would take advantage of that.

He got out of the bed seething, got back into his clothes seething, took two pistols out of supply and moved on. The machine gun was a tempting idea but it would only load him down for a swift attack. Later, later, when he had the enemy massed as he wanted them to be, he could move in with the full clip. Now he would travel light. He went out of the room and down the stairs, past the desk where the clerk lay sprawled in a stupor and outside into the quiet, broken streets of Boston.

There were several cars on the street which he could have appropriated but even as he started toward one he reversed direction. The hell with it. He was not going to fiddle with ignition systems, bypasses, electrical gimmickry at this point. He did not have the patience, every nerve in him was directed to action. A car turned the corner slowly, engine racing unevenly, the driver apparently lost. Wulff stepped in front of it deliberately, waved his arm. The car bore down on him, accelerating slightly as the driver seemed to balance one thing off against the other, finally slowed and stopped. Hit and run was not this driver's specialty although anything standing in a city street at this hour probably deserved it. Good, Wulff thought. Good. He gripped the pistol, stepped toward the car.

The driver, a young man, barely out of his teens came through the door raving. "What the fuck are you, man?" he said. "What do you think you're doing? Who are you?"

Wulff showed him the pistol. "Just keep moving," he said. "I want the car."

The boy's hands twitched. "This is crazy," he said.

"I need the car."

"It's my old man's car. Listen, he'll kill me if—"

"Make a full report," Wulff said, waving the gun. "Go to the precinct. They won't give you any problems."

The passenger door opened, a young girl came out, her face blank and frightened. She saw the gun and screamed, collapsing into the car. Wulff stayed there, holding his ground while the boy came around to grip her. The girl struggled against him momentarily, fluttering, then collapsed. "Oh my God," she said. "Oh my God." The young man dragged her away.

Wulff got into the car, slammed the door. "You'll pay for this," the boy said, leaning in on the passenger side. He had guts all right; Wulff could give him that much credit. "You won't get away with this kind of thing."

"Get in line," Wulff said, holding the gun on the boy as he drove away one-handed. "Join the club." He rolled up the window and threw the gun beside him on the seat.

The car was a '60 LeSabre, not the ideal stolen car from any point of view—would anyone want to go to jail for theft of an automobile worth a hundred dollars, when for the same sentence he might as well steal a new Cadillac?—but it worked well and someone, probably the boy himself, had done some clever work with the engine. It picked up fast, shifted far more alertly through the automatic transmission than was characteristic. Spoiler mufflers underneath, customizing around the dash, a devil's head dangling on string from the rear-view mirror, grinning at him. The boy had put a lot of work into this one-hundred dollar car. Well, good enough, Wulff meant him no harm at all. He would ditch it, finally, in a well-travelled area and leave the plates on, not that there were many customized '60 LeSabres in the Boston district.

He took the bridge, heading across the Charles River. Revere Beach, that was where Tucci lived. He could have suspected as much. Revere Beach was where the people like Tucci in the Boston area would go. In Brooklyn it was Sheepshead Bay, in Northern New Jersey it was Teaneck; further south, for the more elegant, there was Deal but Deal was a different world altogether. Some day, Wulff thought mordantly, he might be able to make it into Deal if only to lay a few land-mines; it was simultaneously the most beautiful and corrupt residential area he had ever seen, the corruption springing from the beauty which was seen only as magnificent, rolling estates located perilously near the sea. Drugs and pain had bought those estates but the walls shut them out just as the sea shut off the estates on all but one side. Deal was another way of life altogether, but the Boston dealers had their Revere Beach and that for them was probably enough. It was a question of settling at your proper level. If they were not satisfied with Revere Beach then they were not smalltimers: they would never have staked out Boston in the first place. They would have fought for their place in the sun to the south.

Coming into the suburb, Wulff saw the houses jammed one upon the other, thin walls making them separate, all of them shapeless in the darkness. No space in Revere Beach, here the houses were huddled, but there was height and the walls gave their own version of impermeability. The LeSabre was the only car moving on the streets at this time. He cut the lights down to park, eased the throttle. The exhaust system growled thanks to the work that had been done on it, but he was relatively inconspicuous. No one would notice him driving near dawn on the streets of this suburb unless Tucci, of course, had kept a watch.

He drove two blocks, approaching Tucci's home. There were cars parked around it, cars wedged into the driveway, spilling out into the street, littering the block up and down and the house, the only one on the block was blazing with light. Driving by at slow idle, hunched over the wheel, Wulff saw that the door was open, in that abcess men stood, half in the house, half on the street smoking, talking. He drove to the end of the block, not breaking the rhythm of his pace, cut right at the corner, began to circle. This was improbable.

It was totally improbable: what was going on at Tucci's house? Surely they were not keeping a watch for him. They could not have possibly anticipated his course of action, and even if they had this was not the way you laid patrol to a house, cars scattered all over, men lounging in the doorway. Wulff shook his head trying to figure it out, took two more rights and came down the street once again.

This time there was a hearse parked in front of the house. It had backed up to the porch and the rear panels were open. Even as he drove by again he saw a group of men walking from the house toward that hearse.

Abruptly, he understood everything.

All of it came together then; he had stumbled into the middle of a wake. Henry Tucci was dead, this could be the only explanation, and now, in the dawn hours, his fraternity was assembling. In Revere Beach it seemed they did things right. There would be no waiting for the morning hours to begin the burial of Tucci.

Wulff kept on driving, heading flat out this time toward the sea, away from the house. He put his headlights back to full, carefully lit a cigarette, thought about it. His best move, doubtless, was to let the thing go; take another tack, another name out of the stockbroker's notebook, go hunting in a different direction. If Tucci were indeed dead there would be nothing productive there, he could hardly bring pressure against a corpse and the house was, to put it mildly, well attended.

"Son of a bitch," Wulff said. Boston had been a disaster from the moment he had approached it and somehow this was the most ominous signal of all. Wulff's instincts told him that Tucci had not died of natural causes: natural causes would not bring lights to a house at three in the morning, or such an assemblage. No, it had been something brief and terrible that had brought an end to Henry Tucci; there were forces at work in this city now which Wulff could not yet comprehend. He knew on every level that Tucci's death had something to do with the quarter of a million dollars of death that had been released into the city. It was the wild card, the unknown equation. He pounded the wheel with mounting fury, accelerated, turned halfway into an intersection to make a screaming U-turn and then headed back.

It had been a disaster, Boston had; nothing was working. Now things were zooming out of control: if a Tucci had died because of the wild card then there would be others. Whatever fragile balance Boston had had, a balance probably built upon the sharp limitation of supply, it was now over. Open season was beginning.

Wulff felt around his belt and took out a grenade. No machine gun and clip was he going to take out on the streets, it was too encumbering. But grenades were portable, inconspicuous and could have an even more spectacular effect. He took it from his waist and looked at it, considered what he was going to do for no more than a minute.

Some innocent people were going to be badly hurt. But he had to remember that there was no innocence in this trade, that anyone and everything touched by junk became irretrievably rotten and then had to pay the price. If he began to think of checks and balances, levels of thought, then he was beginning only to think like a cop or a bureaucrat again. That was why the enforcers were only another component of the disease; because they refused to accept responsibility and follow it through.

To fight vermin you had to be one.

He poised the grenade delicately in his hand, gathered speed, balanced the steering wheel with the elbow of the arm holding the grenade, cranked down the driver window all the way and got back on the wheel. The car was now moving at forty, forty-five miles an hour on the quiet street. He got it up to sixty. At that speed something came free in the transmission and he had the feeling of floating above ice, suspended. The mufflers cut in and he felt the power building.

On to Tucci's block. The hearse had attracted a crowd outside, all of them were watching with interest as five or six men struggled with a blocky shape that could only have been a casket. Henry Tucci's last ride. A flasher on top of the hearse which was wedged well out into the street spun, throwing yellow and red into his eyes. Wulff blinked. He pulled the pin.

Now everything was crucial, it had to synchronize. Seven seconds. He cocked his arm, held the gas pedal steady. Six. He could feel little slivers of heat from the grenade penetrating like splinters into his palm. Nervous reaction. Plenty of time. Don't throw it yet. Five seconds. Four. He was within twenty yards of the house now and gathering speed. Faces leapt up at him in the light. He could see the casket waver in the air as, distracted, the carriers looked at him.

The grenade seemed to be growing within his palm. It was just like combat, a bursting flower spreading under his fingers, a feeling of flinch and underneath that enormous power. Three seconds. Two. All of them were looking at him now. The pattern of bodies on the street had broken. They were running away. They were running into the house. The casket, the last receptacle of Henry Tucci bounced on the ground, abandoned. Life was for the living.

In that last second Wulff saw it all, the sweep of bodies, the scattering, bouncing coffin, open doors of the house, the last frantic twitches of an ant colony as it unconsciously realizes that an enormous foot is about to stamp it to death. He put the gas pedal down to the floor praying that the LeSabre would hold. He threw the grenade.

There was a dull *whoomp:* and the house went up.

Sheets of flame carrying ash and splinters were hurled into the night. The roar of impact covered what must have been the lower shouts and screams. But all of this was happening in a tunnel somewhere to the rear: Wulff was in the pipeline, he was already bailing out. Fifty yards, then a hundred, then two hundred behind him; explosion was building upon explosion as the fragments fed the building fire, but he was out of it.

It was a hell of a wake for Henry Tucci. Surely the dead man would have appreciated it. When his world ended, it ended for so many who had known him. Yes, this would in a way be the ultimate satisfaction.

Wulff drove out of it all. He was laughing. The laughter came out of him harsh, cruel, devastating, painful in his chest, refracted within him. Death laughter known first as pain and only then as knowledge. He heard the roar of the night. He heard the first sounds of sirens.

Ditch the LeSabre, sure. But first, get out of there. He drove on.

VI

An hour earlier, the two men who had been in Sands' house edged the old Impala cautiously onto the turnpike and headed west. The road was deserted; occasionally the headlights would pick up an animal scampering in terror or a faint illumination from the hedges that ripped against their eyes. The men said nothing for a while. Paul who was driving had everything he could do to keep the battered car functioning and stable at highway speeds and the stocky man was slumped within himself, still trying to put together the pieces of what had happened. After a little while a mist began to come up against the windshield and Paul put on the wipers. The right one had no blade, it streaked and smeared the windshield and the stocky man cursed. "I can't see a fucking thing," he said.

"Don't complain. I'm driving."

"Yeah? Well how far are we going to drive?"

"Until we're the fuck out of Massachusetts," Paul said. "We're not going to hang anywhere around Boston while this is going on."

"You mean we'll commute back tomorrow night."

"Something like that."

"Horseshit," the stocky man said and when there was no reply he added, "I don't like this. I don't like any fucking part of it."

"You made that quite clear back there."

"I don't trust the guy. How do we know he just won't take off with the stuff?"

"He's got roots."

"How do we know he can even do anything for us? You heard him say that we had him wrong."

"Don't worry about Phillip Sands," Paul said, playing with the knobs on the dashboard, getting a faster stroke on the wipers, "Phillip Sands is *the* supply man for this area. If anyone can do the job for us he can."

"He'll screw us blind. I don't trust the son of a bitch."

"You don't seem to understand," Paul said quietly. "We're not in any bargaining position. We can't get that stuff into channels ourselves."

"We didn't even try!"

"You're stupid," Paul said. "You've been stupid all your life, Miller, and you'll go on being stupid. We come into daylight with a haul like that and we wouldn't last half an hour. Telephone calls would go right through channels and they'd have a party for us on the spot. A guy like Sands at least gives us a chance. He's an outsider too."

"We could have tried," Mac said sullenly, "we could have at least given it a go. How do we know it's a quarter million? It could be twice that. It could be a million!"

"Sure," Paul said. He worked his blond hair out of his eyes. His forehead was sweating lightly. "We could have turned the stuff in, too. Remember? You wanted to do that."

Very lightly Mac said, "I still think we should have done it Paul. We're in over our heads now."

"We're not in over our heads if we don't panic. Let this man handle it. He'll fence it for us, believe me. We'll go back there tonight and pick up that fifty grand in cash. You wait and see. He'll get the stuff tested and he'll raise the money. He's not going to let something like that go once he knows what it is."

"He isn't?"

"He's greedy," Paul said, "he's a lot greedier than I am. All I want to see out of this is fifty grand."

"Fifty grand is no price, Paul," Mac said. He shifted on the seat. Behind them he could see headlight beams coming up through the rearview mirror. A wanderer, travelling fast. "What are we going to do with fifty grand?"

"I don't know what you're going to do," Paul said, "I'll tell you what I'm going to do with twenty-five though. I'm going to go underground and I'm going to do it alone. You go your way, I'll go mine."

"I don't like it," Mac said, "I just don't like it. We should have delivered the stuff and let it go."

"And picked up a hundred each?"

"Maybe two hundred each," Mac said. "Maybe three hundred. It was a big package. We took risks."

"Fuck that," Paul said. The wipers quit suddenly and he cursed, fumbled with the knobs, managed to get them going again before the mist closed in. "I'm sick of living on the margin all my life. You see a chance you take it. Don't bother me anymore, Mac. You don't like the route, I'll stop the car and you can get the fuck out. Walk to Pittsfield, take a furnished room. Tomorrow you can call them and sincerely apologize."

"Screw you," Mac said unhappily. He hated the son of a bitch. All right, he would admit it, he would face the truth. The man was no good. He was crazy. He really thought that he could buck against the echelons above and he had talked Mac into it against every instinct which Mac had. He *knew* that they would never get away with it. But what was he going to tell the silly fuck when they were driving away, the valise in the back, Paul at the wheel in full control, when Paul said *let's make our own run for it*. Was he supposed to get out of the car and run? Pull out his pistol and shoot Paul? Threaten him? No, he had been sucked in; that was all there was to it. There was something manic and poisonous about Paul's greed, it had infected him.

It had infected him all the way to the professor's duplex apartment and even a little beyond that until, sitting in the living room, listening to that smooth bastard talking away, Mac had realized that he was in completely over his head. Paul was crazy, that was bad enough, to listen to a crazy man, but to turn over goods like this to some son of a bitch in tweeds who would not even admit that he could *do* anything—that was insanity.

He should have shot them. That was all. He should have gunned both of them down in that living room, grabbed the valise and gotten the hell out of there. Turned it over. Turned it back. He would have had a double-murder on his hands but maybe, just maybe, if he had turned over the goods and shown good faith, they would have protected him. His record was clean; he was a good assignment man. He had never gotten into any trouble like this before. They would understand. He would tell them that Paul had pulled a gun on him or something and forced him to go along and he had bided his time until the first opportunity to turn the tables. They would listen to him. They would take him back and put him underground and in four or five months after the headlines over the professor had gone away he would have come out and it would have been just like the old days and he never, never would have gotten involved in anything like this again.

Too late. That was hours and hours ago that they had been in the professor's apartment. Now they were headed west, down the road toward Connecticut, and Paul was at the wheel which meant that if he tried anything he would only wreck the car and it was too late. He didn't even have the goods anymore, which he knew would have been the only way he could have bought his way back.

He had been sucked in, Mac realized, and there was nothing left to do but play along and hope that Paul's maneuvers worked out. Maybe they would. Maybe the guy did know what he was doing. Perhaps he was even right: that you had to take the chance when the chance presented itself unless you wanted to live on the margin all your life.

Mac sighed, glanced at the rear view mirror again. That car behind had come up fast but now it had slowed. It certainly was tailing them close. Going at seventy-five, which was all Paul could coax out of the old machine, the car was no more than two or three lengths behind. Paul's hands clenched the wheel, his face grim. He seemed paralyzed, locked into the speed which was, of course, fifteen over the legal limit. If it was cops and they wanted to bust their balls they were dead. Mac turned, looked out the rear window. A red light on top of the following car came to life, sent panels of light into his eyes. He heard a siren.

"Shit," Paul said. He was sweating freely. "Godammit it, it's cops."

"Slow down," Mac said, "we can't outrun the sons of bitches."

"And what do we show them? License? Registration please? They'll pull us in." He floored the accelerator.

"We'll talk our way out of it," Mac said.

"We can't chance it. They could lock us up. We've got to get to Boston tomorrow night."

"Paul," he said, "Paul you're crazy, they're not going to jail us on a simple speeding, even if you haven't got license and registration. They'll impound the car and we'll have to make some bail, that's all."

"Make bail?" Paul said. He was fighting the wheel, the car groaning along at eighty, beginning to wobble now on the center line, "You need identification to make bail, godammit."

"We have identification!"

"They'll pass it around. You know the cops here, don't you? We'll have a welcoming party two blocks from the station house wherever it is."

He was right. The trouble was that the son of a bitch was right. They were in deep now, deeper than he could have imagined. But there was still just no way that the Impala could outrun a squad car in full cry. He heard the siren, coming at him as if it would shatter the glass and send fibers pierced into his brain. "Pull over!" he said. "For Christ's sake, whatever happens, you've got to pull over!"

"Fuck it," Paul said. With one hand on the wheel he used the other to fumble for his gun. "Get your gun," he said, "shoot them."

"Shoot them? They're bulletproofed, we're shooting through glass—"

"Shoot them!" Paul screamed, wrenching at the wheel and he lost control. Almost elegantly, softly, the car tracked to the right, and at eighty-two miles an hour hit the shoulder. Mac felt the suspension sway, had the sensation that the Impala was almost meditating not only on its future course but its history, the ten years that had passed since it had come off the production line, new and with two hundred and eighty-three cubic centimeters, shortly before a President was assassinated. The car rocked, spewed up pebbles and then came back onto the road with hesitancy, then a growing assurance.

"Shoot at the bastards!" Paul screamed again. Holding the wheel with his left hand he turned quickly and pumped through a wild shot with his right. Splinters of glass exploded, Mac could feel them darting into his cheeks. The rear window cascaded open in colors. The siren shifted to a deeper, more insistent tone and the car behind sprang out, shifting lanes. At full acceleration it started to come alongside.

"You're going to kill us," Mac said, turning with the angle of the police car's roll, now seeing it come alongside them. Locked wheel to wheel at eighty-five miles an hour the motion was slow, elegant, it might have been creeping abreast to get into a parking slot behind. For the first time Mac could see the faces of the occupants. Young cops, faces like apples, both of them staring. The could not believe this and for that matter neither could he. "You've killed us!" Mac shrieked.

"Shut the fuck up," Paul said, hunched over the wheel, "don't tell me what I'm doing, just shoot them. *Shoot them!*" Mac levelled, aimed and discharged the pistol toward the driver's window, hoping the catch the passenger-cop in the head. Maybe it would panic them at least, slow the vehicle.

Just as he pressed the trigger the Impala hit a small stone on the road, magnified by speed. It sent rolling layers of concussion through his body, it shook his gun hand and therefore, quite methodically, Mac shot Paul in the head.

A small hole appeared near Paul's temple. Blood wept out. Paul himself kept on driving for a few seconds, astonishment mingling with confusion in his features. More than anything else it appeared as if he had inherited a terrible itch. He raised a distracted, clawing hand to scratch the itch, the fingers met his hair and only at that connection did he pitch over, sidewise, falling across Mac, falling across his gun, the car now out of control, the steering wheel slack and loose, and the Impala scooted across the lane-separator, hit the police car a rolling blow, rebounded, ducked onto the shoulder and then with the absent grace of a ballet dancer gathering himself for a final leap, the Impala lost all handling whatsoever.

Paul came into his arms with the horrid finality of a lover settling in. Mac embraced him, desperately holding on, his eyes wide. The Impala rolled and rolled, it came off the shoulder at seventy-one miles an hour and onto a little embankment, the embankment grappled with it, the tires split open, the suspension swung, the car heaved to the right, overbalanced and began with lazy grace to roll. Mac felt every bump and hollow as the car took the long dive. He moved between roof and seat, hitting his skull several times, fracturing, hemorrhaging, but consciousness was absolute. *I'm going to make it*, he thought joyfully, *I'm going to make it.* Survival was a great flame ahead of him; it embraced him just as he was embracing the corpse, showered with blood. Nothing, absolutely nothing mattered if he survived. The car rolled down the last yards more slowly, hit a little crevice before the tree-line and it was this which probably unsettled the delicate adjustment which had been made so far. *I'm going to make it*, Mac thought one last time, and the car exploded.

He felt himself as if gripped by a giant hand, thumb and forefinger constricting, pressing against one another, working his life away and then a plunger hit his heart and took it with enormous force; he could feel his life moving up that plunger. In his last extremity he gripped the dead Paul as if Paul's body itself could guarantee him passage, but the corpse was heat and stone, death and ice, it was merely a causeway toward death. Mac slid along and along that path as the car went up around him as if with the arcing of tracer fire.

At last it was very quiet.

The police car dragged itself to a halt a few hundred yards up the road. Both of the cops were quite young, one a rookie, the other only with three years in. They looked at one another and then quickly back at the burning car and then the rookie began to vomit.

The driver thought that he would admonish him but felt himself seized with his own retching; he opened the door and managed to lay it outside, on the pebbling, rather than on the mats of the car.

Christ, it was too much. He began to weep. In just a minute he was all right and he would get on the radio to make a full report but Christ, Christ, it was too much. It was just entirely too much for him.

A job like this: getting involved with drivers like the one in the Impala, crazed gunmen seemingly bent on self-destruction, well—

A man could *die* on this job.

VII

The item on the two punks in the ditched Impala was way, way down on page 27 of the *Globe*, but the firebombing of Tucci's house, the twelve injured and eight dead, that was on page one. Sands didn't even look at it though. He took the paper when it was delivered and chucked it onto the table where Karen could look at it later if she wanted to bother. He had enough trouble already.

He had more than enough trouble; he had a valiseful of junk to feed into channels and no one wanted to touch it. He found that out soon enough. A couple of phone calls into the usual sources not only met at refusals, they were terrified refusals. "Don't tell me!" one outlet who had been particularly dependable said, "for Christ's sake, I don't even want to hear about it!" and hung up on Sands which was doubly impossible because people simply did not hang up on him. They were always eager to hear from Phillip Sands; he brought them their good news.

But no one was going to touch this. Sands got that feeling early on; you were nothing without instincts in his very risky sideline and his instincts from the moment the two men had come into his house had screamed that they were in over their heads and that anyone with the valise was probably heading that way himself. The valise was a curse. It was an absolute curse. If he was right and he was almost never wrong about this, he had been looking at one of the biggest hauls in the history of the Eastern seaboard, all of it tucked away together. And the fact that it wasn't where it was supposed to be meant that there was going to be hell to pay. A man who kept hold of that valise for any period of time could get himself killed. That pair, with all their mumbling and threats, had seemed almost happy to walk out of there and leave Sands with the problem.

He should dump it. He really should; he knew that the right move was to simply wait for the two of them to return which they probably would hours early, throw up his hands and tell them to get it the hell out of his life. But how could he do it? Looking at the valise, feeling his life beginning to shake around him, Phillip Sands came to a reluctant understanding that day. Everything that he had done before had been small time. He had a good, quiet reputation and he could get a job done but he had just been a little man working on the fringes, taking no more risks than an associate professor could afford. He was absolutely, completely out of his depth now.

But he could not give it up. There was a hundred grand for him in that suitcase, maybe more, if only he could move it out. Even after the two punks had been paid off—and he was not entirely sure that he would go the full fifty for them, he might be able to get away with a lot less— there was so much that it might change his life. It was life-changing money. Nothing up until now had been at that level, it had all been nickels and dimes. Now Sands had a decision to make, and that morning, with difficulty, he made it: it was more important of him to dispose of that valise properly than it was to be an associate professor who did a little dealing. When he came right down to it—and he had little choice now in facing what he had become—the valise was more important. That was all. It meant more.

He called the university and reported sick. Upperclass seminar, the hell with it. Teaching, since he had settled into it four years ago, had become increasingly burdensome; now, it was little more than boredom. Part of that had to do with the collapse of a research project to which he had dedicated ten years of his life; when all the curves were skewed there was simply no definite coefficient of correlation between the belligerence of a society and the prevalence of invective. It had been an insight but insights meant nothing, verification was all that had counted. He had been able to fake it through for the doctoral thesis but no further. The work was flimsy, superficial. The Foundation had not renewed. Like it or not, if Phillip Sands ever became rich or important he would not do so in the field of linguistics.

Sitting by the phone, frozen in thought, he calculated his moves. He needed desperately to talk with someone, but he had played a lone hand all his life, never more so since he had begun to move from the casual procurement and resale of marijuana toward the harder stuff a few years ago. There was no one to talk to. Karen was impossible. She might have had a vague idea of what he was doing—she had been in his classes, hadn't she? He had met her at a campus party for Christ's sake—but she would not admit it, would not come to terms. He had hinted around it a few times early in their marriage but she had dropped every attempt at discussion. Soon enough Sands had understood. Her background might have prepared her for a joint or two—she could talk glibly about the varieties of drugs and their effects—but the realities of supply were simply not to be acknowledged. She was the same way about fucking. In bed, often enough, she could be quite passionate, come to him with a frankness which was shocking, but it was only under cover of dark. Any reference outside of the bedroom to sex, their sexual life, any expectation of sexual relations could turn her off for days. Once she had shut him off for a week because he had said, stoned at a party, that his wife was a good fuck.

No, he was alone. At noon, Karen came down carrying a small suitcase—the shape and texture of it was shockingly close to that of the valise, for an instant he thought she must have compressed it somehow and was now taking it away from him—and said that she simply couldn't take it anymore, she was leaving him. Sands looked at her blandly and responded without emotion. This would make the third— no, the fourth time that she had left him within the past six months. It was always for the same reason, the utter collapse of communication, the feeling that he was shutting her out of his life. He could tell her a few things about shutting people off. She always came back. She went to one or another off-campus apartment with one or another of her student girlfriends, and three or five days later she came in, almost contrite, and the sex was better than it had ever been. Her problem, maybe, was dropping out of school when she married him, but that had been her decision, God knows, not his. He had had nothing to do with it. Married to a Ph.D. ten years older, you would have thought that she would have *wanted* to keep up her education. But her parents, for vague reasons not really having to do with the marriage, had disowned her, and she had not wanted Sands on an associate's salary to put up himself the ninety a credit to stay at Boston University, which she called fifth-rate anyway. He guessed he couldn't blame her. There was something about her getting a job and maybe working on an education degree at night, but nothing much had come out of that.

Sands said that he wished her well. At another time he would have tried to have shown more passion but the valise was on his mind. It made for an easier homecoming if he showed passion but it just wasn't in him. "You don't care!" she said, standing at the door. "I just realized that last night. You don't care! You have no feeling! Inside, you're nothing but a machine."

"That's not so, Karen."

"What do you mean, it's not so? It's so clear to me. I don't even know who you are!"

God, she was pretty. She was never so pretty as when she was leaving him. Desertion gave her passions that she could otherwise find only under the cover of night. Sands said, "Karen, we've gone through this too many times before. I just can't—"

"You take it for granted! You just expect me to come back and fall against you, isn't that it? Well it won't happen this time."

"All right," he said tiredly, looking at the valise. He had been up all night thinking about it. He had been on the phone all morning. If she had stripped and invited him in he might have reacted the same way. "Anything you say."

She held the suitcase almost jauntily, then, walked toward the door. "I know what you are," she said quietly.

"I'm glad you do, Karen, because there are a lot of times that I don't."

"I'm no fool. You think I don't know what those two men were here about last night?"

"We were discussing Whorf's theory," he said. "They're graduate students from Western Reserve who travelled East at their own great expense to see me because they know my reputation. They wanted some ideas for their theses."

"Fuck you," she said. It somehow never failed to shock him when she used obscenities so casually; he was thirty-four, she twenty-four, but it was not ten years, it was another condition of life altogether. Whatever he had been and done, he still quailed a little when he heard a woman curse, but they seemed to think nothing of it. Except in bed where he liked to hear her curse and then she bit her lips and wouldn't say a godamned thing except *faster*. Perverse. The perversity of them. "You're a godamned son of a bitch fucking *pusher*, that's what you are."

This was a new element in their desertion discussions. Usually she stopped after telling him that he had nothing inside and went right through the door, swinging that damned little suitcase. But now she was hitting a new key. He wished he had the energy to respond. "That's not true," he said.

"That is true! It's perfectly true! You're selling drugs all over the campus and everybody knows it and it's starting to get back to me and what kind of a fool do you think I am? I won't put up with it!"

"Karen," he said, "please get out."

"I know what you are," she said and this time there was no uncertainty, only a qualified kind of triumph, "that's exactly what you are, you son of a bitch."

"It's time for you to get out, Karen. You should have left two minutes ago. Please don't change the script." He concentrated on keeping his voice mild, professorial. His hands were shaking. "Get out Karen."

"I've checked on you. I know."

"If you don't get out now, Karen, I'm going to have to throw you out."

"I ought to go to the cops on you," she said. She opened the door. So this had been her planned exit line. "That's what I ought to do. It's the only way anyone's ever going to reach you. To get you good and scared. Maybe they'd send you up for twenty years with your graduate students and your fucking Whorf theory of linguistics."

Had this been the woman who whispered *faster* to him in the night? Stone, she was stone, his feelings had congealed to stone against her and he felt the rage beating. "I mean it," he said, "get out." All of his life he had sought for control. Without control you were not a human being. He had believed in it, had had faith in discipline. But how far could it take him? "Get out," he said again.

"I'm going to get out," she said. She hoisted her valise, little flurries of dissatisfaction moving across her cheeks as if she were still not satisfied that she had found the proper exiting stroke. A painter unwilling to abandon a canvas, still looking for the killing dash of color that would bring it alive. "Junk," she said, "godamned fucking junkman."

With a growl, Sands charged her. She dodged toward the door but the valise encumbered her, she could not duck out of the way quickly enough. Her head hit the panelling and she slumped. He grabbed her chin, cupping it as one does a child's face and hit her in the mouth. She crumpled against him. He straightened her up and hit her again, harder. Color slashed across her cheeks. He raised his arm to hit her on the skull, a ramming blow that would knock the top of her scalp toward her jaw and only then did he stop. Something caught him. *What have I become?* he thought, *what is happening to me?* With a gasp, tears in his eyes, he pushed her from him. She slammed into the door. He kicked the dropped valise so hard that he tore a hole in it, saw the glint of underthings.

She was crying. Shaking little tears welled out of her eyes. She raised both hands to her mouth, knuckles against her teeth like an infant. That was all. She was a child. He had never understood her until this moment.

"Cunt," he said, "cunt, get out of my house."

"Oh my God—"

"Get out of my house," Sands said, *"get out of my house,"* and yanked open the door, put his hand on her chest, surprisingly unsubstantial under the bright, pitiful dress and pushed her into the hallway. She fell away from him like jelly. Groaning and gasping she continued to gnaw at her knuckles.

"Fucking cunt," he said, "fucking whore son of a bitch," and seized the suitcase, hurled it violently against the wall. It hit with a crack making the sound a skull might make, fell to the carpeting.

"Don't come back," he said. "Don't ever come fucking back into my life again, you cunt."

Trembling, he closed the door, turned the lock. It was not enough. His whole body was shaking, he could feel the dislocation tearing through him like fever, like knives. He lunged into the living room, took a straightback chair, wedged it against the door in a police hold as once, long ago, he had done against a feared raid that had never come off. To keep this woman out. In rage he stormed through the rooms then, yanking off tablecloths, ripping linens from closets, seizing plates from random points in the kitchen and shattering them against the wall.

At length, all of this burned itself out and he was quiet. Sands sat gasping by the fireplace, holding himself against the great, tearing sobs that arced through him, forcing his respiration back to normal, feeling his heart pound away the small crucial passage of the blood which was his only—which was anyone's—hold upon life. And at the dead-center of all of this, he saw what he would have to do.

Everything came together for him then with a dull and final sense of connection and he saw before him the only way that this could be handled, the only way that he would be able to fit the pieces together. If he wanted to hold onto that valise, make it count, make it work, he had to do it this way. There was no other choice.

All of his life he had worked for the avoidance of risk. It had gotten him a doctorate and a failed project and a wife turned cunt who had walked out on him. And had put him nowhere at the age of thirty-four. Now he had to try it another way.

He had to take the path of risk which he had so carefully avoided. All of his life he had been the one at the head of the class, the one who got the assignments in on time, made a personal relationship with the instructor, took careful notes, never burned his bridges, considered all of the angles of a situation, never did anything whatsoever without careful, ponderous reflection. And this is what it had gotten him. No, now he had to try it the other way.

Every nerve and instinct shrieked against what he was about to do but Sands did it anyway. Everything started in the reversion against habit. He picked up the phone. He dialed a number that he had long known by memory although he had never expected to use it. But there were numbers that you would never use that it still paid to know simply because it was a small advantage. This was one of them. God help him, Sands thought. The phone rang dimly at the other end. After a time, someone picked it up.

Sands said that he had important business and he wanted to talk to a man named Cicchini. The secretary wanted to know his name and Sands said he wouldn't give it but he would guarantee that Cicchini would be interested: it had to do with a quarter of a million dollars. Maybe more. The secretary put him on hold.

After a longer time a man with a lilting voice came on and said that he was Cicchini's confidential assistant, his employer was out of town for the day but could he help him? Sands told the man that he could screw off, this was big business and he was going to talk to the man on top or no one at all. He offered to hang up. The confidential assistant asked him to hold on for a little while.

After a much longer pause than the first two, a man with a curiously flat, dead, dull voice came on and asked Sands what the hell he wanted and exactly who in hell he thought he was.

Sands nodded with a satisfaction mixed with the most terrible kind of fear, and quickly, intensely, levelly, he began to spell out his situation to Louis Cicchini, the head of the Boston family.

Cicchini heard him through without interruptions. A man did not get to where he was without being, among many other things, a good listener.

VIII

Wulff read all about the firebombing the next morning but it gave him no satisfaction. No reason why it should; he was as far from objective as ever. *Firebombing* the press called it: had the grenade been undiscovered in all that wreckage? Apparently. Little satisfaction. He was, for all of the excitement, back to square one.

Eight of them dead, almost twice as many injured, a good haul, but what had it done for him? He had to face the fact, he had accomplished nothing. The valise was still in the hands of the others, the essential structure of the enemy remained unchanged. It was like laying down artillery fire in a country ruled by guerillas, he thought; you could clean out isolated spots here and there but the basic organization would hold because it was dispersed, indigenous to the countryside itself. The only way that you could beat the enemy was to destroy the country itself, but the country was worth saving. You had to work from that single assumption; if you didn't you were dead altogether. Wryly, he thought of Vietnam.

Wryly, he thought of many things as he made his way back cautiously on foot to the flophouse hotel, the LeSabre, like so many cars before it ditched some distance away, keys in, motor running. Walking through a grey midmorning rain which had chased everyone, even the junkies, from the downtown streets—but then again Boston was a tightly-run city, with the levelling of Scully Square they had sent their junkies scattering north and west, east and south, eliminating the problem then by simply denying it—Wulff thought a little of the nature of the enemy, of the nature of his own struggle. Now he could see that everything had just been skirmishes, little forays on the outside. New York had been a joke really because he had not touched the men who controlled the network; San Francisco had been something less than a joke, it was a sunshine spectacular is what it had been, complete with a pier fire and a lot of death. But all that he had been able to take out of San Francisco was a valise, and how long had that lasted? How long would any of this last? If he died today, got himself gunned down on the pavement, which was more likely than not, the way things were going, the enemy would roll over as if he had never existed. They were so deep into the vitals of the country that no one man, no group of men could make a difference. The enemy, in fact, was infinitely replaceable. Everything so far had proven that. Crush one ant in a colony and two would come to take it away.

At the hotel entrance two men approached him from opposite sides, pinning him against a wall. He felt the looming pressure of their bodies, tried to go for his gun but the gesture was blocked and before he could react further they were expertly frisking him, patting him up and down, relieving him of the revolver which one of them shoved into a side pocket. They were tall, indistinguishably grim men wearing curiously elegant hats and they had caught him cold.

Stupid again. To go through all of this to be nailed down on a slum pavement. Wulff calculated briefly the chance of an all-out assault. But the men were professionals. The frisk completed they backed away, pulled guns beyond his reach and looked him over calmly. For the second time since he had come to this accursed city, Wulff waited for death.

"All right," the one on the left said, "let's go. Move."

Law enforcement? Wulff doubted it. Falling into the hands of the cops would not, however, be an improvement. He was in as deep with the one as the other and a quick death was preferable to confinement for life. He swung his line of sight from one to the other, looking for some vulnerability, some kind of weakness against which he might launch himself. But part of his own professionalism was in knowing not only when to attack but when to hold off. These men were impermeable. They had their guns out, they knew how to handle guns and they would put him on the pavement before he could close any distance. It would be a very poor supposition too for him to think they might miss a vital spot.

"I mean it, Wulff," the one on the left said, "let's get going." He reached forward but did not touch him, merely made a directing gesture and the one on the other side slipped behind to prod him gently. There was nothing to do. Wulff walked past the hotel, up the street. No one bothered to look at any of this. In the cities the most drastic and terrifying events could occur before crowds and there would be no interference. It was the only protection these people had.

There was a Continental idling at curbside near the corner, a third man behind the wheel. In an odd touch which indicated that these men had not missed a single detail, he was wearing a chauffeur's hat and reading a newspaper. He would attract no attention at all; just another employee of the gentry bringing some terrified businessman into the slums. As he saw them near, the chauffeur tossed the paper to the floor, adjusted his cap and, gripping the wheel delicately, eased the car out of its space and toward them. Wulff heard the sound of power door locks unsnapping and then one of the men, coming up in front of him, opened the rear right and showing him the gun again, motioned.

"Get in," he said.

Wulff got in. The car was a full divider, the glass probably inches thick and bulletproof. He could see the chauffeur's head only as a vague outline surrounded by what seemed to be clouds of vapor. He moved halfway across the seat and the other man, the one who had been behind him, opened the left door and slid beside him, knee to knee. The one on the right got in easily, closed the door, and almost imperceptibly the big car yawed into gear and began to move.

Frozen in. Wulff looked to the left and he looked to the right. No hope there. The gunmen had merely increased their alertness now that they were seated. They looked at him, weapons exposed, casually, almost pleasantly. In their eyes Wulff saw that familiar look: it was nothing personal at all. The gunmen barely knew who he was. They would, if he moved at them, gut him like a fish on this shiny back seat, but there would in all of it be nothing but the casual efficiency of a job performed for pay.

Wulff sighed, sat straight back and closed his eyes. No conversationalists, his abductors, no conversationalist he. They might be taking him out for the last fifteen miles of his life but in the meantime he was going to sleep.

Surprisingly, he did so. He must have passed into an uneven doze, broken only when the car got free of downtown Boston and began to move north in a clear surge of power. It was the speed which awakened Wulff; he was sensitive to the quality. It looked to be eighty-five, ninety miles an hour and this was both good and bad, bad because the limousine was not strung for speeds like this no matter what the manual said, but good because his abductors, obviously, had a destination. They were not looking for a place to ditch him; they wanted to get directly to where they were going and this was a good sign. Even professionals—*mostly* professionals, in fact—did not drive fast to the site of an assassination. It gave any man pause.

"Should we blindfold him?" the man on his right said. It was the first word from anyone since they had gotten into the car.

"I don't give a shit," the one on the left said in a thick New England accent. "Were we told to?"

"Well, no, not really—"

"Then the hell with it," the man said flatly. He leaned over toward Wulff, again with that strange solicitousness and Wulff knew then with a sense of positiveness that they were not going to kill him. Not now, anyway. And not these men. "Would you like to be blindfolded?"

"Not particularly."

"A lot of people *prefer* to be blindfolded," the man on his right said. "Would you believe that?"

"Why not?"

"They'd rather *not* see where they're going; they think it's better to see nothing. People are really strange," the man said and sighed, toyed with his gun. "Don't make a move or I'll kill you," he added in an obligatory way.

"I wasn't planning on it."

"I don't really want to kill you. I don't want to kill anyone. But sometimes people make it necessary."

"It's a tough racket," Wulff said.

"You don't know the half of it. You don't even know a *quarter* of it, the way some people are—"

"Shut the fuck up," the New Englander said. He bunched his coat, looked down at the folds. "Some people don't know when to quit," he said to Wulff.

"I guess not."

"But I do. So we'll just keep our conversation down if you don't mind."

"Suits me."

"You got a big fucking mouth," the man on the right said but added nothing and looked into the barrel of his gun then the way a drunk might look into a martini pitcher. Gloomily.

Still at high speed, the car broke free of the turnpike, dived for an exit, took a local road north, the driver cutting back to a mere sixty-five, the Continental absorbing the disturbances in the road like a bear grappling with its paws. Marblehead, Wulff saw.

So this was where the higher levels lived. He knew now that the two men were not assassins but delivery boys and he was being taken to the quarters of someone important enough to have a Continental and three men for hire. Marblehead was no Revere Beach, that was sure.

Here the land had opened up in the way that the pioneers moving west must have found it a hundred years ago; the clutter and enjambment of Revere Beach had given way to rolling green land chemically treated, moving right down to the seacoast, the seacoast itself richly colored and coming up to the rear of some houses which were located down at the front. The houses themselves were enormous and separated not only by the walls and hedges of a Revere Beach but *space*; there was space in Marblehead. Here, Wulff thought, was in microcosm the story of the drug trade itself, beginning hesitantly as a congested and horrid series of acts in the back rooms of the cities, moving further and further out then as the poisoned injection held, the poison going into the bloodstream, whirling, dispersing even further, moving through the trunk to the limbs, to all of the distant, departed places....

It was beautiful. Nothing in New York or San Francisco to equal it. You had to go to Deal, to the South, to see something like this, but the Deal estates did not have the aged, carefully molded look that these houses did. Work, restoration, a great deal of money had been put into these houses, but it was careful money, carefully applied. It preserved but did not destroy. Wulff looked at it fascinated, thinking that it would be nice if they, the people who lived in Deal or Marblehead, had had the same feeling about the cities that they did for their own ground.

The car braked, swerved, cut into a long, loping driveway to the right, the driver hitting the brakes expertly, the car skittering a little on cobblestones. At the end of the driveway, a full quarter of a mile down, was a gate; beyond that Wulff could see the house, beyond that the sea itself. The house was set directly on the sea at no rise; in the morning on a clear day the occupants could probably see out beyond the islands. On the other hand, when the mists closed in the house would be like a coin held in a fist: trapped, delimited. The young guard inside the small enclosure blinked as he saw the Continental drive in.

"You got him," he said.

The driver gestured, said something but the soundproofing shut it out. The man to his left rolled down the window, looked at the guard. "Of course we got him," he said.

"I could tell. I know his face."

"Why don't you shut the fuck up and just let us drive through?"

This New Englander had a nasty mouth. Of course considering the various pressures on him, he might even be entitled to it. "When I'm ready I'll wave you through," he said. "This is my post."

"I'll give you a post in the fucking woods somewhere, you want a post."

"Come on," the man to his right said, "why don't you just cool it?"

"You can shut the fuck up too," the New Englander said. He gave Wulff a glare. "As far as I'm concerned," he said, "you're a big fucking pain in the ass. I had my way I would have pulled off the road and shot you."

Wulff shrugged. "I'm sorry," he said.

"I put up with enough shit, you know? All I get is this kind of crap."

"It's tough," Wulff said, amused. "It really is. I know what you mean."

"But then again it's a living. They ask you what the alternative is, I really don't know."

"Why don't you just cut it out?" the man to his right said almost plaintively, "couldn't you do that? We deliver him, we're done. You're just holding up the works."

"I'd like to deliver him with a bullet in the spleen."

The guard shook his head again, went back into the booth and picked up a telephone. Wulff sat rigid, quiet. The thought occurred to him that he had them now in a state of minimal alertness. If there was ever a time to make a break it was now. The man on the right was merely embarrassed, the one on the left was rubbing his hands into one another and whispering vague foreign-sounding threats which sounded promising but which were keeping him completely occupied. And the guard, now talking intensely into the telephone seemed to have troubles of his own.

But the chauffeur, the least noticeable of the three, would of course be the wild card. He wouldn't get three yards, even if he were able to decapitate the other three—which he doubted—before the chauffeur disposed of him. No, Wulff decided and put the thought away carefully, inserting it into the deck next to the wild card, it wouldn't pay. He had gone this far, he would go further yet. What he had to remember was that he was a dead man and that a dead man could not be killed twice. He wanted to believe this. He told himself that he did. But all of the time, the stakes were going up.

The guard made a waving gesture from inside the booth, directing them in. The driver put the Continental abruptly into gear and floored the gas, shoving them back into the seats. The car spun on the gravel, held for purchase, then reared forward and they headed up the pathway toward the house.

"Son of a bitch driver," the New Englander said. "Doesn't he know what he's doing?" He looked at his gun moodily. "Maybe he's got us assigned to take care of the wrong people. I'd like to shoot the fucker."

"Why don't you cut it out?" the other gunman said as if at the end of his patience. "I've had to listen to your shit all the way up from Boston. Couldn't you give me a break, for Christ's sake? I didn't ask for this anymore than you did."

"Yeah," the New Englander said, "yeah, that's right, you didn't ask for it anymore than I did but there's nothing else you could do with your life. I could have been all sorts of things if I had put my mind to it. But it sure as hell's too late now, isn't it?"

"I don't know," Wulff said, "is it?"

"What's that?"

"You could get out of the business," Wulff said. "You could try to break out on your own. Set up your own shop, work as a freelancer. You might have a place like this yourself someday."

The New Englander gave him a look of hatred. "I've got my orders," he said, "and believe me I'll follow through with them, but I'd like to put a gunhole into your fucking skull, would you believe it?"

"I'd believe anything."

The driver yanked the car to a stop, cut the engine and almost instantaneously departed from view. Wulff, leaning over instinctively, wondered exactly what the hell was going on but then he saw the driver stretching out, somnolent and peaceful, on the leather cushions. What he was doing, it seemed, was going to sleep. Well, there was much credit to be given a man like this: he took his percentages where he could find them, and Wulff himself had been able to manage a little doze on the way.

The New Englander kicked open the door, seized Wulff by the wrist and guided him out of the car. Wulff did not resist. It would have been easy in getting out of the car to have felled the man and with the chauffeur now on the cushions there would have been a small but real chance of getting away with this—but he had made his calculations. He would let it ride. He stood on the path, listening to the sounds of the sea.

"Inside," the New Englander said. They flanked him left and right and walked toward the house, set level to the ground, a flat ranch but sprawling and sprawling through layers of space. Someone opened the door and they went inside. At the end of a long hallway which fronted them someone stood at the end. He smiled when he saw them.

Wulff looked at the man, wondering if he could be right and then as the distance closed between them step by step he saw that he was and a sudden, rushing, vaulting sense of connection filled him. It was the same kind of feeling which maybe a not-too-advanced junkie got from the first rush. It was everything for which he might have hoped a few months before when all of this madness had started.

Unless he was very, very wrong, and Wulff did not think he was, he was looking at Louis Cicchini, reputed to be the kingpin of the East, and Cicchini's lieutenants, having been acknowledged and dismissed were already scurrying away leaving him face to face with the man.

He felt like an exterminator without his equipment.

IX

"I want to be very honest with you, Wulff," Cicchini said a few moments later. "There must be no misunderstanding between us and I want to make this as quick as possible."

He was holding a gun on Wulff with the loose, easy detachment of the professional. The boys in the Continental might have been good with all their personality problems but Cicchini with a gun was like Isaac Stern to a wedding violinist. He held it almost absently, dangling from his fingers, a detachment which might have been deceptive for anyone that had tried to rush the gun. Then Cicchini, his eyes still bleary and half-closed, his hand still out of position would have ripped off the shots to have killed him. All in about three seconds. "All right," Wulff said, shifting on the couch where Cicchini had directed him, some yards back of the large desk from which the man had risen to look out the window toward the sea. "I have business elsewhere too, a big appointment list, so maybe we can keep it short."

"I despise you, Wulff," Cicchini said, in a flat, unaffected voice. "I've done a good deal of research on your background and your recent travels and I think you're the most dangerous man by far with whom we've ever dealt."

"That says a lot for enforcement," Wulff said bitterly and then, with an effort, sat back on the couch, wedging the pillows tightly into his back. *Shut up*, he thought, and then, fascinated, followed Cicchini's eyes to the sea. The roaring, vaulting landscape of ocean beyond. Glancing at this a man, even a Cicchini, must have understood the possibility of his own death.

"You got two good people in New York," Cicchini said tightly, "and a lot of bad ones and you've fucked up San Francisco for years to come. Was it necessary for you to blow up the ship?"

"I thought so."

"You're insane, Wulff," Cicchini said levelly. "You take all of this personally. You don't understand that our business is merely that, a business: a lot of people are doing the best they can. If there weren't a demand, there wouldn't be a supply. We didn't create the demand, it was always there. We're merely filling it."

"You're wrong," Wulff said, unable to keep quiet. If he was ever going to leave Louis Cicchini alive, and he doubted it, he could only do so by being silent and letting the man's rage exhaust itself, roll over him like that enormous ocean outside, but he could not. "You're creating the demand. The poison feeds upon itself. If you were just filling a need you'd have opened a couple of heroin clinics twenty years ago to registered addicts and you'd have a clientele left now of about twenty. The rest you would have killed off."

Cicchini's face clotted, abruptly he turned and sat down behind the desk. He took off the rimless glasses he wore, extracted a handkerchief from his breast pocket and very carefully wiped them, the gun swaying back and forth with the motion. *Don't even think about jumping him, not with that desk between us.* At length he sighed, apparently satisfied and put the glasses back on, rolled up the handkerchief and put it away. "I'm not going to argue metaphysics with you, Wulff," he said. "I didn't come up here to have an argument and you weren't brought here so that we could discuss motives." He made an abrupt dismissive gesture. "Let it be."

"Good," said Wulff, putting his knees together, palms flat to knees and standing, "in that case I'll just go—"

"Sit down," Cicchini said, his voice modulated. "Don't be ridiculous. I just want to say one more thing about this and then I'll tell you why you were brought up here—which was, incidentally, not to be killed. If I wanted to have you killed that would have been taken care of twenty miles from here about two hours ago."

"You brought me up to offer me a partnership," Wulff said, "what you need is new blood—"

"I want you to shut up and listen to me," Cicchini said. "I'm going to make you a better offer than you have any right to but you're trying my patience. That girl who died in Manhattan, that Marie Calvante—nobody within my purview had anything to do with that at all."

Wulff felt his breath suddenly become ragged. It was uneven, tormenting, fire in his chest. "Don't talk about the girl," he said.

"I know that this is a sensitive subject for you. I've done my homework on you, Wulff, a man in my position would have to do some pretty thorough checking, and I know all about that business. I don't blame you for being bitter. But no one at any level of the interlocking organizations had anything to do with it. I've gone through this very thoroughly and it's the truth."

"Shut up," said Wulff.

"As I said," Cicchini said, "I know this is a pretty sensitive subject for you but I'm afraid you're just going to have to sit there and take it." He slammed the desk hard with the flat of his hand. "You've gone through all of this under a misapprehension. You've gone around shooting and killing and destroying and generally making a great deal of trouble and it's all been a mistake. We had nothing to do with that. If that girl died it was either by her own hand or she ran into something like a tenth-rate burglar who didn't expect to see her and panicked."

Wulff sat on the couch. He leaned forward and looked at Cicchini, got his eyes finally, met him at every conceivable level of search-and-connection. "If you mention that girl once more," he said "you're going to have to kill me. I'm going to jump you and I guarantee you can put five shots into me before I've stood but I'll have my hands on your throat anyway. I'll get you. I'll cut off your wind."

Cicchini made a gesture of disgust. "All right," he said, "you're never going to listen, are you, Wulff? I'd be better off putting a bullet into your heart now and putting you out of your misery."

"Why don't you?"

Cicchini sighed, stood again and began to pace back and forth behind the desk in a rigid, spaced-out line. "I'd like to," he said. "You're dangerous and stupid and probably I'll get around to it sooner or later. But right now I happen to need you."

"To do what? Mainline junk?"

Cicchini laughed almost boisterously, cut off that laughter almost as quickly as it had come. "You're obsessed," he said, "you're a single-minded man. You have only one purpose and the pity is that we'd never be able to bring you over to a more sensible point of view. No, not quite, Wulff. I need you to get hold of a valise."

Wulff kept himself under control. Inside, the astonishment was ripping out of him like blood. Show nothing. Betray nothing. "What valise?"

"The valise you brought into my territory, Wulff. It's fucking up my life and my work and I'd like you to get your hands the hell back on it and take it out of here if you'd be so good. Is that simple enough?"

"I don't understand," Wulff said. "I just don't understand what you're talking about." He paused and then, almost against himself, smiled. "If you wanted me to keep hold of the valise and get it out of your territory," he said, "why did you take it from me in the first place?"

Cicchini shrugged. "Situations change," he said. "Frankly, it was a very bad idea. It was no worse though than your decision to bring that valise here in the first place. You see, Wulff, I'd like to explain something to you: I've got more or less a very nice, tight operation here. I don't know what you encountered in San Francisco but I suspect that it was something quite behind the times. Here, I like things to run smoothly and efficiently."

"Don't we all," said Wulff. Cicchini, the businessman. But Wulff had to make, however grudgingly, the concession: in his travels Cicchini was the best he had seen yet. He had to admire him. He was everything which Nicholas Severo, the fat little boss in San Francisco, had imagined himself to be, except that Cicchini knew what he was doing and had the obvious strength to back it up. *All levels of competence in any field,* he thought bitterly. This bastard would have made a good desk sergeant. "Don't we all like smoothness and efficiency as long as we don't have to see those who pay the price for order."

"You're getting abstract again, Wulff," Cicchini said, "and I told you, I don't have the time for this. Now bringing the valise in here was a very bad idea, a dumb, stupid idea—it was a New York-cop idea if you want to know the fucking truth—but it was done and it was my decision that it would be best to get that thing away from you before complications developed."

"You fouled it up," Wulff said.

"I certainly did. I certainly did foul it up," Cicchini said. "I fouled it up very seriously and I'll look you in the eye and tell you that because my ego is not involved in this job so much that I can't see my own errors. I misjudged my personnel and I misjudged timing and I misjudged other things and—"

"And you lost control of the valise."

"Exactly," Cicchini said. "Don't interrupt me. That is right. I lost control of the valise."

"And you don't know where it is."

"I know exactly where it is," the man said. Momentarily his confidence seemed to falter, just for an instant tiny chinks, cracks, flaws appeared in his face, eating their way through the thin flesh so that grey bone seemed exposed, Cicchini seemed older, he seemed much older, and Wulff had the total comprehension that this man who was in such control of everything he touched could not truly control his own biology: he would not live long. He would die in two to three years. Not that this would make much or any difference of course. The face reassembled itself and Cicchini was once again forty-three, forty-four years old and polished: "That's the trouble, I know exactly where that valise is. If it had vanished altogether I would just assume that it would no longer bother me and I would write it off. I have learned to write things off in my life, Wulff. This is the only way that you can build and hold an organization. I never wanted that valise anyway, its contents only make problems, its contents as a matter of fact could only flood and depress my market and *I don't need it.* If it hadn't surfaced I would assume that it was out of my territory, which is perfectly all right, and if it had surfaced I would have dealt with it for the usual routes. But I seem to have a little bit of a problem now."

"So why don't you just go out and get it?" Wulff said, "if you know where it is."

Once again those tiny lines and chinks appeared in Cicchini's face and this time they did not go away so quickly. "I wish it were that simple," he said vaguely, waving his hand. "Would you like a drink, Wulff?"

"Not particularly."

"I'm not going to poison you. We'll drink out of the same bottle and you can choose your glass."

"I don't believe in drinking," Wulff said. "I get my kicks from killing stinking drug-pushers and cheap mobsters."

He thought that that might push Cicchini all the way over the line, and frankly he did not care if it did. He was sick of the interview, sick of the gun held on him, and he was beginning to get the clear feeling that Louis Cicchini was as crazy as Cicchini thought Wulff was. This could go on and on for some time at the end of which Wulff would probably be headed for the bushes anyway. Might as well end it sooner than later. He did not care. He did not care. You could not kill a dead man. Remember that.

But Cicchini took it. He did not falter, his face even reassembled. "It's quite hopeless," he murmured. "Really, it's very difficult to try to reach an understanding with you, Wulff. You seem to think that I'm the enemy but I'm really not. I have nothing against you. What you've done in New York and San Francisco leaves me a clean slate as far as I'm concerned. We start from the beginning. But you're not being reasonable."

He ducked, still holding the gun and a glare on him—the man was a professional—burrowed in his desk, brought out a scotch bottle and put it with a crash on the panelling. "Cutty Sark," he said. "It's not the best, but it's only mid-afternoon. Do you want some?"

"No."

"All right," Cicchini said. He opened the bottle and lifted it, took a series of swallows as if he were taking beer, said *aah!* and capped the bottle. He looked much younger now, barely out of his thirties. "I wish it were so simple as to move in and retrieve the valise," he said. "Unfortunately, the valise is in hands against which I'm reluctant to move, but you will not be, Wulff, and that is precisely the point. That is why I think we'll be able to do business here."

"Who's got it?" Wulff said. "Just tell me who's got it."

"I will," Cicchini said. "The valise and what I estimate to be not a quarter but a half a million dollars' worth of uncut heroin stolen from a freighter in the San Francisco Bay is in the hands of a man named Phillip Sands who is a professor at Harvard University."

"Fine," Wulff said, "I always wanted to meet a Ph.D."

Cicchini blinked. "Sands is one of the most significant independent purveyors of hard and soft goods in this area," he said.

"That's a nice way of saying that he's a pusher working the college circuit."

"I suppose so," Cicchini said. He sat behind the desk, his joints loose, oiled by the scotch but his face and hands still alert. "Everything is supposed to be semantics with the college crowd. Sands got hold of the valise because it was put into his hands by a couple of men who are unfortunately no longer with us. Sands expects to see them again but he will not and very soon he will realize that he is by attrition, so to speak, the sole owner of those drugs."

"So I suggest," Wulff said, "that you send in about forty people to Phillip Sands who you seem to know pretty well and just take the fucking valise

away from him. Make it sixty thugs come to think of it; I wouldn't want
to see them outnumbered."

Cicchini concealed a hiccup with a palm. "I told you it wasn't quite that
simple," he said. "Not at all. The fact is that for certain reasons which
I don't want to go into at this time, I don't want to move against Sands.
I find myself very reluctant to get into that area. That's where you come
in, Wulff."

"You want me to go in there and get that valise."

"That's the general idea," Cicchini said. He put a palm to his mouth
again, burped, shook his head. "That's what you're here for."

"You want me to go in and take the valise from this guy, Sands."

"I think that I said that already, Wulff. There's no need for repetition."

"What's to guarantee that you'll ever see the valise again? You think
I'd turn it back to you."

"That's the point," Cicchini said. He made a twitching gesture with his
shoulders, leaned forward. "You can have that fucking valise, Wulff," he
said, "because I don't want any part of it, don't you understand? I
didn't ask for it to come into Boston and since it did it's been one
damned thing after the other. You killed a lot of people last night."

"Who killed a lot of people?"

"Don't give me that shit, Wulff," Cicchini screamed. Abruptly, he
abandoned all pretense of control. "I know what the fuck's going on here,
I know your fucking methods! You bombed out that house! You're
trying to take all of Boston with you."

"I don't know a thing about it," Wulff said. "How many did you say were
killed?"

"Forget it," Cicchini said, "that's under the bridge. If I were going to
shoot you for that you would've been dead in that car. I'm willing to
make a clean slate starting from now. I want you to get your fucking
valise and get out of my area, Wulff, and stay away permanently. What
you do elsewhere is your business. I don't care. I'm responsible for my
area and that's the end of it. You take that valise and get out of here and
never come back again."

"That sounds like a promising offer," Wulff said quietly. "It really
does. Why should you trust me?"

"You know why?" Cicchini said, "because you're crazy. I can trust a
crazy man. The most important thing to you is this crusade of yours and
nothing's going to stop you from going on. If you figure that it pays the
rent, you'll pick up that valise and get out of town. I don't give a fuck
what you do with it. You can drop it in the fucking Atlantic Ocean for
all I care. Just get it out of my life and keep it there for good."

"You're going to let me walk out of here," Wulff said almost unbelievingly. "You're just going to turn me loose and send me off to Sands."

"Would you prefer that I shoot you?" Cicchini said and showed him the gun, spun the barrel absently, clicked it once. "I'll do that if it would make you any happier. The fact is that people like you want to die, Wulff, you don't want to get along, you don't want to live your lives. Deep down the most satisfaction I could give you would be to shoot you dead and put you out of your misery, but I'd rather not unless you make me. I think that we can do business together. This is purely business, there's no sentiment, I don't like you, I don't want to get involved with you on any level, but it looks like our purposes could mesh here. You want the valise and I want it out of here and I don't want to touch Sands."

Wulff stood. Heavily, awkwardly, but he stood and felt the better for it. He had been sitting since he had entered the room, now, standing, proportions seemed reduced to more manageable size. Cicchini no longer loomed over him, the ocean was no longer a malevolent presence through the window. He was merely looking at a tired man of normal height who had troubles that he could not handle, and at a ragged strip of beach, pebbled and rock-strewn, falling into the ocean. "You'll have to give me information," he said quietly. "If we're going to do business at all you've got to give me a lead or two here."

"I don't have to give you shit," Cicchini said, holding the pistol levelly and then flicking it, making a dismissive gesture. "Just get out of here and do your job. The stupid son of a bitch is listed right in the phone book."

X

Wulff remembered how it had been on the squad. The squad was big during the late sixties until the new Commissioner came in and the real shakeups had begun. But straight through to the moment of his bounce the squad had still been golden. If you were on it you could have an income for life. The work was interesting and not too challenging and all in all it was the kind of job that a young man just getting out of high school, say, would have been well advised to take.

Of course it wasn't that easy to get on the narco squad; you had to get into the department in the first place, and in the second you had to politic it all the way. A post like this had to be preferential; no merit system was going to be able to point out who would fit in and who wouldn't, and anyway nine-tenths of the department, easy, would be filing into the examination center if you threw it open competitive. Wulff was one of the few who *hadn't* politicked his way in; when he came back from Vietnam two years later he had made a lot of people feel guilty in and around the precincts and they had decided that the least they could do was to work out something nice for him. The narcotics squad was about the best they could do; it was plainclothes and you could pick your spots, also you could use your own transportation and to a certain extent make your own hours, because so much of the thing was based on coaxing up informants.

Needless to say the vice squad would have been even better. The vice squad was what every cop in the department, homo- and heterosexual dreamed about at night: it was harmless, lucrative and there was the possibility of some pretty good sex in the bargain if you wanted to play it that way, but even a combat veteran couldn't have everything. The department thought that they had done pretty well by Wulff, setting him up for narco. What did he want? Blood?

Actually he didn't even want narco. All that he wanted when he came back was to be in a quiet room alone for a while where he could work out his thoughts and impressions carefully. In three months or six he might have been ready for the world that way. A desk job on the precinct would have been ideal for his purposes, but he never made the suggestion—he was a good cop, his policy was that he would go where they told him to in those days—and since desk duty was mostly for cardiac cases or men who had proven themselves spectacularly unworthy on the streets, but in no way which the department wanted to make public, narco it had been, and Wulff had spent two and a half interesting and complex years enforcing the law, fighting the drug trade in New York City. He figured that he personally had contributed over fifty thousand dollars worth of stuff of varying street quality to the stash room over that period. It was a little embarrassing to find out later that the stash room had merely been another drop and that the cops who had unlimited access to the center were carrying it out of there in car loads and replacing it with sugar; but there had been a time, at the beginning of the assignment anyway, where every small bag or box of stuff he had dropped in there had to him been another step in the right direction, in fighting the enemy, in cleaning out the city.

Well, you lived and learned. After a while if you were the wrong kind of cop the idea might occur to you that the best thing would be to bust the informers. The informers in those days were functioning as if the squad worked for *them*, they were setting up the appointments and naming the conditions and they even had a selected list of bars and restaurants which were the only ones they would patronize. It had gotten that bad. Wulff began to feel that the informants were laughing at them; that more often than not they were manipulating the cops so that the cops went along with the trade, became subcontractors themselves—but that kind of thinking just did not take you very far in the department. It was a very dangerous thinking as a matter of fact and that was what had gotten him into trouble.

What you were supposed to do when you got on the squad was to go along with it, it was a sinecure, a good post, and although it didn't have much of a future it sure as hell had a lot of presence. Wulff knew that he should have considered himself fortunate. All over the city cops were busting their asses to get onto the narco squad, those who had made it would go through their days with quiet eyes and complicated expressions except when there was one or another of the periodic investigations which even then were coming two or three times a year.

That was the only thing you really had to watch: the investigations. Men got transferred or thrown out of the department like fleas when the press began to shout, and one or another idiot on the lowest level would confess to having taken a dollar here or there. For three weeks to three months things would be distinctly uncomfortable; it would be impossible to meet an informant in a place and have a quiet drink, get any real business done at all—and then the press would go on to something else, usually the vice squad, and things got back to normal, except for a turnover of about ten percent. Wulff had gone through five of those in his time and had survived every one. It was not only a question of keeping a low profile which everybody did anyway, it was a matter of honestly not caring, of not allowing the troubled periods to shake you or take you out of the modus operandi. Since Wulff, as far as he knew, had been the only man on the squad who was not overtly or covertly on the take, things never bothered him too much.

His troubles began when he busted an informant. Informants just did not get busted; that was one of the principles of the game. Occasionally it was necessary to warn them when a raid was coming up in case it was in their area: otherwise in addition to a few hapless college kids and a couple of junkies who were mostly glad to go to the Tombs since at least they were familiar with it, you were likely to get yourself an informant in the net and that meant going to all of the trouble of having him turn evidence and getting him out quietly. You could do it, you could work that kind of thing out, but unless you played it very subtly you were likely to lose the services of the informant permanently. It was just too pat the way that they would get out of it while the others stayed in—and sometimes their connections could turn damned nasty. Informants could even get killed that way, not in the Tombs (the junkies might take to occasionally hanging themselves but that, the guards insisted, was only because they needed a way to get warm) but outside of it, on the streets. The fact that this kind of thing might happen to them made informants very reluctant to be a raid altogether and therefore it was sound policy to make sure that they were tipped off in advance. If they couldn't be, there had been more than a couple of raids in the history of the department on which all charges had been dropped before arraignment, simply because it was easier to handle it that way than to get into risky territory. The system did not work, it hardly functioned at all, but it was through ten years or so about the best system that anyone could think of or want to use—it kept the squad, the informants, the big fish and the Commissioner if not the press quiet—so the policy held. Informants just did not get themselves jailed.

Except that Wulff jailed one. He couldn't let it go. He knew that the son of a bitch was dealing with left and right hands together while he used his mouth to pass on messages that would undercut the competition. He was only twenty-two years old this kid, quite young for an informant, but he had a history of involvement with the department, being an old valued friend from the age of fifteen, when he had been caught in car theft and grand larceny, and he was able to graduate, as it were, to the status of informant quite easily. His information was worthless, now and then he would turn up a bunch of West Siders smoking hashish on a Saturday night or some half-dead men crawling around in alleys, but then almost *all* of the information was worthless. Wulff had caught him with a deck of heroin in the right pocket of his sport jacket. It fell out when the informant, at the bar, had been in the process of extracting a pack of cigarettes while he laid some more bullshit on the cop about the general scene uptown and downtown but not in midtown where he operated. The bartender saw it and half of the seven or eight people at the bar saw it, and the couple dancing to the jukebox, staggering around in a haze of either lust or downers saw it as well.

Wulff thought that he had no choice. He couldn't let it go. Maybe he *should* have let it go, and if he had all of it to do over again knowing everything that had happened, he might have, but the situation at that time seemed absolutely clear-cut and without options. He took the man in.

Right away he saw that it had been a mistake. They wasted no time in delivering the message. The papers were late in coming through in the first place, and in the second place he and the kid had been separated at the stationhouse and he had never seen him again. Wulff had sat by himself in a large, peeling, grey room for several hours while they told him that the typist would get onto the material as soon as he got back from a lunch break, but by about one o'clock, an hour past his shift, Wulff started to get the idea, and by two o'clock he was certain. He knew then that he had made a mistake but it was, of course, entirely too late. At three in the morning when he was beginning to regret everything about it, he got to a phone and told Marie that he wouldn't be able to make it to her house as they had planned after all; he had gotten involved in something. As always—she would have made a great policeman's wife—she said that this was fine and she'd wait to hear from him. No questions. She would never have asked any questions but waited for him to tell her, which he certainly would have, except that this one time he never got a chance. That was just two days before she died and he hadn't had a chance to see her in between because of the whole mess that came up. At about four in the morning the lieutenant came in and said that he had gone over all of the charges now and Wulff had no case. He had no case at all. They were improperly filed, the information on the suspect did not jive with identification that the suspect had produced and where the fuck was the heroin anyway?

Wulff said that he had turned it in and the lieutenant said that he didn't think so because there was no record of it. Wulff offered to get the desk sergeant and the property clerk down there right then to settle this but the lieutenant said that the shifts had long since changed and what the fuck was the point anyway? There were no verification signatures on file. At that point Wulff understood everything or nearly everything, but it was definitely too late for understanding. The lieutenant was incensed. He wanted to know who the fuck Wulff thought he was anyway and didn't he realize that he had far more important things to do than to get involved in chickenshit like this. Wulff should not have done what he did next but he did it anyway. He slugged the lieutenant.

Oh, he pulled the punch even as he was throwing it and he didn't do more than ruffle the man but it was enough, quite enough, and from then on things, as they say, deteriorated. The lieutenant smashed him open-handed across the face and Wulff took it, there was nothing else to do, and then he left the room quickly and told Wulff to wait in there.

Wulff was half-convinced that they were going to shift the terms of the arraignment; they still needed a body and the body would turn out to be his instead of the informant's, but that was not the way it worked out. Not quite. After a time, instead, the lieutenant came back with a captain, the captain holding a large bunch of forms and the lieutenant said that if Wulff would now just sign all of them he would be allowed to go home. The lieutenant did not say anything specific about Wulff being held under arrest, because no such thing was possible, but the implication was there. Wulff looked at the papers, which seemed pretty vaguely worded generally, but seemed to have something to do with the fact that he was requesting relief from his present assignment.

He signed all of them. Really, there seemed nothing else to do and under the circumstances it seemed like a pretty good deal. He was sick of the narcotics squad. He was sick of the informants, sick of the junkies lurking in the alleys, laughing at them when they went in to make their trivial busts, he was sick of the smartass college kids who always seemed to know their rights in the trucks going downtown, and showed no hesitancy in showing the cops what they thought of them. If this was the narcotics squad, if this was the way that the city of New York was going to come to terms with the cancer that was invading it and bring the drug traffic under control, well then he had had enough of it.

The captain stood there, arms folded impassively while Wulff completed all of the forms and then told him that he was a fool. The lieutenant nodded at this but made no comment. The captain added that Wulff was a damned fool; he thought that he was doing something worthwhile, he was one of those fuckers who thought that they could write their own laws and put them on the statute books but in actuality he had no understanding, no understanding of what the police department had to deal with, and how did he like that? The captain said that Wulff was a disgrace to the department and had fucked up a number of people in the process, but after just a little of this he said no more, leaving Wulff and the lieutenant alone in the room facing one another. The lieutenant yanked the forms out of his hand and told him to get the fuck out of there and go home. He was being transferred.

By that time it was five in the morning which was no time to visit anyone's girl, even Marie Calvante—although he should have known better: she would have come out of bed wide-eyed and opened the door and embraced him. He did not think of that. He went straight home in his own car, cursing all the way, rolling down the window now and then to spit the bile out of the car onto the glistening surfaces of the Long Island Expressway, and eventually he got home and went to bed for three hours. He was awakened by a telephone call telling him to report to the 24th precinct for radio car duty at his regular shift time and that had been the end of his career on the narco squad. Damned near the end of his career in the police department proper. He had lasted, all told, another thirty-six hours.

Well, that was all water under the bridge now, water under the bridge and all like that but it came back to him. Things like this could not be put away under consciousness forever; eventually they were going to come back and seize you. The Narco squad came back to him vividly, and following that the thoughts of what had happened in the last thirty-six hours of his service came too, and Wulff had to tangle with all of them even though the proper thing to think about was Louis Cicchini and the pact he had made with Cicchini and what he had to do now. That was the important thing. The past was gone, it was locked away; there was nothing that you could do about it except move on. Or cry. Or cry and then move on but this kind of thing could not stay with you.

But it had to come back. Sooner or later he knew it would come sweeping over him, and so it had. The point was that Cicchini was right. The man was right. The man knew what he was talking about. Wulff was crazy; he was out of his mind. Anyone with his mission would have to be. He was fighting a flood with a sieve; they would run through and around him without even knowing, most of them, that he was there. He could storm city after city, knock out San Francisco and give a body-blow to New York, hurt some minor operator here in Boston—but the real power, the kind of power represented by the Louis Cicchinis, who were distinctly not clowns and made the whole thing operate, well ....

Well, the real power was so contemptuous of him that the only purpose Wulff served was one of potential use. Cicchini could use him. He had taken him to his home, given him orders like one of his *soldati* and discharged him with the assurance that Wulff would discharge those orders faithfully or perish in the attempt.

The fact was that where the real power lay, Wulff was merely another employee.

Freelance, of course.

XI

Sands was frantic. His wife had left him but that hardly seemed to matter, not in the context of this new and larger disaster. The bitch should have left him years ago, that was his only thought on that matter. No, he was in trouble now. He was in a quarter of a million dollars' worth of trouble and the trap was springing. But he could not let go of the valise. Damn it, he would not do it. The valise was his way out.

His normal channels wouldn't touch it. Not that he could blame them; this was no nickel-and-dime stuff, it would make a disastrous dent in any market into which it was poured, and the whole business of the fringe operators was working on the margins, making sure that they had no effect upon the overall picture. If they did it was no longer a hobby for them but sheer murder. But up at the higher levels he was completely blocked. "Are you crazy?" the man who he called in desperation said when Sands had finally got through. "Do you really think I want it?"

"I have your name and number as someone who might be interested in this kind of goods," Sands had said. He had tried to be calm, tried to play it cool, even though he knew he was way beyond his depth now. "I'm willing to meet at an agreeable neutral zone and discuss this."

"I wouldn't meet you at the circus," the man had said. "I wouldn't meet you at a strip joint, I wouldn't have a cup of coffee with you on the turnpike. Do you think that I'd get near stuff like that?"

"The price is right."

"The price is *wrong*, the price is always wrong. This is no candystore I'm running here, I'm in business and I know what my business is. I won't touch it."

"You're not being reasonable."

"Reasonable! How reasonable do you want me to be? I'd be very reasonable with a bullet in my head. You take that fucking shipment of yours whatever it is and you drop it in the river, that's my advice. I don't know where you got it from or exactly what you think is going on here, but you're in deep water man and you are sinking. The best thing you can do is to get off the phone."

"Now listen," Sands had said with a series of gestures which were of course invisible and thus of no help at all, his free arm wildly flailing through the air, "listen, you're not giving me a chance—"

"Get the fuck out of my life," the man had said and had hung up on him leaving Sands sitting, sweating in his living room, the valise still between his legs. He could not get rid of it. He could not move it. Achilles heel, albatross, the son of a bitch stood there like a quarter of a million dollars' worth of jewels under glass in a vacant museum and he could not do a thing with it. Not to say that the man he had called had not probably protected himself by putting information around immediately as to exactly what proposition and propositioner he had just heard from. On every level, the pressure was increasing.

Give up. Give up and let it go. But it was probably too late already, Sands thought. The two men would be back in a few hours and they would want to know exactly what arrangements he had made for the valise. They would not believe him if he said that he had not been able to do anything, they might in fact become extremely ugly. What would he do then? He did not think that anyone was going to gun him down for possession of that valise—he had a pretty good idea of working arrangements in Boston and a Harvard professor was just too risky to take on in a gangland-type slaying, it would bring all kinds of pressures into what had been a pretty smooth, tight operation—but that did not mean that he was home free by any means. The two who had dropped off that valise were ugly types. And then too he could not let it go. That at least had been long since settled.

So Sands was in Harvard Square now, four in the afternoon, pacing uneasily, waiting for a man to show. Harvard Square was sinking pretty low, waiting around for a man who was already four minutes late was even lower, but he was committed. The valise at least was locked and bolted into his closet; he did not think that anyone would be getting to that, and the apartment was completely secure. Chalk up another for Karen's walking out this morning; if she had not he might have had to tell her many things, none of which would have done her any good at all. Sands walked back and forth, too restless to sit even in the September temperature, looking at without really seeing the Square. It was pretty bad. Like Tompkins Square Park in New York it was the kind of place where almost everything went on, but unlike Tompkins Square it did not have that sense of near-confidentiality, but instead was open on all sides to the world. Not that the cops gave a shit, of course. Nothing bothered the cops around here as long as it didn't move too fast.

At ten minutes past four, a thin young man with a drooping moustache, wearing sandals, came into the park and, seeing Sands, walked toward him. They had met very casually a couple of times although never intersecting and Sands had not imagined much difficulty in making a rendezvous. As the young man walked toward him it occurred to Sands that the valise had already driven him low indeed; he was not only appealing to but consorting with types who just a day ago he would have felt utterly below him. Still, there was nothing to do. The decision had been made.

The young man came within a few feet of Sands, put his hands on his elbows and waited for Sands to close the distance. "All right," he said when they were face to face, "now what's the deal with this, no shit."

"I told you."

"You didn't tell me nothing. I want to know now and you come straight across with it."

"You're fucking insolent," Sands said.

"Listen, man, you're in no position to talk personality types. You got something on your mind, you talk to me now; otherwise no deal."

Sands sighed, tried to hold himself in check. "I've got a valise," he said.

"What kind of valise? Leather, gold inlay, what?"

"I've got a valise with a large quantity of heroin," Sands said.

"Horse? Junk? Shit?"

"If you want to call it that."

"I call it anything I want," the young man said. "How much a quantity you say you got?"

"Large. I don't know exactly."

"Kilos? Pounds? What?"

"Maybe twenty pounds," Sands said.

"Ridiculous. That's crazy. You're talking about a million dollars street value, maybe half that whole sale."

"I know."

The man raised his palms and shaking his head went back a step. "I don't think so," he said. "No, I don't think I want it."

"Why?"

"Because you're crazy if you think you got that kind of stuff. Where'd you get it?"

"That doesn't matter."

"What am I supposed to do with it?"

"Get rid of it," Sands said flatly, "put it into the pipeline."

"That's not my kind of thing at all."

"It isn't?"

"No," the man said. Up close he really did not look the college student that he did from a distance; he was at least thirty and his outfit was contrived rather than worn. His eyes were extremely clear and cold under his high forehead, an enormous quantity of hair. "It sure as hell is not my kind of thing. I may do a little skag now and then but primarily I'm in soft goods. I wouldn't touch this kind of stuff."

"Yes you would if the price were right."

"You misunderstand me man," the man said softly, intensely. "You been teaching metaphysics in the Harvard Yard so long you don't know what the fuck is going on in the so-called outside world. You think that this is a piece of candy, a lollipop maybe; you stick it in the city's mouth and it starts to suck away. It doesn't work like that."

"You said you'd meet me," Sands said. Instinctively, he drew his tweed jacket around him, the faint breeze chilling him. "Surely you didn't say you'd meet me just to give me a lecture."

"As a general rule," the man said, "I try to meet up with anyone who tries to see me. I am very definitely into soft goods, just like you are, and I got nothing to hide. I've got to meet people, move around, circulate, because I don't have a ready made group of customers dumped into me three times a week for ten o'clocks."

Sands felt himself reddening. He was not a violent man but his instinct was to launch himself against the man, and what would it get him? What would happen then? "Shut up," he said.

"Don't like that, professor?" The man shrugged. "That's your business. I don't mean to offend. It's your life; you can do anything you pretty much want with it. I don't look at you as any kind of competitor. The primary reason I arranged to meet you was I simply did not believe it. I did not believe that you were actually serious and I thought it might be worth my while to come out and check this thing personally. But you are all wrong, professor."

The man nodded, backed away. "I mean you are *all* wrong," he said. "You are missing out on everything. There's nothing that you can do with that valise of yours except to throw it in the river or shove it up your ass or maybe shoot it yourself, although you're probably the kind of guy who doesn't use yourself. All you do is sell. But maybe you could start off by watering it down a little and heating it, you sniff, dig? Or you can even try a taste, that isn't the best way of getting it into the bloodstream but it's fast and easy and you'll get something out of it. But you are definitely not going to *sell* those contents and you are not going to give them to *me* to sell because the truth is that one crazy man in Harvard Square at a time is more than enough and you've got the market cornered on craziness right now I think. You're done, man. You are *done.*"

He turned from Sands and began to walk briskly out of the square. Unbelieving, his fists knotting, Sands watched him go. In a way, watching him go was like watching a quarter of a million dollars walk out of there, but there was simply nothing he could do. What could he do? He could run after the youth and begin to appeal, he could leap upon him and try to beat him up, but that was the stupidest thought of all, because he had not been near physical violence of any sort for twenty years now and he had had a horror of it even back in the schoolyard.

Sands let him go. He stood there, the breeze ruffling his hair, twisting at his hair, poking it, twirling it, turning it, oblivious to the fact that everyone in Harvard Square probably knew exactly what he had been up and to and was amused. A missed deal, that's what it would look like. And he was out a wife, too.

He was in over his head now. He had been from the moment he had accepted that valise. The only thing to do now when the two of them came back was to turn it back, apologize and try to get out of it gracefully, but he didn't think that that would work either. Types like that did not understand or appreciate grace.

Sands, in full view of the various junkies, traders, mothers and drifters of Harvard Square began to shake with sobs that were half rage and a third despair, but the thing that really got him, that really tore him open, was that that left about seventeen percent of those tears for amusement. He could not stand the fact that he could back off from himself and look at himself objectively and see that there was no way around it: Phillip Sands had made one sadass mess out of his life.

XII

Cicchini taketh away but Cicchini also giveth. Louis Cicchini had giveth unto Wulff a black, 1965 Plymouth, which under the hood had three-eighty-three and accelerated like nothing that Wulff had driven since the patrol car days. Cicchini giveth unto Wulff back his pistol, unloaded. Cicchini, as he walked Wulff out the door of his house even gave him some advice and instructions. "The car is unmarked," he said, "the plates are good, the identification is cool, everything's in good shape but it would be best not to be nailed with it if you know what I mean."

"I know what you mean."

"When you're done with it ditch it. I don't want you to use that car anywhere except in and around Boston. You get back on the road, you're on your own. This is a loaner car."

"Where should I ditch it?"

"Anywhere you want," Cicchini said. "You're on your own for that too. Put it somewhere in the downtown area, lock it up, throw the keys in a sewer and we'll find it."

"You really think I'll get out of town when I'm finished with the job?"

Cicchini looked at him tightly, then put a hand on his shoulder, gripped him. Two housemen standing down the walk looked them over with interest. Wulff knew that if he made a single move in resistance now he was as dead as he could have been all afternoon, but the urge to smash the man was irresistible. Resist it. Resist it then. *Later.* "I know you will," he said, "because if you don't get fucking out of town we'll hunt you down and torture you to death."

"That's a nice prospect."

"Don't fuck around," Cicchini said, "just don't think that you're ahead of the game because you got out of here in one piece. That has nothing to do with the future. You're getting a shot, Wulff, because I think we can do business together. You stop doing business though, you screw around with me and you're finished." Cicchini let his arms fall away, looked at Wulff levelly then, locked into position. "I own this territory," he said. "This is mine altogether and no one is going to screw it up."

Wulff opened the door of the Plymouth which was idling softly and said, "You've got to let me handle this my way. I don't want your men trailing me."

"Don't worry about that," Cicchini said, "we're going to give you plenty of rope. I just want it done quickly and I want you the hell out of town."

"My pleasure," Wulff said, "that would be my pleasure," and stepped into the car, closed the door, tested the pedal. At gentle idle the doors began to rattle, the car was simply overpowered. Stick-shift. He put the thing into gear and slowly rolled it down the path.

All the way onto the road he still expected it to be a single vast hoax. The housemen who parted in front of him, stepping to sides of the road, would give him a little bit of a lead and then they would begin to drill the car with bullets. Bullets would ricochet in and around his body and then he would be dead; they would leave him in the car, tow it to downtown Boston to put it on exhibit, and he would lie there on Beacon Street, embalmed for everyone to see, a lesson for the restless in Cicchini's happy domain. But they did not shoot him. Nothing happened. The Plymouth moved obediently onto the road and Wulff cut it right and headed toward Boston as fast as he could, struggling with the gearshift. Something wrong in the transmission: the car did not want to come out of second, but considering that it handled fifty-five miles an hour in second without strain he guessed he didn't have to worry about that too much.

In and out of the Hall of the Mountain King. He had gone into Cicchini's lair and somehow he had gotten out. The circumstances were not to his credit but then, in another way, he supposed they were: Cicchini respected him enough to use him. He seemed to trust Wulff as well. The reason might be obvious—whatever Wulff wanted to do he didn't want to replace Cicchini, just topple the regime into vacuum— but that did not, whatever it was, minimize the accomplishment.

He doubted if the man and his troops would want to let him live. For reasons which he had to accept they did not want to go after Sands themselves, they needed an intermediary to do it, someone to take that valise and get it out of Sands's possession. But once that was done Wulff's use was over, and someone, in or out of Cicchini's organization, would have to figure just as Sands had figured that the valise was worth the risk after all. His prospects were not good.

Unless he made a frontal attack.

Wulff thought about that, driving back to Boston he thought about many things, but he did not allow thought to interfere with the sense of purpose shaping itself below. He was beginning to see now that things were quite complicated, more intensely complicated than he might have thought when he got into this mission. New York had been ugly and sloppy but no real challenge, San Francisco had been a knockover pure and simple. But Boston was turning out to be the burial ground of what he guessed was his simplest view of the matter: that the enemy was aligned against him, that it was just a question of knocking the enemy down one by one until no more remained.

It wouldn't work. Not if Cicchini and he were actually aligned in purposes, not if in effect he was now doing Cicchini's work. He would have to think this matter through.

His impulse was to go straight to Sands's house and get the job over. But there was no way of telling what he might be walking into. It might even be a setup from Cicchini. The house might be covered, Wulff could be killed in ambush in such a way that all the suspicion would turn on Sands. No, it was best to swaddle his impulses and try for the first time now to get this thing logically ordered. He went back to the hotel.

No one there. Empty, the street burned free of people. He parked the Plymouth right outside, suddenly not caring whether he was being observed or not, went inside, past the perpetually-drunken desk clerk and up to his room, a curiously aseptic little box, only the unmade bed breaking up the geometry of angles and lines. In the room he went to the closet, angrily seized the machine gun and full clip. He would go in to this son of a bitch if necessary with full armament; he was going to leave nothing to chance. If Cicchini was setting him up a couple of men were going to be the cost. The room phone rang while he was inserting a round into the chambers.

He hadn't even been aware that a fleabag like this would have a telephone in the room, and who the hell would need it anyway? But there it was, underneath the bed, a fine web of dust over the receiver. The occupants of this room had obviously not had much of a social life. "Yeah," Wulff said.

"Hello," said the voice of Louis Cicchini. "I thought you'd go back to the hotel."

"If you thought I'd go back to the hotel why call?" Wulff said.

"I like to keep in touch. I'm very interested in you, Wulff. I have a feeling of great personal warmth and closeness and an almost excessive interest in your movements over the next few hours."

"I'm very moved."

"This is just a reminder, Wulff," Cicchini said. "You're being kept under observation. Everything you do, every single action is being reported back to me. I know what you're doing and where you're going and you're under the tightest kind of observation."

"Good. I wouldn't want to get lonely."

"You have a sense of humor, Wulff, and a little self-possession and that's good. That makes you more useful to me. But this call is just a little reminder that I want you to carry around with you: *don't get any ideas*. Don't get cute with me, Wulff. You know exactly what you have to do and I want you to go ahead and do it and get the hell out of town.

You get clever with me and I'll push the button. I can wipe you out."

"I want you to understand something," he said, the fury which had been bubbling within finally coming out now through the thin pipeline of his mouth. "I want you to fucking understand something, Cicchini, lay off me. I've had all that I can take; I don't give a shit who you are or what you think you're doing but you let me be now. You let me handle this my way."

"To a point," Cicchini said. "Stay calm, Wulff. A man who has been pushing as hard as you've been, under the enormous pressures you've been tackling, could have himself a heart attack or a stroke if this keeps on. You've got to learn to relax. Thirty-two isn't ancient you understand but you aren't as young as you used to be when you were taking graft on the narco squad."

"Fuck you, you son of a bitch," Wulff said. "You lay off me now."

"Temper, Wulff, temper," Cicchini said with something that sounded like a giggle and hung up on him. Wulff smashed down the receiver, then went through the process of completing the loading and checking of the machine gun. Everything in place. He could feel the deadliness of the stock in his hands, the power exuded from the gun. In Vietnam a few times on patrol he had handled the Browning Automatic Rifle, and that had given him the feeling of this kind of equipment, but what he had in his hands was infinitely deadlier than the Browning because it was mobile, a man of average size and weight could handle it expertly, whereas the Browning was so big that you almost needed a wheeled stand to carry it properly. He thought of what he was doing—taking a machine gun up against an associate professor—but the thought was not as amusing as it could have been; he had a feeling that Sands would give him all that he could handle.

He checked everything out in the room, tossed the gun into a canvas bag and got out of there. His plans, dimly formulated, were already emerging into sharp relief as he went down the stairs and he knew then exactly what he was doing, what he had probably planned to do from the moment that he realized that Cicchini was not going to kill him.

He was going to get that valise back. The valise came first and he would not rest until it was back in his hands. But the valise was only preparation; the real job lay ahead.

He was going to wipe Louis Cicchini out of business.

XIII

On the way back to his apartment, Sands finally caught the item about the two hoods on the turnpike. It had been moved up to the front page of the *Globe*, the afternoon paper, because further investigation had uncovered the indications of gangland involvement. The corpses were charred almost beyond recognition but identification had been made. Sands felt the sickness going through him.

It tore through him as he walked back to his apartment house like influenza or fever, ripping away small sections of his gut and seeming to open up layers of adult reaction and knowledge, peeling them away until he was a quivering eighteen years old again. He remembered that eighteen-year-old who had been Phil Sands—he had been a freshman at college, or maybe again it was a sophomore, hard to keep the years in perspective when time was slipping away from you—but this eighteen-year-old Phil Sands had never been able to bear pressure of any sort. Going to whorehouses had terrified him, dates with girls had scared the shit out of him, any kind of an examination could reduce him to a mumbling, frenzied despair and yet, for precisely those reasons he had forced himself to go to the whorehouses, forced himself to go out with girls, driven himself through cramming for the examinations simply because he would not concede to anyone at all, least of all himself, that he could not bear the simple and terrible exigencies of living. A lot had happened in the fifteen or sixteen years since that time, he had gone a long distance and had indeed probably been the first, although hardly the last, faculty member at the university to get into drugs as a sideline. He had spent the last decade in the process of denying that this younger, frightened Phillip Sands even existed, let alone could have any control of his own life—and yet it was all still there. Underneath it seemed he was the same person that he always had been.

His bowels became watery looking at the newspaper; he crumpled it into a large, tumbling ball and hurled it into a wastebasket, missing, increased his stride, began to feel his teeth hitting against one another in nervous response. This was the worst news of all now; he had intended to give the valise back to these men when they came tonight and tell them that it was hopeless. Coming to this decision, which he had slowly done in Harvard Square after the man had left, had half-killed him—he could not remember any decision he had made in years which had hurt him as much—but even in the act of making it he had felt that characteristic vaulting sense of release and certainty which always accompanied what he knew was a correct choice. He could not live with it. He was clearly and evidently out of his depth with the valise, and the only thing to do was to admit it and then get rid of the thing as quickly as possible. Gone with it was the idea of the ultimate score which would free him, the life-changing break which would take him out of the trap his life had become—but he would be a better man for all of it. He knew that.

And now the men had gotten themselves murdered. Murdered, doubtless, over the valise itself. He could feel the chills gradually becoming warm within him, it was as if a set of bells strung along his nerves, one by one, were all beginning to ring. He felt the ringing moving from level to level, arcing, soaring, in just a moment the gong in his head would begin that indicated he was going to go through one of his migraine attacks and nothing to do to prevent it. He was helpless. He who had always believed in the principle of utter control, who had sacrificed his life in a sense to order and caution, he was now in the grip of a migraine and the migraine in turn was caused by the realization that he had moved far beyond his ability to control the situation and could now wait, only helplessly, for the denouement.

Fool, Sands said to himself, *fool, fool*, but this did not help. What was self-loathing going to do for him now? If he had been a fool all his life, which was indeed quite likely, what was the naming of names going to do? He went into his apartment building, a large cooperative near the University, feeling the sweat coming out from him more freely as he went into the acrid, dusty lobby, signalled for the elevator. He was going to be sick. He knew it, he was definitely going to be sick. Going up in the elevator alone, leaning against the wall for support against the sudden and sickening waves of faintness which lashed him, Sands had one last desperate idea: he could give the valise back. He was no fool, he had a good idea now of whom it had been taken from and who would want it back. But even as the thought gave him some comfort it was snatched away, the doors of the little car sliding open in a sickening jolt to disgorge him. It was too late. Who cared whether or not he turned the valise back? By this time the people who wanted it undoubtedly knew exactly who had it. They did not need to bargain with him, they did not even need to accept the valise gratefully.

They could simply come in and get it and give him a going-away present in the bargain.

Sands stumbled down the corridor to his apartment. He was sick; he was sick, he had never been so sick in his life. Everything had turned against him, and yet it had appeared so innocuous; he was so sure when the men had come to his door that he would be able to handle this. He took his keys from his pocket with a shaking hand, noted the shaking absently, the palsied, uncontrollable quiverings of the hand which caused the keys to jingle. *I'm falling apart*, he thought and opened the door, staggered into the hallway where the men had stood last night. Oh last night was a long, long time ago; it was in a different eternity altogether. Last night he had had a wife and a conviction that he could control anything, now he had neither. Deserted. Abandoned. He took off his coat, hands shaking, sweat streaming down his forehead, gasping at his appearance in the large mirror which faced him across the living room at the base of the stairs of the duplex. A desperate, frightened man. That was all. All his life he had been desperate and frightened but the masks had covered it up: professor, husband, dealer, confessor, now one by one they had all fallen away and Sands saw the face of a boy he had used to know twenty years ago. No help. Nowhere. Simple greed had got him here; if he were going to live, he realized, only simple greed could get him out. The simple greed to live. That was all. He did not want to die. He wanted to live; he was only thirty-four years old. He was entitled to better than this. He was entitled to better than this.

Sands went to the phone. It was on the wall near the kitchen. He looked at it blankly for a moment, his instincts having run ahead of his power to identify. It could have been an artifact this telephone, some curious object from the other side of the Moon. Then he remembered what it was and what he had to do with it. He had never wanted to hurt anyone. Never. He had never wanted to hurt anyone. He had only gotten into his sideline because the demand for soft goods among the students was so visible, the students themselves were so vulnerable that it almost stood to reason that they got them from someone they trusted. It was a service. He was only performing a service. For the kids.

But only soft goods. Never hard goods. Not until this time and that did not count because he had not been able to do anything with the valise. Had he been able to do anything with the valise? Of course he had not, he couldn't move this stuff. It was fate. It was fate stepping from behind a curtain with a pointed finger and showing him all the time that essentially he was slated to be a good man. He was not a junk pusher. Not at all. He was merely a teacher who had the trust of his students and who in turn had tried to help them by providing the kids with the necessities of life.

They would take it into account. They would certainly understand his position when the deposition was taken. They would know just as he did that Phillip Sands was a good man. He was not a bad man. He was a good man who had never wanted to hurt anyone, and they would see this and take all of it into account and they would give him mercy.

God almighty, he thought, picking up the phone, it was not mercy he
needed, it was *protection*. And that was another issue altogether.

Trembling, he had to dial the number twice to get through, the first
time his fingers going utterly awry on the dial. Finally however the
connection was made. A voice came on.

"I want the police," Sands said.

"You have the police."

"I want them. I want them."

"Your name and address sir."

Struggling to remember these facts which slipped in and out of his
mind like stones in water, Sands got them out. He said that he needed
help urgently. Something about a valise.

The desk sergeant told him to sit tight.

XIV

Wulff saw it all. He got there too late to do anything but see it, but he
was not short of details. Parked outside of the cooperative was a prowl
car and that right away had made him revise his plans; he had decided
to sit tight and do nothing at all until the occupants of that car got back
and went away but even as he watched a second patrol car came up and
then a third. Then a fourth and with full siren a fifth. Something big was
going on up there. Wulff had a good idea of what it was. It made sense
to move the Plymouth away from its illegal parking space near the
entrance and he did so, wheeling it around the circle and at the rear of
the line of police cars. He sat there, motor idling slowly, ramming his
hand on the steering wheel, already almost sure of exactly what was
going on there.

He did not have long to wait. After a little while a distracted man in
his mid-thirties, scratching at himself and mumbling ferociously to the
policemen who flanked him on four sides came out of the building and
proceeded straight to the original patrol car. A moment later another
four police came out, one of them carrying a valise which looked
strikingly familiar to Wulff. It should have. He had known that valise,
taken it cross-country as a matter of fact, and its every outline was as
familiar to him as the contours of his own body, not that this did him
any particular good at this time. The valise was within ten yards of
where he sat but it could as well have been in Turkey or on the remains
of that freighter buried in the waters of the San Francisco Bay. The cop
carrying it went to the second car in line and tossed it carelessly into
the back—how well Wulff knew that careless toss, it meant that he

would kill anyone who tried to take it out of *his* car, *his* goods!—and the police fanned out into their vehicles, started a procession. All of this could have taken no more than two minutes. Detention was always quick; the longest flight could end so quickly as to trivialize it.

The cars drove off. Wulff released the clutch and mechanically, fascinated, followed them. It served no purpose, of course—what was he going to do, cut off that second car in line and lunge into it for the valise? No, he guessed that he better stop with this kind of thought—but he felt himself irresistibly impelled. What else was there to do? His mission had been aborted without even the confrontation that he had been goading himself into making. He knew that he would have killed Sands face to face; it would have been a pleasure.

The cars majestically, elegantly, cut through the university area and headed toward downtown Boston. The sonofabitch had probably called some informant inadvertently and without the proper kind of protection had gotten himself booked in instantly. Either that or more horrifying Sands had turned *himself* in because the valise had proven beyond his capacity to handle. Did it matter? Did any of this matter? The valise was out of his hands now, reasons did not matter. Whether the bastard had fouled up on his connections or whether the pressure had been too much and forced him to the police, it all came down to the same thing. He had lost.

He followed the procession, dodging and winking in and out of the traffic. For one instant he thought of trying to take them by force. There was a chance at least, a small chance that he might be able to cut off that second patrol car and get himself into it. But what chance would there be? These cars were moving in a body; immobilize the second and the first, third and fourth would be there in a second to cut *him* off.

Then Wulff saw the possibility.

It was crazy, it was a chance in a million, but it was one worth taking. Trailing the procession, concentrating on keeping them a level thirty yards in front of him—the cars themselves locked almost bumper to bumper, no sirens going—he took out his pistol, checked it, cocked it rapidly. Everything in order. He held it in his right hand then, held the wheel rigid with his left—and he began to gain.

Through the maze of downtown Boston they went. The cars could make no headway on him; Boston's reputation for the worst downtown traffic in the country was well-deserved. The streets were narrow, cluttered, they had been constructed for horse-and-cart traffic rather than automobiles, and the staggering of the traffic lights was awesomely inept. At every intersection now, in early rush hour, the cars were piling up bumper to bumper, not shrilling at one another, simply sitting, the drivers poised in various attitudes of hopelessness and the police cars could not cut through the maze. In downtown New York, a little flasher let alone a siren would have opened up the streets like tubes to the procession, but here these Boston cops knew apparently that resignation was the better part of valor. They stayed inside of the stream, not trying to buck it.

There they were in front of him, laboring in gear, at rest on a side street. Wulff swept the Plymouth right, diving out of the line of traffic. The car beside him gave him an irritated tap of the horn but nothing else. As he drew cheek-by-jowl with the driver Wulff could see the man's irritation turning toward astonishment as Wulff slowly moved the Plymouth along the sidewalk, then cut dangerously back into lane now behind the fourth car, revving the engine as he waited for the light to change.

Now he was directly behind them. That was good because he could not do what he intended to if there were any gaps, then again it would make him more noticeable. That was the way it had to be. Lose some to win some. He could not move in on them at close range, he would have been annihilated. What he was looking for now was a little spread, a little distance, just a little bit of an opening ....

The light changed. The lead car moved out slowly, poked its way through the intersection, was blocked by a huge trailer trying to move left, but finally squeezed its way through, the other cars following. These Boston police were certainly polite; any other large city cop would have been apoplectic. Well, maybe they were in no hurry to go down to the station house to start to fill out the forms. The valise would bring down at least half of the assistant DA's in the county and each of them would have his own individual idea of the best way to process it in. The procession blundered its way through another side street, a less congested one this time, and then broke out onto a little tree-shaded avenue, beginning to gather speed. Heavy traffic here but moving rapidly the way that blood manages to move through a clotted artery. Uneven but pumping away. Wulff, still locked bumper to bumper with car number four, pulled out suddenly, crossed the divider line, ducked an oncoming Volkswagen and began to squeeze against the critical second car of the procession. Now he was being noticed for the first time. Astonished faces under visored caps filled the windows.

He would try not to hurt them. His policy from the beginning had been clear: he was a policeman, he could not hurt a policeman. Rogue, maverick, exile as he might be, his essential loyalties still went toward the fools who were only trying to do or escape from their jobs. But there were limits to his principles, he thought. He hoped that they would not be tested. Rocking the car, holding the wheel, then lashing it on the main divider line in order to create a confusing target, he cocked the pistol, leaned over, quickly rolled down the right window of the Plymouth a quarter of the way and fired at the left front tire of the second car.

He knew that the only thing going for him was surprise. If he could just unbalance that vehicle before they even knew properly what was going on—but the bullet ricocheted off the pavement, he could hear it spit back the gravel and he had to cock and fire again, wasting vital seconds, almost losing control of the car before he was able to put the second bullet dead center into the valve cap of the left front tire. The second car swayed. It lurched toward him. It lurched away.

Then it went completely out of control, through a lane of traffic, toward the curb. Halfway there it was hit by the third patrol car hitting its brakes too late, it spun almost lazily and turned completely around, then it smashed into a streetlamp, the metal quivering. Intensity became stop-action at the moment of impact, the car hung for seconds, minutes really at the point of intersection before caving into that streetlamp with a lazy kind of grace, and then everything happened very quickly indeed.

Wulff vaulted from the Plymouth, twisting the wheel hard to the right, slamming the brakes and ramming it into neutral before he did so, more out of prayer than design. Holding his pistol in front of him he ran clumsily but desperately toward that second patrol car. The third, after the impact, had skidded into the oncoming lane of traffic and had hit a Volkswagen broadside, sending that one out of control into a bench on the other side of the street; the fourth patrol car however was closing in behind the smashed second, the brakes shrieking. The driver, though either instinct or fear had set the siren wailing.

Wulff kept on moving. He had maybe a leeway of thirty seconds to operate, maybe less if things kept on going this way. The first car in the convoy, the one actually carrying Sands, had been caught by surprise and was halfway up the block before it could stop, even when it did so the stop came casually and the driver seemed to be meditating his next course of action. The car was not coming back.

Car three was out of the scene, car one confused, car four gathering its senses. That left car two to deal with, but Wulff had already covered that one. He was in at close range now, his pistol exposed, waving it at the two astounded cops in the front seat. "Don't move!" he said. "Don't move!" He leaped toward the back where he could see the outlines of the valise distinctly.

The driver pulled out his gun, awkwardly. Wulff, not even thinking, shot it out of his hand. The other one, alert, dropped to the floor before struggling for his own gun but by that time he had the back door of the car open. He felt the handle of the valise almost leaping into his hand like a dog's tongue and he yanked it off the leatherette. The valise bobbled against his knees, hit him a glancing blow on the shin. The man on the floor shot at him, the bullet going past Wulff's ear.

Wulff shot him in the shoulder. Even as he did so there was a flicker of guilt. He had not meant to shoot police. Whatever he was, whatever New York had done to him he considered himself a cop. But there was no time now for scruples. The cop who had been shot screamed and grasped his shoulder, his gun falling away from him like a twig. Wulff had the valise in his hands now. He ran back toward the Plymouth.

By this time the first patrol car had wheeled around. It was bearing down upon him, moving the wrong way in the lane but not making good speed. Traffic had, of course, piled up during all of this. Cars had come to a stop, drivers were even now cranking down their windows to see what was going on. They created an obstacle course for the convoy which were now hopelessly separated from one another.

Gasping, he ran with the valise back toward the Plymouth. It was at the far extension of the lane, over the dividing line and the brake had slipped out, it was creeping imperceptibly forward. He felt the heavy breath of bullets passing his skull, two of them, as he dived toward the open passenger door, flung himself, atop the valise, inside. With a flailing leg, he slammed the door closed by hooking his toe into the handle and wedged himself behind the driver's seat.

All four cars, even the wrecked one at the other side of the road had their sirens going now. The beams and horns jolted him. Doubtless at this moment all of them were using their radios as well, frantically calling for aid. In just a matter of moments now the area was going to be sealed off with cars. He threw the car into first, released the clutch, floored the gas pedal.

The car moved outward into the oncoming lane. The oncoming lane was blocked, of course, by cars piled up behind the accident, but he ignored this. There was enough small space in front of him to open up some kind of maneuver and he went to the extreme side of the road, touching the shoulder, feeling the car buckle beneath him. The valise slid into the door with a clang. He put out a hand, supported it in place and brought the car back to the center line. Straddling it, there was just enough room left and right for the Plymouth to pick its way through. He was going forty miles an hour now, maybe forty-five and beginning to feel the disconnection of speed.

Bullets went into the glass. Nonsense. The car was bulletproof. Spatters of glass opened like teardrops to his left and right but the basic structural integrity of the car remained. He passed the first car, going the other way at high speed, opening it up, burning rubber. There was a quick frieze of three faces: the two police, in the back an open-mouthed gasping man who could only have been Sands. So this was the famous Phillip Sands who made even Louis Cicchini tremble. He did not look remarkable at all. Wulff should not have thought that he did.

Now he had the valise and a little distance opened up but he heard the sirens behind him suddenly louder and knew that the real business was beginning. They were going to chase him. Of course the sonsofbitches were going to chase him. What else could they do? It would be their asses if he were able to get away.

Hopeless. By rights he should quit now, pull over and let them take him. How was he going to be able to outrun police cars at full throttle? He had proved his point by taking over the valise—that in itself, unless he was badly mistaken, was going to lead to investigations and shakeups within the department here. How had they let him get away with it? He had made fools of them all.

But he was not in this for moral victories or to score points over the police department. Let the losers worry about their moral victories: he was the Wolf. Opening the car up to an insane sixty miles an hour through the city streets he opened his mouth in a mad grin to the wind, gripping the wheel until his hands turned white, hearing the mutter and jounce of the valise behind him. The losers could have their moral victories, the bureaucrats could have their signals of intention, their shows of strength.

He was the Wolf again and he was in this game to win.

XV

He got them all the way out to the Turnpike. The Plymouth was, as Cicchini had promised, indeed a hell of a road car, all of its troubles and reluctance seemed to go away when he moved the needle over seventy which he was able to only a few blocks short of the interception. Downtown Boston became a pastel of mud colors, faces like pennants, buildings like mottled dreams, he ripped the car through all of this at a speed of gradual intensity, building it, moving the Plymouth toward the Turnpike. He felt that if he could only get there he might be able to outrun them on the flat open spaces of the pike. The state cops would be in on this of course, reinforcements would have been radioed in from a radius of maybe twenty-five miles, but Wulff had a kind of bizarre confidence in his ability and his luck. What had the odds been that he would even be able to retrieve that valise? Yet there it was, next to him. He made himself a vow, rocking the car through dust at fifty miles an hour, looking for an access road to the Pike: he was not going to voluntarily turn that thing over again. They might get it from him, they might not, but they would have to kill him to get hold of that valise this time. Stupid once, dead twice. He ignored the beams and flashers, ignored the sirens, kept on driving. They would not try shooting at him again in heavy traffic. These cops might have been taken unaware but they were not stupid. Whatever they stood to gain by retrieving that valise they would lose by using downtown Boston at rush hour as a shooting gallery.

He stayed with the car. There were police cars ahead of him trying to head him off. It stood to reason that they would call for reinforcements the other way, but it was an open traffic pattern and Wulff did not doubt his ability to deal with any kind of traffic on the open road. Coming onto the Pike there was a sickening lurch as if the chassis of the car was going to take off backwards from the rest of it, he had had the clutch all the way in to avoid a downshift, but he was able to compensate by heavy work with the accelerator and the clutch, working them against one another. The car came back to itself. He was in business.

He went through the toll booth at sixty-five miles an hour, all the windows up, hunched over the wheel, glaring at the road. He was not going to have any dealings with toll booth attendants any more; that was one certainty. Behind him the police cars came in a screaming heap one after the other. He faked left, Worcester, and then sent the car hurtling New York bound. Twenty-five mile an hour speed limit on the access ramp. He got the car up to sixty. It held.

Once he hit the Pike there was a brief illusion of vaulting, of open spaces. The cars were not yet behind him; if there was anything up ahead it was not yet visible. The road was strangely open for a rush hour; a trickle of cars in the west-bound lane but nothing whatsoever eastbound. No one was taking the turnpike at this hour. Then he suddenly understood: they had probably cleared it and blocked it off already. They were not so stupid after all. Now they might have twenty miles of road in which to run him down and he would be open to them.

In his rear view mirror he could see the first police car coming onto the Turnpike now, beginning to close the gap already. In the city the superior mobility of the Plymouth and his skill behind the wheel might give him some kind of balance, but the open road was a different thing altogether. There was no way that he was going to be able to outrun them on open road, particularly if they put solid blocks ahead. He wanted the valise badly but not badly enough to drive into a solid block holding onto it. With one part of himself he held the wheel, concentrated on keeping ground between himself and the following cars, swept the road ahead for the first sign of blocks or a lurking state patrol car. On another level he was making rapid calculations.

His only way off the highway was on foot. That seemed obvious. The thing about the road was that it nailed down everyone on to its two dimensions of speed and distance. No one really thought of going *off* the road and this would be the only way in which he could break out of the lockstep and possibly evade them. But even assuming that he could crawl off the road with the valise, what were the chances that he would be able to make it back into Boston or any other town without being apprehended? These men were no fools. Like Wulff at the toll booth, they had made one terrible mistake in yielding up that valise but they were not apt to repeat it.

Nevertheless: what was there to do? He could see the situation; already they were closing ground. The patrol car behind him, apparently a maverick moving far ahead of the pack was within twenty to twenty-five carlengths, moving to the size of an apple in the rear view mirror. Once they drew alongside to run him off the road, that would be the end of it; these men were accomplished drivers, he would not be able to do to them what he had managed with the fools in the Mercedes in San Francisco.

He hit the brake rapidly, repeatedly, feeling the interruptions of the car's speed as jolts moving up through the floor and into the backs of his thighs, almost disengaging the delicate balance with seat and machinery which had sustained him so far. He kept on hitting the brakes and when the car had yanked itself down to twenty-five miles an hour he spun the wheel, gripping it in his hands, rocking it back and forth like a fisherman whipping out a netful of fish into a bucket. The entire transmission groaned with the shock. He stayed with it.

He rocked the car clear off the pavement and onto the shoulder. On the shoulder, he accelerated.

The patrol car following had come level but the driver obviously did not know what to do. He swayed indecisively toward the shoulder where Wulff was scuttling along, then hesitantly came back toward the center of the road. He had to brake violently at the same time or lose Wulff, and the braking threw the suspension out of alignment, the car rolled sickeningly, overcorrected and went toward the divider-strip. Wulff could see the passenger-cop gesticulating frantically at the driver, who gripped the wheel, struggling in an abstraction of panic. The car rolled into the divider strip and flipped.

Wulff did not watch it further. He had his own problems. For the moment the accident to the patrol car had cleared the road, there was no one behind him, but he knew that any sense of isolation was illusory, and soon the heavy troops would be moving in. He even thought that he might see in the distance some suggestion of a block, shrouded outlines of cars humped over like insects in the haze, but block or none he was committed. He kept the car rocking on the shoulder now, gathering speed, carefully setting it up for what he wanted to do. With a free hand he slapped together the lap-and-shoulder harness dangling free around him, another old New York habit. You were trained to lash yourself in in the dead of night there.

He felt the belts digging at him, holding him now like a mummy in a coffin. He hoped that it was not a coffin that he was driving but a serviceable souped-up Plymouth about to perform its last and greatest feat of readability. He would see. He certainly would see. He thought of Cicchini and offered a small appeal, not to the man or his integrity, because that would have been pointless, but to his common sense. Cicchini would not send him out in a defective vehicle. It simply would not, as the man would himself put it, pay. You did things right. In Cicchini's business you did things right all the time because you were apt to be permitted only one mistake.

The car was rocking freely now. Before he could think about what he was doing further, allowing any kind of imagination to enter, Wulff whipped the wheel all the way to the right, and spun the car off the shoulder.

He was heading into a wide, flat, blasted meadowland, shallow and without protuberances of any sort as far as he could see. This was important, but what was almost as important was that the land was completely level, because everything that happened now depending upon his ability to control the car within the planned geometry of limits. He felt himself launch into a roll like an astronaut and like an astronaut he held on, orienting himself through eyes fixed to the unchanging point of the dashboard, feeling gravity depart. Weightless, he lashed against the ropes.

The car rolled once, came unsteadily to all fours like a dropped cat. He gave it a little more gas, yanking the wheel and the car rolled again. He let it go. He was drifting straight right now, rolling in the meadow like a playful bear, rolling toward a clump of trees about fifty yards downrange.

The car kept on going. He ducked his head in, hunched his shoulders, presenting the minimum surfaces to possible impact. He wished that he had had a crash helmet—open the trunk of this bomb and doubtless he would find one—but too late for that now. The landscape spun around and through him, surrounding him on six sides; he could see the sky through the side window, see the ground through the windshield. Still the car rolled.

Controlled destruction; he hoped that it would not explode. It should not if the gas tank were properly shielded; he had hit nothing hard enough to trigger the flames. Still, you could not tell. You could not tell about the structural integrity of an American car.

To anyone watching from the road—and as far as Wulff was now concerned he hoped that they *were* watching—he had lost control of the car and was in a long, flat deadly slide. The car seemed completely beyond the driver's mastery; the only ending for something like this would be a dead man. He was counting on that. Struggling in the car, storming against the seat-belts he found himself almost smiling. He was preparing for Burt Wulff an exit which, he hoped, would keep damned Boston at least away from him ....

The car came to ground again and this time, with another violent shot of gas, Wulff kept it level, straightened the wheel, ran it parallel to the clump of trees by about five yards. He unbuckled all of the belts, freed himself, leaned over at speed and pushed open the right passenger door. It swayed back at him once and slammed; on the second, more violent try he was able to throw it off its hinge, even against the wind resistance, and hold it into place.

Wulff raised his left foot off the clutch, jammed the brakes violently, seized the valise in his right hand, pushed off, vaulted—and rolled.

He hit the ground at speed, the valise yanked away from him so rapidly that it was as if a giant fist had materialized from the air to jolt it away. All right. Let it go. It could not go too far. At twenty miles an hour, Wulff rolled over the ground, retracted into himself, feeling energy lash him like waves. Even at this growing distance he could feel heat from the car, the burning oil and rubber of the Plymouth. He decelerated, came to rest finally in a shallow grove about a hundred yards from the point of dive, feeling his limbs, ascertaining that he was intact except for a few minor bruises. He risked a quick glance over the terrain seeking the valise, saw it a long ways downrange, a tumbling object coming to rest near a tree trunk.

And the car exploded.

It must have hit a tree dead-on; there was a dull *whomp!* of impact and then Wulff could feel the searing heat, no longer waves now but vast gusts like a hurricane pouring off the car. The first *whomp!* set off a series of others, the car went up in stages, blowing fragments downrange like shrapnel and he ducked into the ground, allowing all of this to pass over him, protecting his eyes, clutching his elbows against his face.

Then, when there was just an instant of silence, he scrambled to his feet and in a blind totter began moving toward the point where he had last seen the valise. He tried to stay low to the ground, anyone watching this from the road must think that he had perished inside the car, but at the same time haste was of the essence. He must have that valise and be gone before the first police or motorists pulled over and came to investigate. The force of the explosion had given him a couple of moments grace, certainly, but nothing like this could go uninvestigated, the convoy must by now have already alerted the state police and soon the cars would begin to sweep in.

He found the valise. It lay, filth-encrusted, one snap open, at the base of an enormous tree. He yanked on it, feeling the hinges buckle as he wedged it out of the ground. The force of the roll had buried it inches in the earth. It was free. It was in his hand. He felt its surfaces against him.

Stumbling, clumsy but somehow methodical in his haste, Wulff held onto the valise and headed toward the wooded area and safety. He dived into the trees, his view of the road being instantly shut off. He collapsed sobbing ten yards deep into the forest, the valise rammed into his stomach.

And then, for a long while, oblivious of anything that might be happening outside, Wulff just lay there.

XVI

"It can't be!" Cicchini screamed into the telephone, but it could be, and he knew with the more rational plane of his mind that it could indeed be, and that shouting would get him nowhere. *Shoot the messenger* might be a popular policy but if you got anywhere in this business in the long run it was in separating the news from the source, and all the amount of shouting in the world would make no difference. "How did it happen?" he asked more calmly after a moment and his informant told him in quick sentences punctuated by the crackle of background static.

His informant, a young state patrolman, was taking a big chance in communicating the news through the radio car, he reminded Cicchini of this several times; anyone could intercept these broadcasts and if they got hold of this one he would really be in the soup, but he just thought that Cicchini had best be told as soon as possible. The state patrolman said that he hoped that Cicchini appreciated the way he was sticking out his neck for him, and Cicchini resisted with effort the need to begin screaming and cursing into the telephone. It would do him no good. He must remember that. The essence of success was to concentrate only upon those actions which would lead you somewhere, and telling the state patrolman what he thought would do nothing except to lose him a valuable informant. So Cicchini took it. He listened to everything that the kid had to say and then he hung up on him.

The Plymouth demolished. Wulff and the valise gone, probably into the woods off the turnpike. Somehow the son of a bitch had gotten away with it, how, exactly, Cicchini would never know. Another police car wrecked. State patrol, Boston patrol, even a couple of federal cars all the hell the way over the area, poking around and absolutely nothing to be done about it. The valise, meaningful evidence, gone. Sands, shaken up in the chase, taken into headquarters and after only thirty minutes, released. No evidence to book him. No one who cared to listen to Sands. Released in his own recognizance.

Wulff now somewhere at large in the area with the valise. Everything, the whole balance he had made of his life wrecked, fractured. "All right," he said into the phone when the man was done and there was absolutely no further information to be extracted from him, "all right, I appreciate this," *fuck you, up your ass*, and slammed down the phone, turning from his desk, confronting his view of the sea, his view of the grounds from the opposite window, not with the familiar pleasure at having gone so far, but rather as an animal might regard the bars of a cage while somewhere in the background he hears the Keeper coming— he was in a palace but the palace was also a trap. Not like the old days when he could have gone out himself and *done* something; now he could only wait for situations to come to him. He had arranged matters that way, successive layers of insulation built over the years to remove him from any responsibility, any culpability if things should go wrong, but the isolation cut two ways. In a sense now, he could only wait for Wulff's to come to him. It was the son of a bitch's move.

Possible, very possible that Wulff would take his advice and get out of Boston with the valise. But Cicchini doubted this. He had never had any intention of taking the man's word that he would do this; the idea was to wait until he had gotten it back from Sands and then, under close surveillance, tail him until he was in the first likely spot and get rid of him. Take the valise away. Cicchini was no fool; he was not going to allow a crazy man like Wulff to walk around Boston or anywhere in the fucking Northeast for that matter with a quarter of a million dollars' worth of drugs. But now the son of a bitch had wrecked everything. It was impossible that one man could pull off what Wulff had just managed. The guy had to be crazy. Absolutely obsessed and insane. Still, there it was.

Cicchini paced back and forth savagely. He wanted to take his gun and go hunting, but it was pointless. He wouldn't even know where to go. The guy had a hundred square miles to play around in if he was going to stay in the territory. Going after him and that valise would be suicidal until he had some sense of direction.

The phone rang again. Cicchini picked it up on the second ring, surprised at the sudden quivering of his hand. He had not trembled like this for decades. What was happening to him? What had this crazy son of a bitch done to him? The man on the wire said that someone wanted to speak to Cicchini who refused to give his name. Did he want to take it? At least the interceptors were on the job. He had the place manned up to the hilt. No one could get him here. He was convinced of it. No one was going to get Cicchini when he was walled into his palace. But there was no way that the son of a bitch could have gotten away with the valise either.

"All right," Cicchini said, "I'll take it." It was probably someone from New York wanting to know what the hell was going on. This was his territory and no one was going to challenge his authority, but they would be interested, damned interested in what had gone wrong here. If Cicchini did not have a good explanation, someone in the Middle Atlantic might begin to get ideas. *He had been fucked up just like San Francisco.*

"Cicchini," a voice said. Cicchini knew that voice. He would know it in dreams or death. "Hello, Cicchini."

"Where are you, Wulff?" Cicchini said. With an effort of will he managed to mask completely the quiver in his voice. The son of a bitch could not possibly know what he had been going through. "Just tell me where you are."

The man seemed to laugh, harsh barking sounds. "Why should I tell you?" he said. "I've done my job. I got your fucking valise."

All of the control disappeared. It was like a rubber band stretched to the breaking point that had been insolently clipped with a delicate pair of scissors. "Where are you, you son of a bitch?" Cicchini screamed. His hand clawed at the phone. "Just tell me where you are and I'll settle you out!"

"Will you?" said Wulff, "I thought that we were partners."

"I'll destroy you, Wulff."

"Come on," the man said, "come on, Cicchini. I'm waiting. I'm waiting for you to come in and destroy me. I want you to do it personally, face to face, but you don't have the guts. You'll send messengers."

"Tell me where you are. Just tell me."

"I'm going to tell you," Wulff said, "I want you to come in and get me.

Are you willing to do that, Cicchini? Are you man enough to come and get me yourself?"

"Tell me where you are," he said again in a low, maniacal voice. "Just tell me where you are, Wulff, I swear to God, I'll get you barehanded."

"I'm waiting," Wulff said, "I'm waiting for you to do that. Where do you think I am?"

"Tell me. Tell me."

"I'm at Sands' apartment, you cheap son of a bitch. I've got a valise full of heroin and a gun and I'm waiting for you to come and take them away. Or will you do it, Cicchini? You said you didn't want to mess with an associate professor."

Cicchini felt the rage covering him like a tent. It blinded him, choked him. "I'm going to get you, you son of a bitch," he said.

"That's good. I'll be waiting."

"I'm going to kill you."

"Please do that," Wulff said and the sound of his laughter slammed into Cicchini's gut like an arrow, "please do that, Cicchini, because you haven't been able to do a fucking thing right *yet*."

And hung up on him.

Cicchini was beyond thought. He grabbed for a gun. The men on duty downstairs had to hold him back bodily and scream at him in their fear before finally he understood what was happening to him and told them. Once he did he was glad.

He would go in there with an army if he had to.

XVII

Sands knew the guy was crazy. The guy was crazy because he had the insane, compulsive purposefulness of the madman and there was no way, absolutely no way that he could crack through it. But then again if the man was insane he was the most thorough lunatic that Sands had ever met, and that only made the situation worse. There was just no way around it. He could not win.

He did not want to win. All of that context had dropped away from him, coming out of the stationhouse all Sands had wanted to do was to get back home, lock the doors, bolt himself in, collapse. Cancel out, quit. The idea of turning himself over to the police for protection was, he saw now, absolutely purposeless, panic-induced, they could protect him from nothing. He had not realized the terror he had had of confinement until he had been in the car, watched what had happened off the road, been taken into the stationhouse. He could not bear it. He could not bear confinement. Better to stay walled in the apartment and wait for them to kill him, better to change his identity and flee this part of the country—but the police were no solution.

So he had come back to the cooperative only with dim thoughts of insulation or escape and this man had been waiting for him in the lobby, a tall, grim man with mad eyes and a set to the mouth which had terrified Sands, terrifying him more was his first sight of the valise, that valise which he knew so well clutched in the man's hand. "Upstairs," the man had said and pointed a gun in the vacant lobby. *Pointed a gun at him!* no one had ever pulled a gun on Sands in his life, just a little harmless dealing, harmless wheeling and dealing to keep the students happy; he had never wanted to become involved in this kind of thing and now a man with a gun and a valiseful of junk had met him in the lobby of his apartment building and had told him to get the hell moving quietly or he would blow his brains out.

No one did this to Phillip Sands! But then again no one had ever dumped a valiseful of junk on him before or had walked out on him saying the things his wife had said this morning. It was all tied up with the junk, that was all, the valise was a curse and he should have barred the men from his place before at the cost of being killed by them but too late, too late for any of this nonsense now. He was in. He was in deep, Phillip Sands was, and no amount of recrimination was going to change the situation at all.

When they got upstairs, Sands struggling with the key which did not seem to want to fit the door until with a click it went in and he stumbled into the apartment, the man said, "I want you to go in the bedroom. Just stay out of my way now and you'll be all right for the time being. You make any problems," and he showed him the pistol, "I'll have to kill you."

"No problems," Sands had said. His bowels had become ice and fire alternately and he had had to stagger into the bathroom, leaving the door ajar so that the man could see that he was not planning to do anything in there. He had never been so frightened in his life. This man was implacable. He held the gun with the assurance of one who had been living with guns all his life and had no imagination about them because he knew exactly what they could do. When Sands had finally gotten up, released from the cramps but just barely able to walk, the man had ordered him into the bedroom. "Stay in there," he had said. "Just stay."

"I will. I won't move. I'll—"

"There's probably going to be some activity around here and possibly a little shooting. If you stay out of the line of fire you may be all right for a while."

"I won't move."

"I'll take care of you later, Sands."

"Listen," he had said resisting the impulse to clasp his hands and fall on his knees, "listen, just leave me alone. Whatever I did, it was a terrible mistake. I'll leave Boston. I'll leave this part of the country."

"It's too late for that."

"I don't want to get into any trouble."

"You disgust me, Sands," the man had said, "you disgust me the more you talk, so you'd better shut up. There's nothing I hate more than a man who won't take the consequences of what he's become."

"I'll take the consequences. I'll do anything; it's just that—"

"It's just that you want to live, but we're past that simple equation now, Sands," the man said grimly. "We can't take into account anymore who wants to live and die. You should have thought of that years ago."

The man was crazy. He said all of this in a neutral tone, flat affect, absolutely not raising his voice at all and it was the most chilling thing that Sands had ever heard. *This man was not afraid of death. This man was death;* this flashed across his consciousness. This abductor, this person with the gun could not be moved by ordinary calculations because he simply had gone beyond all of them. He did not care whether he lived or died. Looking into those eyes, seeing the cool, grey panels of the man's consciousness sliding closed behind him Sands knew that he was dealing with something unlike anything he had ever seen in his life. The man flicked the gun indicating that he should go into the bedroom and Sands scuttled away like a dog or a child admonished by a parent. He would do anything that this man asked him to do. He was quite sure now that any protest at all and the man would kill him.

In the bedroom he collapsed to the bed itself, finding himself unable to stand or pace, feeling the sheets bunch beneath him. The urge to simply sink into sleep was overwhelming. Maybe he would awaken and find that all of this had gone away. But with that cooler, more detached part of his mind which had never failed him and which would not fail him now, he knew that he was not going to be able to sleep. He had been raised to screaming alertness.

The valise. It all went back to the valise. If he could only get his hands on the valise he might be able to save himself yet. The man had said that there would be shooting, very likely, going on within this apartment. That meant that there were people, surely, who wanted that valise, were coming here to try and take it away from the man with the grey eyes. But if only somehow Sands could get hold of that valise himself, turn it over to them, then he would have established his credibility, would have proven beyond doubt that he represented no danger to these people and they would release him. It would be his captor with whom they would have to deal but maybe, just maybe, his captor would not be around.

Sands went to the bureau, opened the third drawer. The gun was where he had left it the last time he had looked at it a month ago. Once a month he just wanted to open the drawer and check to assure himself that the gun was still there. Otherwise, until now he had wanted nothing to do with it. He had a horror of guns, everything that they represented; having it around had been only insurance. But in the sideline he had fallen into it made sense to have a gun in the house even if you were not quite sure that you knew how to use it.

Sands took out the pistol. It felt warm, palpable to his touch although it had been lying untouched under the stack of underwear for months. Had Karen ever found it while stacking his clothes? He had ordered her time and again to stay out of his bureau and she said that she would, but there was no accounting for the woman. Maybe she had seen it, touched it recently. It could be another reason why she had left him so abruptly. That was worth thinking about. How could he have explained to her that he never wanted to use the gun?

No way. She was gone, she was gone anyway, forget it. He held the gun against his side and very cautiously walked toward the door, opened it a soundless crack, looked through. The man was standing in the living room, occupying ground in a position of alertness, the gun held easily in his right hand, his eyes sweeping the terrain with such rapidity that Sands could only freeze into position hoping that he would not see the slight crack of the door. He did not. Finishing his sweep, his eyes cut back to the opposite corner of the room and then, very quickly, he walked to the window and looked outside, down three flights. Checking out streetside, Sands held the gun in his right hand, the gun shaking slightly. He would have to open the door slightly; the crack was too narrow to risk a shot. It could rebound off the wood and hit him. That would be his luck.

He would have to push that door open quickly, as silently as possible, aim and fire. With luck he had one shot, one clear shot before the man whirled and cut him down. If he missed that shot, he was unquestionably dead because he was obviously dealing with a man from whom no second chances were obtained. But he did not even know if he had that one shot, the door might creak (did it creak? he had never noticed) and his finger might slip on the trigger, any one of a number of things might happen, all of which would be disastrous because the man would turn on him before he would even have a chance to guard himself.

The man was still standing by the window, now. Something outside had caught his attention because he was pinned to the glass there, fluttering like an insect in his attention. He had not looked back toward the bedroom for a full minute. The man shrugged his shoulders, flexed them and then, quickly raised the pistol, checking it out. Then he dropped his hand back to where it had been and quickly, delicately, walked through the living room and positioned himself by the door, wedging himself against the wall, his shoulders flat to position.

Carefully, Sands aimed. Both hands were shaking, the gun fluttering like a bird, it took all of his attention to keep it on the man. He realized something of which he had only been marginally aware before; he was capable of killing another human being. Once you got your mind down to it, it was no big deal whatsoever. The man was an obstacle, he had to be removed, that was all. Sands extended his toe and flicked the door open another two or three inches. It moved noiselessly.

Holding the gun with all his strength he squeezed off a shot at the man.

It hit the wall in an explosion of plaster, the man crumpled to his knees, then turned, aiming his own pistol and Sands realized with a sick, familiar wrenching that he had missed. Missed the man and now he was dead. How did he think that he could go up against a professional like this? He must have been crazy, but then he always had been crazy.

In that extended, frozen moment, Sands waited for the man to fire and blow his life away but in the dead-center of it the door behind which he was standing blew open and three men charged into the room. Behind them another man came slowly. The one who had tried to kill him fell to his knees from the sudden impact of the door. Sands, gasping, collapsed to his knees.

And the scene dissolved and resolved like shapes of fish twisting in an aquarium.

XVIII

Rolling on the floor, Wulff got off a shot. It went wild but it managed to startle the man at whom he had aimed, the man twitched and dived for cover, struggling with his own pistol. The other two were looking for him but momentarily disoriented by their plunge into the room. Only the fact that he had sensed something and had, at the last moment, opened that hallway door had saved him. Expecting solid impact they had found only air. It had sent them scuttling through, now they were still scurrying for balance.

The son of a bitch in the bedroom had tried to kill him, but no time to think of that now. Stupid: he had been stupid leaving Sands alone there, why had he not thought that the bastard might have had a gun? He could deal with Sands later, however, assuming that there was a later. Wulff held the thirty-eight in his hand and pumped a shot into one of the men who had stumbled clear across the living room and against the window.

The man fell, screaming, bubbling, bright with instant blood. One down. Wulff, looking desperately for cover, felt a shot go by him, fired at the source. There was another scream and he saw the second gunman fall. Two down. How long could he go on this way? His luck was holding but he was as exposed as ever, now lying full-length on the rug, doubling up his knees, moving them in a rapid low-crawl toward the couch.

Cicchini came into the room. Slightly more dishevelled than Wulff had seen him, holding his own gun, purposeful. Supervising. But Cicchini had not anticipated this line of fire; he had obviously expected Wulff to be taken out with a neat shot or two. Instead of using his gun then, Cicchini backed against a wall, struggling to get out of the torrent of bullets. The remaining gunman was behind the couch now. Wulff saw the protrusion, the thrust, of pistol. He fell fully to the rug just in time to avoid the shot. It took a spray of dust out of the wall behind.

"Son of a bitch," one of the dying assassins said on the floor, "you fucking son of a bitch Cicchini, you got me killed!" and this must have distracted Cicchini's attention. His eyes flicked over to the form on the floor and just in that one brief lapse of attention, Wulff got him in the shoulder. He had wanted the neck but the shoulder was good enough.

Cicchini screamed, the gun leaping from his hand. He sprawled. Wulff took a direct hit in the shoulder. He had forgotten the one behind the couch. The impact spun him, he felt numbness. Not his gun hand at least. He got halfway to his knees, leading the man, and put a shot behind the couch.

Missed. The man ducked and fired again but the shot was wild. Panic. Cicchini was on the floor now moaning, gripping his shoulder. Cicchini was trying to get to his gun but could not make that gap; he got halfway and fell. Wulff put another shot into him, back of the left knee. He did not want to kill him. Cicchini and he had things to talk about later. He was assuming that he got out of this.

Cicchini was merely a diversion. Shooting the downed man was wasting a bullet. Wulff felt another bullet go by him but the man behind the couch was in an obvious panic now. Two others dead, his boss disarmed and helpless, the man must have felt that he was slated to die. Wulff could hear the whistle and sob of his breath. The man was going to ground.

If he had had a forty-five he could have shot him through the fabric of the couch itself, the bullet using the fragmentation for increasing damage. If he had had the machine gun he could have swept the area clean. But that was neither here nor there; he had the thirty-eight and would make the best use of it. He put another shot into that area just to keep the man down, not expecting to hit him. One of the downed men screamed, a last dying scream that went from shrill to bass and then fell away. Cicchini, his knee torn, was sobbing with pain. Wulff rose clumsily to his knees, giving the man behind the couch a full target and was able to just see the top of the head.

He put a shot into it.

The skull exploded like a teacup. The man vaulted to his feet, his head falling off in fragments, looked at Wulff with an oddly purposeful glare, walked straight toward him like the walking dead, holding the gun stiffly and then, his cheeks yellow, fell gracelessly, arms buckling, legs splitting, at Wulff's feet. Breathing heavily, Wulff backed away, surveyed the room.

Four down. Only one alive, Cicchini in the center, lying on the mats, his forehead covered with sweat or dew. Wulff felt the pain beginning to come through his shoulder now, gripped at it, then remembered the man in the bedroom. He turned there: the door was closed. Quickly, without thinking about it, he went toward there, gun first. He had to clean out the area.

The door seemed locked. So the man had bottled himself up in there. This made sense he supposed. He put a shot through the lock and went on. The door caved in against his shoulder in splinters, he hit the floor as soon as he was in the room, expecting a shot. His shoulder launched massive pain as he hit, then as the pressure eased it went away. Not a serious wound. He could not see the man.

Not against the window, not on the floor. Sweeping the room he saw Sands. Sands was lying full-length on the bed, shoulders hunched, face down into the pillow. He was sobbing with terror. The gun lay on the floor beside the bed. Wulff went over there, took it, put it away. It was hot and had a peculiar, dry odor. Probably never properly serviced. The man had been lucky to get a shot off with it at all. It could have blown up in his face.

Amateurs. But the amateurs were the most dangerous of all, they were the ones you had to watch. Until, like Sands, they caved under. He went to the bed, looked at the man with disgust. Sands heard him, folded the pillow up around his head and mumbled something into it.

Wulff reached out with the uninjured arm and bunched the man's clothes, yanked him from the bed full-force. The mewing, whining thing that had been Phillip Sands hung in his grasp like a pendulum. He turned the man around toward him, saw the concavities of cheek, the desperate, stricken eyes, the slack, open expanse of mouth from which saliva rolled.

He hit the thing. It hopped with the impact, put both hands to its face, collapsed toward the floor. Wulff caught it before it could fall all the way. It lay almost weightless in his hands. He hit it again on the cheek, feeling the breaking bone like glass, spatters of bone moving through the thing's face.

The thing cried. It sobbed like an infant, tried to raise its hands against the damaged face, the eyes welling. Wulff felt the revulsion. There was no retaliation. There was no way, ever, that you could get even with them. You might think that you had finally turned around on them, sapped their poison, put the evil in a place where you could deal with it as only evil knew. But then they turned out to be something else. They turned out to be corpses or spent and broken things like this one before him or the one called Cicchini in the living room. At the instant of retaliation they were no longer the thing that you had been attacking. All of the power was drained out of them and they too were only victims.

No. No atonement. No way whatsoever. The score could never be settled because other things would rise up in their place, challenging with their own power and ugliness. For every Sands you laid out on a bed, two or ten would come in his place. Hopeless. It was hopeless.

He felt the bile rising within him and felt he might vomit from a combination of the revulsion and pain. His shoulder was hurting him quite badly now. His head ached from the sudden release of tension. He had not realized how tired he was, what price Boston had exacted.

"Please don't kill me," the thing said. It was crouched before him in a penitential posture. The hands snaked around his knee, cupped it like a breast. He felt the moist, ugly contact and broke it with a kick. The thing, hit in the forehead by a toe, the skull damaged, collapsed to the elaborate orange rug on which it had pranced and danced. It was still begging.

"Do kill me," the thing hawked. "I was wrong, they were all wrong, you must kill me. Bring me death." It flopped on the rug. It was a fish, an insect. It was no longer a human being. Wulff had to remember that.

He kicked the thing again. He was an exterminator and this putrid, ugly thing was in his way so it would have to be kicked. There was no satisfaction in it. There was no satisfaction in anything. Things like this had killed his girl, destroyed his life, were crawling through all of the streets of the cities injecting their death, and yet there was nothing to do. "You don't deserve to die," he said and the understanding came. Death was only for those who could understand it. This thing on the floor never could.

"You don't understand it," he said again. The thing sobbed. The thing that had been an associate professor, that had arrogantly turned children into addicts, that had stolen a valise, that had tried to kill him, began to babble again but this time he could not understand what it was saying.

No matter. It did not matter what it was saying; the message could not change. Only the faces changed, never the message. Wulff took out his gun slowly, reluctantly. He would kill the thing because if he did not it would be like a stray roach going back to its nest; you could not account for it. It might start the cycle again.

He shot it in the head once, precisely. The thing took the shot behind the left ear and with a gulp of mingled delight and acceptance fell all the way below him, seeming to flow into the rug. Blood mixed with blood. Wulff left it there. He went back to the living room.

Cicchini had somehow managed to stand, propping himself on the destroyed knee, gripping his shoulder. His eyes were blind and desperate. "Help me," he said. He was a thing too. In the commonality of pain all men became merely objects. That was the clue. It was the clue to Cicchini's power. It was even why they loved junk. Funnel enough junk in and you no longer had to worry about people taking it. They were people no longer.

"You've got to help me, Wulff," Cicchini said, "or kill me." The stiffened leg on which he was trying to balance kicked straight out and with a scream of agony Cicchini fell to the floor. He tried desperately to keep weight off his knee and shoulder but failed. He took the full impact on the palm of the injured arm. He bellowed the sounds that children make under bombing and then vomited, more as an extension of the pain than for any other reason.

Wulff let him. He had other things on his mind right now. He checked out the three gunmen, found that they were already freezing into the postures of death. Rub-a-dub-dub, three men in a tub. Butcher, baker, candlestick maker. Their faces had the shrunken, wistful petulance that he had seen in open coffins. Nothing became life so much for these men than the leaving of it. He stumbled into the bathroom, took off his jacket and ripping off the shirt in clumps, checked out his wound.

Not too bad. Relatively superficial. The bleeding had already stopped, which was not necessarily a benefit, but feeling within the edges he could touch no bone. Delicately, expertly, he checked out the depth of the wound, only a half an inch, if that. It would leave a shallow scar, might limit the mobility of the left shoulder a little. All right. Not the gun hand.

He opened the medicine chest, went through it. Feminine ointments and palliatives tumbled into the sink while he looked for alcohol. No such thing. The Sands household had never concentrated on the basics. He settled for some after-shave lotion, poured it clumsily but directly into the wound.

The pain was intense. It was like the shot all over again but worse, seizing and shaking him in deadly little fingers. He gasped, tears coming to his eyes although he tried to hold them back, leaned over the basin, vomited. It hurt. Everything hurt. You paid and paid the price and at the end it was as it had all been at the beginning. Still, you had to go on. What else was there to do?

The pain ebbed a little. It always would. Unless you were dead the pain would go away, you would forget how it had been until the next time. It was the forgetfulness which kept you going. The same thing for sex. He found some gauze underneath a box containing a diaphragm, ripped it out not bothering about the niceties of it and with a couple of bandaids in another box managed awkwardly to secure the taping. It would hold out. He might need to see a doctor about secondary infection but he even doubted that. The alcohol would have taken care of that. If you could stand the pain you could clean out anything. For a little while.

He turned. Cicchini had crawled into the bathroom like a dog. The man was sniffing at the air that way too, completing the image. Wulff saw the slow drip from the two wounds, heard the uneven exhalation. The man's eyes were bright and sunken.

"Get me out of this," he said.

"I intend to," said Wulff.

"You son of a bitch," Cicchini said. "I never went up against anybody who beat me. You beat me, Wulff."

"That's great," he said, thinking of the three corpses in the living room, the dead thing near the bed. "That's a real thrill."

"Get me to a hospital. Don't leave me like this."

"You won't die, Cicchini," he said, finished with his bandaging, turning to the man, "not quite yet."

"Take the valise. Take it." A stab of pain caught the man crosswise, he slumped to one side and collapsed, rolled to his back, drew up his knees. He barked in his pain. *Dog.* That was what he had been dealing with all the time.

Wulff finished his taping, turned to the man. Cicchini had not fainted. No such luck for the man. Fully conscious, pinned to consciousness like a butterfly, he lay on his back, strapped to pain, looking up at the fluorescent light. "I can't stand the pain, Wulff," he said almost matter of factly, "you can't leave me like this."

"Why not?"

"Shoot me then," Cicchini said. "At least give me that. Give me some dignity."

"Dignity?" said Wulff, "you were never worried about anyone's dignity in your life." He resisted an impulse to kick the man, stepped over him instead, walked back to the living room. The smell of death assaulted him, strong, almost like whine in his nostrils. A thick, dusty odor like an untended corner of a museum.

"It's no good to you anyway," Cicchini said weakly, "what have you gained? You can't do anything with the valise. You win but you lose, Wulff. I never wanted the valise anyway. Nothing will change."

"I know that."

"You can't change a thing," the man said, rolling his head to look over at him, "so at least you can kill me."

"Beg for it."

"I'll see you in hell," Cicchini said. He tried desperately to get to his feet but pain had sapped the motor capacities of the body. He could not stand. He lay there like timber grounded on a beach.

"Kill me," he said again. "If you want me to beg for it, then I'll beg. Kill me."

"I have a better idea," Wulff said.

He went to the valise. It was where Sands had dropped it. Tugging at the clips, he opened it. The effort took more out of him than he had thought; he was weaker than he had conceived. Sweat came off his forehead, dropped into the contents of the valise lightly.

He looked at the contents again. For all that that valise had gone through the contents appeared intact. That was it; the junk remained secure, inviolate. The world revolved around it, men lived and died, distributed and ate, shot and drank it, crawled through a thousand alleys in its pursuit or evasion, but the junk could not be touched. Nothing would ever change it. Like money, like death, like sex it was a neutral quality, all of the torment imposed.

The heroin was arranged in loose decks. He took one out. It felt surprisingly light, almost weightless in his hand. A pack of cards. Running his fingers over it he could feel the little granules of powder moving beneath. He opened one corner, looked for the first time at what he had. He had never bothered in San Francisco, cross-country, Boston. It was beautiful. He could have expected nothing else. Death was always beautiful. Why else would men accommodate themselves to it, administer it so easily if it were not beautiful?

"I've got a much better idea," Wulff said.

He took the deck and went into the kitchen. Poking through a cabinet next to the cheerfully-humming refrigerator he found exactly what he wanted, a huge water tumbler, sixteen-ounce capacity, decorated with merry little floral designs. Red and green and yellow flowers beamed out at him. He went to the spray tap, opened it to cold, put six or seven ounces of water into the tumbler.

Then he tapped the deck against the sink and—very expertly, you learned a few things anyway on the narco squad—he poured half the contents of the deck into the glass. Folded it over, put it away. Took a spoon from the drawer on the side and stirred in the granules until it had the lumpy color and consistency of sour milk.

Delicately, very carefully, he sniffed at it. The odor seemed to be about right. He carried the glass back to the bedroom where Cicchini lay, resisting an impulse to whistle. He passed the telephone on the way. How long did he have with four and a half corpses here? he wondered. Not too damned long, he supposed, but long enough. There was something to do. No matter what happened to him he would not leave here until it had been done.

"Here," he said extending the glass toward Cicchini, "here, this will fix you up. Drink it down."

The man's eyes flickered. There was intelligence in that face and perception. You would have to shoot Cichini in the brain to take that quickness away and then where would the fun be? No, he wanted the man whole. Cicchini twisted on the floor.

"No," he said, "I won't do it."

"Of course you will. It'll take away the pain."

"I know what that is," Cicchini said. "You think I'm crazy?"

"I doubt it very much. You're as sane as I am, anyway. Drink up."

Cicchini shook his head. "I won't," he said, "I won't do it."

"Yes you will," Wulff said, already getting weary. The glass was becoming heavy in his hand. He knelt, extended it. "Take it now."

"You're crazy," Cicchini said, "that's junk in there."

"Is it?"

"You don't drink that stuff."

"Of course you do," Wulff said. "You can shoot it, roll it, sniff it, taste it, smoke it, fuck it or shove it up your ass. Shooting happens to be the fastest way, but different strokes for different folks. It'll get into the bloodstream, Cicchini. Have no fear. It'll go right through the stomach wall and hit the nervous system and you'll feel better than a triple dose of morphine. Come on."

Fear came across the man's face. It was a different fear than the one before; it opened into a chasm. "It'll kill me," he said.

"I'm not a doctor," said Wulff. "It might, though. But what the hell? You were asking to die just before, weren't you? What a way to go!"

"No," Cicchini said.

"Yes," said Wulff. He fumbled for his gun, patted it, took it out of his pocket and showed it to the man. "Drink it," he said, "or I'll shoot. Not to kill. Just in the neck. You ever been hit at close range by a bullet in the adam's apple? I know a man who was once, in Vietnam. He was trying to tell me all about it for forty minutes but he couldn't make a sound until he died. He wanted to die very badly, though. I could read that in his eyes."

"I don't want to take it. I don't—"

"Of course you don't," Wulff said softly, holding the glass trembling against the man's chin, "I know you don't. You never touch the stuff, you see. You'll build a palace on it and kill to keep it moving but actually, of course, you don't indulge. You're the Pied Piper, Cicchini, except that you're tone-deaf and that's not a flute you're playing, it's a needle. But you're going to get a taste of it now. You're going to get a taste of what you've been doing."

The man's cheeks bulged. He gagged from deep inside, retched thinly. When he opened his mouth to let it run out a little blood came with the sputum.

"Internal injuries I guess," Wulff said. "It must have gotten in somewhere, that shoulder wound. So you're in trouble anyway, Cicchini, you might as well enjoy yourself."

He cocked the gun. He did not think that it was going to be necessary to shoot the man but he was perfectly willing to do so if it were necessary. He did not care. He would just as soon shoot Cicchini in the adam's apple if it came down to that. The Vietnam story had not been a lie. The man he had seen it happen to had been someone who he cared about; he guessed that it would be much more interesting in the all-around sense to see it happen to Cicchini.

Cicchini saw it. He saw the purpose in Wulff and the movement of the gun and this was what broke him. He did not want to be shot there. Wulff could hardly say that he blamed him. Cicchini reached for the glass. Wulff let it slide into the open hand like a block of wood.

"All of it," he said, "every bit."

Cicchini's hand fluttered. The fluid shook in the glass but did not spill. He raised his hand and put the glass against his lips, drank.

The first swallow made him gag. His stomach heaved, mouth opened, it ran out of him. Wulff saw that the man was not faking, he was genuinely sickened. All right. "Try again," he said, "now that you know how it tastes."

"I don't want to. I want—"

"Take it again."

Cicchini drank. The rest of the glass went down quickly. He took it down in a series of choking swallows like a freshman drinking beer from a pitcher. His eyes rolled. The glass slid away from him.

"How long?" Wulff said, still kneeling. "You're the expert on this. Two minutes, three minutes to get into the bloodstream? That's all right. However long it takes. Have fun, Cicchini."

"You son of a bitch," the man said. "You rotten, filthy—"

"Don't tell me sons of bitches," Wulff said, standing. "You scum, I could torture you to death for a year and you would still be getting off easy." He felt the rage coming out of him in great gasps but held it back. No point, no point. Nothing would be accomplished. "You'll never pay," he said, "you'll never pay for what you are."

He stumbled out of there, the rage weakening him, taking almost the last of the physical reserve out of him. But there was still too much to be done; he could not stop now. He bypassed the three men in a tub, went back to the valise, closed the clips. This valise had travelled with him from San Francisco to Boston, it had cost him a lot, it had taken many byways and pathways to meet him again but he guessed that he was not going to give it up. Not quite yet. In a mystical way he felt united with it.

Leaving Cicchini already feeling the first effect of ten thousand milligrams of only slightly adulterated Turkish heroin, Wolff hoisted the valise and weaved his way the hell out of there.

XIX

He was a little boy. He was a little boy named Louis Cicchini who lived in a burning barn and then he was someone else, a man with the same name who lived in a castle but in between he had lost the touch, the connection, he was sliding on paper, encased in ice and the transition was so smooth and deadly that he could not make the connection between the one and the other. The boy was dead, the man in the castle was dead, they shared this but there was nothing else; they spoke a different language.

He felt the smooth, even flow of the drugs. They worked their way into his body like power through the distributor coils of a car. He was a machine. He was not a man but a machine; he had pistons and a crankshaft and distributor coils, through them the oils and waters of the drugs flowed. The machine was broken now, malfunctioned and burnt, it would be tossed soon enough into the junkyard for pressure-and-reconstitution but in the meantime there was just a little space left, enough space to know what was happening to him.

The boy and the man lay on the floor, the drugs working through the two of them. He had not known that they would take hold so quickly nor that they would do what they had to cancel sensation. He felt no pain, pain could not be recovered even though he sent his mind scurrying down the corridors of recollection looking for it; it had gone. There was blood but it was not his blood, there was emptiness and waste but that was not his either. He lay on the floor, his eyes locked to the ceiling, and he did not blink, the ceiling pressed down upon him but he could not close his eyes against it nor did he want to. The blink was supposed to be the only way in which men could survive in the world, the world being so unbearable to them that they had to close their eyes against it five or six times to the minute, once every ten seconds just to shut the world out but he did not feel that he had to shut it out nor could he have.

The boy lived in the burning barn and turned to him and said, "I don't want to, I don't want to do this."

"You've got to," the man Cicchini said in the logical, reasonable voice of the adult. "You've got to do it son, because that is the world."

"No it isn't, it doesn't have to be, I can't take it, don't you understand? It isn't worth it," the boy said, and the barn flamed around him, the shingles and cinders caving in toward ash, the animals trapped within, mooning and baying, and he reached toward Cicchini as if Cicchini could somehow pull him out of those spaces and save him but Cicchini could not. He lived in a castle by the sea and that castle arched far above the waters, being surrounded by gates on all sides and the gates were impermeable. He could no more get out through them than those outside could have broken through, and so the boy shrivelled and screamed in the barn, his cries for help falling away, weaker and weaker until at last Cicchini realized that he stood alone, the boy being quite dead, all of history smashed inside him, and yet that did not change the message, did it? Was there any change? You had to go on, that was all, you had to go on because all of the alternatives were worse. He would have told it to the boy if he had had any more chance, but all chances were gone ....

Ten thousand milligrams of heroin working through the liver, spleen, digestive organs. He had a moment of relative lucidity during which he thought he could see them, could see the distinct granules oozing their way through the various organs, into the ruined blood and then at last to excretion, kidneys and bladder screaming with the weight of it. The granules were small and frail but they would not dissolve, in fact they became stronger in the blood, pelting through, and each of them had a face. Each of the granules had a face: mouth and eyes, personality and voice, and they were talking to him, talking inexhaustibly as they channeled their way into and out of the central nervous system. "How do you like it, Cicchini?" the little granules sang and spoke. "What do you say now, now that you've said that you're sorry?" And he writhed on the floor, writhed because he could not answer them, how could you answer something inside of yourself? "You don't like it at all Cicchini," the granules noted as they bobbled and swam in the blood. "You don't like it, well how are we supposed to like it? We've got our problems too, it's not easy being junk you know. You've got a bad reputation, why, people won't say a good word for you actually, and yet the fact is that junk is curative, junk is restorative, it acts to take people out of their lives when those lives are unbearable, and besides that, do you know that until 1913 it was actually approved for us by licensed medical practitioners at their discretion? But then there was a panic in Congress and a law was rammed through making it illegal and the hysteria began to build. Now isn't that a point, Cicchini? Consider our position, here we are bum-rapped all over the states when actually it isn't our fault at all, we're just a neutral quality."

"Right!" Cicchini said to the granules, "right, you're right, now doesn't that say something for me, that I allowed you to be used, that I helped people to use you?" Thinking that this was an important point, a vital point on his behalf in fact, and then the granules turned on him and began to laugh.

"You fool," one of them, apparently the spokesman, said. "You stupid fool, don't you know that's all been taken into account already, and besides that times have changed? Times have changed a great deal, Cicchini, the whole nature of the business has changed, things aren't the way they used to be in 1913 or even 1963," and the granules laughed and spattered within him, then massed and began a sidewise thrust through the delicate membranes covering the old brain.

Cicchini knew he was dying. In and out of rationality all the time, he had a great roaring sensation of collapse as perspective began to slip in and out of him like a surgeon's knife. He kicked and scuttled on the floor, still trying to raise himself but even though the drugs had cancelled pain they had done nothing to restore mobility. They whisked through him on ice skates. He was a frozen pond; he was a reservoir. Cicchini, lolling on the floor, felt his bowels open as if all of this was happening to another man somewhere and he voided thickly, everything below mixing and congealing toward the darkness.

"You killed us, Cicchini!" the little boy said, stepping from the burning barn, "you killed the two of us, it's all your fault," and Cicchini could only agree: yes, that was true, he had killed the two of them. It did not seem to matter whether he had or not. Flames arched from the barn and embraced the boy in arms of fire, dragged him back into the barn and everything collapsed around him, embers and ash.

Cicchini had one last moment of lucidity. In it he was staring not at the ceiling but toward the window. He had convulsed in a half-roll, now he saw the bodies of the three men sprawled throughout the living room; through the open door of the bedroom his fixated, staring eyes saw the clumped corpse of the professor. Four dead men in a room.

Four dead men in a room, soon to be a fifth. That was all that it came down to. He had spent forty-five years swinging wide of this pattern, avoiding it, moving in greater and greater circles from the burning barn of his childhood, but this was the way that it had all ended. Maybe it was supposed to be this way. In some dark, final abscess of the heart, Cicchini understood, accepted that his life was meant to end in this way and that everything that had preceded had only been a preparation for this moment. And all else had been lies. A man was only his ending, the rest meant nothing. The death defined the man. That was all. That was all there was to it. It was as simple as that.

He tried to let out one last bellow of anguish and rage but his lungs would not take the air. They choked on the inhalation, his eyes bulged and everything broke within and tumbled down. Submissive, he went inside himself.

And Cicchini died.

XX

Karen decided to go back. His conduct this morning had been impossible but she guessed that she was no great shakes either. As a matter of fact, she had said things to him that thinking it over she probably had no right saying. Anyway, better left unsaid. If he wanted to push drugs as a little sideline it was his business, and what was the difference anyway? one way or the other everybody was into it. Drugs were no big deal. Every freshman in the dormitories blowed a little pot, dropped some speed now and then. If Phil wanted to give them what they would have gotten anyhow and make a few dollars on the side, that was his business. She had no right to complain. Did she walk on water?

Anyway, staying with a girl-friend was a bit of a drag now. Admit it:

she was twenty-four years old. She was no longer an undergraduate, it was one thing to hang out with roommates when you were still in college, or barely out, but the whole life was shallow, superficial. She had better things to do with herself now, even if she didn't want to go to graduate school, and he had no right to push her. Maybe she would get a job. In any event, part of the point of fighting was the making up. He was never so tender and considerate of her as when she came back, and sometimes the good times would go on for weeks. Days anyway.

She got out of the cab in front of the building, paid off the driver and went inside. Five o'clock now, he ought to be back. It was possible that he had stormed out as he sometimes did after one of their fights, and might not come back until late at night or even early the next morning, but she had a feeling that Phil would be waiting for her. Usually he was. He would come toward her, his face open with gratitude, his arms already reaching and she would drop her things, hold out her arms and let him touch her. The touching was nice. Sometimes the sex wasn't so good but she really liked the beginning of it at times, and because of his fear and gratitude he would hold back for quite a while and just touch her and let himself be touched. That was good. That was just the way she liked it.

Into the vestibule, up the elevator. She had never liked this building. She had wanted to get a house right away, rent one if not buy it, have some space, but Phil had said that houses in this area were ridiculous rentals, there was no point in getting into a mortgage situation at this time, and what was all that space necessary for anyway? It was just the two of them, and would go on being the two of them for a long time. She couldn't fight that, even their living in a tall apartment building was just so depressing that she could scream. It was her childhood all over again. She had grown up in Forest Hills and had sworn when she got out of there to go to Radcliffe, that she would never live high off the ground again. Well, everything just went to show you. The style of living here was just like Forest Hills too. People had no contact, they avoided one another. You could get killed here and it might take weeks for someone to find you. Well, it was the only defense, she supposed, against being piled on top of one another like this.

She walked down the hall, smelling a strange odor. Her senses peaked, curious, she found that she was slowing her pace, trying to find the source of the odor. It seemed to be in front of her. She continued down the hall. Phil would probably know what it was.

The apartment door was open.

That was strange right away: you never left a door open, even if you were just carrying a bag of garbage down to the incinerator. But worse than that, she now understood, the odor seemed to be coming from inside her apartment. Closer in, she felt she could identify it; it was a sticky, dense, trapped kind of smell, the kind you would get if you bent down to an ant colony.

Suddenly she did not want to go inside.

But that was ridiculous. That was ridiculous, too: it was her home, hers and Phil's and what could be inside there that could keep her out? Karen pushed the door and calling Phillip's name walked inside.

And saw all of it at once.

The bodies, two of them jammed together, lolling in the shroud of bloodstained clothing, fornicating in death it seemed to be, the wizened, transparent faces looking at and past her with the dead man's peculiar perception; further behind, under her window another corpse, more shrunken than the other two, trapped in what seemed to be the odd, precise gesture of pulling down the windowshade; blood all over, congealed, dry blood already coming off the furniture, the floor, the corpses in scabs; the blood, the odor, the corpses almost casual in their posture, as if death had only been an interruption of something interesting and important that they were doing, were going to continue. Karen lifted her hands to her face, inhaled, waited for the scream to come but the scream did not, she tried to hawk it out, past her voice box, fill her throat with it and explode the syllables, but her throat was dry, nothing would come out of it, not even gagging, not even vomit. She knew instantly that she was not going to faint. Fainting would be easy, slide to the floor, collapse, be out of it, but then she would lie amidst the corpses, would be yet another body on the floor. She felt herself slide out of all relation to the room, walls and panels shifting. In some trick of neurasthenia she saw the corpses coming much closer, bearing down upon her, the bodies floating through the air, inflated, suspended, closing the gap, the death drawing her in ....

The scream came at last but it was a pitiful thing, a forlorn bird cry in the dense room; it might have been only the sound of leaking blood. She collapsed against the near wall, dropping her suitcase, the wall bracing her, bringing her up again, she felt the plaster coming up behind her knees and she stood, extended an arm blindly, felt the thickness of the air and it was as if the air had become aqueous. She was swimming within it, the air sustaining her, floating her forward; she began to move then to the bedroom.

The door of the bedroom open, everything in the bedroom open, things pulled apart as if a man in agony had been looking for an antidote, ripping through possessions, furniture, laundry, for the bottle of elixir which would save him, and on the bed, my God, lying on the *bed* ....

She saw him, saw Phil then. Dead, he had somehow at the last moment turned on his back so that he could see light rather than darkness during the passage. His hands were folded on his chest, the blood which lay in streaks on his body covered him like gay strips of rag. There seemed to be no pain in it. Fascinated, compelled, she moved forward, saw the staring, bulging eyes of the corpse and that was all it was, merely a corpse. She had seen a dead dog once in a roadway and he had looked like this.

She looked down at the body of what had been her husband thinking that she should scream now; if there were ever going to be a time to scream, this was definitely it, what with the horror in the living room and the horror in the bedroom—but she could not. She did not even try to force it out of herself, the screaming was cancelled. Phil looked so casual, that was all, so much at peace with himself and his condition, nothing could have left him as relaxed and easeful as this death by violence had; and to scream here would have been like violating a church with curses: it was not appropriate. It did not fit in. Dimly Karen realized that she was hysterical. She was absolutely hysterical.

She raised a hand to her hair, felt it, felt the little puffs and strands, and backed away from the bed, her other hand touching her stomach. That had always aroused him. When she lifted her arms and touched herself, that had been the gesture which most inflamed him, he would come off the bed sometimes laughing, laughing pursue her around the room until his hands disappeared around and inside of her and she had felt his need slamming at the doors of himself, groping and gathering until at last she had submitted. She had always submitted. Did he want her now? There he was, lying on the bed, she was certainly doing everything possible to arouse him but nothing seemed to work.

She put her hand behind her, dropped the zipper of her dress, parted it to the waist and spread it open, dropped it off her arms. Now in her brassiere she confronted him, held the hand behind, opened the brassiere and her breasts shook free. How he had loved her breasts! He had drowned in them, played with them the way, he had once said, children liked to play with crayons, endlessly rolling and squeezing them—but now he seemed to show no response. What was wrong with him? What in hell was wrong with him?

Well, she wasn't going to go on, carrying on this way if he was going to ignore her, that was all; she didn't have to put up with this humiliation. She was a married woman and a very pretty one, ten years younger than this drug-pusher of a husband, and if he thought that *she* was going to stand here all day playing with herself for no response, he had another thought coming. Funny, he never touched drugs himself.

Blew a little pot now and then, but said that he didn't like to mix business with pleasure, wanted to keep tight partitions between the two. That was the way he had put it, "tight partitions." Well, so much for *him*. She gave him a last contemptuous look and, gathering her dress around herself, left the room. She would show him. She'd leave him all over again.

Coming back to the living room though, in the center of her determination, the odor and the corpses hit her all over again, and she fell like an arrow to the floor, head first, rocked on her skull for an instant, then fell limp. The blow must have stunned her, or then again maybe it did not stun her, maybe everything that was happening was really happening. One by one the corpses came over to her, covered her with their bloody clothes as if performing an ancient ceremony, and then the three of them, pallbearers, took her into the bedroom and tossed her next to the body of Phillip Sands, where Karen lay for three days and three nights before one of the neighbors finally got curious about the open door and poked her old lady's brow in. Such shrieks and foolishness! Such an explosion of police! But Karen did not hear any of it, being happily catatonic, and so she remained for many months while the kind physicians of Austin Riggs filled her up and emptied her out, emptied her out and filled her up with the best and most modern varieties of various drugs which perilously restored her sanity to her, and at the age of twenty-five sent her out to make a new life for herself in the wilds of Rego Park, New York.

EPILOGUE

Wulff with the valise took a taxicab out to the bank of the Charles River. The driver wanted to know if he should wait or just go on his way, and Wulff said that he better get going, he had things to do. The driver said that was all right with him, and Wulff gave him five dollars and sent him on his way, taking the valise out to the bank and then standing there inert until the car was gone.

He looked at the muddy surface of the Charles River in isolation. The day had dissolved into grey foam and mist; he could no longer see Cambridge or its university across the shore. No one was out here. Years ago he understood that students, even in bad weather, would come down to the banks of the Charles to make love or just to be together, but that had been a long time ago. All of the dormitories were coed now and half of the students were living off-campus in or out of wedlock. Nobody took a bottle and went down to the Charles in 1973. The dormitories permitted liquor but most of the students used pot.

Wulff stood there quietly. People might still be after him but he had a feeling that they were not. He had a feeling that his Boston siege was over. Cicchini dead, his henchmen dead, Tucci dead, Sands dead, all of the elements of the network fallen away from him. Without Cicchini at the center, the hunt would have to be called off. The Northeast had been a tightly controlled sector. Everything emanated from Cicchini. Now, with him gone, reorganization would have to start at the bottom.

The time of the wars would now be beginning. No one was looking for Wulff.

He looked at the valise. He had had it for one week, two days, and about four thousand miles. For all that it had been through, for all the hands that had touched and clawed at it, it still looked curiously impermeable. He ran his hands over the surfaces, felt the damp of the city festering through his fingertips. The valise merely conveyed qualities. Of itself it meant nothing at all. Its contents meant nothing either. It was only what they could do to men that had caused men to die ....

Men had sought this valise, men had died for it; men would seek it again. What lay within the valise was of such importance that lives itself meant nothing. The lives were merely conveyor belts, vehicles for what lay within.

What lay in the valise began on parched empty fields under the foreign sun, the sun drew it out inexorably on its journey of thousands of miles, hundreds of hands, adulteration, manipulation, until finally it ended or some of it ended within the living flesh of human beings.

But only the journey itself mattered. The final trip did not; what happened when these contents intersected with the users could not be mapped out. Only the externals, the consequences could be, and it was these that now possessed Wulff, caused his vision to momentarily blur, until even the muddy waters of the Charles became merely another element of the inner design.

The price was too high, that was all. It was too high from start to finish, too many lives snuffed out, bodies destroyed, futures blotted, children smashed and left broken in alleys, all of this coming from the one weed that sprung under the foreign sun. And yet, high or not, the price had to be paid. It had to be paid in the coin which the drug itself extracted: pain, illusion, terror. Because if you did not pay it the drug would burn and it would consume the world.

But with this lot too much had happened. Too much had been invested, the cycle had to be broken. He had carried it from San Francisco from a burning freighter, he had killed the men who took it from him to get it back; four men lay dead up the hill because he had to have it—but Wulff could see now that he had been wrong. He had been wrong about this valise. It had cost too much.

It meant starting from the beginning. It meant going back to New York and, as if for the very first time, two endless months ago, to begin to dig. The valise could not be a crutch. Its possession meant nothing. For every Cicchini dead three would rise. And he would have to combat them from the start every time.

Wulff sighed. He had never felt so tired. And yet in a way he had never felt so sure of himself, convinced of his purpose. He knew that he was right. A half million dollars of junk was now out of the streets forever, San Francisco was hurting badly, the Northeast sector was wrecked. New York was tottering.

The war was going well. The war would go on.

Wulff hoisted the valise, felt the weight almost tenderly, like that of the girl who had nestled against him in San Francisco. He brought it to chin level and held it poised, looking out at the waters. Then he walked the three closing steps to the bank, slammed his other hand on the valise, lifted it and flung it into the waters.

The waters took it.

The valise bobbed once, slid out of sight, was gone. Convinced that it would sink, Wulff did not follow it. He turned his back and began the long, long trip toward the next campaign. The next campaign had started now.

The dark, ruined waters of the Charles heaved once in the place where the valise had sunk and then, dense and oily, rolled over to placidity. The river lay in the mist. Cambridge poked lights like little fires through the fog.

THE END

THE LONE WOLF #4: DESERT STALKER

by Barry N. Malzberg

Writing as Mike Barry

Those convicted of selling hard drugs to minors ...
should be sent to prison for life.
—*Nelson A. Rockefeller*

Why waste the room and board on them?
I have a better idea.
—*Martin Wulff*

PROLOGUE

TO: NETWORK
FROM: L
SUBJECT: MARTIN WULFF

This man, an ex-New York City narcotics officer, is demonstrably insane and extremely dangerous. *He must be killed on sight and details of the bounty will be distributed in a further memo.*

This man's movements in the last three months have been tracked from New York to San Francisco to Boston. Presently his whereabouts are unknown. After killing several valuable men in New York (details also in a further memorandum) he appeared in San Francisco where, after another series of murders, he seized and disappeared with a quarter of a million dollars or more of raw materials whose shipment he intercepted. Efforts in Boston where he next appeared to retrieve the materials were not successful. A top northeast official was murdered and Wulff, with the materials still in hand, disappeared. It is indicated that the materials may have been destroyed. No substantiation of this can be found, however.

This man, from internal evidence and from statements he has made to various personnel, intends to "destroy the international drug trade." He has already affected operations seriously and must be considered a menace. *His elimination is top priority.*

The basis of subject's motivations has been inferred from various sources. Subject, while still in NYCPD (although transferred from Narcotics Division for failure to comply with policy) was affianced to one Marie Calvante, who died of heroin overdose which may or may not have been self-inflicted. Subject was in radio car with partner at the time that anonymous tip on Calvante came in and it appears that he was the first to see her dead. Immediately after, records indicate that he resigned from PD and it was then that his "war" began. Thus, the "war" may be considered to have been personally motivated by the death of fiancée although subject's record while with Narcotics Division indicated an extreme impatience with conventional means of drug-suppression.

No known personnel were tied to the death of Marie Calvante. This has been researched carefully and it is clear that no member of this or interlocking organizations was in any way responsible for this incident. Nevertheless, all indications are that Wulff believes the interlocking organizations to be responsible and, needless to say, he cannot be approached or dissuaded.

Subject is six feet four inch veteran of combat (although granted draft exemption by virtue of employment in PD he enlisted in armed services in 1965, apparently out of patriotism) and displays an extremely sophisticated knowledge of explosives, incendiary devices, armaments of all kinds and hand to hand combat. He is directly or indirectly responsible in three months' period for at least one hundred and fifty deaths and it appears that his "war" is now accelerating. Since he left Boston a few days ago, his whereabouts are unknown.

A photograph of the subject accompanies this memorandum. *He may be shot on sight* and all members are advised that considerable benefit will accrue to them should they be the ones to shoot him.

In the twelve years of the interlocking organization and the important supply pact of 1963, no such danger has appeared. Wulff is only one man but for that precise reason, retains a great freedom of action. He is a cold, remorseless killer and the danger he represents is not to be ignored.

It is indicated although not proven that he may at present be back in the New York City area.

Further memoranda, as noted, to follow.

I

Wulff, tired but still functioning, the Charles River where he had thrown the valise with a quarter of a million dollars' worth of uncut heroin bobbing mindlessly in his brain, came into New York tired but not fulfilled, still with a sense of beginnings. He had taken a car from a shopping center in Cambridge, a new Buick LeSabre which the owner had left keys in, motor running, and had driven down the three hundred miles of turnpike, thinking. In the case behind him on the seat he had the more portable of the armaments he had brought to Boston: a machine gun, hand grenades, a couple of pistols. He was perfectly willing to use them on any police officer who wanted credentials on the car. He didn't want to. He still thought of police as brothers. But it was just the way it had to be now.

All out, no quarter. Cicchini, the boss of the northeast who he had killed face to face would have killed *him* if it had not been for luck and he would have done it more brutally. The war was on in earnest now. The quarter of a million dollars he had dumped into the Charles raised the stake. The men who controlled drugs in and out of this country might tolerate a Wulff who only picked away at various echelons, leaving corpses here and there. In that business it could merely act to straighten out the line of succession, clean away the ranks. Survival of the fittest. But a quarter of a million dollars was another kind of thing. Now he was actually meddling with their business.

They would kill him, all of them would kill him. No doubt now as to where he was: he was in the game for the rest of his life. Death was the only exit and ripping the car down the thruway at a hundred and ten miles an hour, only parking lights on, he thought that death itself might be a release, not an unwelcome way out of it. But he was a dead man already; he had died on the fourth floor of a walkup building on West 93rd Street and death could not come twice. Only oblivion but never release. And that was a different issue.

Wulff rolled the car into the Deegan expressway, cutting down there to a graceful seventy, but it was only as he rolled onto the Triborough Bridge that he realized where he was going. For hours he had been driving *away*, the only purpose had been to put Boston and its horrors behind him and New York, as familiar ground, was the first place he had thought of but now, as he saw the flat and dead buildings of Queens before him in the late night, very few cars around him, he realized where he had been going all the time. He was heading for St. Albans. He was going straight for the home of a black cop named David Williams.

Williams had been in the radio car the night that they had gotten the call on the girl o.d. on 93rd Street, the anonymous tip that had sent Wulff up three flights and into hell. Williams was twenty-three, only a rookie, but there was nothing of the rookie about him: he was as purposeful as a knife and, Wulff suspected, at least as deadly. In New York, at the very beginning, it had been Williams who had come to him offering him assistance in his war. In San Francisco, it had been Williams who with a phone call had uncovered the shop from which he got the armaments to blow up the ship. Wulff had the uncomfortable feeling that the black man was laughing at him; that he was using Wulff as a tool without risk. But, then again, the man's offer had been sincere. And the help had been real.

He needed to see the man. Wulff had the feeling now of being closed in on all sides—by this time, across the country, the network must be on fire with panic and rage—and yet at the same time he had the vague feeling that he did not know precisely what the next move should be. Throwing the junk into the Charles after killing Cicchini: that had been all right, that had been closing off for all time the first part of his war, but now he felt like a machine at deadly idle, waiting to be pulled into gear.

He drove into St. Albans.

St. Albans was quite, respectable: the streets were wide and hushed now in the darkness, the houses were as good as any in the middle-class sections of the city. At this hour, two in the morning, you could not have told, looking at the landscape, that the people here were black and that most of them were living in St. Albans not by choice but simply because there were very few areas in the great, liberal city of New York where a black man with a little money and a handhold on the middle-class could move his family without the risk of getting his home burned. If he could even find a broker to sell him a home. Lower-class blacks were struggling out of Harlem and Bedford Stuyvesant into areas of Brooklyn and Queens which five years ago had been white but they were carrying their poverty and misery with them. St. Albans, though, was a place where you had to get your ticket punched first. It was depressing, Wulff thought, but he was not really concerned with race relations. He had other, much more terrible problems to deal with, than what was being done to the black man. And, of course, if his doomed war could succeed, which never in his lifetime would it, things would have to get better for the black man for he was the one on the bottom, most of it, keeping the machinery going, keeping the Cicchinis in their mansions on the river.

He ditched the car at 69th Road and Queens Boulevard, double-parking it there, leaving the keys in, motor running as he snatched the heavy valise off the seat and walked briskly away. If the owner was lucky someone would snatch the car right off the street this way, drive it to the nearest junkyard on Pennsylvania Avenue and have it dismantled by professionals, buried deep. Otherwise, if he had left the thing parked and locked, there was at least a small chance that the police would have found it and that would have done the owner no favor. The thing only had seven thousand miles racked up but already the fan belt was squealing, the shock absorbers were failing and the transmission starting to slip; the car would be major trouble before it got to 20,000 miles. Now the owner could collect close to new-car price on it and try his luck again. The owner would never know, Wulff thought wryly, what a favor had been done him unless of course the cops found the car first, noted the Massachusetts license plate and impounded the thing to track it down. But that was doubtful on 69th Road and Queens Boulevard in Forest Hills. It was a lightly-patrolled area, and everything was going on at least five stories up. No street action at all, the high-rise had shifted the structure and occurrence of crime into the air and the police department was still at least ten years from coming to grips with it. You could always trust civil service to be ten years behind the realities, unless it was in relation to drugs in which case it was fifty.... Wulff took a cab the rest of the way to St. Albans.

He still had a good deal of money. He had lifted five thousand dollars off Cicchini's corpse after he had disposed of the man and five grand could take you a fair distance when you were a freelancer. Money was not his problem; the problem was a vague feeling that the enemy was closing in on him from all directions, while he was sitting at idle, trying to find his next move. If he could find the moves he would be all right. It was kind of nice to be back in New York in a way; the sullen slump of the driver's shoulders, his vague cursing when blocked by sanitation trucks on the Boulevard and when Wulff deliberately undertipped him at Williams's door were somehow comforting. New Yorkers had cultivated the attitude of despair; if they had not seen everything, they acted as if they shortly would, and it kept them from seeing anything more. A healthy way to act except if you were a narcotics cop and couldn't avoid seeing and feeling. "Fuck you," the driver said and went away.

Wulff stood for a moment, looking at Williams's neat little two-family house on the deserted street. Two-family, that was the way to do it: live on one level and use the rent from the other to pay off the mortgage so that the only thing out of pocket was the down-payment which in the long run you could absorb too. Williams had all the angles covered, he wasn't doing badly for a black man: wife, quiet little house, income-producing house. But, Wulff wondered, exactly what the percentage could be in safety if you knew that you were the one in ten who had staggered out of the wreckage of your race and that there were men like Cicchini who all the time wanted nothing other than to put you back there ... decided that this was none of his business and exactly the kind of thinking which would make Williams angry and went back to the door. He rang the bell, hefting his case, feeling tentative, noting by his watch that it was now one-thirty. This was a hell of a time to come in on a man, even one who had offered to help you. But it was Williams himself who opened the door, dressed in street clothes and alert, smoking a cigarette and in all ways looking as collected as he had been the last time Wulff saw him in the Manhattan rooming house. "I expected you," he said quietly. "Come in."

Wulff went in. He had never been in this house before, but it came back to him like bits and pieces of a recollected dream: the short hallway, the spare furniture in the living room, installment plan all of it, the curtained windows, the color television set in the corner playing a movie now. "I figured you'd be along," Williams said, "and I'm not surprised to see you at all." He motioned for Wulff to sit on the couch. "I just got off shift about half an hour ago and I can't sleep," he said and then looked at Wulff alertly as if all the time for social conversation had now passed. "I heard about San Francisco," he said.

"Did you?" Wulff said putting the case on the couch beside him and leaning back. "That was nothing. San Francisco was nothing. It was Boston that was the killer."

Williams shook his head and chuckled. He looked much older, could have been forty or fifty: it was something to realize that a black cop was probably fifty inside before he took the exams. "I haven't heard about Boston yet," he said, "but the word will filter down. But San Francisco was nice." He paused, exhaled. "San Francisco was very nice. New York wasn't bad either. That townhouse ..."

"I'm not here to discuss what's been done." Wulf said, "that's over with."

"It's not over with. It's just beginning. You took a fucking ship out in San Francisco, you know that?"

"I know it."

"A whole fucking freighter. Man, reports are getting around, people are in a *panic* out there. And in here too," Williams said. "You are upsetting the natural order of things. What did you do in Boston?"

"I got to a man," Wulff said, "and I got rid of a shipment."

"The same shipment you picked up in San Francisco?"

"You know about that?"

"You learn," Williams said, "you come around resolved to listen and, oh my, you learn a good deal. But that's not what you wanted, is it?" He looked at the case lying next to Wulff. "You travel light, don't you?"

"That's equipment."

"That's what I mean," Williams said. He sighed, stretched on the couch, stood. "There's a pretty big one for you," he said, "if you're interested in going in on it."

"I call my own shots."

"I *know* you call your own shots," Williams said. He smiled vaguely, walked into the archway separating kitchen from living room. "You want some coffee?" he said. "My wife's asleep or I'd give you better than that, but there's some cake ..."

"I'll have some coffee," Wulff said. "What's the big one?"

"Ah," Williams said. He went into the kitchen, let Wulff look at the prints on the walls for a moment while he seemed to be struggling with some plates, then came back, balancing a cup of coffee precariously balanced on a palm. "Never make no waiter," he said, passing it to Wulff, "I *had* to get into the sub-professional classes because the fact is that I simply could never make it in the servant class, isn't that right, Wulff?"

"I don't know," he said and took the coffee. Williams had his points, the man was valuable ... and the man had been at his side the night they killed him, that was not the kind of bond you could break ... but even so, Williams got on his nerves. Probably he always would. There was hatred one inch below the surface of any black man and all in all, Wulff guessed, they were entitled to it, they would be crazy if they did not hate ... but it was tough to take, working your way through a network of feelings that could blow up on you. "Tell me what you have to and let me go," he said.

"But you don't know *where* to go, Wulff," Williams said. He stared at him blandly. "You are a fighting fool, you are a mass of energy, you are going to take on the pushers and the dealers and the organizers and the suppliers and the channel men single-handed but you are a weapon without direction. I got to point and *aim* you man. All right," Williams said, waving his hand in a dismissive way, sitting across from Wulff on a straight chair he dragged from the side of the room. "Let's not even get into that." He looked at Wulff for a while, his eyes flickering to intensity and then suddenly, convulsively, deadening. "You know about all that shit in the evidence division," he said.

"Indeed I do."

"Two million dollars street value of heroin missing in the last three years when they finally get around to investigating the place. That was real nice," Williams said, "that was a credit to the department."

"Did you expect anything different?" Wulff said. The evidence division, where criminal materials were checked in by police to be used later at trial had, according to the headlines which all broke about the time Wulff left the department, been about the biggest stash room in the history of the international drug trade. Pounds and pounds of uncut heroin, most of it of high quality, which had been seized by police in raids and turned in to the materials room which had the equivalent of one full-time clerk, had been found missing when the state had finally sent in some investigators. The commissioner, of course, had been acutely embarrassed by this. He promised a merciless investigation. If indeed New York City police officers could be tied to these thefts, they would be confronted by the full force and majesty of the law. In the meantime, an investigation, vigorously conducted, was in progress. The commissioner had assured the populace that if any police personnel were involved they were the exceptions to the rule, the few dishonorable men who had flawed the image of a great department ....

He had no further comment. "I didn't expect anything different," Wulff said, thinking about all of this, the little snatches and pieces of the story he had gotten while otherwise engaged in New York and San Francisco. That stuff is lying there, not even inventoried, just logged in for years, there are a couple of part-time clerks there who may make eight thousand dollars a year, everybody on the inside knows where that room is and what's inside .... "No," he said, "it didn't surprise me at all. It would have been a surprise the other way, if that stuff had actually been in. Why bother? They might have figured they'd never catch up to it."

"Just about," Williams said softly, "but recently there's been a little movement on this. It's not for the press yet; you know why."

Wulff guessed he knew why. At the beginning of the investigation suspicion had moved in on a suspended New York City detective who had promptly committed suicide, not even doing the department the favor of leaving a suicide note admitting to all before he did the job with a point thirty-eight caliber. If he had left the note that would have been a great help to everyone, condolences could have been paid and the books on the investigation closed, whereabouts of the heroin forever unknown. But the detective had left no note of any sort, which at least left open the possibility that he had been an innocent victim hounded to an unjust death. So the investigation had continued in a desultory way; the state arm kept on plugging along on it, just releasing enough to the media every now and then to indicate that the Governor somehow believed that the Mayor of New York was directly involved in the matter, probably using all of the heroin himself both for injection and distribution and in reality, the police department investigations division which was doing the only actual field work although prohibited by the commissioner from making any statements to the press at all, had kept on staggering ahead and had developed a couple of leads although no recovery of the heroin. The heroin would be long gone, of course, cut up, shipped here and there, driven into the arms of ten thousand mainliners, sniffed by half that many more experimental types. "So we turned up," Williams said, going through all of this quickly, somehow indicating a disinterest in all of it, "or I should say they turned up about a week ago some informer who actually had a couple of bags of stuff in the original labels and everything in his apartment. They had him on a rape charge and a couple of assaults and even an unsolved murder or three they could have pinned on him, so he started to do some talking."

"That's a change," Wulff said, straightening out his legs which had stiffened on the couch and from the exertion of the long drive. "In my day the informers never talked. What the hell, an informer wasn't to give *information*. He was just there so you could list him on the sheets as an informer and explain why you spent three hours in a bar and what was happening to your expense account. An informer *talking*? It'll break down the whole system; next time they'll actually start to solve crimes instead of log them in and what's going to happen then?"

"Don't be bitter, man," Williams said softly. "That's the system you're talking about and it's the system which has given me this nice little house and this good civil service job to say nothing of my pension rights. I'm a believer."

"I know all about the system," Wulff said. "I've been all over this country and I've been able to see what the system has created. It doesn't work any more. Nothing works. The only way to get anything done is to go outside of it."

Williams smiled, a tight, controlled smile that had overtones of evil in it. He never knew the man at all, Wulff thought. He knew the organization men fairly well, he thought: he could gauge what they were after and how they intended to get it, living in their large or middle-size houses off the water, picking up the phone and sending their contact men around. There was no problem in tracking out the enemy; he guessed he knew them now as well as he had ever known any class of men and yet this young black patrolman was of a different stripe altogether. He simply did not understand him. Abruptly Wulff felt uncomfortable, almost desperately so, driven by fatigue to a point where he would go out of Williams's house and never come back, drop the whole war if necessary simply because he could no longer see things clearly ... but he put that thought away carefully as he had put away so many impulses during this time. Depressive reaction. It meant absolutely nothing. You went on, you did the best you could, and he was hopelessly committed. The enemy was counting on him giving up, but he was not going to. "Don't tell *me* about going outside of the system," Williams was saying. "That's an option you may have but I don't. You take the system away and all of this little home is in flames, you understand that?"

"I understand a good deal," Wulff said tiredly. He eased the cramps out of my legs by standing, putting his calves flat against the sofa and as he did so he felt the shaking for the first time since he had left Boston, all of the tension and terror of what he had gone through working through him in little rivulets. He held his stomach in tight, consciously, took slow, deep breaths and flexed his sphincter, an old combat trick until the trembling began to ease. Williams looked at him with an expression of concern.

"You've really been through it, haven't you?" he said.

"First I get lectures on the system and now I get a medical checkup. Screw that," Wulff said. He sat. "Finish," he said. "Tell me what you're leading up to."

"You can crash here tonight, man. We got an extra room down the hall which is going to be for a kid someday but right now it's filled with nothing. We can rig up a cot ..."

"Just tell me," Wulff said. "Don't worry about sleep. I can take care of that anytime." Now with the tension partially released he felt coming back into him the old, desperate sense of urgency. Everything was getting away from him, the enemy were so many, so clever, so far ahead of him that he was whipped before he started, could only deal with that by excesses of effort. Still, he was so tired ... "get to it," he said.

"All right," Williams said, suddenly disengaged. "I'll get to it. There's a lieutenant or at least there was a lieutenant named Bill Stone who this informer tied pretty closely to that stuff. Stone's name had been on the checkout list more than a few times—shit the investigation was the first time anyone ever *read* that checkout list—and the informer said that he wasn't taking out that stuff for an appearance in court which is supposed to be the only reason for it getting out of there. He had other plans for it and he wasn't turning back smack, he was turning in sugar. No one looked in those bags."

"All two million dollars of it?"

"A goodly chunk," Williams said, "a very goodly chunk. Our man who started to talk like hell once they brought some rape victims into a lineup who were very interested in him, our man thinks that Stone might himself have been tied to a million dollars of that stuff all on his own."

"Beautiful," Wulff said, "that's beautiful. A new York City lieutenant, a man who could walk into that evidence room anytime, sign for it, take it out, perfect cover, perfect disguise, turning back false samples which no one even looked at ... it's perfect," he said. "It's a major distribution setup."

"That's what they seemed to think," Williams nodded. His eyes had begun to moisten with excitement and suddenly he did not look so implacable after all; he looked like a young cop who was chasing down a lead. "So there were a lot of people who got interested very quick in talking to Bill Stone. In fact, it could be said that for a period of about eight hours Bill Stone was the most sought-after, popular man in the history of the department."

"Bill Stone bugged out."

Williams nodded bleakly. "That's exactly what he did," he said. "He is whereabouts unknown. You'll enjoy this one though, Wulff. Some of those state investigators, already into this, are beginning to compare your dropout with his. Both of you quite without notice, just dropped and disappeared. They're beginning to theorize that the two of you might have been connected in some way."

Wulff smiled although it was no such smile as any of the investigators might want to see and said, "That's very interesting. Where's Stone?"

"You get the point."

"Of course I get the point. You think you've got a lead on Stone and you think I might be interested in looking him up."

"Something like that," Williams said. "You like to look up people, I've noticed."

"If I've got a lead, then a lot of other people would have it too. Why don't they just follow it and pick him up?"

"Because you're right," Williams said candidly. "The system sucks, it really does, it doesn't work at all; it's just that for me it's the only thing I've got and I'm holding on. But by the time those clowns get coordinated and decide how they'll go after him and when and get authorized pay vouchers or decide to turn it over to the FBI or maybe just cover it up and forget it altogether, by that time Stone can be out of the country or so far underground that they'll never find him. I think he's worth finding," Williams said. "I really do."

"I see what you mean."

"I think Stone is big. I think he may be one of the biggest. A lieutenant with those kind of opportunities, that kind of access could be very big."

"All right," Wulff said, "where is he?"

"He's somewhere in Las Vegas," Williams said. "We know that pretty well, our informant is sure on that point. Exactly where he's not so sure, but there are a couple of hotels owned by a man who might be tied in with Stone on one side and drugs on the other. It's likely that he's in one of those two hotels."

"With maybe a million dollars' worth of shit," Wulff said.

"Or at least a lead on it. A good lead."

Williams stared at him impassively and Wulff could feel the excitement building could feel even against his will the old anticipatory tremor. San Francisco, the quarter million in the valise, seeing Cicchini in Boston, killing the man, ripping open the Boston drug trade itself, bombing out the freighter in San Francisco—that was nothing as against what Williams was talking about now. Williams was talking about a million dollars but it was more than that, he was talking about a man, this Stone, who might or might not be a key-in to a distribution system so central, so large that it would go even beyond the Cicchinis or Marascos who, when you came right down to it, were small-time. All of them were small-time out of the big town; you had to remember that, New York might have collapsed but the city which had once been the crown of the world was still the crown of the underworld; what could not work the right way could still work the wrong. Wulff felt the breath fluttering unevenly in his chest, with an effort calmed respiration and looked at Williams who, his black man's mask fallen, was looking at him intensely, his hands twisting. "You want him bad, don't you," Wulff said.

"Yes. I want him very bad."

"Why don't you go and get him?"

"That's not my move," Williams said. The hands were twisting more energetically now. "Don't you understand that? I've got to stay by here and play by the rules. But you don't."

"Go to Las Vegas and bring him in, is that it? They'll give me a medal and pension rights back, and if they're really feeling generous I can come back at patrolman's pay."

"You don't want to bring him back," Williams said. "If you wanted to bring him back you wouldn't be here at all. You'd be Mr. Law and Order, still busting your ass in a blue uniform, unless they put you back in plainclothes which is a bad bet."

"A million dollars' worth of shit."

"I'm not saying he has it," Williams said. "I'm not saying anything about that at all; I don't know what he's got. That stuff probably went into veins years ago. But he's got to have some of it left."

A small woman appeared at the archway, delicate, her face slightly blurred now from fatigue although then again her self-possession for someone in a nightgown at three in the morning was more than Wulff would have expected. "This is my wife," Williams said to him. "Martin Wulff, this is Henrietta. Henrietta is kind of an elegant name for a lady in St. Albans but then again there are a lot of maids named Jezebel so I guess it's all right."

"David," the woman said, "David, stop it now."

"Henrietta keeps me together," Williams said vaguely. "It is either her or absolutely nothing; Henrietta is why I believe in the system. Henrietta *is* the system. Henrietta, this is Martin Wulff of whom you may have heard me talk then and again." He stood swaying, opened his tie all the way and let the edges flap. "I'm tired," he said. "I am going to go to bed. All of this is in your hands now, Wulff; I have nothing more to say. There's a man out in Vegas who is worth seeing and you're the man to see him." He began to walk toward the archway.

"Mr. Wulff," Henrietta said, "if you want something to eat; if you'd like to rest here ..."

"Don't bother the man," Williams said. "Look at his attitude of dedication. He's not a man, he's a machine. He's got things on his mind."

"No man's a machine," Henrietta said. She walked toward him, touched his hand and Wulff felt a vague tingle, somewhere between tenderness and apprehension. "You look tired," she said, "stay."

"I told him that already," Williams said, "to stay. He said he didn't want to."

"Yes he does," Henrietta said. She held his hand and looked up at him.

"David's a very angry man," she said, "but he doesn't really mean to be unkind. You know that, don't you?"

"He don't know anything, Henrietta, except how to get to Las Vegas."

"Leave the man alone. Will you stay?"

Wulff looked at her and something within him uncoiled slowly like a spring retracting and then going loose. "I can't stop," he said. "Don't you see that? I just can't stop. There's no time."

"Then a night won't matter. If there's no time at all what difference can a night make?" She reminded him of Marie Calvante. Somewhere within this woman the quality lurked. He felt pain and yet the pain was kind of a release. "All right," he said, "if you want me to."

In the corner, Williams kicked at the wall. "I wanted him to," he said, "you should know that."

"You don't know how to talk to a man, David."

"It's an old police habit," Williams said. Momentarily he seemed completely at odds with himself, disengaged. "The hell with it," he said and headed out the room. "I'll leave you the information," he said. "I'll write the thing down, the names of the hotels and so on. It'll all be there in the morning. I have to pull overtime. I'm going to bed."

"I came here in a stolen LeSabre," Wulff heard himself saying, somewhat wildly, "a 1973 LeSabre with full power and air conditioning. Power seats, tape deck. I lifted it out of a shopping center and took it all the way in from Boston and I took it to within two blocks of Rego Park and dumped it. It's probably on a joyride now."

"You had your reasons," the woman said.

"Did I?" he said. "Did I really? Do you want a man like that staying in your house?"

"Why not?" Henrietta said. She tugged gently on his wrist, he did not have the strength to resist her. The man who had called Cicchini struggled lightly and then yielded to the grip of a five foot woman. "Come on," she said, "I'll show you to the room. There's a cot there and everything. You should be comfortable."

"You're kind," he said, "you're too kind."

"You don't understand," she said and put an arm around his waist to steady him as he staggered with fatigue. "You just don't understand."

He tried to say that he did, he understood everything now, there was nothing that was beyond him, understanding flooded him like light but he was too tired, he felt himself spindling out of there at great speed and soon with the sheets of the bed around him, the door of the room closed, he heard nothing at all, not for ten hours or more while slowly dreams cleansed him of Boston.

The enemy had half a day's breathing spell. After that, pity them.

II

Come seven. Stone leaned over the table, digging his hands into the furry surfaces of the mat, not conscious of the bodies around him, only dimly aware of the background of the casino itself which under the fluorescence shook with the controlled panic of men climbing out of bed at six in the morning to find their wives gone, their lives smashed. Three hundred riding on the roll; he tried to focus down his attention to its narrowest point, just a pinpoint of perception, looking at the little man shaking the canister as if he could not let it go. The houseman smiled. The little man shook, fussed, finally let go of the throw convulsively, the dice bouncing, yanking themselves to position on the table. Eight. His point was eight. There was no way that a son of a bitch like this could come through but there he was, out the other end, the two fours on the die glinting at him. The houseman took Stone's chips. Stone felt himself beginning to shake very subtly within his suit, little fingers of sweat running to the edges of his body, then ominously rolling in. Three hundred. Why was he sweating? It was house money, all of it house money: it wasn't his own that he was playing with at all and, anyway, what the fuck did it matter? But it was an omen, that was all it was. It was an indication of luck rather than luck itself rolling in from this craps table. "Going to make it!" the little man said, the canister trembling in his hand. "Going to make that point, going to break the place!" Only some used car salesman from Des Moines or a bank clerk out of New York could talk that way in front of a table, surrounded by half a hundred people under the lights but the son of a bitch had no shame, no understanding. You *couldn't* lose betting against a bastard like that; if there was any right, any sense in the world you had to make money betting against them. The houseman lifted his palm, restraining the little man from throwing the canister and called for bets, the little man's face yanking up like a windowshade as he stopped dead, shaking, holding the canister now as if it were a drink. Stone went into his pocket.

Never carry all the chips in front of you; always keep a reserve. In his left pocket he had at least five hundred left, maybe nearer a thousand, he hadn't counted, but it was his reserve, all of it and he would rather go broke now playing against this bastard then hold onto it. It all went back to the house anyway. Didn't it? Didn't everything go back to the house, sooner or later? He put two hundred dollar chips, two fifties on the don't come line, then impulsively went back into his pocket and went for all the rest of it, five hundreds as he counted them and a few miscellaneous chips, seven hundred and eighty-five dollars altogether on the don't come line. Bastards like this, in or out of the world, never made their point. The houseman gave him an encouraging look, winked at him. There were other people on the course, at least ten on the line right now but the communion between him and the houseman Stone thought, the tendrils of connection which seemed to link them were real and special. There were really only three of them at this table: the little man, Stone and the houseman. The heavy woman to his right, the businessmen, glasses gleaming beneath their foreheads on the pass line, the hard little girl with mad eyes who was betting on the field again and again, none of them existed. *Mano a mano* on the houseman. Stone wondered if he knew that he was playing with Vinelli's money, if there was some communications network floating down from the big room up there to all of the croupiers, dealers, security men, housemen so that they knew everything about the players before the players even came up to the tables. Probably. Probably it would have to be something like that.

The little man was back with the dice now. He waved them above his head like a defensive end plunging over the line, brought the dice against his waist, then, with a curious tentative gesture, holding himself back, he threw them on the table, the canister following. The dice floated, struck, floated again—Stone found himself thinking how such an essentially boring act as the turning of dice became fascinating once you had a stake in it, well say that about most of life—and then staggered to position the table, two fours again, everything falling away from him quickly.

"Point," the houseman said and reached out his rake, caressed Stone's chips and drew them in. The little man, as if he had been some creation of the house rather than a self-propelled human being told the houseman that he wanted to cash in. His movements seemed awkward, like those of a junkie under stress as a matter of fact: why, Stone thought, the little son of a bitch was probably deep into speed or even stronger stuff and here he was now a thousand dollars of Vinelli's money gone and some of his own funds too. He felt the rage within him but it was almost beside the point: what was anger going to do? The houseman gave him a quick glance and then looked away, behind him, denying all contact. "I always try to get out when I'm ahead," the little man said and picking up his chips into uneven handfuls staggered away from the table.

Stone followed him. There was no purpose to it; it was just something to do. Nothing else was in his mind. He had been locked up inside this complicated whorehouse for three days now, three and a half, and was going stir-crazy even though he supposed that his position was enviable, now he had lost not only all of the play money that Vinelli had given him but had gone into his own funds as well and Stone could feel the first edges of panic beyond the age. The situation was getting out of control. It was more and more out of his hands now; when he looked at it objectively he was not a guest in this hotel but a prisoner, Vinelli was not helping him to pass time, sheltering him, protecting him during a bad time but in fact was keeping him prisoner. And it was then that all of the feelings which had been swirling within him for the last few hours suddenly coalesced into a shriek: *I've got to get out of here*, Stone mumbled, passing a crazed old lady who was trying to loosen the handle on a slot machine, *I've got to get the fuck out of here*, passing two bright whores on the day shift who looked at and then right through him, probably knowing as everyone in the hotel seemed to know exactly who he was and what he was doing here. He walked up a winding ramp traced in brilliant orange and green, into a massive hallway where the one-armed bandits and their customers were lined up like urinals and into an elevator with an operator lounging on its seat, sullenly reading a form sheet. "Five," he said.

"Five?" the operator said. "What are you going to five for? Your room is on eleven."

"Are you a fucking social director," Stone said. "Take me to five." He felt his fists clenching. It would be so easy to ram this bastard through the wall, ram all of them for that matter, take them on one by one until the sneers had changed into whimpers, but he could not think that way now. He was in trouble. He was a man in deep trouble, and really Vinelli was trying to help him and if he could not adjust to this it would only be worse. "Fifth floor," he said more quietly.

The operator slammed the paper against the wall, stood, kicking dust off a shoe and slammed the gate closed, yanking on the handle. "I don't think you should go to five," he said. "The man is busy now."

"I don't care what you think. How do you know who I'm going to see?"

"I don't know anything," the operator said. The car swayed in the shaft, moved above the number *six*. Cursing he dropped it into position. "I just work here."

"Then shut the fuck up," Stone said as the door came open, "and mind your own business." He walked out, kicking the horsesheet into the hall. The operator scrambled after it, picked it up and put a hand on Stone's elbow. He could not have been more than nineteen years old but his eyes were as crazy as the eyes of the women against the bandits.

"You watch it," he said. "You don't mean anything to anyone here; you're going to get your ass handed to you."

"Fuck you," Stone said, yanking off the arm. "Fuck you again," and in panorama in his mind could see what might happen next, he could knock down the boy with a heavy right, use his left to yank him again to his feet and then he would give him an old-fashioned PD going-over, the kind that had gone out in the last ten years because of the courts and the press and the fucking pressures in the department but which never, like love, went out of style. That was what he needed but he could not do it. A door was opening way down the hall, little shafts of light spitting out of it, a man who looked like Vinelli peering through that door, apparently having heard something, and Stone backed away. It had been close. Looking at the face of the kid, the way his hand shook as he gathered the sheet against his arm and walked back to the elevator, Stone knew that it had been close. Much closer than he had thought. His control was lapsing, he was not really sure of himself at all, and if he was actually going to go around beating the shit out of the hotel staff how long would he last? The figure down at the end of the hall was gesturing toward him. It was Vinelli. The elevator dropped behind him like the sound of money falling down the shaft.

It was Vinelli all right and following the curve of the arm, moving toward him now, Stone realized that it was a damned peculiar thing all right. He had come here to see Vinelli, to lay it on the line to the man, to tell him that he could not go with this anymore ... but now that his man was there, open in the hall, his arm moving in that florid, commanding gesture as if Stone was another of his lackeys, Stone felt a reluctance tugging at him, a reluctance which was telling him to go the other way or at least to stay rooted at the spot, let Vinelli come to him. The terms of this were all wrong; he had come up here to demand a plan, a set of alternatives, a change ... hell, he had Vinelli by the balls, not the other way ... and yet now it did not seem so easy. He moved grudgingly, conscious of his footfalls like an old man, seeing Vinelli waver in his vision, becoming larger, a sense of consequence overtaking him then, like a man who was willingly taking his doom ... what the hell was happening to him? Three days in Las Vegas, he guessed, could get anyone crazy, particularly someone like Stone who had never understood gambling. Not even now. "I was looking for you," Vinelli said, gesturing him into the room. "How convenient of you to come right up and save me the trouble of paging. Get inside."

Stone went inside. He was a big man, six feet, two hundred and forty pounds, still in good shape for a man just forty but Vinelli had always given him a sense of reduction even though physically Vinelli was much shorter than he. He guessed—all right, admit it, face up to it now—that he was afraid of the man. There was no disgrace in it, a lot of people were. But somehow he had never imagined himself being at Vinelli's mercy. It had always been supposed to work the other way. Until last week ...

He walked into the small, bare hotel suite, unmarked, in which Vinelli did his work. No offices, he had explained, nothing elaborate, the stuff upstairs was only for show. He worked on the fifth floor where no one could find him and he travelled light. Stone looked at the bare walls, the spare furniture of the room, such a contrast to the decor of the rest of the hotel and he felt the fear beginning again. Vinelli closed the door quietly and went over to the desk, hovered there rather than moving into the chair. "Been having fun?" he said.

"No. I don't like craps or roulette and I don't understand blackjack."

Vinelli shrugged. "Your fucking problem," he said. He reached into a desk drawer, took out a *New York Daily News* and tossed it into Stone's lamp. "Very quiet, huh?" he said. "The whole thing under wraps, right?"

Stone unfolded the paper and stared at it. He didn't have far to look; he was a liner on page three: COP TIED TO DRUG THEFTS DISAPPEARS BEFORE GRAND JURY APPEARANCE. His picture was there, a bad one, about twelve years old, from the files, probably when he had been promoted. The story was set in four columns of dense type for the *News* and broke over to page forty-eight. Stone found that he couldn't read it. He folded the paper over, feeling nauseous and carefully passed it back to Vinelli. Vinelli raised his hands.

"I don't fucking want it," he said. "You think I fucking want this shit? It was all supposed to be quiet, right? You know what? They got informants tying you to Vegas."

"I can't understand what happened," Stone said. He tried to keep his voice level, keep his palms flat on the arms of the chair. "There's no way ..."

"I know what fucking happened," Vinelli said. He slid into the chair now and somehow this gesture was more ominous than the standing; it brought the man who had an abnormally large torso in relation to his height above Stone's level, forced Stone to look upwards like a schoolboy being reamed out. "What happened is that you sold me a bill of goods. They knew all along that you probably were heading this way and you dropped the word all over town. So now I got you here and all of a sudden it isn't a quiet job at all, it's a big problem."

"They won't find me," Stone said. "How can they find me?"

"They're bloody fucking well not going to *look* here," Vinelli said quietly. "You think I'm going to give you room and board while the FBI comes crawling all over my hotel? You're out of your fucking mind, that's what you are."

"It's not an FBI matter. It's just the *News.* They ..."

"Don't tell me about the fucking *News.*" Vinelli put his hands together with odd precision, leaned across the desk, looked at Stone flatly. "We're not going to play it your way anymore," he said, "I seen how it goes playing it your way. It's going to be mine. I want the fucking stuff."

"That's impossible," Stone said although with an odd thrill, clamping the gut he knew that it was *not* impossible, it was what he had expected all along. How could it have not come to this? Vinelli was no clown, he was no fool: it was only a matter of time until they had this confrontation and for these three days in the hotel and all the frantic days just before his flight Stone had tried to avoid thinking about it, concentrating only on moving inch-by-inch along some path of survival. But now it had happened and somehow the fact that it had gave him strength. It could not have been avoided and it could not now get any worse. From here on, it would have to be downhill. He had to believe that. "I told you," he said, "at the beginning, now this is nothing new, Vinelli, you knew from the start, there's no way I can lay my hands on the stuff until the heat goes down. It shouldn't take long, a week, a couple of weeks tops before they go onto something else, you'll see. They have no real lead on me, they wouldn't know where the hell I am, it's all newspaper stuff." He was babbling. This was not coming off as it should. "Just wait a little while," he said, "until they get onto something else and I can move in on it."

"You know what I fucking think?" Vinelli said as if Stone had not spoken at all, "I think that you don't have the stuff at all. It was all bluff and bullshit so you could talk me into putting you on ice for a while."

"That's ridiculous," Stone said. He concentrated on leveling out his voice, keeping his face expressionless. "I know exactly where it is and how to get hold of it but can't you see, this isn't the time ..."

"I'm dumb," Vinelli said and put his elbows on the desk, tearing little pieces from a blank sheet of paper which had been under the blotter. "A dumb, greedy, uneducated, fucking wop, that's how you had me figured, wasn't it? I'd sucker into anything; you said that you could get me a half a million dollars' worth of materials you'd figure that I'd trip myself up, fall over my hardon running but even the stupid ones learn eventually." Vinelli opened his desk drawer again, took out a deadly silver letter opener and ran it casually over his nails in the single most threatening gesture that Stone had ever seen. "The next thing," he said, "they'll be crawling all over the fucking hotel. They'll wind up closing the joint on me for aiding and abetting, Lieutenant, and there are some people above me who are going to be made very unhappy by that."

"You've got me wrong," Stone said. He concentrated now on modulated voice, slow gestures, reasonable, easy talk: the same kind of talk you might try with a suspect if you were playing the soft guy on the team and were going in for something final. Once, as a rookie, he had been backed up in an alley by a mob at a public school who thought that he had shot a kid lying on the steps who turned out to have been having an epileptic fit and he had gotten out of that one with this tone of voice. "I can lay my hands on the stuff. I'm not bullshitting you, I've never bullshitted you, I can key in on it and I promised and I'll deliver. But not now, Vinelli, don't you see? There's too much pressure on us now. Wait a couple of weeks and they'll let it die, go onto something else and then I'll be able ..."

"And give you room and board and fucking partners and two hundred dollars a day gambling money, right? Set you up here in style. You'll never move."

"I don't want the gambling money. I never wanted to gamble. You told me to go out, have a good time, mingle, get around."

"Well that was a fucking, crazy, stupid idea," Vinelli said. "That was one of the stupidest wop ideas I've ever had in my life, letting you move around in the casino. I thought you were clean, Stone. I thought that you were on a leave of absence, that everything here had been managed right, that half of the fucking law-enforcement personnel in the state weren't looking for you." His face became clotted, his cheeks pulsing. "They've probably got your picture from fifty fucking angles," he said. "They're probably tacking them up in a gallery somewhere." He stood again and his hands were white against the flat, dead surface of the desk. "You're through Stone," he said.

Stone saw it. He saw it in the man's eyes twice: first in the conviction, the terrible concentration of light coming from them and then, an instant later he saw it another way: as a flash of recognition as something came into Vinelli's line of sight that he had waited to see. Stone knew with his old instincts that the situation was developing too fast for him to do anything but witness, nevertheless he turned in the chair, saw the two men at the doorway looking at him impassively, the taller of them holding a small revolver pointed at Stone's temple: the other one, much smaller, smiling, smiling, he had never seen anyone smile like that. Jesus Christ, was that what the man was on the payroll for? To circulate among the guests and *smile*.... no, he guessed not, he dodged as he saw the gun being lifted, hit the floor, then turned to Vinelli on his knees, arm outstretched. "For Christ's sake," he said, "give me a chance, at least let me tell you where the stuff is. Don't you want to know?"

Vinelli shook his head slowly, softly. "No," he said, "you don't know where the stuff is."

"Yes I do ..."

"You don't know anything, Stone, you're full of fucking shit, you've always been full of shit," and then Vinelli smiled too, this just an echo of the terrible smile behind and almost imperceptibly nodded ... but Stone caught all of it, knew what was going to happen then. He rose to his feet, tried to get balance, slammed to his knees again and then he felt something like a needle penetrate his temple, opening up inside there like a flower, the flowering needle, the swing of his blood pouring around it and he fell heavily under Vinelli's gaze, drawing up his knees like an obstetric patient, palpitating, looking at the ceiling through sight that was already failing. Half a million dollars, son of a bitch, half a million dollars there for the taking and now no one would ever take it. Stone died.

Vinelli put the letter opener into his desk drawer, slammed and locked it away and then turned to the two men still standing by the door in locked position. The smiler had turned solemn, looking down at Stone's body. A little pearl of saliva formed at the corner of the smiler's mouth, dropped like a pearl to the carpet.

"I don't want no fucking part of it. Get this dead meat out of here," Vinelli said and walked through them, parting them like sheets, out into the hall.

Sucker. It was all a sucker game. If he was in luck it would all end now. Unless that fucking lunatic that he had heard about, the one bombing out San Francisco and Boston with land mines, the one that had blown up the townhouse in Manhattan ... unless the scent of action drew the madman here.

III

Three miles out, maybe two, it is all desert, all emptiness and the ruins of land which will never sprout. But nothing goes into the desert except madmen or teenagers loaded up with spare gasoline and blankets against the night, looking for a little fucking under the stars. Yet the madmen and the teenagers never meet, the madmen being locked inside the skull, the teenagers in the groin. Coming into the town without a downtown, only one vast strip slashed through the desert, gnarled and glowing, its lighted tendrils like those of an enormous plant, Wulff felt the New York fatigue and depression beginning to lift even as the clouds themselves were lifting against the jagged blue of the sky. Valise in hand, enough dynamite and wiring to level Las Vegas—but it would only go underground and burst through the planet the other way—he listened to the driver as background, thinking of Bill Stone who was somewhere in that plant ahead, a rogue cop this one, the worst kind or the best depending upon which side of the street you were working this Thursday, and worked out what he would do.

Vinelli, this Vinelli was the one who was probably sheltering Stone: Williams said that the informants were very clear on that fact although exactly what relation Vinelli as manager of the *Paradise* might play to Stone's activities in New York, what Vinelli had to do with those above him, that the informants were not so clear on. There were not even any guarantees that Stone would be here; the whole thing might have been a false lead, and, then too, Vinelli becoming aware of the increasing heat back from New York might have gotten rid of Stone. That was a possibility. There were many possibilities including whether he actually wanted to check into that hotel himself; his face would be all over by now and his hotel was no hotel at all if it wasn't filled with people with access to that picture. But for the moment he could let it all slide, all of it washing over him, filling in little chinks of the present while he left the bleak spaces of the future to sketch themselves in. His first glimpse of Vegas. He had read about it, heard of it, seen the movies, knew the stories ... who didn't? ... but seeing the place was something again. "Stay away from craps," the driver said to him.

"I intend to."

"Craps is deadly. They suck you in by saying the house percentage is lower than roulette or even blackjack which it is, about one and a half percent, but they're taking that bite on every roll, four rolls a minute. So in twenty-five minutes they've eaten up everything. Did you ever look at it that way?"

"I've thought of it."

"The races, keno, they take out fifteen, twenty percent but you only get one race every half hour, fifteen minutes if you're playing a couple of tracks so that way you can stay in action longer. It's a question of staying in, you understand; if you can keep on going you can go for luck, but craps blasts you right out of there."

"You can get hot in craps too."

"You can get cold in hell," the driver said vaguely and then said no more, apparently the conversation having posed some complexity with which he could not deal, either that or his caution about craps was the extent of his dealings with passengers; after that they were all on their own. Wulff leaned back in the seat thinking that gambling had never meant much to him, it seemed to be a characteristic of police in general that after having been on the line playing for real stakes the manipulating of money and risk could only seem counterfeit. Of course the years in Vietnam could be responsible too .... A car came across his line of sight moving parallel to the long line of the highway, moving on the bypass road within a few yards of them, the bypass flowing into an intersection lined a hundred yards down the road. The car was moving fast, much too fast. It came into the intersection, its brakes screaming, turning it halfway around still at about thirty miles an hour. The driver had to brake down frantically, cursing as the other car, a beaten-up Cadillac now reacquired momentum, came off its side of the two-lane highway and headed toward them.

"Sons of bitches!" the driver said. "Sons of bitches, what is this? They're after us," and Wulff hit the floor as the first shot came through the side-paneling shattering glass, exiting the other side with the sound of wind. They had wasted little time at all. They had been much closer on him than he had really expected. And he had felt himself prepared. But it had seemed that the hotel itself would be the first gauntlet he would have to run ... but now the road was exploding underneath him, shots lacing the cab, and Wulff could feel it sliding out of control. You could always tell, when the chassis and frame seemed to float away from one another, a sensation of water filling that split space, then the car was going or gone; he had known it in police vehicles and he knew it now. He kept low to the floor fighting inside of himself to get his revolver. No time to go inside the case for the other stuff which would be worthless anyway in a situation like this. The revolver was pretty worthless too when under fire but it was at least something, it was in his hand. The driver must have been hit. He felt a terrific impact, sound and disconnection through the cab and was smashed into the surfaces of the back seat which held him. He came off of it in one piece, knowing that these men were taking no chances on him, they were professionals or then again simply very desperate and had hit the cab broadside, door-to-hood in order to have a stationary target. He heard doors slam, behind that a thin wailing which meant that someone had been hurt. That would not stop them of course. They traveled at least in pairs, probably in threes, and someone in the car smashed up would have nothing to do with the assignment. It would be considered by everyone except the injured man to be a kind of necessary loss. He hunched down, pulled the safety back on the revolver and did the only thing he could do; he came out of the back in one motion, already shooting.

They might have taken him for dead, at least they had not expected him to come up like this, and the first shot hit the man in the head and dropped him cold. There was another behind him who hit the ground as soon as the shot went off, his gun falling from him, he scrambled for it and Wulff was unable to get another clear shot because the car that had hit them was on fire. Smoke was coming from under the hood, underneath he could see the clear, yellow flames of an ignition fire and the man on the ground could see it too, he picked up his gun, leveled a shot at the cab and then began to run for space. Wulff did not even feel wind from this shot; it must have missed him by yards, the man had other things on his mind. In front of him the driver was lying in an odd quiescence, one hand curled under his ear, his eyes closed, he had been knocked unconscious by the impact, a small delicate stream of blood coming from the top of his head, deep in the bald spot but the wound looked superficial, Wulff thought, in any event, he was in no immediate danger. They might try to kill the driver later just to make sure that there would be no loose ends, no witness, but that was later, now it was focusing on him.

Within the Cadillac the wailing had picked up in pitch and intensity and had now turned into words. "Get me out of here," a voice was saying, "I'm bleeding, burning to death," and Wulff felt the situation in that cry wheeling around; it had been three on one, assailants and victims, but now the wheel had turned and there was no recovery. One of them was dead on the ground, the other trapped in the car. All that he had to worry about was the one who had run, but that one, confused by the crash or the smoke or simply by the fact that Wulff was still alive, had not even gotten off another shot. He was walking in crazed little circles behind the Cadillac listening to the shrieks and at a certain point the shrieks must have gotten into him. Wulff, kneeling inside the car, still leveling down for the one, careful precise shot that would end it saw this man point his gun into the driver's compartment of the Cadillac. There was a thin high sound, a sound like a bird poised for flight and then another thinner sound behind it, a peep or a cry and then, as Wulff watched, the Cadillac blew up. The fire had hit the gas tank, the car was a '59, fifteen years old, almost all of the shielding must have been rusted away. The sound of the explosion was almost incidental, coming as it did between the bird sound and the series of peeps, an anticlimactic *whomp!* and a sheet of flame came from under the car and embraced it. There was a secondary explosion, this one scattering little fragments of detonation which rattled against the cab and then it was over, the explosive part anyway, the car sitting, very quietly eating itself up from the inside. Wulff could not see any figure in the driver's compartment now. He could not even see a driver's compartment.

They were far enough downrange from the fire to be safe; car fires never spread anyway. Everything began and ended at the center of the machinery. So he could leave the driver on the seat without having to worry about him now and he did so, opening the door and sliding out carefully, protecting himself against the possibility of a shot by using the cab as a wall, dropping out of the line of sight of the living gunman if he was still there. Then, very cautiously, using a low-crawl and working himself toward the other car patiently, he stalked the other man.

Still no traffic on this road. But then there never was, that was what the driver had said; he would take him in on an almost unused bypass that almost no one knew about, that was eight miles around but would end up getting him in faster than any of the main roads. He had gone along with that; he didn't want to be in a situation where they were contending with other cars, any of which might have been on the Cadillac's mission, but the gunmen had simply fallen into a kind of unfortunate luck. They had planned almost certainly to hit him in heavy traffic where for all the seeming obstacles there would have been almost no risk other than the getaway itself and instead they had been led into the desert where, city lifers all, they had not been prepared to cope. Wulff low-crawled the hundred yards toward the other car, his revolver at the ready, not worried now about his exposed position, unconcerned that at any moment the man might rise to his feet and level off the shot that would kill him. He was pretty sure that this man would never stand again.

He found this gunman behind the Cadillac, huddled over in a posture of death. There was a thin hole underneath his temple, almost bloodless, where a piece of steel must have been thrown in the explosion. He had been a heavy man with a face which some people probably thought of as affable; full folds of skin, gaping lips, but now, with his eyes opened in death he did not look affable but simply surprised and somehow reduced. He was crouched over, his forehead leaning against one of the ruined doors. Wulff wedged the gun out of his hand, checked the clip, and then threw it into the desert. The fire had eaten away the metal.

He moved away from there finally and checked out the first gunman, the one he had dropped as the man foolishly bolted from the car. This one had a small wound in the neck through which he already seemed to have bled everything that was in him, the blood still coursing through five minutes after death in a steady, unending stream, the reflex action of the viscera just grinding the blood out and when he had had enough of that he walked back to the wrecked cab where the driver was now sitting, rubbing his hand over his head, talking in a confused manner. Concussion. There was no sign of recognition in the man's eyes as Wulff pushed him over from the driver's side and got behind the wheel. The man lay rigid against the seat, his body tensed, babbling.

The only humane thing was to take him to a hospital and get some kind of treatment, in a way Wulff was at fault for this and in another way by taking the route he had the driver had saved his life ... but as he considered that possibility, Wulff decided that he did not like it at all. That was no way to come into Vegas, a town he did not know, coming in a taxicab with an injured man, having to find a hospital in a strange place and then put up with all of the questions which there would have to be, questions which even if he did not answer would serve to pin him in space and time, reduce his mobility, draw an attention that he could not bear.

There was no way around it. There was just no other way to handle the situation. He did not like it at all; it put him in a way on a level with the enemy, but then again he was at war now and the only troops he had were those in the case behind him. He reached for the case, took it, gathered it in like a football, meditatively, then he sighed, put the case between he and the driver on the seat, got out of the cab, went to the other side and pulled the babbling driver out of the car. The man came into his hands like paste, unresisting, unremitting, easy to get hold of, hard to dump. He pulled him well off the road to a position where he would be visible, propped him against a boulder where if he did not move much he would have support against falling and left him there. "Crap on all of the sons of bitches," the driver said. "The nine's an eleven and don't believe otherwise."

He didn't believe otherwise. He was beginning to accept everything that he heard, closing the books on none of it; this was one of the keys to any workable campaign. He got back into the cab, pushed his case over, slammed the door and started the engine. A '72 Impala, already 85,000 miles on the thing, smashed up before the impact, worse smashed after it but still drivable. It would have to do. You made do with what you had and let the rest of it go to hell.

He hoped someone would pick up the driver. Wulff took the wrecked taxicab into Vegas and the *Paradise*.

IV

He left it a few blocks down from it on the strip after having circled once to establish location. The strip would eat anything up alive; an hour from now the cab would not be there or it would have been changed into another slot machine and slammed into a lobby somewhere. Nothing could survive outdoors on the strip, the heat was terrific, dry, pounding, moving upward from his shoes on concrete and lunging then into his body, unlike the New York humidity which always moved down from the head. Wulff carried the attaché case lightly, loosely, walking toward the hotel, hoping that he looked like everyone else on the strip although no one there looked exactly like anyone else. He was not noticed. It was not the kind of place where people considered other people.

No. Here it was machinery. It was the perfect place, perhaps the only place where the wolves at the height of the drug trade could have dug in and built their castles. The money had to go somewhere, somewhere where the stench would be lifted or if not that buried. And it had been buried here in a hundred hotels that rose or spread, in fifty casinos filled with light and noise so overwhelming that it would be possible to forget, if only for the time spent in them, exactly what had built them and where the money would go after it passed through. Somewhere around 116th Street and Lenox Avenue right now people were staggering and shuffling, gathering in the shooting galleries like flies, conferring over the needles, somewhere right now people were dying, the last frozen moment of an overdose when the impure heroin hit the central nervous system—somewhere all of this was going on, but it would take a saint or at least a philosopher, Wulff thought, to make the equation between the two, to point out that Las Vegas and the shooting galleries were exactly the same thing, in different decor but the same thing nevertheless. People were all over the streets but they moved in them like roaches in an open space, only to scuttle from one abscess to the other, no one looked at the sky here or even at anyone else. The action was all indoors. Las Vegas was the ultimate indoor city. Holding the case, walking toward the *Paradise,* Wulff did not feel at all conspicuous. He could have undressed on these streets or taken out his revolver to begin shooting; in both cases people would have dropped away from him and dived into their pursuits. Las Vegas was either the last city of escape or the very first; he couldn't make out which.

Hotels on the Strip were built two ways, *up* or out, *those* that were *up* ascending twenty or thirty stories of sheen and concrete, the ones that were *out* using their materials to lunge over an acre, shallow domes topping them off. The *Paradise* was definitely an *up* construction; he could see it a few blocks away, rising over the surrounding buildings, gleaming against the lights from the casinos and as he came nearer the place seemed to overwhelm him. It was an enormous construction which Vinelli managed; this was probably one of the three or four biggest hotels on the main strip and momentarily Wulff felt a sense of insignificance: it was just too big, there was too much, it seemed impossible that one man could have any effect upon a network which had managed to throw up something like this ... and then he thought grimly that the people who ran the network had thought enough of him to send out three semi-professionals in a Cadillac to greet and kill him; he was not as insignificant then as all that. Nothing was too big for them, nothing was too small: they protected everything frantically, and he was beginning to get into the center .... He walked into the hotel.

No one *walked* into these places; you were conveyed, usually by a limousine direct from the airport, and he felt a momentary conspicuousness. Then, entering the lobby, he was absorbed by the noise, the crowds, and the effect was shocking. It was as if this lobby was a glove which had snatched at him, seized him in a hand covered with satin and in that clamp dumped Wulff into another plane of existence. There were the machines lined up against the walls, there was the flicker and the roar of the casino, out of sight but ripping through to him through that satin covering and there was the lobby itself, an open space filled with oddly ornate furniture which was only an abscess carved into that noise, not set off from it at all. At the machines people were yanking frantically at handles, most of them muttering and cursing. A few, older women seemed to have moved beyond energy, though, into some state of transfiguration in which every clawing at the handle was merely a prayer, every spin of the wheels an offertory and these were the most frightening—the old ladies that was, because they were not people but merely appendages of the machines. Like junkies in the last stages were simply an extension of the drugs which clamored at them, so these women were not to be set apart from the machines: they looked as if they had been fastened on them with wire and as demonstrators of the movement of the machines had found their last purposes. Coins rolled within the bowels of these machines; he heard the damp, silvery twang of money being vomited into canisters and Wulff's own insides roiled from the sound of it. He had seen enough of this, he had dealt with the junkies, seen the map of drugs spread through the cities and that form of corruption he could understand and had now become literally deadened but this matter of gambling opened up a new level of feeling entirely. These people were crazy. They were genuinely crazy, all of them, and yet if you settled for thinking that you would be entirely off the track ... because the craziness was normal, built and patterned deep into the country that had sent them there, and once you began to look at things that way, there was literally no end to the line of speculation that this would bring.

So enough. Enough thinking. Wulff moved with his attaché case through the lobby of the hotel, knowing that he was being seen by a hundred eyes, that at least three or four pairs of them would be checking his face back against a register, recorded and unrecorded, that somewhere, someone was going to make the necessary connection and that in almost no time at all Vinelli would know exactly who he was and when he had entered. He was walking right into the maw of the enemy, presenting himself to them. It was not subtle, it was extremely dangerous, but Wulff knew of no other way to handle it.

He thought that he could handle Vinelli. Then again perhaps he could not. He might have misjudged everything. But he suspected that he might be able to deal with the man because although this was Vinelli's turf, controlled entirely by him, Wulff had something on the man as well. He knew why he was here and so did Vinelli and if Vinelli was as nervous about Stone as Wulff suspected ... well, then, an interview could work two ways, couldn't it?

Regardless, he did not know any other way. He never really had; it had always been a question of walking into situations, taking them at the level confronted and making the best of them. It had been that way from his earliest days on the force as a patrolman pounding up the filthiest alleys of Harlem; it had been that way in Saigon when, in what seemed to have been another lifetime, he had once walked through a minefield alone and taken out a nest of twelve guerrillas. No medal of honor on that one; the company commander had fucked up everything, had not accounted for the presence of that team and had been about to order the company into the area until Wulff, on the point, discovered the mines and then the embankment ... not a bronze star nor a silver medal nor a cross of distinction, not even a three-day pass for that matter from his panicked young captain, but he had not minded. It was a lesson. Everything could be a lesson if you approached it in the spirit that almost nothing good would ever happen. So he had kept on walking into things; back in New York he had done it on the narcotics squad which was the plum they thought they would assign him for his self-sacrifice in enlisting in the army, and it was that which had finally gotten him into trouble, bounced off the squad for turning in an informant, back to the patrol car, the dead girl and everything which had followed. Walking into situations with his eyes open, willing to pay the price of prices. A smarter man would not have functioned that way. A smarter man would not have blown up San Francisco either.

He walked through the lobby into the casino. They had him spotted by this time, he was sure. A man who had been lounging against a pedestal reading a racing sheet and smoking a cigar, apparently a relaxed horseplayer, had taken one quick look at Wulff and almost dropped the paper, scurried then toward the bank of elevators. A well-dressed girl who might or might not have been a hooker looked at him sidelong as he passed and then went to a lobby telephone; two middle-aged men with menacing faces had conferred with one another and then had hastily moved toward the desk. These people were not fools, security was strong here and Martin Wulff was famous too, never forget that: he was probably one of the best-known names in the world now to the people with whom Vinelli circulated. Fleeting thing, fame, but real while it lasts. So it was only a matter of time now: five minutes, ten minutes until they made their move. He decided to let them come to him.

Plenty of time. He felt the old combat calm coming over him, that deadening sense of certainty with which he had walked toward the embankment knowing that the worst thing the mines could do would be to blow up and kill him. Only one death however in a lifetime, and he had had his. The calm leveled him down, gave him a cold sense of purpose. He wished that Williams had been with him now, right this moment, so that he could see how Wulff could operate when the pressure was on and that vision would have wiped the contempt from the man ... but Williams, no fool, was on patrol duty right now, his part of the assignment finished. Who was using who? Wulff thought vaguely and kept on moving into the casino.

Here, the noise overtook him. On an upper level grim men in evening dress watched everything going on below; below, over an enormous area, half-partitions thrown up here and there to split it, the roulette wheels were grinding, the great lights of the casino were fluttering like birds, the croupiers and housemen were grinding away. It was the kind of sound you might have heard at the end of the world; a sound of gathering, forces meeting at a concentration of focus and even in terms of the situation he had to react with awe to the sheer power and dimension of it. Here it was all out in the open: drugs were quiet, drugs went inside and broke down the mind and the body in a series of smooth, deadly implosions but gambling was public, an extension of heat and light in which the evil became stretched so thin as to be almost transparent. Wulff felt that he could look through it, almost, down to the center to see the souls of the people at the tables, their little dead souls encased in the wood called greed and pain ... but then again maybe you could tell nothing about them; it was an exaggeration to think that gambling revealed anything other than the sheer results. The hell with it.

He moved into a roulette table. In a short period, men with huge palms would grip him by the shoulders and spin him upwards to Vinelli; for the time being one way of waiting was as good as any other. He watched the wheel spin, the mottled, crazy wheel ticking and brushing away all possibilities as a woman in front of him put her hands to her ears and closed her eyes breathing deeply. She seemed to be in anguish. Then the wheel stopped, the croupier said *"quatre noir"*—the black four hovering under the brush, even here they must have thought that using French gave the operation a touch of real class—and the woman leaped, one tiny bounce and ran toward the table, her hand extended for the chips. "Double your money!" she said, "Double your money!" Her mouth hung open, her hand scrabbling at the table. At another time she might have been pretty but all of that was behind her now. Wulff watched her take handfuls of chips, sprinkle a few of them at the croupier and run from the room, her buttocks moving unevenly under the dress. It was impossible to tell where she was going.

"Chips," a girl in a short costume on his left said, "do you want some chips, sir?" She looked up at him in an appealing way, holding a tray on which glasses were balanced. Impulsively he took one and drank from it, raw scotch on ice; choking. "You shouldn't do that, sir," she said, "these are for the players ..."

"I'm a player," he said, "I'm a player," and walked toward a cage on the end leaving her behind, looking for some chips but down the line, swinging his case, he felt a hand hitting his shoulder with a finality which was unmistakable. He turned, holding steady under that handhold and saw the two men, one very tall, the other short. The short one was the one with the hand on his shoulder and he was smiling, smiling, Wulff had never seen a smile like that in his life or then again perhaps he had; coming into a shooting gallery once, a man clamped against a wall had turned to him, his face breaking open into an expression so ecstatic and terrified by turns that Wulff had been almost unable to deal with it. This was the same smile and dear God, he had it now and it all came together, Vegas was a shooting gallery.

He slowed. The smiler kept on the grip, applying some pressure now, surprisingly forceful for such a little man. "Well," the tall man said, "you're wanted upstairs."

"Right away," the smiler said. His fingers became sharper. Wulff felt them hit bone. He tried to shrug them away but the pressure only came in harder. No one was looking at them. There was nothing you could do in a casino to attract attention except to die or break the bank.

"Let go," Wulff said.

"Make me," the smiler said. With his free hand he reached inside his coat. "Just make me."

"We can do it easy," the tall man said quietly, "or we can do it hard. Your decision."

"Don't try it," Wulff said.

"Why not?" said the smiler, his hand fondling his chest. "What's to stop us?"

"Easy or hard," the tall man said. He seemed to be enjoying himself. They were both enjoying themselves. That was the kind of thing you liked to see, all right, people who enjoyed their work. A light heart was the most important thing.

"All right," he said.

"Just walk toward the door," the tall man said.

"Tell this clown to let go of me then."

"I don't think he wants to let go of you."

"I don't want to let go of him. I really don't want to let go of him."

Wulff turned on the smiler, came down across his wrist with a short, heavy blow. There was no sound of impact but instead a high, thin sound as of wood snapping. The smiler gasped and his hand came away, shaped at an odd angle. It was jammed up against his arm. The wrist seemed to have vanished.

"He broke my wrist," the smiler said in a sobbing whisper. "The son of a bitch broke my wrist." He started to draw something out of his jacket but the tall man stopped him, one easy gesture, and the smiler abandoned the idea. He clamped the broken wrist between his knees and screamed soundlessly with the pain, semi-crumpling. At a table near them a woman screamed. The field had come in, tens twice, apparently she had a parlay working. There was a trace of blood at the corner of the smiler's mouth.

"Forget it," the tall man said, "let's just take him upstairs."

The smiler had sunk to his knees now. He was small; pain was compressed within him, far more intense than it might have been in the taller man. Wulff stood, looking at him. He felt something prodding his back in a familiar way.

"That was stupid," the tall man said, "that was really stupid of you."

"I told him to let go of me."

"Now what the fuck am I going to do with him?" the tall man said with disgust, looking at the smiler. He had come in on himself like a snail now and was shaking on the floor. For the first time, a little attention was being paid to him. Chips, after all, might come rolling out of his pockets.

"Leave him there," Wulff said, "the sweepers will be along."

The tall man seemed indecisive. He functioned well under orders apparently but something out of schedule threw him off balance. Vinelli could hardly be in such a good position after all; not if the help could not even handle a simple job like this. The point seemed to be that almost all of them were incompetent. Only Cicchini in Boston seemed to know what the hell he was doing and he had gotten through to Cicchini as well. The smiler, no longer a smiler but a pale little man whose eyes had rolled up beyond the sightline weaved to his knees and crouched on the floor. "Kill the bastard," he said.

They were drawing a crowd. The flow of play seemed to have eased off at the tables; one by one, as if word was being passed down the line telegraphically, people were turning, looking at them. The tall man seemed to tremble, doubt and indecisiveness pouring through him like water. He seemed, however slowly, to come to some kind of a decision. He reached inside his clothing.

Wulff beat him to it. His revolver was in his hand and then he was holding it, jamming it tightly into the tall man's ribs, closing off the contact by turning his body so that it would have taken someone very close in to see what was going on here. "Don't think of it," he said, "just don't think of it."

The man's hand fell away. He turned toward Wulff, his face falling open. "If you shoot," he said, "you'll never get out alive."

"You botched the job," Wulff said, "what kind of clowns are you people?"

The tall man said nothing. He lifted a hand weakly as if in greeting. The smiler had managed to get to his feet and stood there, holding his wrist with a broken expression.

"All right," Wulff said to the tall man, "let's go."

"Go? Go where?"

He prodded him with the gun indelicately. High above he could see the attention of a houseman focusing down on him. The man leaned over a railing as if he were trying to fix everything in memory. Then he turned and reached for a telephone.

"Where?" Wulff said, "where you wanted me to go, of course. Take me up."

"I'll kill the bastard," the smiler said. Rage seemed to have given him new energy. He lunged toward Wulff and Wulff kicked him in the ankle, hard. The smiler screamed and fell to the floor on the broken wrist. He opened his mouth then and vomit came out.

Definitely, the flow of play began to break in the casino. Housemen were coming toward them. People were moving away from the tables, not toward the incident but rather the doors. In a moment, the situation might get out of control.

"Let's go," Wulff said. He prodded the man in the ribs hard, again. The tall man began to stagger toward an exit. Wulff kept on top of him, allowing not even an inch of space to open between them. They got through the door without any trouble.

"You're crazy," the tall man said, "you're crazy. Don't you know what you're walking into here?"

"I'm walking into a place full of people like you," Wulff said. Expertly, pivoting, he frisked the man, removed his gun. They were in a long, curving hallway filled with light. No one came out of the casino in pursuit. No one looked for them at all.

He took the gun and put it away, gave another prod with his own. "Come on," he said, "let's go."

"Let's *go?*"

"To see the man," Wulff said, "to see Vinelli."

The tall man began to move again. He moved ahead of Wulff in twitches, like an aged beaten man, dragging his leg. A door opened down the corridor and like a sunbeam an arc of noise hit them, high, panicked shouting from the casino. Then the door closed, and they were in silence again.

The tall man shook his head and plodded on, his shoulders heaving slightly against the impact of the gun. "You're just out of your mind," he said, "if you think that you're going to be able to get away with this. No one takes on Vinelli. No one gets near him."

"I'm off to a start though, right?" Wulff said. The tall man said nothing to this, and they went on.

V

Vinelli remembered the great councils of the early 1960's. That was when it had all started to come apart. Up until then it had been a clean, tight operation, dispersed, of course, but run through a central committee and with a remarkable degree of efficiency and union considering the personalities involved .... But the councils had signalled the beginning of the era of breakdown—the 1960's when everything had started to come apart and nothing could be done about it. You could not go back. That was clear, anyway. Whatever happened, you could not go back.

The councils had had to do with the drug trade. What it came down to very simply was that the people at the very top, the older men, wanted no part of the drug business. The great wars of the 1930's had convinced them that there was a clearer, easier path in gambling, loan-sharking, smuggling, prostitution to say nothing of getting into construction and all other areas of so-called legitimate business. They did not need drugs, which only served to bring a lot of crazies into the organization and were far more trouble than they were worth, what with the problems of controlling traffic, watching for adulterated supplies and so on. Also a number of the old bastards had simply been against drugs on so-called moral grounds: they did not like the idea of people putting shit into their veins when there were so many more pleasant ways of getting out of the world like fucking or running policy. Back in the 1930's that had probably been a good idea, there was no rhyme or reason to the trade in the thirties, all kinds of shit was coming in from all over the world, a large part of it smuggled in by students and vagabonds and there was no way of clamping a lid on it. Also that stuff could kill you.

So the Mustache Petes had a point. The trouble was that the point had to do with the situation as it was twenty or twenty-five years ago; in the fifties the situation had broken open. Drugs were everywhere now, they were already a highly refined, organized business and in the absence of organization control and administration a lot of independents had moved in, most of them blacks getting their chance for the first time at the kind of independent organization and money which was enabling them to set up a distinct counter-organization. There was no way to cut off these interests short of getting into drugs on your own and knocking them down that way with the old organization power and coercion.

Also, things were not going so well for the organization at the time of these conferences. A lot of things had turned sour on them: the Appalachia business in 1957 had put away a lot of people for good, and almost no one who had been nailed at that meeting could be said to have been the same afterwards. A new generation was coming up and taking a look at the organization which in the 1940's had been so all-powerful and in control that no one except a madman or a leader would want to take an overview ... but the organization had gotten soft. Two decades of relative peace between the gang wars and the conference had eaten away at the hard edges and there were a lot of men in control who could hardly speak decent English or whose kids would care to be seen in the same room with them. Definitely some kind of shaking up was needed. It looked like drugs were the coming theme—gambling was holding up but sooner or later the government was going to move in as either a partner or competitor; prostitution what with kids fucking in the streets and a whole older generation who believed in wife, home, family and the secrecy of purely sexual relationships was dying out—and if the organization did not go for them the blacks were going to keep right on pushing and in just a little time, no more than ten years, might be in so deep, might have so much money, power and control over the trade that the organization might never get in ... might, in fact, find itself competing with the monstrous organization which the blacks had built, block-by-block for everything. That was not to be faced. The organization in many ways was so soft now, so mindless, so much in the grip of men who had not had an original thought since they decided to try and make peace with Capone that they might very well fall to a clever and sustained attack unless they moved and changed fast. That was the really frightening thing that came out of the meetings about drugs. The drugs were not only important in themselves, they were, when you took the longer, more sociological view of things, possibly the very key to the organization's survival.

Vinelli had been in the forefront of those arguing for moving into the drug trade. "It doesn't mean we have to take them, it only means we've got to supply. It has nothing to do with moral issues," had been his line of argument and it was such a simple, obvious line that it became clear soon that he was in the majority. Maybe that was why, come to think of it, he had taken that position in the first place: not because he did not have real convictions on the matter but that this seemed to make the most sense. He had been in a fairly vulnerable position at that time, painfully trying to put together a Kansas City operation, which had been absolutely moribund when he found it, and it was good to know that, if you got into conferences at this level, you had taken a position where a lot of important people would be on your side ... and a lot more would then fall into place. Really, he had had almost no business participating above the regional level. Kansas City was a territory that had been completely fucked up and mucked over and being head there was roughly equivalent to being a street man in New York, but what the hell ... it had been the senior organization, the Mustache Petes themselves who had set the ground rules providing that each region was to be represented by its top man, and he was the top man in Kansas City, even if there were only about four or five people in the whole fucking place to take orders from him.

But at that he had been lucky. When the decision had been made, had come out of those conferences that it was to be full-speed ahead, although with caution, on the drug business, a lot of the old bastards hadn't liked it. Some hadn't swallowed it, and, as the first moves were made to recover lost ground and get into the drug trade, the wars of the sixties began, which in bloodiness, pain and publicity were even larger, although not as mythical, as the stuff of the thirties—which as far as Vinelli was concerned was a pack of crap anyway. He had been twelve years old at that time, reading it in the papers, and it had been a lot of shit, guys killing one another when they could have just sat down and divided up the United States, what was left of it with the depression. The wars had raged on both coasts. They had cut into Chicago and on a less publicized level the south and the northwest had been torn apart, but sitting where he was in Kansas City, where there weren't even that many drugs to put his finger on, you could go down to the railway terminal and pick up a few kilos on a cross-country switch now and then—but that was practically petty graft, not trade. Vinelli had been in a nice tight spot to watch everything that was going on and to pick up a good deal of incidental seniority without lifting a finger or losing an ear himself. So things had rolled on and around. New York had gone through a whole series of dislocations prefiguring the almost complete organizational collapse that was to come in the seventies; Los Angeles had gone through three separate and warring administrations with bodies falling all over the Hollywood Bowl and to points up north as far as the San Andreas fault line. And all this time Vinelli had hacked it out in Kansas City, armpit of the nation maybe, but the absence of competition meant that it was possible to get what work you could done without being blocked on every end. He started to acquire a reputation. He was a man without much imagination with a foul mouth and a vile temper, but things around him seemed to get done pretty much quickly and the right way which was more than you could say of most of the clowns around the country who were far more interested, it seemed, in killing each other than in putting any kind of organization together.

Also the fact that he was the only one at this level in the country without family ties of any kind counted to his advantage. All of them had wives, children, residences with gates, relatives pressuring them all of the time, mistresses, homosexual connections, the full paraphernalia of the middle-aged, upper-echelon businessman who was in too deep to really have the freedom of action that was necessary, whereas Vinelli had nothing. If he had ever had a family of any sort no one could account for it; certainly there were no wives or mistresses, let alone children. He was simply all business, none of that stuff hooked him in at all. It was possible that he would see a whore of one sex or the other once a month just to get his load off, but there was no way of even accounting for that. The man simply did not appear to function on any personal level at all. This meant that he had mobility; he could live anywhere, go anywhere, do anything. There was no detail so petty that he could not, if necessary, oversee it himself and nothing so large that he would have to dodge it for fear of putting his family in a more exposed position than he could risk. He was a man who could live out of a suitcase or a penthouse, usually both, sometimes neither; it just did not seem to matter to him. And as early as 1966, just when the war was beginning to really move along, millions and millions of dollars of new junk were pouring into the country every day from this glistening new supply area. Vinelli had gotten himself a reputation in the organization which went entirely beyond his accomplishments. He appeared to be, whether they were right or wrong, a man who could get things done and to whom calculation would never enter into a decision because on the personal level he just did not seem to function at all.

His break came when an enormous load came in from Saigon, straight to the Midwest, funnelled in little packages through the service clubs and the USO and then simply disappeared. It was not where it was supposed to be, the men who were committed to delivery vanished, the people waiting for pickup were ambushed and apparently a million dollars, maybe more (no one knew enough about it to put a real price) of the best Asian gold was off the map, all of the payments to the NCO's to get it through, all of the logistics of the supply apparently down the drain. It represented an enormous loss for the organization. They could absorb it of course, by this time profits were such that they could absorb almost anything ... but still it looked bad, if a load like this could slip away from them in the night it might make a lot of people, particularly the dangerous blacks in Harlem who were always thinking about coming downtown and staging a last war for the territory, the idea that the organization was losing its grip. Also, business was business: the fact that you could absorb a loss was no excuse for taking it. Once you began to think that way you went in the direction of Nash, Studebaker or the Hudson Hornet.

So Vinelli had been detailed to find the junk if he could and get it back into the supply channels if he did. He had gone at the job utterly without humor and with tremendous cold efficiency, virtually closing down all but the routine operations in his area (because he insisted on overseeing everything) while he went into Chicago to see what he could see. No one, frankly, expected that he would come up with much; it was a hopeless kind of job, a suicide mission at best, but there were a lot of people in the organization by that time who were already becoming a little frightened of Vinelli, and it seemed a pretty good deal, then, to put the man in a spot like this. Let him sweat it out, make a horse's ass of himself or best of all get killed. He was the kind of man whose death would make thirty or forty others sleep better nights. But Vinelli had not screwed up the job. In fact, he had found the stuff.

He found the stuff and he got it back into the stream. It had been necessary for him in the process to kill eight people, five of whom were buried so deep that they were not even connected with the situation for years, it had been necessary for him to literally remake the relationship between the service clubs and the organization so that the service clubs had to make it on their own and without drug supply—leading to the revelations about them and the complete collapse of the system some years later. It had been necessary for him to coldly and systematically torture to death an important Chicago second-echelon man who turned out to have too much information. That had been very risky, but Vinelli had made a clean breast of everything as soon as he had finished the job. He had taken it right into the council, to prove that he was functioning perfectly above board and was only trying to protect the organization against traitors and he had been forgiven. There was some questioning of his methods but absolutely none as to his work; the man got results. The council had approved. The junk had gotten into the network, turning out to be slightly adulterated and resulting in a lot of sickness and deaths about three months after it began to hit the streets, but that had not been his fault either. Vinelli was on his way at last now. He had been taken out of Kansas City.

Las Vegas was the ideal place to put him. Las Vegas had originally been a diversion for the organization, a place to carry the spare money and wash it clean by burying it in the sand and causing it to sprout. It had sprouted casinos, hotels, nightclubs, vegetation in the desert beyond the wildest hopes of the organization at the time they had started because all that they had really had in mind was finding a way to keep the money occupied and maybe in an attractive way create a setup which would someday be their private property. That had cost them a lot of money, but the state of Nevada went cheaper than most even in the nineteen-fifties and things moved along pretty much according to plan. Then they moved beyond plan. It turned out that Las Vegas, Reno were not merely utilizing money, they were making it. They were making it out of all proportion to what the organization had figured. In fact, thanks to the efforts of some publicity men, contractors, state senators and travel agents who were above and beyond the call of duty, Nevada soon turned from purest silver to gold. The grosses were not all that fantastic, drugs could top them in a good year, but the net was fantastic. Eighty-five percent of the money bet at the casinos, being run through the tables and machines over and over again, would eventually wind up with the house. And the overhead, except for union salaries which was chickenshit, was almost constant. You could graph it out for the year ahead and unlike almost anything else it would hold to ninety-five percent.

It became apparent to the organization or what was evolving from it that in the years ahead Las Vegas might be the foundation of something they had never even considered previously: an international empire. Linking up with the Saigon sources had been the first inkling that not only business but real expansion might be accomplished by going international, now there were people investigating as never before the possibilities in continental Europe which had heretofore been wild territory, absolutely sealed off from the organization. But continental Europe had been facing its own problems through the sixties. There was a new breed of management there who were interested, however tentatively, in some kind of cooperative effort, long-range planning, foresightedness. Las Vegas could be the crown of the international in thirty years if things moved along.

Meanwhile, however, it was necessary to protect the operation as never before. The trouble with Vegas was that it was just too open, too accessible, by definition it was a public place, a gathering point, a spa if you will, into which almost any element could circulate and by definition it was impossible to maintain a tight access, real security. Putting a lid on the place would, for one thing, have shut down eighty percent of the profits. So it was necessary to get a very special kind of man in there, or putting it another way, it was necessary to get two special kinds of men because by definition almost no one was capable of performing both functions. One kind of man would have to be a press-agent's dream if not a press-agent himself: a legitimate, polished, sophisticated kind of man who without a taint of involvement could manage the property and its interests in a way which would ingratiate almost everyone, satisfy everyone, keep the ball rolling ... and behind or under him there would have to be another kind of man, one like Vinelli, someone who could make sure that the first type of man was not looting the place to the ground and that the essential control of the organization would never be challenged. There was nothing worse than a public-relations type who got ahead of himself or began to believe his public image. It was the function of the Vinellis to make sure that the administrators were reminded all the time of exactly who they were and what was sustaining them ... and what could push them off a cliff if they should happen to wander cliffside.

For the organization, this was pretty advanced-type thinking: as subtle and far-ranging as anything which might have been thought up in the government of that time. It showed what a truly great distance they had come from the councils of the early 1960's. Of course most of the people who had been at those councils were now dead or otherwise indisposed.

Vinelli was sent to manage the Paradise Hotel in Vegas. Actually it was far more than the Paradise that he was going to manage. On paper he was going to look like an underling, a hired hand who was taking care of the scub-work while a guy named Walker who was on a first-name basis with everyone in Hollywood would use his ownership of the Paradise as a wedge to explore more and more real estate in Vegas. But behind closed doors Walker called Vinelli "sir" which very few people in his life had ever done and palpably trembled at everything Vinelli said, dreaded to pick up the phone when Vinelli called intercom and always did on the first ring and all in all, blew his nose whenever Vinelli sneezed and quite loudly. Walker should have been glad to have had Vinelli there, it meant that the organization was taking an interest in him and that Walker's position was secure—if it was not secure they simply would have bounced him, but he was not at all glad. He did not think that way. He was, in fact, terrified.

This did not bother Vinelli. Nothing much bothered him at all; you just did not get to the age of fifty-two after thirty-three years in the organization and allow much but the highly necessary stuff to touch you. The business about shielding the fugitive lieutenant, Stone, had been taken in stride; you did this kind of thing all the time and his contact with Stone went back many years; the guy would come up with the goods sooner or later. Having Stone wandering around the Paradise with play-money was all right too; routine courtesy to a guest. But when the word had come that this lunatic, this Martin Wulff, might well be heading toward Vegas and the Paradise itself ... that had bothered Vinelli. It had bothered him a good deal. He knew the organization's affection for nice, tight operations; he was a nice, tight operation kind of man himself and anytime someone like Wulff headed this way it meant problems and difficulties. He knew that he would have to do something about Stone right away and even then he had kept relatively calm. Wulff was bad news but, all right, it was a tough life; you tried to take this kind of stuff in stride, and he was sure he would be able to nail the clown if he ever showed. Vinelli was no Cicchini.

But then, falling into the suspicion that Stone had been full of shit from the beginning, that the New York stories were just bluff and cover and he probably had no line of junk to peddle at all ... now that had bothered Vinelli a good deal. Fifty-two years old, thirty-three years in the organization or not, there were certain things that you simply could not tolerate and this was one of them. It was one thing to shelter a potentially valuable fugitive who would eventually show his gratitude by handing over a million dollars tax-free worth of gifts to show good faith. It was another to get taken for a ride by some pig's-ass lieutenant who was just desperate enough to take advantage and not farseeing enough to know what he could do after the string ran out. And when it tied in with this Wulff and his portable explosives factory closing in on his entrusted territory ...

Well, he had really regretted dealing with Stone in the manner that he had. Contrary to all the books on him, Vinelli was a man who held no brief for killings or other rough treatment. He was not a sadist, he got no pleasure out of it. He got no pleasure out of anything except being efficient, that was his secret. That was why no one had ever been able to touch him. But then again Stone had offered him no way out. If the man had nothing to trade for the risks that Vinelli was taking, then he was nothing other than a pure menace, pure minus factor on the balance sheet. So Vinelli had had to do the necessary and the proper.

He would have to do it all the way down the line. There was nothing personal in this—his viewpoint on life was gloomy, no one got out of it alive and essentially it was just a matter of filling in seventy years or so until you went back where you came from so you might as well do it with as few loose ends as possible—but it was not quite impersonal either, it was something between the two. A job had to be done well for its own sake.

He heard that Wulff had broken through the first line of defense in the desert and had made the casino no more than thirty seconds after the man had come in. He called up to Walker and told him to sit tight and then he put the second line into action. If they failed which they probably would not (but you had to take everything into account) there was a third line and a fourth. Maybe a fifth. No loose ends, whatever you did, all the way down the line. No loose ends, ever.

This was the kind of man who Wulff took an elevator up four flights to see.

VI

Wulff said, "Knock on the door and tell him the job's done and you're alone and you want in." He prodded the man down the hall. There was no one there.

"It won't work," the tall man said. He was not arguing, only a desperate reasonability in his voice. If there had been any spirit it was well broken. "He knows everything that's going on there downstairs, don't you understand? He's no damned fool, he's hooked right in there and he probably knows everything."

"We'll try it that way," Wulff said.

"We'll both be killed before we get into the room."

"So what do you suggest?"

The tall man stopped bringing Wulff up sharp behind him; he took another prod from the gun and stumbled but held himself against a wall. "I'll tell him that I've got you and that you're disarmed," he said. "It's the only way."

"And what will I walk into?"

"How the fuck do *I* know what you'll walk into? I'm trying to stay alive too, friend."

"Are you now," Wulff said softly. They began to move again in a soft huddle, the tall man motioning toward the suite that was Vinelli's. Only a few yards now. "What happened to Stone?" Wulff said.

"What's that? Who?"

"Don't give me any shit now; it's too late. What happened to him?"

The tall man turned. His eyes were burning. "I can't talk about that," he said, "that's something I just can't talk about at all."

"Even if I shoot you in the ass?"

The man shook. "I'm afraid of you," he said flatly, "and I'm afraid of dying. But there are some things I'm even more afraid of."

"Vinelli."

The man looked at him, said nothing. Involuntarily, his head jerked.

"All right," Wulff said, "play it your way. Knock on the door. Or why not try it and just go in?"

"He always keeps it locked."

"What the hell," Wulff said, "try it anyway."

The man reached forward, caressed the knob, his hand bouncing. He turned it. It slid in his palm, leaving little stains of gloss on the metal.

"I told you," he said.

"All right, knock."

"He could just open that door and shoot the two of us down. You don't know. You don't know Vinelli."

"I'm going to," Wulff said, "I'm looking forward to it very much."

The man knocked. The sound came back on his fist rather than resounding the way that solid doors always do. He knocked again.

"Who is it?" a voice said from the inside.

"Thomas," the man said. "I've got him. I've got him with me."

"Got who with you?"

"Wulff."

"The New York freak? You've got him?"

The tall man looked back at Wulff as if he expected to be shot for this. Wulff held the gun very steady and looked at the door, leveling down, trying to find a sightline. He had made a decision the moment he had heard the voice; he was not going to go in to Vinelli to negotiate, to give him any chance whatsoever to maneuver. He was going to shoot the man instantly and negotiate later.

The tall man must have seen this. He looked at Wulff hastily, looked back at the door. "Yeah," he said quietly, "I've got him."

"Where's Witt?"

"Not with me," Thomas said. "Downstairs."

"Why?"

"No reason," the tall man said. "All right, fuck, plenty of reason. The guy knocked him down. But I was able to wrestle him into control."

"That was fucking stupid," Vinelli's voice said. "That was really fucking stupid."

"I guess so. But I got him."

"All right," Vinelli said. "Bring him in."

"I think it's better if you open the door," the tall man said at a jab from Wulff, rubbing his back then in real pain, trying though to keep his voice flat. A fuckup but a professional. You had to respect that. You had to give him that much. "I've got him under tight control here but I don't want to start fucking with the knobs."

"Oh," Vinelli said. There was a sound of motion behind the door and then it stopped. "How do I know you've got him under control?" he said.

"I do. I do."

"And what if you don't?"

The tall man shrugged, almost as if he had been speaking the truth. "What can I say?" he said, "I sure as hell can't prove it behind a closed door."

"I'm coming," Vinelli said after another pause, "but I'm coming with a fucking gun. I'm going to answer that door, open it right up with a fucking gun in my hand and if I see any fucking thing wrong I'll kill you and then the other guy and Witt too if you're lying and he's with you. I'm not fucking around with fucking games. This guy is dangerous."

"I know he's dangerous," Thomas said, "that's why I wanted you to open the door."

"All right," Vinelli said. Wulff gripped his revolver, bringing it in slowly across the tall man's body, easing it toward the door. At some level of reasoning he knew he was calculating the most possible angle at which Vinelli's body would confront him at the opening of the door. The thing to do was to play the odds just the way the suckers did downstairs and hope that there was no percentage in this one to eat you up alive.

The tall man in that bleak, compressed instant before Vinelli opened the door, must have seen exactly what Wulff had in mind. The comprehension moved from his eyes down the cheekbones and into his neck. He trembled. Then he must have made calculation of his own.

What happened next happened very quickly. Looking back on it Wulff could see it clearly, could plug the sequence of events to tell exactly what went on but at the time it lacked any sense of continuity and he was working only on the ancient cop's instinct. What happened was that the tall man, pedaling backwards, tried to throw his weight into Wulff, catch and pin him by surprise against the opposite wall just as Vinelli opened the door, hoping that Vinelli would see what was happening instantly and using that moment of surprise, shoot over him to kill Wulff. It was a simple plan, certainly one which came out of vast respect for Vinelli and looking back at it Wulff could only admire the man. Right to the end, even defeated, he had been thinking like a professional.

But it did not happen that way. What happened is that the tall man caught Wulff all right, threw an elbow into his solar plexus and sent him back against the wall gasping, losing that one crucial instant and handhold on the gun which could have been the story as Vinelli opened the door ... but Vinelli, either misjudging the situation or overreacting or perhaps (this was the most frightening of all) doing something which he had planned to do anyway, shot directly at the tall man and hit him in the chest, killing him.

He must have been killed instantly. He fell away from Wulff the way a sheet falls from a naked girl doing a final strip and gasping against the wall, holding his solar plexus with one hand, trying to get a decent grip on the gun with the other, he was open to Vinelli. The man raised his arm for the killing shot.

Wulff fell. He plummeted straight down, no longer trying to protect his stomach and hit the floor like a carpet, scrambling behind the corpse of the tall man named Thomas. Plaster sifted into his hair behind a quiet pop. Vinelli had been using a silencer. He fired off the silenced gun to kill Wulff, but the bullet only hit where he had been.

Vinelli had an instant of confusion. He was a big man with experience and no fool in situations like this but he was also fifty-two years old and the reflexes were simply not where Wulff's were. He took a fifth of a second to try and see exactly where the hell Wulff had gone. By the time he found him on the floor, Wulff had rolled part way on his back, arched himself, pointed the gun and gotten the shot off.

No silencer. The gun screamed in the confines of the hallway. It threw up dust, the recoil slamming him straight back into the corpse.

He hit Vinelli in the left kneecap.

It was where he had wanted to put the shot in the first place. He could not have done better if he had wanted. Vinelli, pivoting, raising his leg to aim the next shot had presented that target directly to Wulff, and Wulff hit him dead center. Blood leaped from the knee like a bird.

Vinelli screamed.

The scream was harshly feminine, unlike any which Wulff had ever before heard. At the same time that the bird of blood carried him upwards, the scream must have carried him down, the leg arching up straight into the air, inclined toward the ceiling, little bone fragments spilling. Vinelli fell straight into the carpeting still screaming. His body, two hundred and forty pounds of it, unprotected, not guarding against the fall hit hard, like a mass of gelatinous material, and he screamed a second time.

Wulff, half on his own knees now, finished off the job by shooting Vinelli in the foot of the same leg.

The scream came again, ripping out in little waves, rivulets of effeminate sound that combined with the pain in Wulff's plexus to carry him to a place where only noise existed. He could not have been there for more than ten seconds, probably less and when he came out of it he found himself embracing a corpse while a live man squealed before him, his face brightening ... but he would never be the same again. He knew that. He had simply never seen pain like that in a human being before.

Dogs yes, plenty of dogs and there had been a stray cat he had once seen on patrol which some madman had literally opened up so that its guts were falling out of it like a series of pendulums and the cat's agony had brought it to humanity. It had looked at Wulff with gratitude as Wulff had pulled his revolver and instinctively shot it. But the cat was something else, so were the dogs, Vinelli, whatever else, he was a man, a man now with a destroyed knee and a ruined foot, clubbing and howling himself to death in a hallway and Wulff knew that whatever he did now he had to get the man inside, had to get the two of them inside along with that corpse because the screams were surely going to draw reinforcements, had probably counselled reinforcements already and what would happen when men poured down this hall went beyond description. At least inside the room he would have a post; he would have a line of defense.

Wulff staggered upright and looked at the man before him in the hallway. Vinelli was the man all right: he was the one to whom Stone had fled, the one who had sent four men to kill him, the man who might have been the most dangerous of all that he had faced, but in the posture of agony they were all the same, weren't they? the faces drawn to the same translucence of anguish, the mouths uttering the same words of hurt and shame. Remember that Wulff told himself, looking at the thing in the hallway, clutching itself almost senselessly on its left side, at the end all of us are the same. Pain is the great leveler.

He left the dead man, Thomas, in the hallway. The dead were the dead all right, there was nothing to be done with them. He might not even attract attention out here, at least from guests. He would look just like any other loser, busted out, lying facedown in the hallway. They would lie in the hallways after a disastrous night at the casino, sometimes in their own vomit, and the considerate staff would not help them into their rooms, often because to awaken in the knowledge that they had been seen would be the most unbearable of all. He kicked the man aside, feeling the odd resiliency of the corpse and put his hands on the shoulders of the semiconscious Vinelli. He poised himself behind the man.

He dragged him into the room.

The left leg dragged and bumped on the carpeting; Vinelli bellowed once, that piteous effeminate wail and then lapsed into unconsciousness. His head lolled off to the side. He was dead weight, dead meat. In the room, Wulff dragged him clear of the door, left him lying there, came to the door and kicked it shut, chain-bolted it. Alone in the room now with a wounded man, one dead in the hallway. He saw the little trickles of blood pooling from underneath the pants leg, billowing onto the slick, yellow carpeting of the room. Vinelli must have been proud of that. The yellow carpeting must have been his taste, all right: he was exactly the kind of man who would take pride in a touch like that.

The phone was ringing.

He allowed that fact to penetrate his consciousness, standing there, looking at the man, then he went over to the phone itself, alive with its piercing sound and considered. Then he picked up the phone, inhaling, allowing not even the sound of his breath to hum over the wire and listened.

"Sam?" a man's voice said finally, "Sam, are you all right?"

Wulff said nothing. He held the phone. Eventually, if they had something to say, they would come right out with it anyway. You could count on that. An open line for a man under stress was a request to speak.

"Sam?" the voice said tentatively, uncertainly, "there's some trouble down in the casino. Sam, there's something going on down there. Are you all right?"

"I'm all right," Wulff said in a monotone. "Everything's under control." He kept his voice expressionless, level. There was always the chance that you could get away with it. It was worth a try anyway. "I don't want to be disturbed," he said, "I want to handle this my own way. Everything's under control."

"You sure? Are you sure now?"

"Yah," Wulff said and slammed the phone down. He tracked the silvery coil of wire into the wall, yanked on it hard. Expansion material, the coils bulged in his hand but did not come free. Impatient, he took out his revolver, put the nose of it against the wire and blew it free. Then he picked up the disconnected phone, carried it to the window, pushed open a latch with difficulty and hurled the phone out the window, quickly closing the pane against the sound of impact.

That would take care of that for a while.

He had a few moments leeway he supposed. He walked over to Vinelli, checked the unconscious man who was now beginning to breathe in deep, whimpering gasps and kicked him once in the ribs, feeling bone shatter. That would bring him back to consciousness, sure enough. Then he went back behind the desk, took a straight chair against the wall there and carried it to the door, wedged it underneath in a good tight hold. Going back to the desk he ripped the remainder of the phone line out of the wall, took it over to the door and, grunting, plugged it into the lock. It just fit. It might not do much but then again it could possibly be something of a help if they tried to shoot their way in.

Then he went back to the body on the floor and kicked it again, then once more until the eyes fluttered and Vinelli, his eyes rolling, looked up at him.

"Let's talk," Wulff said, almost affably.

He was going to get some answers.

VII

He squeezed what he could out of the brief conversation and still it was not enough. He did not like it. Walker did not like it. Whoever had picked up that phone was not Vinelli and yet that knowledge was not enough; Vinelli maneuvered around a lot down there and generally speaking his moves were not to be questioned. If he didn't want to be bothered Walker should have left it at that, but sitting on the topmost floor of the Paradise, Walker turned in his chair, looked out past the strip to the clear dark spaces of the desert in the distance and decided that this one time he could not let it go. Whatever the risks he had to follow through.

There was the problem in the casino for one thing; the little man who, reports said, had been beaten up and had been taken out of there by ambulance. There were the two other men in the casino who apparently had been with the hurt one and who had left, headed, it was said, to Vinelli's office. And there was a whole feeling coming over Walker that something happened which was off the books, not to be controlled, outside entirely of the normal routine.

Thinking about it and what he would have to do next, Walker felt himself beginning to shake. If his luck had held he would have been in Europe today on a public-relations tour disguised as a vacation, an actress next to him, reports clustering to ask the latest decision of the man who had come to be known as the miracle magnate of the strip. If they knew! if they only knew! later on he would have gone back to the hotel with the starlet, he to his room, she to hers, and there lying under the ceiling in the dark he probably would have jerked off to her remembered image behind his eyelids, the only way it got off, the only way that he had been able to get it off for ten years. And all the time there would have been the phone calls to answer from the states, the memos and lists of things to be done to be followed up while the starlet who was part of the package deal grinned mindlessly for the press and stayed out of the way otherwise. But the godamned thing had been canceled, they had wanted him here for some reason which they did not explain and that had been that. They never explained anything of course, and Harry Walker was sure as hell not going to ask. That he had understood very early in the game; that he had one function to perform and if he did it for them he would live very well and within limits contentedly but if he started to fuck around with them there were sure as hell a couple of hundred others who would do the job *without* fucking around ... and it wasn't that bad a life, he would get along with it.

So all right, go to Europe—he went; go to Los Angeles and tour a studio or two—he went; hit New York and do the celebrity circuit—and that was fine too; stop, go, wait, reverse—anything they wanted was fine, and if there had been a change of plans on Europe he would accept it without question. But now, suddenly, Walker had the feeling that what had been dumped on him was the biggest mess that had hit the Paradise, maybe had hit the entire strip and it was his responsibility. No one else was going to handle it.

He was a weak man. He accepted that weakness; for the most part it had not hurt him. He had known plenty of strong men in his time, men like Vinelli, and had survived most of them because strong men tended to get themselves, time and again, put into positions where they were tested by men equally strong and that was often fatal. Whereas weak men like Walker lived within the circle of their limitations willingly, almost eagerly holding onto their weakness as their strength because it protected them and kept them from taking the chances which time and again broke the strong ones. In weakness was strength, and if he was only a figurehead, well, then, the Paradise itself was only a figurehead, he knew that quite well and the two of them went together well. He booked in the entertainers, did the public relations bit, tried to keep the entertainers, even to the two-bit old men working in the lounges on Sunday mornings, happy ... and the rest of it Vinelli could worry about. But now he was deep in and the responsibility his.

He could duck it of course. Wall up in the penthouse or duck out of town; say that he knew nothing about it. Let them when they picked up the pieces later decide whether or not Harry Walker was responsible. By that time he could be out of the country. But no, he felt the weakness rising within him and in a kind of disgust knew that he just could never get away with it. If the place blew, responsibility would be traced to him, and he would be dealt with almost as an incidental, their main thrust of revenge running over him like the sea over pebbles. He had to confront the situation.

Slowly, painfully, Walker picked up the phone. He dialed the security desk and waited until the chief man on duty picked it up. Three rings. They were getting sloppy. Three rings and even then there was a five second lag while the man fumbled for a cigarette or somesuch. They had gotten arrogant. They had become slipshod all the way down the line and acted as if they had gotten beyond any position where they could be touched. Dangerous. That was dangerous thinking. It all just went to show you.

If they got through this there would be a lot of people paying and at least he could take some satisfaction in knowing that probably, likely, one of them would be Vinelli.

"Who the fuck is this?" the security man asked when Walker had not responded the first time.

"This is fucking Harry Walker," he said, and the guard gasped which helped his morale a little for what he was about to do. He asked for full security, he asked for reinforcements, and he told them to hit Vinelli's room full out. He told them that he thought the manager was having a little trouble and it was more sensible to come in with full firepower. He told them that it was a matter of protecting Vinelli. The man sounded worried.

VIII

He squeezed everything out of Vinelli that he could. It did not take long. It took only a few moments in fact to get everything he thought he needed and then the only question was what to do with him. He knew that it would not be very long until they unloaded everything they had at this room. They were no fools.

"Where's Stone?" he said when he knew the man was conscious. "Where is he?"

"I'm dying," Vinelli said. He did indeed look like a dying man. Amazing how they crumpled. Time and again it was shocking for Wulff to realize the leveling effects of pain.

"You won't die," he said, "not soon enough anyway." Soon enough would have been thirty years ago. "Where is he?" he said and held his revolver backhanded as if to club the man. Vinelli held his face rigid, his eyes unblinking and looked at the ceiling. A crying sound came from his throat. Wulff put the revolver, butt-first into the back of the man's

hand, hard. Vinelli whimpered, but then the whimper shook his leg and
he screamed.

"Where is he?" Wulff said.

Vinelli was trying to talk. His throat bulged and little sounds came out
of it. Wulff leaned over and looked at the man in a gesture as intimate
as the beginning of a kiss. He spat into the man's eyes.

"Speak up," he said, "or I'll hit the leg hard."

"Stone's dead," Vinelli said in a croak.

"How?"

"We killed him."

"Why?"

"We had to," Vinelli said, his voice somewhat stronger. Thinking about
Stone brought him back hours to a happier time when he had been the
one on top. "The son of a bitch was holding out on us."

"Was he?"

"The junk, the junk. He said he had a million dollars ..."

"And he didn't?"

"There was nothing," Vinelli said. He gagged and tried to vomit but the
angle was wrong and the vomit fell back into his throat. He purpled.
"Kill me," he said, "go on, just kill me."

"When I'm ready."

"I'm better off dead than talking to you." He inhaled, tried to force
volume. "You son of a bitch cop," he said.

"I'm no cop."

"I don't know what you are."

"Where's the half million?"

"I told you," Vinelli said with tears in his eyes, "there's nothing. He was
holding out on us."

"How do you know?"

"I know."

Wulff stood, went to the window, then came back. The office was
sparsely furnished but he knew that the desk drawers probably held
enough material, put in the hands of an honest staff, to give the drug
trade a staggering, perhaps final blow. In time. The question was
getting out of this room alive, let alone with files. "So you had him killed,"
he said.

"I told you that."

"You told me nothing," he said. He pointed the revolver at the man's
leg which had now become warped, was lying in a peculiar angle to the
floor. "Where is the stuff?" he said. "Tell me or I'll shoot you there
again."

Vinelli convulsed. "No," he said, "you can't do that."

"Try me."

"I told you, it isn't. We found out he was holding out on us. There never was any stuff at all. It was just a way of getting out of sight. Of getting us to take him in."

"So you killed him," Wulff said. "Naturally."

"Wouldn't you?" Vinelli said hoarsely.

That was a question. It was an interesting question. At another time he would have to think it through. Now he only looked at Vinelli levelly. "I think you're wrong," he said. "I think that the stuff is here. He never would have left New York without something."

Vinelli said nothing. Wulff looked at him. Probably if he did not receive medical attention shortly the man would die. The central nervous system was wrecked, overloaded by pain and there was considerable blood loss. Blood was draining out no slower than it had five minutes before. High blood pressure no doubt, the carotid blowing the stuff out unclotted under stress.

"It's probably in a locker at the airport," Wulff said, "that would be the most logical place." He paused. "Did you search him? Of course you searched him," he said. "Did you find a key?"

Vinelli's eyes narrowed. Pain or not, he seemed to be thinking. Wulff could see the thoughts like little dogs chasing one another across his eyes.

"Don't hold out on me," Wulff said. He motioned toward the leg. "You're in no position to get clever." And neither am I, he thought. He heard the first faint sounds in the hallway. Time. Time enough. They were starting to close in.

"There was a key," Vinelli said. A bolt of pain went through him, he put his palms flat on the floor and looking at the ceiling wrenched with agony. "Sure, there was a locker key in his clothes. We thought nothing of it. We ..."

"Didn't get around to it is what you mean," Wulff said. "You would have though. You're thorough. I'll give you that. Where is the key?"

Vinelli shook his head, closed his eyes. Very methodically but with a shade of distaste, Wulff kicked him around the kneecap, the injured one. He did not like to do it. Unlike the Vinellis themselves he took no pleasure in inflicting pain, it was only a device. Still, he was willing to do it without worrying. That made him still more than two-thirds a cop.

"In the desk, top drawer," Vinelli said when he was able to talk again. "It's in there. We would have gotten around to checking it out ..."

"Yeah," Wulff said and went to the desk, flung it open, found the key where the man had said it would be, "after you killed him first of course. It's always a good idea to kill first and check after the fact, right?"

He could hear the voices in the hallway. Security was lax here; they did not know how to come up on a position silently but instead conferred with one another every step of the way, most likely for assurance. Arrogance and ease, no doubt. They probably had never had a challenge in this hotel. Taking drunken losers quietly out of the casino was just about their style, this was beyond them. Vinelli inclined his agonized head toward the door and his eyes lit with hope, then he closed them when he saw Wulff looking.

"Don't worry about it," Wulff said, going over to the door. "You're not getting out of here alive."

Vinelli said nothing. His hands were folded tightly over his stomach and he appeared to be praying. Prayer would always get them at the end. He wondered if this man had laughed when he gave the orders to kill Stone. Vinelli's lips moved, his body convulsed again.

There was a knock on the door. "Vinelli?" someone said, "are you in there?"

Wulff gave the man a warning look. Vinelli said nothing. His voice would probably not have carried that far anyway.

"We're coming in," another voice said, "unless you tell us you're all right we're coming in."

Wulff checked the chair to make sure that it was solid and well-set in place. Then he backed off from the door and lifted his gun.

"No you won't," he said.

"What's that?" someone said, "what's going on in there?"

"You're not coming in," Wulff said. He paused. "Your boss is in trouble here. If you come in he's in worse trouble."

There was the sound of anguished conference. "Who the fuck are you?" someone said hesitantly.

Wulff went over to the body on the floor and, kneeling, pressed his revolver into the temple. "Tell them who I am," he said.

Vinelli's eyes rolled. There was knocking on the door, increasing in volume.

"You really better tell him who I am," Wulff said calmly, "or I'm going to have to start shooting. In the crossfire, you'll probably get hit in the leg."

"Please," Vinelli said, drawing in his breath on every syllable. "Please don't come in. I'm hurt. He's in here with me."

"Who's in there with you?"

"Wulff," Vinelli said. He gasped, his face turning yellow, he nodded in an agonized way, trying to show Wulff that he could not speak further. Wulff gave him a prod. "Martin Wulff," Vinelli said, "the cop from New York. He's hurt me. I'm hurt bad. I can't ..."

"Vinelli?" the voice said, "Vinelli, what the fuck is going on there. We ..."

"Stay out!" Vinelli screamed, "for the love of God, stay out!"

Wulff gave him an approving pat, a *well-done* and went to the door. "I'm afraid your man is in trouble," he said. "I'm in here with him and he's helpless. If you don't back off I'll kill him."

"He will!" Vinelli screamed, finding full volume. He hawked in air. "He will!"

"That's right," Wulff said, "I really will. So you'd better carry the message downstairs to stay the hell out of this room. Isn't that right, Vinelli?"

Vinelli said nothing. It was not from failure of effort but simply a lapse of strength. He looked up at Wulff and licked his lips. "It would be better if you had fucking killed me," he said.

"We'll get around to that."

"It would be better to be fucking dead than to be like this."

"Not necessarily," said Wulff. He felt almost cheerful. He felt that the situation was now beginning to come under control.

There was a sense of voices in conference in the lobby: murmurs, movement as if someone were pacing. Finally someone said quietly, "Vinelli? Vinelli is it really you in there?"

"It's him in here," Wulff said, "you can count on it."

"Show us," the voice said, "show us that it's Vinelli in there and he's alive and we'll spread the word."

"You think I'm crazy?" Wulff said. "You think I'm going to throw open this door for open house? You must be out of your mind."

The voice dropped back into conference again. There seemed to be three of them there and Wulff could understand their problem. They simply did not know what to do. They had been sent here to blow someone's brains out, preferably his, but hardly to be confronted with a series of choices. Choices were just not the specialty of this group. That was the trouble with the organization he thought wryly, it was very hard to get a good class of help. Those that had the intelligence to make choices or adapt were usually too intelligent for their jobs and had to be gotten rid of. The ones who were left were trustworthy but stupid. Modern personnel practice. It was a shame. The trouble was that the organization had to compete with too much private industry offering similar salaries and better fringe benefits to say nothing of a more guaranteed kind of life-span, and they were falling by the wayside. Already they were starting to import cheap labor; the classic solution for an industry under pressure. But how long until the cheap labor itself picked up the ground rules? No, he did not envy their position.

"Hold a gun on one of us," the voice said, "and open the door. Just so that we can get a look at Vinelli. If it's all true we go away."

"Hold a gun on one of you?" Wulff said, "and what about the other two?" He was beginning to enjoy this perversely, it was like labor bargaining. Give a little, gain a little. He had all the time in the world. His plan had formulated slowly, now was densely coming together below the reach of consciousness. He was staying right here. No pressure. He was going nowhere. "What are the other two going to do; where are they going to be while this is going on?"

"I've got to get to a doctor," Vinelli said from behind him, almost matter of factly. "If I don't get to a doctor I'm fucking going to die."

"Be happy you're not in pain right now if you can think of a doctor," Wulff said. "Well?" he said through the door, "how about that?"

"We'll all be in sight with our hands up," the voice said sullenly. "We'll stay in front of you."

"Why not take my word for it?" Wulff said.

"We can't take anybody's word for anything. We've got to check it out."

Wulff eased the revolver out of his jacket and considered it, considered the door. The voice said, "That guy outside is dead."

"I should hope so."

"You must be some kind of a fucking maniac," the voice said, "what are you doing going around killing people?"

"It's an old habit," Wulff said. "Drop your guns and put your hands up, line up in front of the door. I'll open it now."

"I'm going to get killed," Vinelli said hoarsely on the floor, out of some terrible instinct. "I tell you, I'll get killed."

"Be calm," Wulff said. "Take the long view of the situation. In fifty years we'll all be dead." Except for me, he thought, I'm dead already. They killed me once and they can't do it twice. Only a dead man could go ahead to do what he was doing now.

He threw the bolt on the door, unzipped the chain. Then, Wulff delicately turned the knob, poised the door in position holding his rifle straight out, extended, like a quarterback on a statue of liberty play and then he pulled the door open, dodged to the side and came down on one knee.

What happened then happened very quickly. You could think things out, play them in your mind a hundred or a thousand times: meditate, consider, but when it came right down to the activity everything went much faster than you thought and that was why preparation was the key. A shot came over his head fast as soon as the door was opened. It passed through the place where he would have been if he had not dropped quickly and hit the wall above Vinelli. Vinelli screamed. At the same time he saw the three men, they were in various positions: see no evil, hear no evil, speak no evil, the three of them with guns in their hands desperately trying to locate him, the one in the middle already firing. He dropped that one with a spinning shot, then rolled, changing his position as a shot hit the floor, came out of the full roll to a position dead center behind the door and extending the revolver he shot another one of them, the one nearest to the door. This man hung in and out of the entrance staggering, gripping his stomach, blocking the third from a shot. If it hadn't been for this the third one would have got him because he was the cleverest, the one who had used the most foresight. He was using the corpse in the hallway as half a blind, tugging the dead tall man by the back of his collar to half an upright position so that he was shield and cover and he fired methodically, steadily at Wulff, the bullets being intercepted by the dying man in the entrance who died more quickly, collapsed, rolled away. With the man out of the way now there was a clear shot: one clear shot for each of them and Wulff got his in first. He leveled it in tightly, looking for the spot in mid-forehead where the man would die most quickly but his roll as he got the shot off misdirected it slightly and instead the shot lodged in the throat, dead on the jugular. The man's neck exploded, his own shot hit the ceiling and throwing blood into the air like a fountain. He fell into the carpeting in the absurd way a child draws sheets and blankets over his head, huddling, gathering. Wulff staggered to his feet, kicked the man in the entrance out of the doorway and bolted and chained it again.

So much for that.

Three against one; it must have looked very easy to them. On paper nothing could have been simpler: three men to take out one who was cornered in position but once again the troops were not at the proper level of competence. These were a much better group all in all, as you got closer to the center you got a higher level of man but nevertheless they were not very good. Wulff wiped his gun and put it away, looking back at Vinelli who was moaning. He had almost forgotten about him. The man had lapsed into unconsciousness; his face had turned bright yellow.

He thought about killing him but decided not to. Vinelli might prove himself useful later on. Even if he died, the *believing* outside that he was alive might be worth something as the situation developed.

Wulff put his revolver away and sat down in the chair behind Vinelli's desk. He let the emotions of the kill filter through him and he waited for their next move which would surely come. He had killed six men and badly injured another in only a couple of hours and he had just started.

Their move. Next customer.

Wulff waited for Las Vegas to come to him.

IX

Walker felt the thin edges of his control dissolving. Up until now he thought he had handled the situation adequately, better, perhaps, than anyone could have thought, certainly better than he would have expected of himself. He had gauged the matter correctly, not underestimated the menace which Wulff represented and had put the troops into action, handling all of this without panic and with more control than many would have thought. No one, whatever the outcome of this, could say that he had underestimated the danger or had not come to grips with it quickly and alertly, he was entitled if he said so himself to all the credit in the world ... but now Walker felt the control dissolving, the edges beginning to muddy. He was a man in over his head and he knew it. He had never had any trouble at all in admitting his limitations, that was how he had been able to survive so far, because he had never thought more of himself than he really was and he knew now that he was deep in. He did not know what to do.

Four dead men lying in the hall, Vinelli, badly hurt, locked up with this lunatic who seemed to be in control of the situation. Using Vinelli as hostage, Vinelli's suite as a center of operations he had the place under siege. Whatever name you wanted to give it that was the fact of the matter; he was in a strong position if not an impregnable one and short of emptying the hotel and literally trying to firebomb the room out, Walker did not know what to do. He could empty out the hotel, of course. But that would bring in police, it would bring in reporters, it would in short bring out a large attendance of exactly those kind of people who would be least likely to let Walker handle the situation in the way it had to be. No, that was impossible. Discard the idea. Forget it completely.

He had taken up the phone and put a call through to the room, immediately after reports of the murders had come to him. That made sense; he had to make contact with the enemy. Feeling like a corporal who had taken over command of a platoon because the captain, the lieutenants, the first sergeant, all the sergeants had been killed, with just that raging sense of helplessness, he put through the call and asked Wulff what he wanted. He came right out with it. There was just no point in fucking around with the guy, not when they were so deep in.

"What do I want?" Wulff had said, "I want your hotel, that's what I want. I want all of Las Vegas but I'll start with the hotel."

"You're going to get yourself killed," Walker had said, "you know that, don't you? That's the only thing you're going to get out of this. You can't get away with it."

"I'm doing all right," Wulff had said, "I'm doing fair. Ask Vinelli. He'd tell you how I'm doing if he could talk which unfortunately he can't."

"All right," Walker had said, his hand shaking, "tell me what you want. Tell me your terms."

"I don't really know. I don't know what my terms are yet because I'm not sure what I can get. I have a key to a locker at the airport which I want to use eventually but I won't be able to get to that for a while. You men are stupid, you know. Stone could have delivered all the time. You just didn't give him a chance."

"I don't know anything about that. I don't know what you're talking about."

"Sure you don't, Walker," the man had said almost cheerfully. He was incredible; the control seemed absolute. Walker had always it seemed moved in and around people who could do all the things that he admired under stress, this one had it too, you had to give it to him. "You're just the front man. They take your picture and you make the corporate statements. You don't dirty your hands with business, do you."

"You're going to get killed, Wulff."

"This may be," the man pointed out. "I may well get killed. What should I do, walk out of the room, turn myself in?"

"What's that ..."

"Let's face it, Walker," the man had said flatly, "let's face it and be done with it; the only way that I'm going to get out of this thing is if I do it my way, if I can carry it through to the end. If I try to deal with you I'll get my brains beaten out."

"Maybe I'll negotiate."

"You couldn't negotiate yourself to the men's room. No one's going to let you negotiate, they're going to tell you what to do and from a safe distance. No, Walker, let's face up to it. I've got to go through all the way now. It's too deep and too late."

"You'll get killed."

"You said that already," the man had said. "You said it and I believe you but you see no one can kill me, that was taken care of a long time ago," and he had hung up the phone leaving Walker there, choking on it and nothing to do but to go ahead. Because the man had been right.

Wulff had been right, he had judged the situation correctly, he had come back to Walker the only way that he could. Of course there was no way to negotiate out of this. Wulff couldn't trust him, Walker couldn't trust himself. He was no free agent, he was just a man left holding an impossible situation but pretty soon the orders would begin to come down and the orders would be for Armageddon and nothing to do but to go right ahead. Left to his own devices Walker thought that he just might have talked his way out of it at least to some kind of stand-pat. The man could have been guaranteed safe passage out of the hotel, he could have used Walker as hostage and at least he would have saved the Paradise if not the four men that had been killed. He would have turned himself over to Wulff as hostage; he thought that he could trust the man that far. It was not a matter of courage becoming a hostage, only the likelihood that things would even be worse the other way.

But now he could not do that. They would never stand for it back in New York; they would make sure that any deal he tried to make with this man was blown up, at their safe distance they would press buttons and fling bombs and what it amounted to was that the hotel was finished. Couldn't they see that? The only way out of this if any way at all was to do business, deal, try to hold onto the operation, but the way of conciliation would strike them only as weakness. There was nothing he could do that they would back up. He was only the front man, the hired hand. Pity unto the peacemakers; for in this as in all other generations they shall be cursed, Walker thought grimly and locked himself up in his office, waiting for the New York call that would surely come within a matter of minutes. They had observers all over the place; by now a telephone council rigged in candy store booths all over the city was probably being constructed.

Pity unto the peacemakers. Walker thought of his life, of its fruits, of where he had come from and what he had been and in a way it was a shame to give it up because it was not that bad. He had the women, he had money, he even had a certain amount of mobility as long as he made sure to clear his destinations first and keep in constant touch with them. It wasn't a bad outcome for a man who had crawled out of the fringes of the music business in the fifties, more dead than alive, smashed up and broken, two ruined marriages behind him and almost nowhere to go. He had always had contacts though and he had been able to make an appearance. That was what had saved him. Saved him for this, however? Well, that was another thought. That was another thought altogether. You just never knew where you would end up, did you? It was a wheel and it spun.

He did something that he had not done for a while; he went to the wall safe at the corner of his room and hit the combination, reached inside and took out a small, pure white deck of heroin. He had never really had the habit, this business about one snort of horse and you were theirs for life was so much bullshit—shit, half of café society was on it every now and then and no one was wandering around the streets looking for a fix—he took it occasionally, that was all, for medical purposes really. The last time that he had touched horse—"horse" was a genteel fifties term for it, well that had been his generation, do him something—had had to be a couple of months ago ... but he needed some now. He needed something, that was for sure and it might do him some good. Delicately, Walker extracted the deck, used a nail file to wedge off a tiny white corner and dropped these grains on a sheet of notepaper. He restored the deck to the safe then, locked it in once more and set the grains on the paper until they were centered, then he folded the paper over, brought it very carefully to his nostrils and with economy of effort sniffed it in.

The poorest way to take horse, of course ... it took longer to hit the bloodstream, little grains of it got caught in the cilia of the nose and were lost completely, the entire effect was diluted ... but still, back in the fifties, that was the way the genteel folk took it. Serious users mainlined, people who could take or leave it (they thought) would sniff and none of the modern-day intricacies applied. Nowadays they tasted it, dissolved it, drank it, injected it, smoked it, found as many ways of putting heroin into their system as men could figure out a way to stick their cocks into a woman. The fifties were a better time, Walker thought, crumpling the paper and putting it into a wastebasket, you knew where you stood then. If you didn't use the needle you weren't an addict and that was all there was to it. You were being social. You were taking a high.

He felt the rush overtake him, feebler by far than mainlining he knew but still like nothing else he had ever had. Liquor couldn't touch it for force, the soft drugs, whatever the potheads were saying, lacked any of the concentration and focus, the sheer *disconnection* which smack—now that was a better term, there was a sixties term all the way, *smack,* if he kept it up he would get to *shit* and that was pre-seventies but fuck that—could give you. He felt the stuff hitting his system in little odd granules and spurts of energy; it burbled through the nerve endings and Walker at least momentarily began to feel not like the hounded figurehead owner of a hotel-casino that was going to burn but like a man of substance who did not have to take shit because he had achieved a position in the world where no one, nothing except death could touch him ... and if you could take death with horse in your system, well then you could beat that too. Heroin was a line of defense against mortality; it didn't hurt so much, had no hold on you if you simply didn't care and right now Walker did not care. He knew that sniffing at this time was probably, objectively speaking, not the wisest move he could have made but he did not care. He simply did not care. Nothing mattered. He picked up the phone again, put it on the house intercom line and dove into

Vinelli's room. The big New York clown picked it right up as Walker knew he would. He must have been thinking too, sitting in a room next to a dying man with four corpses in the hallway beginning to realize what he was taking on but he did not have horse to beat it with. No, he was an ex-New York City narco this one; they traded in it all right but they sure as hell didn't use it. Strait-laced. "You're a dead man, you know," he said to Wulff.

"So are you. So are you all."

"We can rush that room and take you out. We can tear-gas you out."

"Try it," the voice said, "come on, I'm waiting."

"You'll never get out of here alive."

"I'm not alive now."

"You don't give a damn, do you?" Walker said, heroin or not feeling rage. "You just don't give a good godamn."

"No I do not. I absolutely do not."

"You're crazy."

"There are people who've said that."

"We're going to get in there and take you out of the place, Wulff."

"I'm waiting," the man said, "believe me, I'm waiting for just that."

"I mean it," Walker said. "I really mean it."

"You'll be the man who killed Vinelli," the clown said, "that's how you'll be marked up on the keno charts. Do you really want to be remembered that way?"

"Fuck you," Walker said. The conversation was all wrong. *He* was in control now. Why didn't the fucker realize that? "I'll kill you," he said.

"I'm waiting," the man said with cold precision. Almost offhandedly. "I'm waiting for anything you have to do, Walker."

"You can't get away with this."

"I think you're starting to repeat yourself," the man said and hung up, leaving Walker holding a dead phone, feeling the little crystals stirring within him to a newer, more menacing beat. He put the phone down slowly, beginning to feel the high turning rancid within him, beginning to feel the whole edge of that high turn ninety degrees and cut against him. He was a fool, that was all he was. He was a fool and now he had done the most dangerous thing of all, he had exposed himself to the enemy. He had made his plans visible. There was no way that you could do that kind of thing and get away with it. If Walker had learned one thing in years here it was to keep his mouth shut, and now all of it was blown.

He felt a self-loathing more profound than any he had known before. Part of it was the panic, another part was the high, cutting back on him the other way. He hung up the phone, sat stupidly in the chair, feeling his body go slack under him. That was the trouble with horse; you couldn't count on it. The closest you could come to it in alcohol was gin. One moment you would be feeling pretty good, very much in control of a situation, prosperous and content and in the next things would shift and you would see them in an entirely different way so that all you knew was a staggering futility. He knew it now. He was conscious of his respiration, the fluttering of his eyelids, all of the hundred, small unconscious acts which the body committed every moment merely to sustain the processes of life. He hated himself. He had been close to that knowledge for a long time and now it was clear. He was a hateful, loathsome man.

Someone was trying the doorknob of his locked office. Walker looked at it incuriously. The knob turned, squirmed around, returned to rest. He had, of course, taken the precaution of locking himself in. That made sense. The knob turned again and there was a light tapping. He said nothing. Eventually whoever it was would become bored and go away, leave him to himself again. Then he would have to figure out what to do. He did not know what to do.

There was the sound of a key in the lock and with a whisper, like a girl's lips opening for a kiss, the lock parted. The door slid open and a man came through. Walker found himself looking at a man who he had never seen before and at the same time he thought that he knew this man as well as he would ever know anyone. He had seen this face in a hundred dreams, conjured it up on a thousand nights, every outline and detail of this face, and now it was before him. His guest walked toward him quickly, lightly, balancing himself gracefully on the balls of his feet, an ex-athlete perhaps, unostentatiously dressed, somewhere in his forties with a cold, compressed face but these were merely the trappings, the outer part of the man who Walker had seen and dreamed. He clamped his hands on the top of the desk feeling them go cold and then colder against the wood. The man looked at him for a long time, his eyes seeming to take in the little scattered grains of heroin which Walker had not even noticed leaving traces on the desk, the decor of the office, the set of Walker's eyeballs as they floated in a face that seemed to have turned to water. He put his hands on hips and looked at Walker coldly. Walker felt his heart scrambling away at the walls of his body like a scared little animal in a cage.

"You silly son of a bitch," the man said. "You really fucked it up this time."

Walker was speechless. He found his hand involuntarily brushing at the grains on his desk, trying to sweep them into the carpet. The man looked at this and a smile worked its way slowly, across his face. It was a terrible thing to see, that smile and Walker was suddenly unable to move his hand anymore. The man had trapped it. Now he leaned on the wrist slowly, hitting a pressure point with his thumb and Walker felt the paralysis begin to work its way, stalking, up his arm. He almost screamed then but looking at the man's face he saw that that would do no good. This man liked screaming.

"You're picture looks all right in the papers," the man said, "and you do all right fucking starlets but you want to know something Walker? You really want to know something? You're just a lot of shit."

Walker gasped. His arm was dead on him now. Yet he could not struggle against this man. He knew, whatever else, that struggle would be worse.

"Just a lot of shit," the man said quietly, almost as if he were amusing.

He released the grip and Walker's arm fell like stone across his lap, hitting him in the groin, hurting him. The arm felt nothing.

"And a godamned junkie," the man said, the smile now fully on his face. "Don't you know that you're supposed to keep business separate?"

He reached into the pocket of an oversize tan jacket and took out the largest revolver that Walker had ever seen. Walker could do nothing but look at it. It was too late to run and nowhere to run to. Somehow, he supposed that he had played out this scene in dreams a hundred times. It always ended this way. It would have to. There was no other way, and fuck all the good times, that it could have ever ended.

"You fuck up everything," the man said and shot Walker in the teeth.

Dying across the desk, Walker's last thought was that he probably agreed with him. Halfway. Not *fuck*. Not present tense. *Fucked*. Past. He was done.

Vinelli slipped in and out of coma like a man being washed by waves on the beach. The comas were not too bad, like being packed in mud and ooze with the smell of blood, but the dreams were twisted and not too terrible. But coming out of coma was always bad; again and again he relived the moment when the man had shot him. Stupid. He had been stupid. He had underestimated the son of a bitch. Nothing like this had ever happened to him in his life; you just did not get where he had gotten by underestimating people and yet he had gone off the track on this one. Badly. The bastard had been much more dangerous than Vinelli had thought and now it was too late to retrieve the moment and handle it the right way. How could he have been so stupid? Had Kansas City, the lessons he had learned both in the field and observing what was happening to the others, hadn't that taught him everything he needed to know? Hadn't they taught him respect? But it was too late for any of that now. Fat and happy and stupid. That was what Vegas did to the best of them. He was just another fucking loser. Then he would slip into coma again for thirty-second periods that felt like hours and come out of it remembering nothing, piecing it together all again. Everytime it was the same. Stupid. He had underestimated the man. You simply did not underestimate people and make it all the way through to the end. He had been stupid. Fat and happy. Vegas did that to you. Stupid.

Coming out of it one time he felt clearer than he had since he had been shot and, turning his head toward the window, saw the man. The man was working over in a corner, doing something with wiring. He was wrapping a long silvery set of wires to something that he was cupping in his hand. Alongside him was an open attaché case, the same case that the fucker had carried into the room, the same one that surveillance said had been with him when he came into the casino. He must have lived with that case. Check it back and he had probably left New York with it. Stupid. They had been stupid.

The man looked toward him and Vinelli quickly turned his head but it was too late. The man had seen him looking, and now the effort of turning rapidly sent pain working through his leg again, some of the worst pain he had felt yet and he screamed with it. He almost lapsed back into coma then, but the pain held him in place, the pain bound him into the room as if with ropes. Then Wulff was over from the corner, looking at him, hands on his hips in an appraising stance. Apparently having decided that Vinelli was in no position to preoccupy him he went back to the corner and resumed work. He did not care then whether Vinelli saw and for Vinelli this was the last assurance he needed. Not that he had thought differently anyway. He was never going to get out of this room alive. He would never see the sky again unless this man drew the curtains and let him look at it.

"You're crazy," he said yet again. His voice sounded surprisingly controlled. The pain was localized now in his leg; the rest of him was weak and empty but capable of functioning. Not a mortal wound at all then, it had probably clotted on him. Given reasonable medical care, he would walk out of the hospital in a week and go back to work. Well. That option was closed.

"I guess so," the man said, not turning his head. Having evaluated Vinelli, Wulff seemed to have lost all interest in him. He was fully concentrating on his work. A true professional.

"You're going to dynamite this fucking place out, aren't you?" Vinelli said almost conversationally. Now that he could do nothing to stop it, it was as if it was totally outside of him, happening to other people in a different city and he could look at the thing objectively.

"I might do that," Wulff said.

"You've got dynamite and fuses and wires in there, haven't you? You're probably working off a couple of monster grenades."

"Could be," Wulff said, "could be."

"What's the point?" Vinelli said. "You blow up the fucking place we'll all be killed."

"Not necessarily. *You* may be but I've got a chance. Anyway," Wulff said in that conversational tone, his hands not breaking rhythm. "What's the difference? I've got no other chance anyway."

"You're going to kill a lot of people."

The man seemed to shrug. "That's my problem," he said.

"There are close to a thousand people in that casino, playing day and night. The nightclub, the lounges. The rooms. The casino's an open area, there's nothing to take the shock there. You could kill hundreds."

"That would be a damned shame, wouldn't it?" the man said. He looped some wire in a final knot, put down what appeared to be one of the grenades with an *ah!* of satisfaction and picked up the other one. "And of course you've got the interest of innocent people at heart, don't you?"

"They won't bargain," Vinelli said hoarsely. "They fucking won't bargain."

"What does that mean?"

"If you think you can blackmail them into giving you safe passage by threatening to blow it up it won't work," Vinelli said. "Never bargain and never submit to blackmail. *Use* blackmail of course, use it all the time, but never let it turn the other way because that's a sign of weakness. You can't show weakness. They'll turn it down anytime. They'll never let you out of here."

"We'll see," Wulff said. "We'll just see."

"You want to get out of here?" Vinelli said hoarsely, "*I'll* get you out of here. You don't have to blow up the fucking place to do it, and you'll just get killed in the explosion anyway. I can get you out."

"Not interested."

"You just want to get out, don't you?" Vinelli said. Negotiation was making him feel a little stronger. He still could not move, but his mind was clear and with the pain localized, shoved away to his left side below the waist he could begin to think with a little of the old cunning again. Unless the guy came over and kicked him in the leg ... that was a possibility.

"I'll get out," Wulff said. "Don't you worry about that." He finished turning wire again, looked at what was in his hands, shook his head and unwound it to try a different angle. An explosives expert. A fucking explosives expert too. How were you going to deal with someone like this? Didn't any of them know what they were up against? Well, Vinelli thought, *he* hadn't, and that was why he was on the floor.

"There are closed passageways," Vinelli said, "right down the hallway, sealed off which lead directly to the outside. You don't think they'd build a hotel without that kind of safety margin, now do you? I can get you out through one of them. But you've got to get *me* out too. I'll be your hostage and you can use my car and dump me at a hospital and that'll be the end of it. No one will even know you're out if we handle it right. I don't give a shit what you do after that, it's not my affair. You can take my car. It's a Cadillac in pretty good shape, you should be able to push it cross-country in a day, day and a half if you really want to push it."

The man shook his head. "No," he said, "we're not going to do it that way. You really don't understand what I'm after, do you Vinelli?"

"No," he said, "no I really do not."

"That's your trouble. You look at me in terms of your own motives, your own reasons. What you think you would do in my position. But it's not that way at all. I'm going to destroy the business, Vinelli. I'm going to blow the whole fucking thing up. I'm not looking for skirmishes and I'm not trying to make a few million dollars myself and get out. What I'm out to do is to put you and everybody else out of the business."

"Then you're crazy," Vinelli said again, "if you think you can touch this, that a hundred of you can touch it you're out of your fucking mind. It's too big for anyone to break down."

"That's what they tell me. But we'll see. I did pretty well in San Francisco, starting from scratch."

"They don't know what the fuck they're doing in San Francisco," Vinelli said, "that's a marginal operation."

"And Boston?"

"I don't know anything about Boston."

"How about New York?"

"You're dealing with New York. That's exactly what you're dealing with right now. The orders are coming out of there by this time, and they'll eat you up and burn you out."

"I did pretty well in New York," the man said softly. "The show opened in New York."

Vinelli stretched slowly, felt the pain beginning in his leg again but it was better this time: gangrene was setting in or at least something anesthetizing and it was becoming progressively sealed off from him. He could live with the pain now. He could even think like the man he knew he was. "Kill me," he said to Wulff and he meant it. "Kill me then."

The man looked up from his work, for the first time really engaged. "Why?" he said. "You're feeling better now, I can tell. Survival instinct; you think you might hang in through this after all. So why should I kill you?"

Vinelli said honestly, "Because I don't want to be around if it just happens that you're right. Because if you bring this off, whatever the fuck you're trying to do, I don't want it to be the man in whose place it happened. It wouldn't go well for me."

"Ah," the man said, turning back to his work. "Well, if I've got no chance as you say there's really nothing to worry about now is there? You'll come out of this a hero yet, Vinelli. Just keep on hoping."

Vinelli said nothing more. What he believed now and always was that you talked when you had business to transact, something to work out, some definite purpose in mind and otherwise you didn't talk at all. Silence made more sense than horseshit conversation. He looked up at the ceiling and closed his eyes expecting to go into coma again, but his frame held. He was still in the room. He would not get any worse for a good long time now and then, eventually, the infection would go out of control, and he would convulse and die. But that might be hours away. Maybe days.

He listened to the whisking sound of the man setting up his devices and finally when that sound stopped—it might have been five or fifty minutes, you lost all sense of time with your eyes closed. Vinelli had no internal sense of ebb and flow to orient him, he had always been a man who worked in terms of *events*. He opened his eyes again and looked at him. The man looked back. He seemed calm, utterly relaxed, totally at peace with himself. He sat in an armchair, breathing evenly, looking at the ceiling.

"Well?" Vinelli said, "what now?"

"What now?" Martin Wulff said. "What now?" He stood, went over to the sofa, got a pillow and almost tenderly tucked it under Vinelli's head to make him more comfortable, being careful not to move the man. "What do you think what now? Now we wait."

Silently, they waited.

XI

Maybe the metaphysical theories about gamblers and gambling are true after all—although the house does not believe this and in fact will send a chartered plane anywhere, anytime, to pick up a load of metaphysical gamblers—because sometime around ten that evening the casino began to empty, not in any purposeful fashion but rather in small clots and clumps of people. The roulette tables emptying first when black hit consecutively ten times, a sequence which mathematically occurs only one in half a million series' of ten turns or more. But half a million or not was sufficient in this instance to send a couple of progressive plungers out with close to a hundred thousand dollars apiece while the remainder of the players, most of them experts who had simply come back harder and harder on red were wiped out. A certain air of discouragement spread out from the roulette table after all of this, two one hundred thousand dollar winners hardly being sufficient to raise the spirits of fifty others and the empty space must have become noticeable through the floor. There is nothing like an empty space to discourage gamblers. A coffin in the gaming area could not have had a more dramatic effect. Surely if something was wrong with the roulette wheels, chasing all of these people away then something must be wrong with the craps too, with the blackjack, with the chemin de fer ... even the slotmachine players caught the sense of gloom and dispersion in the area and almost all of them, except for those who seemed to be permanently locked into the machines by gout, wandered out of the casino looking for bigger crowds and more hope further down the strip. The nightclubs had good crowds, of course, they always did, but the crowds were not exceptional, much of them was composed of people who drifted in from the casino on impulse ... and the casino was down to one-quarter capacity or even a little less than that. Even the guests, huddled, fucking or sedated in their rooms, must have caught the odors which drifted upwards from the casino because a surprisingly large number checked out that evening, others wandering down to look for action were dismayed by the sight of the casino which when opened up could have doubled for smoke and size with an enormous graveyard filled with mourning potheads ... and decided that they would take their action somewhere else. All in all, by midnight, the Paradise was functioning at something less than one-tenth of its true capacity downstairs, something which had not happened in ten years. Even when the snows hit Nevada which they did occasionally it had not been as disastrous as this. Croupiers, blackjack dealers, craps housemen looked at one another across the empty spaces of the room; cigarette and drink girls conferred in the corridors and then went over to the housemen and dealers for a little bit of negotiated action. Discipline, in short, seemed to be very close to breaking down. There had just never been anything like it. No one connected it to anything which was going on upstairs, of course. Why should they? Nothing in the hotel had anything to do with anything else; that was one of the selling points of Las Vegas. You could establish your own world in perfect isolation and integrity and have absolutely no relationship to the outside; this is what they were selling and if that ever broke down, if the separate fates became meshed they were in deep trouble. It was just a bad night, that was all. They would always look on it, right up to the end, as being one of those bad nights which very occasionally happens. Black can come up ten times sequentially in roulette too.

On the upper level, in the business and residential suite which had been Sam Walker's, they could not have cared less, of course. They did not know what was going on down there and it did not matter to any of them. All night they had been drifting in alone and in pairs, the tight sullen men from New York, a couple from the Midwest, one from Cicchini's old turf in Boston which was already up for grabs, a couple of experts in from San Diego who had been on the freighter the night that Wulff blew it up and were in a position to give some firsthand advice, if not any real solution. Now, near midnight, the room was filled with twenty-five to thirty men, stretched out easily on the couches, a couple perched over the desk, more filtering in all the time from the side-rooms where they had been pretty heavily into the whiskey.

Lazzara, the man who had killed Walker, decided early on to let them get into the whiskey. This was a tough crowd, they were going to be rough to handle any way you looked at it, cutting them off from liquor would make them even uglier. The best thing to do was to let them at the liquor early, as soon as they came in as a matter of fact, and hope that the liquor would blunt them down a little, take some kind of edge off them. Lazzara had been occupied with other things; he was certainly not going to entertain the men of the council as they came in. He was on the phone to New York, he had the problem of disposing of Walker's body (by a side-exit right into an unmarked limousine in a box and straight out into the desert, this was one of Walker's goddamned exits that the press was not going to cover), and mostly he had the problem of framing exactly what he was going to say, what tack he could take that they would both believe and follow. This was a tough crowd, all right, it might well be the toughest crowd that had ever been put together in one room at the same time, and he was going to need all the preparation that he could get.

The thing was that they had really bought it this time. This time they were in almost over their heads, and yet the one way to blow the council up at the start was to take that tack, let them know exactly what had happened. They had been in an increasingly exposed position for years and years, Lazzara had warned them of this back in the East seeing it long before they did—that the trouble with going legitimate and putting the money on top of the ground was that any fool could walk in and try to take it—but no one was going to listen. Las Vegas looked like the sweetest racket which any of them had ever found. It looked good, no question about it; there was no limit to the take and all of it could be declared as long as taxes were paid. But how long did they think that it would last? How long until someone or a lot of people went for the visible goodies that the organization had protected for so long by keeping them subterranean? Well, there was just no way to answer a question like that, and Lazzara was not going to try. He was not a thinker, he was a man who performed. That was why he had been rushed out of New York, private plane, to what was obviously a building crisis-center, that was why the situation had been put into his hands, win or lose, full responsibility and no approval necessary for his decisions, whatever they were. He might hang, indeed he might hang ... but he would hang very high.

He let them drift in and drink then and finally at around midnight when he decided that there was nothing to gain by letting the preparations drag on further, he called them to order. A gavel and everything, the works, a formal meeting. These types would be impressed by formality if nothing else. Downstairs he knew that the guy was hanging in there, hanging tight just like Lazzara was but he was pretty sure that there were a few hours' margin. The man was waiting for them to come to him. That was obvious. He had all the time in the world, he was holed up in there with Vinelli, he had heat and running water and maybe a bottle of Vinelli's booze and there was no way that he was going to be starved out but then again he had enough there that he was not in any hurry which gave them some operating margin. It worked both ways. Everything worked both ways, in the long run, if you took that kind of view.

Lazzara told them what was going on. He laid it on the line for them, right up through the crooked New York lieutenant who had come to Vinelli for hiding but turned out to have been bluffing which was the reason, probably, that Vinelli had killed him. Killing Stone was dumb of course, the lieutenant might have been worth something to them as negotiating material—but then Vinelli had gotten his too. He asked for suggestions.

Someone from San Francisco, naturally it would be San Francisco, asked why they couldn't just go into Vinelli's room, bomb out the place and take this Wulff by force. Vinelli was probably dead anyway, they certainly had to figure that and even if he wasn't, he was dead in their calculations. What did they have to lose? This one was probably the youngest in the room, a sick-looking kid in his late twenties who had probably gotten into the operation two weeks ago and was now heading it up. That was just about the way that Wulff had left things in San Francisco.

"Because it won't fucking work," Lazzara said, skipping the amenities, "you think we're dealing with some clown here, you schmuck? This Wulff is an explosives man; he hit town with armament. He's locked up in there with enough shit to blow this place into the desert, and you can bet that he's got it triggered. If we rush him he's going to hit the key."

"Are you sure of that though?" San Francisco said. His face had become mottled. Lazzara wanted to take out his gun and shoot him, but that was not the way you did things nowadays. The organization had changed in the last ten years. Still, every now and then ...

"No," Lazzara said carefully, "I'm not sure of that. I'm not a hundred percent sure, nothing's a hundred percent in this world or out of it except that you're dead eventually, but the odds aren't good. The odds are that he's got it rigged up. Do *you* want to go into that room? Do you want to break in and face him on the gamble that he hasn't got a setup? If so," he said, taking out his gun after all and handing it to San Francisco with a slow, exaggerated gesture, "be my guest."

The kid said nothing. He huddled in his chair, squirmed around. Others looked at him and several with an air of disgust got up and began to walk around the room in aimless little circles. Lazzara looked out on them. They were probably as representative a group as you could pull together on short notice, at least every part of the country had a voice here, but they didn't know what the hell to do either. Nobody did. That was the trouble.

"I'm open for suggestions," he said quietly. He looked out on them. No one said anything for quite a while, and then a short man from Chicago stood holding a cigar with curious formality.

"There's only one thing I see," he said, "we clear the hotel and call the cops. Make it a police matter. If it blows up it blows up in their face."

"What do we tell the cops?"

"That we got a fucking madman in the place. We ain't the first who've had that, are we? Maybe he dropped twenty grand in the casino or something. Maybe he's got a thing against women and his wife deserted him or some hooker couldn't make him come. What do we care? At least we can get off the hook."

"Ah," Lazzara said, "we can get off the hook. What then? Suppose the cops even decide to rush the room. You know cops these days aren't that stupid, our friend there is an ex-cop himself, which says something about the PD, doesn't it? But assume that they decide, okay. They rush the room, and the fucking joint gets blown up. Not on you or me, of course, we're out in the desert or someplace, trekking it. But there are one hell of a lot of dead cops lying around, aren't there? They'll be bouncing off the scaffolding like bowling balls."

"Maybe so," the short man said. He put the cigar into his mouth and puffed to show how calm and controlled he was and how unmenaced by Lazzara. It didn't work. His hand trembled. "All right!" he said, "so what? So we're off the hook, aren't we? We get rid of the son-of-a-bitch and we end the blackmail. Remember, we don't even know what he's going for."

"Yes we do," Lazzara said, "we have a pretty good idea what he's going for, he's going to try and finish us off but that's long-range, that's neither here nor there. Yeah, sure, we get rid of the son of a bitch and a lot of cops besides." He paused and let them think about that for a while. "What do you think that does for public relations?" he said.

"Who cares?"

"Who cares!" Lazzara said, "you tell *me* who cares? There's about twenty years invested in this town, twenty years of hard work, planning, cultivation of a lot of friends to say nothing of about five hundred million dollars in capital overhead. Where are we going to stand, how are we going to look if the hotel comes down on half the fucking police force?"

The man from Chicago tried another weak puff on the cigar, failed completely and began to choke. He clutched at his chest in a fainting way, like a man swooning or having a heart attack. Laughter went through the room, although not of a pleasant, relaxed sort. Well, it was a break, anyway. "Don't laugh at him!" Lazzara said and slammed the gavel, "at least he's raising the fucking questions which is more than can be said of the rest of you clowns. These are the questions which have got to be answered, which have got to be considered before we decide to do anything." He looked at the man from Chicago, nodded approvingly and the man seemed to take heart from this, tried a slightly more energetic puff on his cigar, even wafted a cloud of smoke or two.

"All right," Chicago said, "all right, my question is why do we have to be tied to it? Why can't it be some madman up there who got pissed off at the casino or gambling or his wife or cops or something and decided to blow up the joint? It doesn't have to come out, does it? Besides, I don't believe half of this Wulff stuff anyway. I don't think the guy's for real."

"He's for real," San Francisco said and everybody looked at him. "You ask me if he's real."

"All right!" Chicago screamed, "so he's real but if he's dead he's not so real, and then maybe nobody gets the answer! What's the difference? Answer the question!"

"All right," Lazzara said, hitting the gavel once, gently, and they all quivered, "I'll answer the question. The question is why it has to come out who he is or what they've walked into after the job is done and maybe in all the excitement nobody ever finds out. Or then again, here is a point you didn't bring up, Chicago, even if they do find out they can't be sure that *we* knew who he was. As far as we're concerned he was just a menace to public health. But that won't work, and I'll tell you why too. It's *all* going to come out. It's come out already." He paused, waited on this. "The cops know exactly who he is and what we're going through," he said. "Vinelli made some calls, you see."

The room broke up. Chairs moved, shouts, curses, the pacers who had been wildly working the walls through the meeting stopped cold while others bolted out of the chairs to come toward Lazzara. He had to use the gavel several times, but finally he got a kind of stricken quiet. "It won't work you see," he said, "the world's all over on this one. Vinelli made no secret of what was going on and even before the guy came he warned local authorities. Everybody's got his picture. They know exactly who he is and do you know something? I don't think they want any part of him."

They took their time, thinking about that. Lazzara let them think; it had to be understood by them all the way. "So you see," he said, "we're in a bad position here."

"All right," someone said from the rear obscured by bodies. One of the pacers; Lazzara could not quite make him out. "So leave him sit there. Leave him with Vinelli and his explosives. What the fuck can he do? Eventually he'll get tired and go away."

"Will he?"

"He's got to."

"No he doesn't," Lazzara said, "I mean he may want to go away, but this man is not stupid. A lot of people got into trouble or are dead now because they thought that he was stupid. He isn't at all. He's smarter than most of us. He's not going to give up and go away because he knows that we won't let him. Eventually if he goes out he's going to get grabbed. He knows that he's on our turf and if he can't negotiate his way out he's going to get killed. So he'll stay put."

"So let him negotiate his way out!"

"No way," Lazzara said, and then with enormous patience he put the gavel aside, leaned both hands on the table and catching the man full-faced—a heavy, confused-looking man, probably another of Cicchini's abandoned troops—"and you know why? because he hasn't even given his demands. We don't know what his demands *are,* and that's probably because he doesn't have any demands at all. He's just holed down there with Vinelli, you see, he's already killed at least seven men that we know about, and when he's good and ready he'll go on to the next stage."

"Which is what? Is he a one-man suicide squad?"

"I doubt it," Lazzara said. "I don't think that he wants to get himself killed if he can help it. He doesn't *mind* the idea of getting killed as far as we can figure out his methods but he's not looking for it either. No, he's just looking for a spot and that spot is probably going to get this hotel blown up. Maybe when we're in it. Maybe right now for all we know. It would be a good time, wouldn't it?"

They didn't like that. Throughout the room, men looked at one another frantically, some of them moving instinctively toward the door. At the back someone began to curse Lazzara, the words were hard to make out but the meaning was clear: what kind of a crazy sonofabitch would call a setup like this, run such a risk? Did he want to get them all killed? "No," Lazzara said, "I don't want to get us all killed. I want to save our ass. I think we've got a little margin, not much, but a little bit, because he's still waiting on his moves and because, essentially, he'd prefer us to come to him. He won't want to come to us unless his hand is forced or some time-limit he's set up in his own mind expires."

Now was the hard part. Nothing to do but go ahead. He picked up the gavel, hefted it, waited against the explosion. "Okay," he said, "we've reviewed the situation, and I think that it is clear to all of us where we stand. We've got a man down there with enough equipment to blow us up at will. He's probably got it rigged. We can't call in the cops because they won't come and if they do we can't take the risk of what would happen if it wipes them out. We can't wait him out because he's got some kind of time-limit in his mind after which he'll move first and we're just signing our own suicide note if we let him do it. We can't negotiate with him because as far as we know there's nothing to negotiate."

Lazzara took a deep breath. "So we know what we've got to do," he said.

"What?" someone said, "what do we do?"

"Isn't it obvious?" Lazzara said, "if the cops won't do it, and we can't wait him out, and he won't negotiate, then we've got to do the job ourselves if we want to save this fucking hotel. Maybe if we want to save

Vegas.

"Gentlemen," he said, "this is no discussion meeting. This is a company maneuver. You're all recruited for the operation, crack troops of the organization so to speak and *you* gentlemen, and me of course in a command position, *we* are going to go in and get that son-of-a-bitch out of here."

And then he let them explode.

XII

Wulff knew the time of waiting was coming to an end. It was more than a feeling; it was a deep certainty, they had waited just about as long as they would if they were going to make a concerted, well-planned attack and within the next half an hour they would strike. The first danger point was almost immediately after he had secured the room; a hasty, impulsive follow-up and of course the three hoods had come up just that way; the second danger point was a larger group which might have come after him on the heels of those three, but that was where they had deviated from panic for the first time. They had backed off, giving him all the opportunity in the world to set up the equipment. But then again the backing off had been ominous because it showed that they were trying to pick their spots, that they were trying to figure this situation out in a disciplined manner and that meant in the long-run more trouble than him. A couple of hours, he figured then. After a couple of hours they would have had their meetings, the intercontinental lines would have been filled with their discussions, a party would probably have been put together and then they would come after him. Whether they would clear the hotel or not was an open question. It could go either way. It would be humane to clear the hotel, but then they weren't so interested in being humane. They were interested in protecting an investment which he menaced and hotel-clearing was very poor practice, generally speaking. People might get the idea that the hotel was unsafe. They might even take to leaving and never coming back again.

But all of that was behind him now; the real action was beginning. Wulff had the old combat feel. There had been nothing out of Vinelli for a long time, the man had lapsed now into a heavy doze, not quite a coma but not a real sleep either, lying on the floor. If he awoke he was bound to be feverish and disconnected. Wulff felt sorry about that in a way because Vinelli, in certain fashion, had been the best of those that he had run up against, and he hated to lose his company. The man was a realist and had interesting things to say and probably if he could have probed Vinelli he would have learned a good deal more. Pity that he had shot the man so deeply and painfully; if he had it to do over again he would have settled for a foot or hip. But that was neither here nor there of course, Vinelli was out of the picture and out of all reasonable accounting. He could not save the man nor did he even want to. All that he could hope to do when the real pressure began was that they wouldn't come down on the room too hard for the sake of Vinelli, that they would take a chance on his being alive and take that into calculation. Probably they wouldn't, however. No one was valuable enough for the wolves of the organization to show mercy.

So he sat there, huddled over his explosives and he waited but after a time the waiting got monotonous even for him and he decided that he wanted to make a phone call. He considered calling Williams just to let him know what he was up to and what an interesting situation Vegas had mushroomed into but he decided against that. The phones were tapped, they were probably linked into him now with pliers and it would be very very bad to give them a lead on Williams. Williams was too valuable to him, too dangerous to them, and if they got a tracer on it Williams would be over his head. That would not be fair to the man, although, Wulff thought wryly, it would pay him back in kind for what Williams had done to him. Who was the tool? Who the agent? He had thought about that for the last day or so without coming to any real conclusion. It could have gone either way of course. Call it a question of mutual use maybe and leave it go at that. But it was interesting.

No, he would not call Williams; he could not do it to the rookie. But he found that he wanted to call someone else so strongly that he would take the risk: take it for her and for him together. He wanted to speak to Tamara, the hippie girl who he had met in San Francisco, the girl he had met in amphetamine jag and had murdered to save, had coaxed through, had slept with for one night and had then sent back to her parents with a prayer that this time she would stay and that someday he might see her again. Although he doubted it. The girl had given him the first spate of feeling he had had since Marie Calvante had died. She had been the first thing to convince him that feeling was not necessarily over and that had been exciting but terribly dangerous too because feeling raised you to a new level of possibility ... but he did not want to go into that now, he only knew that simply and terribly he wanted to talk to her. They had the phones lined in: that was all right. It was doubtful that there would be anything to happen to her because of the call. If he survived this they certainly would be afraid to go at her because of the possibility of retaliation and if he did not survive ... what would she matter? She would be an old friend of a dead menace.

He knew her parents' address by heart although he had heard it only once to tell the cab driver into whose car he had committed her and he gave that address to the information operator in Sausalito; she gave him a number and that sounded right too so without thinking about it further he put the call through. There were, come to think of it, no clicks or buzzes on the line. There was a chance then that they weren't tapping after all. Come to think of it, it would make sense that Vinelli's phone would be rigged to be impermeable to tap. Yes, when he thought about it that was the most likely possibility of all and the guilt fell away from him as he heard the phone ring. He knew now, was willing to admit, how badly he wanted to talk to her.

A woman got on and he asked for Tamara, then remembered, catching himself, that her name was not Tamara, that was only what she had traveled under in the subsociety she had bounced through and asked for Louise. The woman asked who was calling and Wulff said that it was an old friend and please hurry and the woman said she didn't know if she could take that, she would really need some better identification. Wulff said to her without thinking about it that she was no godamned switchboard operator and he was no job-applicant and if she didn't get her daughter on the phone right now both he daughter and she might regret it. The woman gasped and threw the phone down. For a time he thought that she had simply hung up on him—and he would have let it go, he really would have because now as he thought about it for the first time he did not know how sane this impulse was—but she had not hung up, only wandered away and then a girl's voice came on. Wulff looked at his watch and realized that it was three o'clock in Sausalito. Yes, that would make anyone a little testy he thought and forgave her mother a little.

"Who is this?" the girl said.

"Tamara?"

"This is not Tamara," she said, but with a little intake of breath. "My name is Louise. I am not ..."

"This is Martin Wulff, Tamara."

There was another intake of breath, much louder this time and then the girl's voice changed. "Martin?" she said. "This is you, Martin?"

"It's me," he said. "It's me all right. I see you got home all right."

"Yes," she said, "I did. I've been home for a month. Has it been a month? It's hard to believe ... my God, it's three in the morning. I've been sleeping. I was ..."

"I'm sorry," he said. "I forgot the time. I wanted to talk to you."

"It's all right," she said. Her voice was starting to come through to him now. It was the old voice, unmistakably Tamara and he found, huddled over the phone that he had a slight erection and this pleased him for some reason even if it was painful and nothing to be done with it because it meant that the girl was still there. She was really still there. "How are you Martin?" she said.

"I've been busy," he said.

"Yes. I've been reading ..."

"It doesn't matter," he said, "it just doesn't matter at all."

"Really?" she said, "then why do you do it?"

He thought about that for a little while. She had a way of asking the dumb question that was central and exactly right. "I guess because I have to," he said. "Are you going to stay at home?"

"For a while."

"That's good," he said, "that's good." Vinelli stirred and moaned on the floor, let loose a quivering sigh, found another position. The man was coming apart now. Without treatment he might be dead within twelve hours. Meanwhile, he sat clamped over a phone, making conversation with a girl, the enemy forces coming toward him. It just didn't make much sense, did it? "I'll see you again," he said.

"When?"

"I don't know," he said, looking over toward the window. There was a sudden interruption of light as if someone had worked his way around the building toward the room. The lights from the strip blanked and then came in again. "I just don't know."

"You're going to get yourself killed, Martin," she said, "unless you stop this."

"That's highly likely."

"But you don't care, do you? You want to get killed."

"I don't know about that either," he said, looking toward the window fascinated. The light was broken again. They were clambering either up or down the building then, they were going to try and close off all exits, doors and windows. He hadn't figured them on being that ingenious but then again they had had plenty of time for discussion. "It's possible," he said, "that I want to get killed I mean. Look, I just wanted to talk to you and to tell you that somehow I would see you again. But I've got to hang up now."

"I miss you," she said.

"I miss you too."

"I have a pretty good idea now of who you are and what you're doing and I still miss you. Isn't that crazy? Good-bye Martin, wherever you are."

The phone clicked. "Good-bye," he said to it anyway, then held the receiver away from him, looked at it incuriously for a little while and put it down. Oddly, for all the pointlessness of the conversation he felt restored. Contact: that was what he had needed, some kind of contact, some assurance that there was someone out there to whom he mattered and who wanted him to come back. Because he wanted to come back badly. Wulff understood this now. The easy despair of the townhouse maneuver in New York, the mood in which he had cut his way through San Francisco, cut his way through Boston—these were gone. He was not the same man. Feeling had been restored to him in little particles and swatches of sensation and he was willing to admit that not all of him had died on West 93rd Street looking at Marie Calvante, a little bit of him, maybe most, certainly the parts that mattered ... but there was still something left, the capacity to feel and as long as you were alive you were going to have to feed that capacity or become a monster. He looked at Vinelli and conceded that he even felt for him. He would have done anything to the man to get him out of the way but having done that the need to punish was gone. Vinelli was just a man. That was all he was. He was a man like Wulff was who had been put in a position because of many things and—Wulff finally was ready to see this now— the same thing could have happened to him granted Vinelli's background and opportunities. It could have been him. It could have been him on the floor.

Well, no time for that now. He was changing, he was shifting, things were happening to him and he was not the same man. He still had a situation to deal with and there was almost no time left. He heard the noises from the hallway now, the faint sounds of attack; they were gathering out there; the fluttering in the window line of sight was becoming more perceptible all the time. They thought they had him at both ends. It was a good plan, he had to give them credit. They had worked it out carefully, they had not, after the first moments, really panicked; they had gone at their offensive with patience and guile.

Wulff took out his revolver, put in a full clip and moved carefully to the door. He had only one last advantage to work after which the game was all theirs; he had surprise. They did not know when or how he would come out of this room, they did not know what he had planned for them. But his options ran only in a thin line and through a narrow time-wedge. The revolver felt good in his hand. He hefted it.

Then he went back to the device that he had so patiently spent two hours rigging. It ought to work but then again there were no guarantees. He checked out the wiring, looked at the grenades packed full of death, traced out the wiring toward the plunger-lever he had over in the corner.

No reason to think any more. He knew what he had to do and it had to be done quickly.

He took the plunger and pressed it in all the way. Slowly, it began to come back at him. If he had calculated it right, it would take five minutes to return on a full time-release.

If he had calculated it right.

He looked at Vinelli lying on the floor. The man had lapsed into coma again. Vinelli was out of this; he was no longer responsible. He had been in it for a while and now he was out of it and he was going to die most horribly. Fragmentation is a terrible way to die; he had seen it in Vietnam more than a few times, the knives of fire and bone tearing into the flesh, the body imploding ... he did not want this to happen to Vinelli. Whatever the man was, whatever he had been, he deserved to be immersed in that final sleep now, not to come out of it for the one instant of unbearable pain which would go on and on ...

He delivered mercy to the man in the forehead, one dull shot springing open the bone and leaving a clear, aqueous hole through which colorless liquid sprang. Vinelli's eyes opened in death and he might have given Wulff a look of gratitude or then again he might have not but he was gone and no factor anymore. He would not suffer.

Wulff replaced with a full clip. He wanted all the shots the revolver could give him.

Then he went to the door, crouched by it, his hand loosely on the knob and when he thought that the time had come ... he sprang; like blood.

XIII

He launched himself into the hallway, the revolver extended and got off the first shot. The first shot was of critical importance, miss it and he had drawn fire on himself. A confusion of forms hit him in the hallway, five or ten men, he could not tell, in a panic-situation anything between four and thirty was the same number and the shot went into the nearest of them, a dead-hit, right in the chest. This man, oblong in the dim hallway, for they had extinguished all the lights except an emergency bulb, let out a peep like a chicken and fell, opening up a space in the middle for Wulff. He ran through this space, screaming. The screams were deliberate; like a football linebacker, he was trying to create as much terror as possible to give his charge greater effect. They dove before him, instincts taking over as he rushed, and then he was through, every one of them behind him, hurtling down the hallway, bouncing off a wall as a knee twisted, getting space between them.

They were screaming, and the first of the shots came then. It hit slightly above him in the wall, the wall yielding like rubber, then there were a cannonade of further shots, shots coming in from all directions surrounding him like insects but by that time he had turned a corner, come momentarily to a clear spot and bolted toward the bank of elevators. Behind that turn he could hear their rising sound as they plunged after him. Perhaps someone was in the room itself investigating the device he had prepared, but he did not think so. Those who had come from the outside as well as those who had attacked frontally; they were all in pursuit. That was the major purpose of his flight—to preoccupy them. He was counting on their impatience and desperation. Of course if they got to him he may have won the calculation but lost his life.

He had a decision to make now—elevator or stairs to the first floor—and even as he stood there balanced, deciding, one of the elevators whisked into place, the down indicator glowing red, the doors opening. Self-service of course. A few unhappy people inside the elevator glared at Wulff. The sounds in the hallway were getting louder. He had at most now a few seconds leeway.

Elevator then. All right. He showed them his revolver. "Out!" he said and when no one moved, *"Out!"* screaming it like a curse and they moved, three men, an old woman in a tight evening dress shambling out of the elevator. He pushed them all in front of him just as the pursuit massed, stumbling to a halt, turning the corner. The front men stopped short and the others, coming up behind them, toppled the leaders. For an instant they were knocked off balance.

Wulff gave the nearest of the men a violent shove and got into the elevator just as the doors closed. The lobby button was glowing and he held his breath hoping that he would make it in one drop, hearing the pounding above him now but something else happened ... the lights in the elevator dwindled, then they darkened and the elevator stopped, the floor indicator switching off just as it had hit 3. A sickly emergency bulb blinked onto his rear.

They had him bottled.

He should have thought of that. He knew that he should have thought of it; of course they would hit the power and cut him off that way. That he hadn't thought of it meant that he had been stupid which was something that only the enemy cold afford to be ... but afford or not, here he was, trapped between floors in a hotel, the power failing, the attack forces coming on him on both sides, probably up and down ... and, Wulff thought, the detonation devices, if they were properly timed would be going off by his best estimate in no more than six or seven minutes. He put his palms flat against the walls of the elevator as if he could somehow yank it up the shaft and toward safety, but the feel of the walls, their lick unyielding passage against his hands only brought him into closer contact with the unbearable reality and he dropped the hold, hung in the shaft, feeling the slight sway of the ropes as the elevator, devoid of power, drifted upon them.

Locked up. They had pulled the plug on him and now he was a bug in cement, mannequin in casting, corpse in the coffin waiting for the final blow. He could feel his life ticking away then in the cavern of the elevator shaft as the shouts increased and what they said was true: one's life did indeed pass before one's eyes in moments of crises. It not only passed, it seemed to flow and in ragged, smashed recall Wulff saw all of it. He saw the dead body of the thing once called Marie Calvante looking up at him, he saw the face of David Williams as he turned from the corpse, barely conscious to confront his partner, he saw the townhouse on the East Side, the face of Albert Marasco as he had tortured the man to death, the freighter in San Francisco bobbing unevenly at pier. He saw the desert, the flat open deserts that he had driven to his path of destruction in Boston and then he saw them again, unreeling before him, those deserts to which he had returned and the rotten little secret heart of them called Las Vegas in which he now rolled like an insignificant pendulum, dangling in an enormous uterine shaft. It had all come to this then, all of the struggle, the bodies, the blood ... and Wulff let go a howl of fury because it should not have ended this way. It was not fair, it should have been, he should have died in open spaces face to face with the enemy, not closed in waiting for the final blow, the waves and waves of power coursing through, the explosion ...

The explosion! He felt power coursing through him, power as an enormous bursting of that shell which might have held it, light and sound, heat and darkness ripping through him, and hanging that way in the shaft Wulff became aware of what was going on outside, up there on the fifth level, came out of himself like a penknife being retracted from housing, saw and felt the power of what he had done and then the waves of heat hit him, the whistling of fragmentation. *My God,* he thought, *I could burn to death here* and that would be the final reparation for his stupidity, wouldn't it? incinerated by his own explosion; but even as he thought this the elevator was swinging like a great bird in the darkness, the cable humming and snapping, Wulff scrambling for some handhold on the walls, gasping for breath, trying to hold his lungs against the fire for that one last chance ...

And the elevator fell. It seemed to balloon in the shaft, then dwindle, all dimension going out of it and he felt the cable snap; felt that snapping as a great release of tension within himself and then he was plunging in that box toward the cellar. Weightless now in the fall he bounced into the ceiling, almost striking his skull against the emergency light on the rebound, then falling to his knees and the collapsing of the elevator was a movement away from the heat as well. It was a fall, indeed it was, but it was also a rising, a rising toward life itself as the heat fell away and then the elevator hit at the bottom of the shaft with a dull clang, shaking him and the very walls seemed to splinter and break loose around him.

Wulff put his hands between the heavy doors, wedging his fingers in tightly and then with all his strength he pulled, separating the doors the way the lips of the vagina are tugged open in a virgin, the doors oozing rather than parting, slipping away in his grasp, the steel moist with his sweat but he was finally able, gasping to get a knee into that deadly splice, the doors circling the knee but not getting past it and after that it was somewhat easier. Rotating his leg in the opening, exerting pressure on the doors with hands and leg both he was finally able to squeeze open a parting just sufficient to admit him and he came out then into the basement.

The doors slammed behind him leaving him in darkness, in the clinging, clamorous mysteries of the basement of a great hotel. But even as he tried to get his bearings down there he saw a slice of light coming from some abscess and as he headed toward that light it wavered before him; Wulff brushed against clinging ropes which felt like vines, felt metal on his forehead, felt all of the engines of the basement closing upon him ... and then, like thunder, he heard the explosions beginning above him again. They were shorter and fiercer this time like the deep jolts of fucking after orgasm and he thought, *Jesus, maybe it's out of control* now and even as he thought this one last, great impact took him by the scruff of the neck, the waves soaring upward and he shook as if in an embrace. One of the cellar walls tore out and he was looking at concrete. He fell through this, gasping.

XIV

Lazzara from a position well back was trying to direct traffic but the sons-of-bitches would not listen. They would not follow through, they had no poise under fire and now everything was beginning to fall apart under them. They should not have panicked, they should have been prepared for exactly what the bastard was doing but most of them, he realized now, had not been in the field for years, if ever. They had gotten fat and happy sitting behind their desks, issuing orders, and controlling from a distance, put back to the ground level they were almost worthless. Still, what was to be done? They were the only troops he could have massed at such short notice; turn the recruiting over to them and it might have been days before they worked through their prerogatives and local councils to the point where they would take some action.

But this was bad. This was really bad. The son-of-a-bitch came out of the room shooting, drawing their fire and scattering them, then got down the hall and around a turn so quickly that there was no time for a shot. Laying back of this Lazzara saw it all developing before him; saw the way that the flying wedge of the attack had been blunted. He ordered himself to get off his own shot, prong the bastard as he ran down the hall but his reflexes were shot, he had gotten fat and happy too and he could not make brain and arm connect fast enough to dump him. Standing in the hallway then, the men tumbling around him, Lazzara had his first real premonition that this was going to be bad. He had mucked the whole thing up. They had underestimated this man yet again, that and his position and now he was going to escape.

"The power!" he screamed into the mass of men, "for Christ's sake, cut the power now!" hoping that the men by the huge generators in the basement had had the sense to have thrown the switches. No coordination. No coordination from first to last but even as he let go a wail of fury, his troops turning to look at him, the lights in the hallway flickered, the emergency bulbs coming on. So at least that had been done. If nothing else they could hope to bottle him up ... but power off for him meant power off for them as well. The men were shooting and cursing at one another in the darkness. He could hear bullets spanging. They were coming apart in the darkness.

"He's in the elevator!" someone shouted, "we've got him in the elevator!" and Lazzara understood then that they had, after all, stumbled into the right position. The man had run into the elevator without thinking and now they had him closed in the shaft. "Come on!" the same voice said, "now we can move in and get him!" Some kid this one, probably one of the youngest, most ambitious people at the council, not that he could associate voices with faces or he gave a shit if the kid was going to try to make points by being the one to kill Wulff. Let it go that way. Ambition was as useful a method as any to get people to do the jobs they should have done anyway.

The flow now was away from him and he let them pelt down the corridors, the men who had come in through the window running out the door. He went into Vinelli's suite and saw what probably none of them had even bothered to look at—Vinelli's corpse lying on the rug, blood surrounding him, blood, dried and crusted on the clothing and in the center of the forehead a neat, tight bullethole. Vinelli looked old in death, a hundred years or more lying on the floor that way, a shell of a representation of a man and looking at him Lazzara could see that suffering and death had transfigured Vinelli, that this was not the man he had known. The sunken, yellowed eyes showed knowledge, the fingers were clasped across the face allowing those eyes to shine through, the bullethole an almost incidental ornamentation in the forehead. He must have suffered but at the end, Lazzara thought, he must have known something beyond suffering, that was fairly clear and he was struck by a sense of mystery. Men could deliver death coldly, they could manipulate and apply it like a compress but they would never, never understand it, nor could they bring its reversal. It was final all right. Maybe men killed precisely out of a knowledge of that finality; death was something that they could not face so that they administered it from the feeling that if they could give they could also taketh away ... but death could never be taken. Vinelli had learned that at the end.

Lazzara kicked the corpse without malice and went on his way. Now he could see the silvery glint of wiring tracking its way on the carpeting. The wiring had been implanted by a quick yet subtle hand, it had been buried in the nap of the carpeting in such a way that it might have escaped a casual glance ... but Lazzara was a professional. Now he saw the wiring and he bent over almost languidly, picked it up in his fingers, felt the little circumference and then incuriously, almost mechanically, he began to follow it to see where it led. His mind was almost blank. After the tension of the day, now drained by the knowledge that Wulff was bottled up somewhere in the bowels of the building, trapped in an elevator where they could pick him off or gas him out at leisure ... after all of this, Lazzara was not thinking very well at all. There was nothing to think about. There was only the mopping up.

But he followed the wire anyway, running his hands along that silvery glint, following where it would take him into the room and as he tracked it from the far edge of the carpet toward a wall, the wall separating the bathroom something began to register, however dimly. There was an appliance of some sort over in that corner, at least it looked like an appliance at this distance, a squat boxlike little thing holding two objects like eggs, a plunger on the top of it. It looked comically like plumbing. Lazzara found himself giggling; it looked something like a portable toilet holding two little brown turds. Turds that looked like canvas.

Canvas! Suddenly he was moving much more quickly. He dropped the wires almost as if flame had lurched through them although they were cool to the touch and moved at a quick, lumbering pace over to the corner; there he saw the device that he had been looking at and Lazzara reached out a hand; almost instantly however he drew his hand back, trembling at the thought that he had almost touched it. He looked at the device and then Lazzara knew exactly what it was and what the man had been doing in this room and what had been prepared for them. Rage, rage was there of course because of the cunning of the plan and the destructiveness, and it was rage which took him toward the device, his hands extended, trying to smash it; but a second wave hit him on its heels and that wave was called *fear.* Lazzara realized with terror that he was playing with a live incendiary device which could detonate at any time and tear him into a thousand pieces.

It was a thought of these pieces, of the living flesh of him being exploded throughout the room, the blood and fibers and filaments of nerve circulating in the desperate light, it was this which drove him away from the device in a reflex action even more rapid than that which had taken him toward it. He couldn't defuse it. He couldn't even begin. He had a little technical knowledge of explosions, everybody did if you hung around long enough but he didn't know how the hell to disassemble this thing and certainly not under the time pressure. He might have seconds left, no time in which to patiently work it out, explore the seating of the wires, find out what would work against what inside that plunger to set off the dynamite.

He couldn't do it. He didn't have the time. Lazzara scuttled backwards reeling, dizzied made sickened by the thick fumes which were now coming off the device mingling with the odor of death in the room. Abruptly he realized that he too was only one in the long succession of people who had underestimated Wulff, taken him too lightly, not understanding what the man really was or what he was capable of doing. Revulsion, self-hatred mingled with the fear, he turned toward the door of the room and began to scream. He caught a glimpse of himself off-angle in the mirror as he scuttled away and saw himself then for what he was; a fat, middle-aged, awkward man with the fear for self turning his body white, loosening the muscles, saw what he had become and diving toward the door he did not know in that moment if it was merely age which had turned him into this or something harder and more specific, no way of knowing. He had to get out of the room. He had to get to safety. Somehow he would have to warn the others, would have to sound some kind of alert, would have to make sure that at the very least Wulff was killed quickly; no man like this could be permitted to go on alive ...

He almost made it. He was halfway through the door, head out, buttocks in, reaching toward the hallway when the detonation hit him as light, a bright orange coming up against the haze of his vision and the light had force, it blew him into the opposite wall ... which he did not hit because the wall was no longer there.

Lazzara never heard the sound.

There was nothing with which to hear.

XV

Wulff, stumbling, blinded by smoke and the fumes, staggered through the rubble and into the air. Blindly he had gripped his revolver, the last instinct being that if he was dying he wanted to die with a gun in his hand. The air hit him like a cold sheet though and he felt himself reviving. He was able to walk; if he could walk, he supposed, he could do all of the other things as well and reason would return.

The basement must have had one of those obscure side-exits which luxury hotels have, it had dumped him not at the plaza on the strip, not even on a sidestreet but apparently in some kind of courtyard filled with refuse and as he backed through it, looking for the doorway that would lead him into the street he looked up for the first time and saw the Hotel Paradise coming apart. Halfway up the ten stories, at the site of the explosion, the walls appeared to be buckling, searing apart and through those walls were little flames and gasps of smoke, below this blocks of plaster and stone were falling. He could hear nothing; the detonation, past the first impact, had occurred in a small, soundless area walled off from all expectation or reaction but as he staggered through the doorway and came then into the street, crowds and crowds of people huddled there looking toward the hotel, he heard the sound for the first time. It was not the sound he would have normally associated with an explosion, not a dull, booming roar this, not at all but rather a thin, higher sound like then thousand sheets of paper being crushed in an enormous fist, then crushed and crushed again: the Paradise was on fire.

He stumbled into the enormous mall setting back the hotel from the strip, seeing then in front view what he had wrought. The essential structure of the hotel seemed to be only faintly altered but there was a buckling which was moving down in waves and rivulets, like drops of sweat running down the face of the building and the sweat was fire. The secondary explosion, the dynamite itself feeding off the grenades had probably blown the halls out and the fragments as they fell became firebombs, igniting the building below. The wound was not mortal so far; the hotel might survive. But unless something were done quickly the Paradise was going to go to the ground.

And it did not look like anything was going to be done. Far down the line Wulff could hear sirens, hear the whooping of horns, the familiar baying of the hounds who came into disaster sites but they were too far away and the press of the crowd around the hotel was too large, too mobile to probably permit in the kind of equipment that would be necessary to save it. Wulff was surrounded by people in all states of dress and reaction, some of them obviously just out of the hotel, roused from bed, others in evening dress from the Casino; a large crowd of those having nothing to do with the hotel had begun to swell and fill the courtyard ... and still people were streaming out of the doors, most of these escapees in progressively worse condition as they emerged; some of them with blackened faces, women screaming, men trying to support the women or themselves as they stumbled to the air. Wulff felt himself fascinated in the old New York fashion, the old New Yorker's taste for a disaster which utterly confirms his certainty of inner disintegration and he found himself looking at the scene almost dispassionately, almost as if not he but someone else had been responsible for this and he merely a spectator. He was deep into narcolepsy, he knew that. There was blood on his hands, he had probably scraped himself badly clawing out of the cellar, there was a wound over his eye which was dripping blood jaggedly across his vision and his entire frame felt weightless, distant from what was happening. What the effort of rigging the explosion and getting out of it alive had cost him he did not know yet. He suspected that he had come close to the end of his reserves. He had to get out of here. He had to get away from this.

What he had to do, what must be done now was to get to the airport somehow with that locker key and find what it bought him. He suspected that it was going to buy him a great deal, a prize so significant that it would make what he had dragged out of San Francisco look very small ... but he just could not will himself to move. He felt himself behind glass, felt himself sliding on the pavement, supported by bodies. "What the fuck is this, friend?" someone said to him and Wulff reared to his feet, the sirens much closer now. He started to move away from there.

But the man who had spoken to him was still at his elbow, holding, detaining, locking into step with him. "What the fuck is this?" the man said again in a more penetrating way and Wulff looked at him; he saw the recognition in the man's eyes and it rebounded upon him; suddenly he knew who the man was and why the man's grip on his wrist, tentative at first, had become harder. "It's you," the man said, "it's you, you son-of-a-bitch," and Wulff recognized the man fully, saw the face of a man he had passed fleeing down the hallway, one of the men of the attack force who had somehow gotten onto the pavement and the fingers were now digging in more tightly to his wrist while with a free hand the man began to fumble in his pockets.

"I'll be goddamned," he was saying, "be goddamned," and Wulff knew what the man meant, what he was saying was that he could hardly trust his luck, the luck of the journeyman who does his job and expects nothing and after thirty years suddenly finds himself confronted on the sidewalk by the Main Chance ... and he yanked his wrist, broke the hold in a sidewise gesture, plunging *into* the man to knock him off balance and calculating the situation only for an instant, Wulff ran. There was nothing to do but run. The crowd offered him protection only if he used it to cover his flight. They would certainly not save him from being shot.

In the midst of the burning, starting to choke now from the smoke, Wulff bulled his way through the crowd, the rising sirens adding impetus to his flight and finally finding an open space he ran. Behind him he could hear the man screaming. He was calling for reinforcements and then he heard a confusion of voices behind him and knew that he had found them.

Wulff ran. It was as if all of his life had coalesced to this one last flight and he thought nothing, knew nothing, only worked to put space between him and the assailants. Two blocks or five from there, he had no way of judging distance or time the Hotel Paradise exploded. The joints around the fifth floor gave out and the massive hotel came in around itself like a terrified virgin being skewered by a rapist, falling within, falling within, and then the burning.

XVI

His flight had no sense or direction for a while; he only knew that space was the answer. He had to put distance between him and the remains of the attack force; there was no question of making a stand and fight with only a revolver. But as his heart began to slam and bounce through his rib cage, as his respiration and pace began to give out Wulff began thinking again, realized that he would never be able to get away on foot. Already he had gone most of the distance along the strip, the avenue was becoming highway, the desert lay before him. He had opened no ground; they were still after him, on foot, shouting instructions to one another and surely by now others had been dispatched to get a car. Once they got a car they would run him to ground. If there was escape for him it would have to be in a car as well and thinking no further, he ran into the middle of the avenue, weaving slightly, traffic screeching around and tore open the door of an idling

Pontiac Tempest at curbside, its young driver sitting there, shaking his head to the beat of a radio, looking at two one dollar bills in his hand. He showed the boy his revolver. "Give me the car," he said.

The boy looked at him. "The transmission is shot and I think the driveshaft is going," he said.

"I didn't ask for a diagnosis. Get out."

"All right," the boy said. He shrugged and languidly put a foot out of the car, touched the pavement with a toe, then hoisted his frame through. "They're not going to believe this," he said.

"Come on, get out of the way."

"They won't fucking believe this," the boy said, handing Wulff the keys with a flourish. He could only have been nineteen or twenty, unshaven, wearing a polo shirt. His eyes showed indications of a three-day bout. "They won't believe it but I'll tell them. They took three hundred and ninety-eight dollars out of me and now they're going to send me out of here on foot."

"Nothing personal," Wulff said. He idled the engine. There was a strange clatter somewhere inside there, a miss and a squeal. Fan belt? Camshaft? He put it into gear. The car grudgingly dropped into drive.

"I would've given it to you," the boy said as he moved it away, "you didn't have to pull a gun on me. Believe me, it's not worth fifty dollars."

Wulff shook his head, rolling up the window and pushed the car out of there. The Tempest accelerated unevenly, the engine hammering as it pulled reluctantly to forty and then he had to drop it back quickly at an intersection, a limousine pulling out without stopping; the car lurched down into first gear and stalled. He tried to start it in motion but the starter was blocked; it was necessary to bring it to a complete stop, put the lever into P and then grind at the starter hopelessly, hearing the solenoid miss and click and then, finally, reluctantly, the car came over again and feathering the gas pedal against another stall he pushed it up to thirty, then thirty-five miles an hour. At forty everything in the car finally began to pull together, bolts soldered, rattles tightened as if the sheer effect of speed had been all that it ever wanted and he got it up to fifty and then sixty in easy stages, Las Vegas beginning to fall away from him. The strip had been thrown up on sand and now the sand was overtaking it once again, two miles off and he was already into desert. He checked the gas gauge which was close to the empty level, decided that like it or not he would have to stop somewhere for a fill, got the car up to sixty-five feeling better all the time, convinced that somehow he had managed to evade them, they had not figured that he would be able to get off from foot so quickly. He even fondled the locker key which along with his revolver he had held onto through all of this desperately and single-minded and wondered whether he could cut back from the desert and get into the airport. Then he risked a checking glance into the rear-view mirror.

They were behind him and growing.

He tried the side-mirror, they were doing the same. There were two Fleetwoods behind him, black, closed-over sedans laying back no more than forty or fifty yards, moving side by side, pacing one another. At any time these cars could have overtaken him; the fact that they had not was probably indication that they were waiting for him to get into the desert, into the open spaces. Once there he would be in a trap of sky burning isolation: they could take him at leisure.

This time he had bought it. Everything that he had done since he left the hotel room had been wrong, he had trapped himself in an elevator, mingled in a crowd filled with the enemy, appropriated a car which did not work, sentenced himself to a desert which would destroy him. Wulff pounded the wheel in rage, feeling his control beginning to break, waves of self-loathing lashing at him but all the time he was working on the car as well, putting the accelerator through the floor, trying to work more speed out of the car. Somehow, he thought, he would get out of this. He had gone so far, he could go a little further, they could not finish him off so easily now. If the desert was a trap it cut two ways because not only they but he was isolated. Things would play themselves out there and finally there would be a conclusion to this and it would be done.

He checked the rear-view again; they were keeping pace. They were not accelerating. They figured, no doubt, that they had him anytime they wanted; they could wait, there was no hurry. They were playing it with patience and calculation but then again these people were not fools. They had been clumsy from beginning to end here, that was true, but now the first-string was coming in.

Feeling terribly exposed, feeling like a fly in a bottle, not a man heading into the desert, Wulff drove. After a time he ignored the rear-view mirror and its news. There was just nothing to be done about that now.

XVII

The man in the front seat of the Fleetwood said, "Let's take him now."

"Plenty of time," the driver said. There were only two of them in the car. Behind them the other Fleetwood, carrying four had fallen back, now they had opened up a hundred yards of distance. Protecting the flank.

"I want to get it over with," the passenger said. He was no more than twenty-five years old and looked as if this was his first assignment. The driver knew that this was not so and that the man next to him had been at this for years but it was no comfort. They were both nervous. The stakes on this one were high and mounting.

"Just a little longer," said the driver. "We've got him in a box. Anytime we want we can take him; it's best to get the hell way out of town."

"I don't like it," the passenger said. He shifted in the seat, fumbling with a gun. "Look at what he's done already. Look at what he is. I think we should get rid of him now."

"We'll do it," the driver said. The nervousness was infectious; he felt his hands fluttering on the wheels. "Shut up," he said, "think of something else. Don't bother me now."

"I think Lazzara is dead," the passenger said. "I think he killed him."

"I don't know anything about that. We've got a job to do and we'll do it."

"We've never gone up against anything like this. There's never been anything like this guy before."

"Wait until you've been around a bit," the driver said. He squinted through the windshield, observing the Tempest. It was weaving on the roadway now, greyish clouds pouring out of the exhaust as it wobbled on the center lane. Coming up through it he could smell the stink, pumped through the intake vents.

He put the air conditioner on *recirculate*. "He's breaking down," the passenger said.

"I don't think so. He's slowing."

"No, I think the car's busted," the passenger said and then leaned forward with the driver. The Tempest threw out another explosion of exhaust and then abruptly accelerated. It came over on the right lane and blew momentarily out of sight behind a signpost. The driver accelerated to keep pace.

"He's doing eighty now," he said. "I don't think the car will take eighty."

"I don't care what he's doing," the passenger said. He cocked his gun. "Let's get rid of him now."

The driver looked through the rear-view mirror. The other Fleetwood was almost invisible now, dropping back half a mile or more. Maybe the sudden acceleration had caught them by surprise. But the car was lagging.

"I don't think we ought to," the driver said. He rubbed his eyes against the glare, shook his head and shut off the recirculating mechanism, putting the car on intake again. There were black smudges under his eyes and suddenly he looked quite old. He could not have been more than forty.

"Yes you do," the passenger said. Suddenly the gun was leveled at the driver. "I'm not going to put up with any more of this shit. Now hammer him down."

The driver's hands convulsed around the steering wheel but otherwise he kept calm. The car accelerated imperceptibly. "This isn't the way to handle it," he said.

"Don't tell me how to handle it. I've had enough, you understand me?"

The Tempest bucked off the road a few hundred yards up, white exhaust spilling from it again. It came to an apparent stop. The driver hit the brakes.

"What is he doing?" he said.

"He probably broke down," the passenger said. The car slowed more. "What are you doing?"

"I told you," the driver said, "I just don't like it. I don't know if I want to come up on him like this." He checked the rear-view yet again. The other car was now entirely out of sight. Was it a double-cross of some sort? Was he being set up for something? He brought the car to a halt about fifteen yards behind the Tempest. There was no movement inside the car now. He could detect no sign of head and shoulders.

"I don't like it," he said again. He turned toward the passenger. "Get that fucking gun out of my face."

"Drive up alongside him," the man said, turning the gun aside, "and I'll pump one through the window."

"Maybe he's waiting for us to do just that. Maybe he'll pick us off."

"The fucking car is bulletproofed," the passenger said, "if you don't listen to me now, I'm going to blow your head off."

"Who's in command here?"

"Not you," the passenger said softly. "Not you."

The driver put the car into neutral. "I don't want no part of it," he said, "I'm not coming up alongside him. You want to do something, you do it on foot."

The passenger switched his attention fully to the driver now as if an itch of which he had been semiconscious had finally prodded him into activity. His eyes had a peculiar coalescence and purpose. "Don't make me do this," he said, raising the gun.

The driver held the wheel steadily, looking out in front of him. "We're supposed to kill him," he said quietly, "not each other."

"Move the car."

"No. I don't like it."

The Tempest slewed onto the road abruptly, tires screaming. It burst out at full throttle skittering several hundred yards down the road and then came to a full stop. Laboriously, it cranked through a U-turn.

The passenger let the gun fall to his lap. His eyes were glazed with interest. "What the fuck is this?" he said.

The Tempest came directly toward the Fleetwood, gathering speed. It was moving thirty, perhaps forty miles an hour on dead-collision course.

"For Christ's sake!" the passenger said. His hands were loose at the wrist, he raised and flapped them like wings. "What's going on! The son-of-a-bitch is going to ..."

He choked, dived into the compartment under the dashboard. The driver grabbed the wheel, dropped the Fleetwood into drive and floored the accelerator, trying to ditch it on the side of the road. He had never seen a head-on collision, never believed that such a thing was possible with modern roads and cars, but the Tempest seemed to be looking for it.

The maneuver did not work. As he came onto the shoulder at the side of the road, the Tempest, implacably, swung left to meet him. Maybe fifty miles an hour and gaining. There could not have been more than ten yards between the cars.

"My God!" the driver screamed, "he's going to hit!" and still fighting with the wheel tried to pull the Fleetwood out but they were in a box now, the Tempest coming in at an angle which cut them off the road, the shoulder to the right looking out at rocks and boulders. He closed his eyes then and took a deep breath, waited for the impact that would be the last thing he would ever know. Underneath, the passenger was babbling, seemed to be praying.

The roar increased, the droning, scattering sound coming from the Tempest's mufflers. Then, having hit a peak, it began to diminish. The driver felt a slight wind through the bulletproof windows although this was impossible. Then he opened his eyes to see the Tempest disappearing down the roadway, the engine screaming.

The passenger scrambled upward from hiding, his face very pale. Everything seemed to have gone out of him. "Son-of-a-bitch," he said, "son-of-a-bitch."

The driver put the car into neutral and took several shallow breaths, trying to force air into his lungs, trying to find normal respiration. "That won't work," he said, almost matter of factly, "the other car will get him. He didn't know that we have two cars."

"Son-of-a-bitch," the passenger said. His gun, which he had forgotten lay on his lap, he picked it up and looked at it incuriously, as if it were an alien artifact, something pulled out of the desert. "I thought that we had bought it," he said.

"He's good," the driver said. He put the car back into drive, feeling a tentative kind of control again. "The man is good. He's a police driver. Let's go back and see what happened."

"No," the passenger said, "no, I don't want to go back. I give up." He paused. "I admit it," he said then, "I don't want to die."

"Nobody's going to die except him," the driver said and rolled the car into a broken U-turn, headed it down the empty road. "It's all over for him. The other car will get him."

"Leave me out of it," the passenger said. "Just leave me out of this."

"You're never out of it until you're dead," the driver said, thinking that this was a large, philosophical thought; oh my, indeed he was becoming metaphysical, well there was nothing like a little sight of death to get you to take the longer view. The Tempest had laid down tracks on the roadway. Following them he found himself thinking, I'm getting old, I'm not what I was, I don't know if I can take this anymore ... maybe, maybe, I should try to find another life.

XVIII

The maneuver with the pursuit car had worked as he thought it might, an old high-speed maneuvering trick which Wulff had never performed but which he thought he had worked out in sleep time and again, he knew that he could intimidate them and pound them out of the pursuit if he only performed the unexpected of going right into the strength rather than away for it. There was still the other car; it had been dropping behind but not *that* far, was probably only a mile down and at the rate he was going he would cross it in a half a minute or less. Wulff stared down the road driving one-handed, his other hand gripping the revolver, and concentrated on what he had to do next. It was difficult and precise, two qualities that he wondered if he really possessed in this state of physical siege. Then again, there was just no alternative to failure and if he had gone this far he could go a little further. The balance wheel was always there hovering in his mind. It would be easier by far to have given up at the start rather than to become what he had, but every challenge conquered was a further investment in going on; if you did not go on then what had already happened meant nothing. He would not yield it. Not so easily, not now.

The other Fleetwood came over the horizon, mounting in vision. The car had been tooling along, acting as a backstop and as a kind of patrol site just as he had expected. That had been clever of them, not committing both cars to the attack at once. This way they would always have reserve. He put the Tempest over the center line, the wheels just straddling it on the left side and flicked on his headlights, floored the accelerator and sent the car staggering directly toward collision. The Tempest was holding up, the motor gasped and he smelt rubber and oil, fumes coming back at him through the open windows but the car would hold up. He had confidence in it.

The Fleetwood picked him up. He saw the car weave, stumble as the driver moved from recognition through indecision and he locked himself into a tunnel of perception, focusing his attention, seeing nothing but the car. They were closing rapidly, it was only a matter of seconds. The Fleetwood held course for a moment and then dived toward the side of the road. Wulff pursued it, holding it in a trap. The car squalled and screamed, kicking up little absent puffs of dust and he came in on it hard this time, closing the gap with force and he sideswiped the sliding Fleetwood hard, smashing it onto the shoulder, then moved out of the trap.

The impact of the swipe made the Tempest yaw, it seemed to be considering spinning out of control completely, but he worked the brakes and transmission evenly, coaxing it back under control and finally it yielded. The Tempest came out of the collision pulsating like a fist, and he kept it going on course, down the wrong side of the road, pumping the brakes for control this time, then coming in a long, sidewise drift to ten miles an hour and he wheeled the car around.

He came back toward the Fleetwood.

Well thank the desert roads anyway; five miles out of Vegas and it was as barren as Beach Channel Drive at dawn on a Sunday morning. However it ended, this last act of Las Vegas would be played out by the principals. There would be no walk-ons here. The Fleetwood was in a cloud of exhaust and sand at the side of the road, the body quivering and as he brought the Tempest down he saw the doors begin to flutter, just as he had hoped they were, moving tentatively like butterfly's wings and men were peering out. In the panic of the collision that had been their first, expected impulse, to get clear of the car and he had been counting on it. He brought the Tempest directly toward those doors.

The doors closed as he came in at forty miles an hour and he swiped the car again, wheeling left at the last moment, delivering a smashing impact to the side of the car, then, before he could take the full jolt of it himself he was away, skittering free over the road, the car twice damaged once again diminishing. He repeated the U-turn movement again, a few hundred yards down, concentrating on whipping the car in short, precise strokes, the least amount of wasted movement, no play in the steering wheel, no false movement in the brake. He had done panic-driving in his life on the pursuit end, now all of it was coming into focus for these enormous stakes. He reached for the revolver which he had dumped at his side while holding on for the first impact. Then he came toward the Fleetwood again.

The sight of the Tempest bearing down on them must have lurched the men inside into panic. They had been the pursuers in a bulletproof limousine, following a miserable junk. It had been for them nothing more than a quick and interesting job, but, insanely, the Tempest had become the attacker. He was counting on the effects of this reversal bolted onto that older, more familiar element of panic for what would happen next ... because if it did not he was as dead as he had been when he left Vegas, came onto these roads. If they behaved sensibly, if their professionalism did not desert them he was finished. All that they had to do was to stay within the car and wait him out. After a certain amount of time they could start pumping shots.

But this did not happen. They did not stay within the car. The doors came open, this time on the desert side and a form hurtled into the sands, then, a little further along another form leaped and they began to roll. Seen from this angle they were a target, a possibility, but Wulff did not want to risk it, not when there was a better opportunity. He clutched the gun, jolted the Tempest to a stop and before it had even finished its roll, clearing the Cadillac, he was outside, bearing down on them.

What happened then happened quickly, although now for Wulff, in the intensity of the action and the depth of his concentration, it seemed to go on for an extended period giving everything that he did the aspect of stop-action. He leveled the gun, standing and pumped two shots into the man nearest him, tearing off an ear, sending the man reeling and vomiting into the sands, then he felt a stab of pain in the shoulder and realized that he had been hit. The second one, the man now running from him had had the presence of mind to desert the car with his gun, either that or he had held it instinctively and now, surprised that it was still with him had decided to use it.

It was not a serious wound, just a minor scrape of the shoulder fired off by a man blocked by terror but it had been bad enough. If the man's luck had held just a shade more strongly he would have been hit and doomed. As it was, Wulff paused only an instant, yanking back from the pain, then aimed his revolver at the man who leaped into the air like a dancer. "Don't!" he screamed. It was the first time he had heard a voice through all of this; its effect in the desert was stunning. This desert had existed five million years before speech; it would last five million after speaking beings had left, it swallowed all sound. "Please!" the man said, and dropped his gun; it sparkled in the air. He showed Wulff his empty hands. Wulff shot him in the head.

The man turned around once, a dancer caught in the ropes and reached toward him gracelessly, Wulff shot him again, this time in the gut and the man kicked, fell. He took a long time falling, falling slowly through particles of sand and at the end of it Wulff had another bullet for him, soldering him to the ground, blood running in the arid desert, the sands devouring it.

He turned and the other Fleetwood, the one he had chased off the road above had come into sight and was rolling down from the horizon.

He had to credit them for their persistence; he thought that they more likely would have pointed in the opposite direction and kept on going. But if he was desperate they were desperate too and Wulff, feeling the pain beginning to lance from his shoulder now knew that he could not take them. He was too exposed, he had to reload, the wound, superficial or not was hurting. This time they would not be stupid, they would not leave the car. He put the gun away and began to run toward the two cars at the side of the road, his side hurting, arm hurting, flashes of pain all the way through. Then he dived into the Cadillac, the keys still in it, the motor running, put it into gear and let it go.

It went. The two blows had done bad things to the suspension, the car seemed to be hanging down on its springs but acceleration, transmission, power were unaffected. The car burned out of there, grabbing the road at forty miles an hour and then beginning to gain.

Now it was a flat run back toward Vegas. He was in a better car than the Tempest, albeit a damaged one, he thought that he had a chance to outrun them and, even if he did not, he thought—using the power switches to seal the windows up tight—he was behind bulletproofing. He was living right, things were getting better all the time. He had traded up so to speak and he had, he noticed, not only better transportation, he had a very good-looking revolver on the seat next to him, dropped by the passenger when they had fled the car. He picked it up, driving one-handed and put it on the dashboard, wedging it in tightly.

Then for the first time he checked his rear-view, to see how closely the other car was following.

But they were not following. Far back he could see the outline of the car by the side of the road, two tiny figures bouncing around it. And then, finally, he understood what had happened and Wulff began to laugh.

He had to laugh: it was such a fitting conclusion, and there was a little bit of irony in it too, the Vegas kind of irony which even the losers back at the Paradise might have appreciated. Their luck had turned against them and with it, as so often happens, their judgment had gone too. They had not pursued him because they thought that *he* was *they* in the Fleetwood, moving away from the scene and that the two bodies on the sands were his and one of the assailants, the other one taking off either out of fright or in such of some kind of help.

They hadn't figured that he had driven away at all.

Wulff felt the pain from the wound but it wasn't bad at all; he could live with it. The bleeding had already stopped and in a little while it would congeal into nothing more than itching. He would have to get some treatment of course but there was no rush. It was a light wound, he was sure. He could probably go around for days like this. He had the car, he had two guns, he had four men behind him on the sand, two of them dead ... and he had an airport locker key in his pocket which might mean more than any of this.

They might eventually get back into that other Cadillac and chase him but his lead-time was absolute. They would never catch him. And there were no reinforcements.

Singing, Wulff drove on into the airport.

XIX

Five minutes after he had come out of the locker in the men's room with the valise Stone had left, Wulff was still trembling. It had nothing to do with the wound. The wound was fine. He had stripped his shirt and washed it with a little soap and water and that would keep him going all the way to New York. It was just a small burn, the size of a dime, the bullet winging him, bringing a fair amount of blood that had cleansed the wound and promptly clotted. The body had its own cunning. No, the wound was fine.

Carrying the valise he walked toward a phone booth. No one at the terminal looked suspicious; they had been bombed out back at the Paradise and probably had no troops left to send. The last *soldat* had gone into the desert with him.

He locked himself into a booth. Nine A.M. All of this had happened after the dawn; it was impossible to realize what had gone on in three hours. Nine o'clock. Six back in New York then. Everybody sleeping except cops, garbagemen, subway motor-men and criminals. All right. Fuck it. Sleep had nothing to do with anything.

He dialed direct, a little shakily, holding the valise between his knees. Williams's wife answered right away. That was smart, letting your wife do all the picking up. That way they had to go one level to get at you which was critical. Marie would have done that for him. Marie would have picked up the phone and protected him. Marie was dead.

"Let me talk to David," he said.

"Wulff? That you, Martin?"

"Yeah."

"You all right?"

"All depends. That all depends."

"But *are* you all right?"

She was a good woman. "Yes," he said, "I'm all right. I'll do. I'm still here. Let me talk to David. Is he there?"

"He's sleeping."

"Wake the son-of-a-bitch up."

"All right," she said, "I don't mind. Break up his sleep for a change."

There was murmuring and rustling in the background. Bedroom phone then in the nice, tight little clean house of St. Albans, Queens. Wulff looked through the dead spaces of the terminal. Nobody. Nothing. This town might be an all-night proposition, the casinos roared ... but between flights nothing at all happened at the airport.

"Wulff," Williams said, "what happened?"

"Plenty."

"You all right?"

"We've gone through that already. Yeah, I'm all right. I survived anyway."

"Good," Williams said. He paused. "Did you find Stone?"

"Nobody will find Stone. Stone's dead."

"That's good," Williams said unhesitatingly. "That's mighty good. That saves what you might refer to as a so-called administrative problem."

"Found his baggage though."

"Oh," Williams said. "Oh." He said nothing for a moment. Wulff waited it out. He would wait it out forever. He didn't care.

"What kind of baggage?" Williams said.

"What do you think?"

"I don't know. You're the one placing the call, aren't you?"

"So I am," Wulff said. "So I am. Stone brought out the biggest load of shit I've ever seen in my life."

Williams said, "I could have figured that."

"I've never seen anything like it," Wulff said and thought again of the decks and decks, lined up like little soldiers in the coffinlike expanse of the valise, neatly strapped in, pure white, pure gold, pure death ...

"Bigger than that San Francisco load?"

"Nothing like that. San Francisco was just a match to the cigarette. This is the real thing."

"All right," Williams said. His responses were picking up now; he was recovering fast. "So you got it. What are you going to do with it?"

"I'm thinking about that," Wulff said, "I've really been thinking about that."

"You better get the fuck out of town, man. I don't know where you're calling from or who's watching you but you better get that mother out of town."

"I intend to. I have a flight out of here in fifteen minutes. I intend to make it."

"You going to bring it back to New York? Or you going to dump it?"

"I don't know," Wulff said. "I'm thinking about that. There are about forty people dead out here and a lot of structural damage. It would be a shame to just dump it, wouldn't it?"

"That might be so," Williams said, "that just might be so. So where are you?"

"I'm in the airport."

"Why are you calling me?"

"Why am I calling you?" Wulff said. He found that his hand was shaking. "Why I'm just reporting to you, don't you see? I'm the weapon, you're the hand, wasn't that the arrangement?"

"You're full of shit, man."

"That's the way you said it was, Williams. You're Mr. Inside, I'm Mr. Outside because people like me are expendable." His hand was beginning to shake somewhat more rapidly. He concentrated on evening out his respiration and locked the hand in between the valise and the wall.

"You don't understand what I was driving at," Williams said, "but this is no time to define our relationship, Mr. Wulff. You sound to me like a man who's jammed in and who ought to get the hell out of wherever he is and get some rest. The valise is your decision."

"Is it?"

"I don't give a shit," Williams said, "turn it back to the supply room. Give it to the commissioner at high noon; he'll give you a medal. The man who broke the ring and came back with the fucking goods. Maybe you could get an honorable discharge and run for Mayor."

"I don't think so," Wulff said, "I don't think I'm going to give it to the commissioner. But I'm taking it back to New York."

"Yes," Williams said, "I figured that you would. You're a New Yorker tried and true."

"What would this stuff do if it were dumped into the market?" Wulff said.

"Make a lot of junkies happy."

"Sure it would. But what would it do to the *market.*"

"I don't know," Williams said. "I'm getting bored with this conversation, Mr. Outside. If you think it would blow the market up you're crazy, though. They're a big organization, just like the government. They got price supports and a subsidy program and a regulator of supply and demand and nothing is going to drop the prices."

"I thought of that," Wulff said. He switched the phone to the other hand, checking the terminal. Police had appeared in a clear area and in a bored way were talking with the receptionist. He ducked his head low in the booth. "Okay," he said, "enough. I'll be back with it."

"Don't bring that shit over to my house."

"I didn't think I would," Wulff said, "I'll work out a better plan."

"You'd better do something," Williams said, "you better figure out *something* because if you think I'm directing you you're out of your fucking mind."

He hung up.

Wulff straightened in the booth, very carefully took the valise, kicked open the door and went outside. The police did not look at him. He walked to and past them and leaned then across the desk to catch the eye of the receptionist. He confirmed the New York flight and its departure time in front of the police and they did nothing at all. All right. It was the only way to play it. The receptionist said that he could board now if he wanted; the plane was ready. He could check his bag if he desired. Wulff said he guessed that he would hold onto it.

He turned and walked back the other way, passing the police again, out the door and into the loading area. The police hooked their hands in their belts, one of them chewing gum and did nothing at all. He walked up the ramp into the empty plane, the motors whining gently and tossed the valise on a rack above and sat with a sigh. He waited it out.

It was only until he was up in the air, two hours later, the businessman behind him mumbling in a thick doze, that Wulff remembered as if in a dream that the police that last time he walked past had not looked at him so impassively at all. They had, in fact, been smiling.

And unless his memory, coming back to him now in little bits and pieces of subliminal incident was wrong, one of them had winked at him.

Had distinctly winked.

Wulff, three hours later, winked back.

And then he folded his hands and went to sleep.

THE END

Afterword to Boston Avenger and Desert Stalker:

Living Here In The Heart Of The Heart Of The Country

By Barry N. Malzberg

"Cohen felt channels opening and closing in his mind and he pitched forward against the enormous bulk of the intruder, moving through a long dark passage, a clinging wet cunt of oblivion." —*Boston Avenger*/page 49 of the Berkley edition.

By the third novel I felt I had found my stride, my balance, some tendentious but passably agile voicing with which to approach this murderous project and although not comfortable within it, that would not come until the very last line of the 14th and final novel, I was able to maneuver within the perimeters, no longer embarrassed, just angry that it had been left to me, not Warren Murphy or William Martin Smith to tell the tale. Burton Wulff (name in the original draft Wolf Conlan) had become comfortable with his mission or at least less uncomfortable; he was crazy of course, a madman on a mad Pilgrim's Progress. That had been clear to me from my initial nodding rendezvous with the series, the twelfth or fifteenth novel skimmed in front of the rack in Rocklin's Confections and Magazines, the guy was out of his mind but his author not necessarily. Pendleton, a pro, was going for the market, the vigilante fantasists or maybe practitioners and he knew what they wanted: the justification of immersion, the immersion of justification. Wiping the criminals, racketeers, godfathers off the planet in the names of justice and retaliation. Revenge porn. It was paying off for Pinnacle and Pendleton and in its down-rent version it was paying off for me too. Truths ballooned for me, emerging from the portable Smith Corona. Here I was at last, truly in the heart of the heart of the country. Science fiction was displacement, the contemporary "realistic" or "naturalistic" novels were codes for the reality of the situation.

That reality was Vietnam and its war, not a "police action" like Korea whose active span ran before me from my eleventh to fourteenth years; I was safe in the cocoon of chronological immaturity and when Adlai Stevenson in the 1952 Presidential campaign pledged to "speak sense to the American people"; his lectures had less to do with that police action than it had to do with hinting that one could be a Good American and yet suspicious of Joe McCarthy and the House Un-American Activities Committee. Quietly suspicious of course and more concerned with the bad manners than with the intent.

That intent, not to fatally digress, had to do with the homogenization of the country, the acceptance of the Cold War; McCarthy was not a proper guest but he was on the trail of the evil Soviets, it was only the methodology which concerned him. Stevenson passed for daring in 1952. A few years later Joseph Welch ("have you at last no decency, Senator?") at the fabled Army-McCarthy hearings at least hinted that the Korean malaise might have more danger and a spurring insanity than had been conceded, but Vietnam was down the road. Spillane and his Hammer might have been proto-Bolans and all of the pieces were on the table, ready to be assembled, but Korea neither enacted nor seemed to have been triggered by that national insanity which found capsulation and a kind of insidious profit in the offices of Pinnacle Books, the needs and half-concealed desires of the Executioner's audience.

Where it was leading was toward the homogenization of the country; the heart of the heart of that country was the uniform dye, bleak and black, which was spreading in its subterranean (and later visible) fashion all over the map; the Lone Wolf caught notice itself, it came late in the series but at last in the 13th volume became explicit on page 53 in what I took then to be the second best paragraph I had ever written. (The best was the concluding paragraph of *Screen* which dealt with the normalization of another kind of madness.)

"So Wulff had picked up the trail. Coming into Shreveport had been like coming into any of the hundred American cities that he had seen or passed during the months of his odyssey; once again he had been overwhelmed by the flattening of America, the gathering of all its cities into one, so that not only difference but any sense of partition had been obliterated. Now it was truly one country, all of it United by highways, loops, cloverleafs, abandoned downtown districts, hamburger stands, in the flat, blank surfaces of the screens of drive-ins, coming up hard against the broken horizon; through that corpse where all cells had become one flowed the deadly, silvery milk of heroin, which had first killed and was now embalming the corpse in clear and frozen strips of hard poison, which yet glistened like something beautiful in that darkness—"

And that darkness which both inspired, drove and destroyed Wulff had leached into the heart of the heart and had rendered a central, a crucial, an active part of its population undone to any emotion other than rage. Like Wulff I drove that terrible, rusted, poisonous vehicle through all of the hills and valleys of the heart of the heart. Wulff was a one-man wrecking crew like Bolan but unlike Bolan he did not have virtue as his impulsion. "Have you no sense of decency, sir?" The decent know the answer to that but it is pure paradox; in the affirmative is the denial, in the denial is the corruption. The series had to navigate that balance. Boston, Las Vegas, Miami and Detroit in the future, a return to New York, they loomed like tombstones on the rooted Avenues of necessity. *Off with their heads* cried the Red Queen. *Off with their hearts* cried Wulff.

January 2022: New Jersey

BARRY N. MALZBERG BIBLIOGRAPHY

FICTION (as either Barry or Barry N. Malzberg)

Oracle of the Thousand Hands (1968)
Screen (1968)
Confessions of Westchester County (1970)
The Spread (1971)
In My Parents' Bedroom (1971)
The Falling Astronauts (1971)
The Masochist (1972, reprinted as Everything Happened to Susan, 1975; as Cinema, 2020)
Horizontal Woman (1972; reprinted as The Social Worker, 1973)
Beyond Apollo (1972)
Overlay (1972)
Revelations (1972)
Herovit's World (1973)
In the Enclosure (1973)
The Men Inside (1973)
Phase IV (1973; novelization based on a story & screenplay by Mayo Simon)
The Day of the Burning (1974)
The Tactics of Conquest (1974)
Underlay (1974)
The Destruction of the Temple (1974)
Guernica Night (1974)
On a Planet Alien (1974)
Out from Ganymede (1974; stories)
The Sodom and Gomorrah Business (1974)
The Best of Barry N. Malzberg (1975; stories)
The Many Worlds of Barry Malzberg (1975; stories)
Galaxies (1975)
The Gamesman (1975)
Down Here in the Dream Quarter (1976; stories)
Scop (1976)
The Last Transaction (1977)
Chorale (1978)
Malzberg at Large (1979; stories)
The Man Who Loved the Midnight Lady (1980; stories)
The Cross of Fire (1982)
The Remaking of Sigmund Freud (1985)
In the Stone House (2000; stories)

Shiva and Other Stories (2001; stories)
The Passage of the Light: The Recursive Science Fiction of Barry N. Malzberg (2004; ed. by Tony Lewis & Mike Resnick; stories)
The Very Best of Barry N. Malzberg (2013; stories)

With Bill Pronzini

The Running of the Beasts (1976)
Acts of Mercy (1977)
Night Screams (1979)
Prose Bowl (1980)
Problems Solved (2003; stories)
On Account of Darkness and Other SF Stories (2004; stories)

As Mike Barry

Lone Wolf series:
Night Raider (1973)
Bay Prowler (1973)
Boston Avenger (1973)
Desert Stalker (1974)
Havana Hit (1974)
Chicago Slaughter (1974)
Peruvian Nightmare (1974)
Los Angeles Holocaust (1974)
Miami Marauder (1974)
Harlem Showdown (1975)
Detroit Massacre (1975)
Phoenix Inferno (1975)
The Killing Run (1975)
Philadelphia Blow-Up (1975)

As Francine di Natale

The Circle (1969)

As Claudine Dumas

The Confessions of a Parisian Chambermaid (1969)

As Mel Johnson/M. L. Johnson

Love Doll (1967; with The Sex Pros by Orrie Hitt)
I, Lesbian (1968; as M. L. Johnson)

Just Ask (1968; with Playgirl by Lou
  Craig)
Instant Sex (1968)
Chained (1968; with Master of Women
  by March Hastings & Love Captive
  by Dallas Mayo)
Kiss and Run (1968; with Sex on the
  Sand by Sheldon Lord & Odd Girl by
  March Hastings)
Nympho Nurse (1969; with Young and
  Eager by Jim Conroy & Quickie by
  Gene Evans)
The Sadist (1969)
The Box (1969)
Do It To Me (1969; with Hot Blonde by
  Jim Conroy)
Born to Give (1969; with Swap Club by
  Greg Hamilton & Wild in Bed by
  Dirk Malloy)
Campus Doll (1969; with High School
  Stud by Robert Hadley)
A Way With All Maidens (1969)

As Howard Lee

Kung Fu #1: The Way of the Tiger, the
  Sign of the Dragon (1973)

As Lee W. Mason

Lady of a Thousand Sorrows (1977)

As K. M. O'Donnell

Empty People (1969)
The Final War and Other Fantasies
  (1969; stories)
Dwellers of the Deep (1970)
Gather at the Hall of the Planets
  (1971)
In the Pocket and Other S-F Stories
  (1971; stories)
Universe Day (1971; stories)

As Eliot B. Reston

The Womanizer (1972)

As Gerrold Watkins

Southern Comfort (1969)
A Bed of Money (1970)
A Satyr's Romance (1970)
Giving It Away (1970)
Art of the Fugue (1970)

NON-FICTION/ESSAYS

The Engines of the Night: Science
  Fiction in the Eighties (1982; essays)
Breakfast in the Ruins (2007; essays:
  expansion of Engines of the Night)
The Business of Science Fiction: Two
  Insiders Discuss Writing and
  Publishing (2010; with Mike
  Resnick)
The Bend at the End of the Road
  (2018; essays)

EDITED ANTHOLOGIES

Final Stage (1974; with Edward L.
  Ferman)
Arena (1976; with Edward L. Ferman)
Graven Images (1977; with Edward L.
  Ferman)
Dark Sins, Dark Dreams (1978; with
  Bill Pronzini)
The End of Summer: SF in the Fifties
  (1979; with Bill Pronzini)
Shared Tomorrows: Science Fiction in
  Collaboration (1979; with Bill
  Pronzini)
Neglected Visions (1979; with Martin
  H. Greenberg & Joseph D. Olander)
Bug-Eyed Monsters (1980; with Bill
  Pronzini)
The Science Fiction of Mark Clifton
  (1980; with Martin H. Greenberg)
The Arbor House Treasury of Horror &
  the Supernatural (1981; with Bill
  Pronzini & Martin H. Greenberg)
The Science Fiction of Kris Neville
  (1984; with Martin H. Greenberg)
Mystery in the Mainstream (1986;
  with Bill Pronzini & Martin H.
  Greenberg)

Made in the USA
Middletown, DE
27 December 2022

20540549R00126